THE CHOICE

S.J. FORD

First published in UK in 2022 by Head of Zeus
This paperback edition first published in the UK in 2022 by Head of Zeus Ltd,
part of Bloomsbury Publishing Plc

9 7 5 3 1 2 4 6 8

A CIP catalogue record for this book is available from the British Library.

ISBN (PB): 9781801101370
ISBN (E): 9781801101363

Cover design © Emma Rogers

Head of Zeus
5–8 Hardwick Street
London EC1R 4RG

Printed and bound by CPI Group (UK) Ltd, Croydon, CR0 4YY

To my mum

PROLOGUE

Let me ask you a question – do you believe in moral absolutes?

What I mean is... do you believe there are some things that, regardless of circumstances, you must never do?

If your answer is 'yes', then you won't like me very much.

I did it, you see. All those things they're saying about me are true.

I *killed* him.

It fills my mind: How could I have done this?

But deep down I know: How could I not?

I saw him outside our houses, he was walking towards his wheelie bin to bring it back in. He was furtive. I was driving home. It had been a bad day. I had a floaty skirt on, the kind that swished and caressed my legs as I moved. It had got trapped in the door as I shut it that morning – ruined, dirt streaking through the grey – such was my distress.

I'd just rounded the corner onto Wesley Street. His hand

was closing around the wheelie bin handle. I pointed my car at him and slammed down the accelerator as hard as I could.

I crushed him between the car and the wall. He was a mangled mess.

Some people are calling me a murderer; others, a hero. I don't know what I am.

I suppose they're both correct.

You see, I saved the children.

PART 1

ONE

NEIL

The first I know of the drama is when I pull into my street after work on 16th January. There are blue lights outside our house – flashing methodically, silently. Two chequered, fluorescent cars form a V across the pavement outside our neighbour's house. The cars have POLICE emblazoned across them. They're blocking the view of my driveway, but I can see uniformed men and women swarming around, the peaks of their hats sharp. I know it's grave when I see the yellow tape streaming in the breeze.

Police line – do not cross.

My home. I never imagined. It's like a photo from a news article. There are *so many* police officers amongst our pansies and inside our slightly crooked garden gate. Whilst they are all slightly different – a whole spectrum of skin tones, varying heights and numerous builds – they are all the same in their dark uniforms and it's *too much black*. Panic grips me.

I ram my car over the curb and judder to a halt behind one of the police cars. That's the moment I see my wife, Jane. Flanked by two police officers, held beside one of the vehicles, she looks so small. Scared. Small lacerations newly splitting her face and glassy eyed with shock; the eye of this veritable tornado. I notice a glinting from her wrists, flashes alerting me. She is wringing her hands – Lady Macbeth... out damned spot. The moment I see those handcuffs around my wife's wrists, I feel it form. It is a sickening ball of knowing before I actually understand. You must know what I mean?

I try to make eye contact with Jane, but she is unseeing. Then I'm surrounded, guided around the police cars to within the arms of the V. He is an unrecognisable shape on the ground beneath a coarse sheet, but I have no doubt about who he is.

'Where are my children?' I ask desperately, my voice strangled and deformed by panic.

'Are you Mr Bell?' a firm voice asks. I can't really make out the policeman's features – the peak of his hat shadows his face. I nod.

'Neil,' I manage, my voice full of cracks that have never been found there before.

'You'll need to come with me, sir. Your children are safe, with a friend called...'

He pauses, checking a worn looking notepad. 'Rachel.'

My panic melts away, and I glance down at the shrouded mound on the pavement again.

I feel a flash of pride for my wife, for what she's done to protect us all, but it is eaten by the horror of the act almost immediately.

A hand grasps my shoulder and I'm too stunned to shrug it off. It pushes me down into the back seat of one of the chequered cars, grille in front of me, doors locked. I am caged.

I stare once more at the lump under the sheet on the ground, at my wife, trembling uncontrollably, and at the army of identical officials. They are all cloaked by the ominous blue flashing.

Jane and I have been through hell with our neighbour, but it's been Jane who has shouldered the burden – she had the encounter, found out what he was planning, fought to get help and was rejected time after time. I know we're a tough neighbourhood, but still. All these task forces, yet they couldn't find their way past the protocols to catch the monster living right next to us. Someone had to do something. That someone shouldn't have had to be my wife.

It wasn't hard to believe Jane when she told me about him – she's nothing if not honest and down-to-earth. Fiercely protective of our children, absolutely, but that's not what this was. This was a terrorist; on the loose; just a wall away from us. This was desperation, love, parenthood.

I should have known. It should have been me behind the wheel.

TWO

BILL

It's 4.55 p.m. I'm preparing to head home, when across the police radios a road traffic collision is called through with the officer detailing a pedestrian fatality at the scene. Officers are dispatched; not me though. I'm a Detective Inspector and it isn't protocol to send us out initially for such incidents. However, when I hear the code, I have a strange feeling settle over me – a sense of foreboding gnawing in my chest. I decide to wait at my desk a while longer – I have reports to finish anyway, I tell myself. A quick text to my Becky telling her I'll be a bit late – she likes to know; it stops her getting worried.

'Okay, love, we'll wait for tea then xxx' comes back.

My phone rings at 5.25 p.m. and I'm called to the scene at 44 Wesley Street – which is in a poorer, but not rough, Birmingham suburb.

'Just get here fast, Bill, please, it looks bad.' Is all I get told. My heart quickens, my stomach knots, and I never get like that – 'calm, steady, and strong' usually appear in my performance evaluations.

I'm guided into the otherwise unremarkable address by

the flashing blue siren lights. There is a hive of activity – neighbours are flanking the road, buzzing with expectation, like a theatre audience waiting for the curtain to rise. A cluster of police officers is gathered next to an old car with a crumpled bonnet. A tarpaulin loosely covers a human shaped lump on the ground. Paramedics guard it.

I step out onto the pavement, grateful I've had a high coffee count today, and am immediately greeted by a constable who fills me in on the situation.

'Sir, we've established that one of the residents of forty-two, a Mrs Jane Bell,'

I write her name and the house number in my notepad, 'ran her car into the resident of forty-four, crushing him against the front wall of his property.' He speaks clearly, gesturing to the car and the scene as he talks. 'The victim was pronounced dead by the paramedics on their arrival.'

'Where specifically was the perpetrator – Mrs Bell – when the first police officer arrived? I need exact details.' I interject, following my honed practice of getting a clear image of the situation straight away so that my brain doesn't fill in the gaps wrongly. The constable flicks back a page in his notepad and scans his eyes across quickly, sweat beading on his temples, shifting from one foot to the other. Homicides hit hard in the early days. In all the days, really, you just get better at coping.

'Sorry, sir, just wanted to check I'd remembered it exactly right.' I give him a single nod of approval. 'When we arrived, Mrs Bell was waiting beside the body, frozen in shock, until my partner touched her arm in an attempt to get her to respond. All she said was, "He's not breathing!"'

'It was you and your partner who were the first officers here?' I confirm. That explains his jitters.

'Yes.' He nods rapidly. I dip my chin to encourage him to continue. 'I asked her what had happened, and she became frantic, urging us to go inside the victim's house. That was the moment everything changed.' Colour is setting onto his cheeks, his blinking more rapid – they are tells of the heat of this memory. Fresh, raw, terrifying.

'She was adamant. "Bombs," she implored. "He has bombs inside."'

Protocol is that officers on the scene do not investigate bomb threats due to the danger. I'd been called at the same time as the bomb squad.

'Obviously we couldn't go in,' he continues, 'so we called for assistance, followed the protocols. It seemed like as soon as she heard help was coming, she just shut down. She was trembling so badly, wouldn't utter another word.'

'Good job, officer, thank you.'

I go to stand beside the police car Mrs Bell is sitting in, wanting to see for myself the woman at the heart of all this. I look down and am struck by her gentle eyes. Her cheekbone and forehead are split with oozing gashes and the right side of her head is shadowed by grazes. My first impression upon observing her is that her muteness is from shock rather than from a lack of cooperation. Gut instincts are a police officer's ticket home each night.

The constables had held her in handcuffs but hadn't officially arrested her; they'd waited for a higher-ranking officer to arrive, given the nature of the situation. That higher-ranking officer is me.

I'm initially sceptical of her bomb claims, just based on probability rather than anything in Mrs Bell that seems dishonest. However, I'm painfully aware that as the senior officer on-site, I am responsible for every single life here, which now amounts to a lot. Therefore, if the bombs are real and active, we are all in too much danger gathered only metres away from the house they're contained in. I have to take a look for myself, assess the situation since the bomb squad still hasn't arrived.

Any doubt I had about the integrity of the bomb threat is annihilated as I step through the victim's kitchen door. I see three full rucksacks on the table along with a detritus of chemicals, nails, and related debris, which form a sea surrounding those three fatal islands.

I feel it deep in my bones, in my fibres – this is the real thing.

My stomach seizes and falls to my feet.

Now I know why it's called terror.

I immediately shepherd the officer who has accompanied me out of the room, and I call in to see where the bomb squad is. Just minutes out. At this point I am aware that the deceased may not be working alone and that these bombs could well still be active, with a huge variety of remote detonation methods possible.

I return to the car where the rigid and silent Mrs Bell is being held. I bend down to the level of the open window, lean in fairly close to her and ask, 'Did you run this man over, Mrs Bell?' She is unresponsive.

A neighbour who is standing behind the police tape shouts over, 'Yes, officer, it was Jane who did it.' I wander over, letting out a heavy sigh before I reach the neighbour.

I need a witness to give me enough evidence for an arrest.

'Did you actually see it happen?' I question the small, bony, confident lady wearing a dishevelled tracksuit. She nods, hard and fast. If I were to give her the benefit of the doubt, I'd say she's trying to be helpful, but my harsher side is recoiling from her busy bodying.

'I saw her drive straight into him – the engine was roaring – which is most unusual for our quiet Jane. We've got a good thing going here on Wesley, officer. Jane's a big part of that. She cares about people, you know, more than most these days. She checks in, does the little extras – takes mince pies round in December, gets her husband to mow the lawn of her neighbour on the other side now he's too unwell to do it himself.' She's earnest, before shaking her head clear and returning to her memory. 'After a moment or two, I saw her stagger out of the car, and go to look at him, like. Then, she covered her face with her hands and screamed. Everyone else came out then like, and my Nev called the police.'

'Thank you. I need you to remain close to give your full statement okay, madam, Nev too?'

'Course, officer. I'll make sure to tell him. He always does as I tell him.'

She nods proudly, with a grin and a wink that makes me shudder, then pushes her chest up a fraction.

I stride back to Mrs Bell and motion to an officer to get her out of the police car. She winces as she unfolds and I make a mental note to get one of the paramedics to check her over more extensively. 'You are under arrest, on suspicion of murder.' I read her her rights. 'Do you understand your rights as I've read them to you now?'

Jane is unresponsive and staring at the ground.

'Mrs Bell?' I ask, loudly and sternly – this is a situation that's still highly dangerous and could turn volatile at any moment; I need to progress it. She turns to me and nods slowly, vacantly. Her response will have to do. I motion to one of the constables who leads her gently back to the car and tucks her inside.

I dispatch officers to clear the onlookers, given the imminence of the bomb squad's arrival.

Minutes later, the bomb disposal team appears and after a brief update swarms into the house. It's a tense wait for all of us outside, every scratch and clunk making us flinch or jump, like a Mexican wave of fearful reactions. They emerge as from the bowels of hell. The leader gives us a nod, signalling the threat was real but we are safe. He then fills me in on their findings. He is concise and direct, turning blunt. His eyes never break contact with mine.

'The three rucksacks each contain large propane nail bombs, rigged up to mobile phone detonators. They're no longer live so won't go off.' He pauses for a moment before landing the disabling blow. 'If all three of those bombs had detonated in a densely populated building, there would have likely been a hundred casualties per bomb. There's a massacre waiting to happen in there.'

THREE

ANEESA

I'm in the middle of typing up an article about the new superstore that has been granted planning permission this week, sipping my sixth coffee of the day when my editor, Eliza, calls me into her office. I work for Birmingham's most prestigious newspaper, the *Gazette*, as the features writer. It's been a slow few weeks... hence the superstore feature. Eliza gestures to the plush chair opposite her desk and gets straight to the point.

'Aneesa, I have a story for you,' she begins.

'Okay, great.'

Eliza steeples her fingers in front of her. She lets a pause hang in the room. An uncharacteristic choice for this freight train of a woman.

'It will require delicate handling. A young family is involved, and sensitive subject matter. There will be a media circus descending on this – all the national papers as well as the vultures at television news. This is huge. But it's ours, Aneesa, it's Birmingham's story.' I notice a tightening around her eyes, a wrinkling to her upper lip. 'It's your story. I know how hard you've been working on the features side to get the experience I asked you to get before I could move you to investigative.' I take a gulp, desperately hoping this is going where it sounds to be. 'I think this will straddle features and investigative and that your style will be perfect for it.'

I can feel my mouth gaping open a fraction, chased closed by the buzzing of excitement humming through my fibres. I snap up from the chair and start pacing back and forth in front of Eliza's desk. I glance at her with a grin and catch the tail of her raised eyebrows and concealed sigh. 'You'll have to keep yourself reined in, Aneesa, I mean it. This will bleed controversy all on its own. We need to keep our credibility here. No messy fingerprints.'

I nod impatiently and perch back on the edge of the chair.

'Okay. Go on then, tell me. What have I got?' I beseech, leaning forward.

'An hour ago, a local mum drove her car into her next-door neighbour, killing him instantly' – Eliza pauses – 'she claims he'd built bombs and was planning to detonate them at the local primary school. Today.'

I lean back in my chair, grateful for its firm support in propping me up, and stare at the ceiling for a few moments, absorbing this.

'If she's right...' I muse.

'I know. Go.' Eliza instructs.

FOUR

JANE

I barely notice my surroundings, wrapped up by the repeating thoughts in my head. I know that I'm seated in a ten-foot by ten-foot cell though, with tiled breeze blocks forming the walls, and a locked steel door in front of me. I reach beneath me and feel a wipe-down vinyl covered pad passing as a mattress. There is a folded blanket over one end of it. I go to pull it towards me but I don't know whether I'm hot or cold. My thoughts pull me back in. I know I got it right. He was going to do it. Nearly three hundred innocent lives saved in exchange for one evil one. *Children*, even. How could that not be right? Yet it's still so wrong. I am the sum of my parts, and those divisions make it complicated. There is nothing else to do in here, so I run over and over it constantly, checking with myself. Every last detail. Every single clue.

The elusive man with the battered cardboard boxes, the dirty blond hair, the thick beard and the strange behaviour moved in next door about six months ago. At first he seemed fine.

Private, but... harmless. I shudder, now. We're not a shiny neighbourhood, but we care about each other, we try to forge a community. I baked our new neighbour a lemon cake and knocked on his door to welcome him to our street with one forlorn tree.

I waited for five minutes but he never came out so I left the cake on his doorstep. The only clue I got was an envelope hanging out of his letterbox, his name above the address:

James Foster.

He came and went in the shadows, leaving before 6 a.m. and getting home after

8 p.m. About three months ago, things changed. From then on, he rarely left. His curtains were always tightly shut. No one else ever arrived or departed. He began building his fence oddly high, like a barricade, and stained it in a dark creosote. He did the pavement side in the middle of the night.

My unease really started with a slip of white receipt paper ten days later. It fluttered to the wet ground like a butterfly. Only this butterfly stung like a scorpion. It was dusk, we were coming back from tea at my closest friend Rachel's. Our neighbour was slipping back into his house, arms laden with heavy-duty shopping bags.

My husband and I have raised our children to be kind to the planet so my little girl scampered into his driveway to pick up the litter. She lifted her prize aloft, her tiny hand clasped around the soggy paper, a grin stretching her chubby cheeks wide.

He hadn't noticed us, but after he had put his bags down inside his door, he turned around to come back to shut the gate. He froze when he saw Molly standing there, waving the receipt around. Beneath his full beard his mouth hardened, his jaw set as rigid as steel. It was his eyes though that flipped my stomach over. Those eyes met mine for the briefest of seconds before slithering away. They glittered with hatred. Fear bolted through me.

Dragging my son behind me I rushed to scoop Molly into my arms and hurry us away from that place. I only let my breath out when I'd locked our door behind us. The look in James' eyes had sown a seed of suspicion that settled heavily within me.

I unfolded the receipt Molly had proudly thrust into my hand.

Fertiliser

Nails x 500

Electrical wiring

Our back windows overlook his rear garden... fully patioed now, another recent middle of the night project, laid on top of new lawn he had seeded and tended for months. There isn't a blade of green in it anymore. It doesn't even have a garden shed for DIY.

What on earth could he have needed fertiliser and five hundred nails for? That seed of misgiving inside me took root.

Since the moment I'd felt his body crumple against my car those thoughts had tumbled through the folds of my mind so determinedly that I hadn't paid attention to the blur of the buildings outside the police car windows on the way here, the dark tints making the shades of grey even more miserable. I blocked out the sirens; I only heard my screaming conscience. It was doing a bloody battle with itself.

Earlier, I was escorted through a door and entered a

network of rooms and corridors. Noises seemed sharper; edges blurred – the shock settled deep. It feels like I've been absorbed by the stomach of this place; it has digested me – processed they called it –and I am now stored. I've settled myself onto the edge of my narrow bed and put my head into my cold hands. I stay this way, frozen in position. I only snap out of it when, sometime later, I'm taken to a room where an important man, the one who arrested me, awaits. His shirt hangs a little loosely, as though he's lost some of his filling lately, and his face looks older than his hands – the hallmark of stress. His eyes are grey, and hold tight to compassion. His silvery, deep widow's peak gives way to pale skin that hasn't seen sunshine for a long while but he has the posture of a man who could command the sun out in this bleak January. I know he is important because I can tell that he *sees* into me immediately, and because he has the weight of the world on his shoulders. Just like me.

'Mrs Bell.' He gives me a steady nod and holds out his huge hand to me, rigidly.

I take it. He shakes gently, his palms cool. This gesture surprises me.

'Please take a seat.'

I sit down in the hard, stained chair, careful to mask the screaming pain of my injuries, allowing myself only the almost imperceptible moans I'd negotiated the pain into with the help of a pain relief schedule. The airbag winded me as it exploded out of the steering wheel and the paramedics tell me my seatbelt cracked a few of my ribs as it snapped me tight to the seat. I remember the struggle of not being able to get it to release afterwards – the claustrophobia, the sound of my screaming. The silence from beneath the wheels. The blissful relief.

'I'm Detective Inspector Bill Simmons. I'm leading this investigation.'

My memories are interrupted. Detective Inspector sounds like a high rank.

'Are you comfortable? The paramedics told me you've got several cracked ribs and extensive bruising. That you could have been killed in the crash.' He cocks an eyebrow.

I wish I didn't have to care.

'My pain is manageable, thank you, I've been provided with pain... relief.' I hope he didn't notice me stumble over the final word, my last-minute swerving around the natural choice –'killers'. I try to cover it up by hurrying on. 'They're taking the edge off.' People ask such silly questions in a crisis. As if a few cracked ribs are even registering amongst all the true pain – relief from what's happened will never come.

'Why don't you tell me what happened today?' he begins.

The thought snaps through my mind like an elastic band stretched to breaking point, released at the last possible moment: *but that's the tiniest part of the story, you can't understand from that alone.* As if you could know mankind by studying an amoeba. I want to refuse to do it his way. I need to lay out before him every moment of this fight, from the early feelings of curiosity, confusion, to the suspicion and creeping fear, to the panic, the anger, the hopelessness, the protective fire. I don't even try though. I realise there's a way to do this now I am sitting here, smelling disinfectant, cold coffee, and an array of fetid body odours. I have to stay smart, not let my feelings ruin this for my children. Nobody could know with greater clarity than I that this isn't a game. Nevertheless, Molly and Joe need me to win.

FIVE

BILL

I return to my office and to the three cold mugs of coffee on my desk left at various stages of being drunk. It feels like a lifetime ago that I brewed the last one.

A lurching vibration against the side of my thigh makes me start and I open my phone, noticing twelve missed calls from Becky. Six o'clock tea is long past. *Another one*. I picture the faces of my two teenage sons as Becky served the food and told them I wasn't coming – snark forced over chagrin. Guilt swallows me whole, leaving my chest heavy, the back of my tongue bitter. I phone Becky back and explain, my voice croaking at odd moments – the ones where I leave out the most terrifying details. I ask her to put the boys on, I tell her it's so I can apologise to them for not being there once again, but I also want to be reminded of the reason I do this job. I need to be taken far away, even for just a moment, from terrorists and bombs by the voices of my boys – Scott's, filled with glee when he tells me about his lunchtime football game and Sean's, who with a quiet pride informs me he got a B in his Maths test. When I hang up, I sadly shake my head clear of their traces, but I'm ready to laser in on the next steps of the case.

It's mind-bending for me that this *perpetrator*, Jane, locked in my cell, may have just *saved* hundreds of lives. I'm unused to the villain also being the hero. It's deeply uncomfortable, weakening the walls of the boxes that let me survive this job.

At 8 p.m. my phone rings, the name of the terror task force leader written across the lit-up screen as the mobile scuttles across my desk on the legs of its vibrations. I clear my throat of the thickness that has just grown there. Professional detachment can't survive cases like these. I take a deep breath and wrinkle my nose at the stale smell of my own shirt, the stress of the day tainting the fabric with evidence.

'Bill speaking.' They would only have called if there is a significant development.

I take a swig of water; my mouth having dried up by the third ring. Dread tastes disgusting.

The office windows have been darkened by the night without me realising, so I haven't drawn the blinds. I glance up and see my face reflected, all the blood drained from it. A ghost.

'I wanted to update you. There were maps. In the front room. Showing the five square miles surrounding Wesley Street. He had clearly identified one target. Three bombs, three circles.' His voice is weighted down with what his words carry with them. Horror.

I know it will have infected him the way it has me, a cement mixer dropping its load through your limbs, while you just hope you can get enough done before it sets – make it home; get everyone else home. 'He was targeting St Oliver's

CE Primary School. The three circles were around the most densely populated areas of the school which touched the bordering streets. The bombs on the kitchen table were tagged with corresponding locations.' I rub my left palm across my eyes as if I could push away the boulder that's been dropped into my gut. 'He was fucking doing it. No doubt. They were ready to go too, nothing left but to detonate.' It winds me, words alone making me double over and clutch my chest. I wonder if I'll breathe normally again for the next few weeks. Then the ice turns to flames searing through my veins. Red-hot, branding me with fury. 'Motherfucker,' I hear down the line. 'Two hundred and eighty-nine kids.' I pull myself together enough to reply, though when I speak my voice sounds robotic, distant, echoey.

'Thanks for keeping me in the loop.'

'Course. Take care, Bill.'

'Thank you. You too.' I give myself precisely two minutes to recover before I start to make a slog of calls.

It's still sinking in, the overwhelming evidence that this man had planned to detonate his three bombs imminently, all in St Oliver's CE Primary School, which educates two hundred and eighty-nine of my city's children.

I'm a law enforcer, and I have loved and lived for every letter of it each day of my adult life. Yet those same letters state that this Jane Bell, saver of innocent lives, protector of people, may be judged as needing to be locked behind bars, maybe for the rest of her life; and I must be the one to put her there.

It's just gone 9 p.m. the same night, four hours since it happened. Those four hours have felt like they've passed both in an instant and as a painful drawn-out ache. Seated opposite me at the table in the interrogation room is an enigma. She exists as a conundrum to me, and my lack of certainty about her unsettles me.

As a Detective Inspector of Birmingham's police force, I see things in one overwhelming way: as black and white as the colours I wear.

This Jane Bell, she is both.

She is black for the killing. She is white for believing so strongly in implementing good that she has potentially sacrificed her future for it.

I don't really know how to treat her. I'm an officer who tries only to think about what is in front of me. I'm also an officer who tries not to feel too much – in this job that would be tantamount to a resignation. *I feel so much* right now.

I feel shame, for letting her down, for making this her action when it should have been ours.

I feel respect, for a civilian who has found such courage and moral conviction.

I feel embarrassment, for missing this monster lurking in my city; for nearly costing my city its children.

Anyway, enough of that, that won't get this moved on. Lord knows what will, though. The letter of the law, I suppose.

Jane Bell was right.

SIX

JANE

'What happened today?' Detective Inspector Bill Simmons wants to know. Where to begin? 'Isn't it obvious?', I refrain from saying.

It is so simple really.

'It seems I killed a man who was going to detonate bombs and murder hundreds of children.'

Bill's eyes widen a fraction. There is a weighted pause; I'm getting used to those.

'Okay, that's as good a place to start as any, Mrs Bell. Can you tell me how you knew that he was planning the attack?'

'It started with a receipt he dropped, that my little girl picked up.' I have to pause here and choke down a huge lump that presses hard against the back of my throat. I feel bare without Molly's hand warm in my palm and Joe's weight settled on my hip, as though pieces of me have been torn off. I know they're safe now, which is more important than any pain I can feel. They have been in such danger. I'm their mother, if I can't protect them from dreadful harm what use am I? I hope Neil can make them understand, one day.

Bill coughs quietly, and it draws me back from images of their twinkling eyes and toothy smiles to this barren room – metal, breeze blocks, and sharp edges. I notice the crumples lining Bill's shirt and blazer, like crow's feet and laughter lines – storytellers.

I suppose those lines mapping across his clothes today speak of *me* being a story he'll tell in the future. I love it; I hate it; I need to make sure he tells the right one.

'That receipt, it was for nails, fertiliser, electrical wiring. We found it after he changed – all of a sudden, James began barricading himself into his house with the big fence, he stopped going out, he patioed over his lawn. Then the receipt. I know it probably sounds silly to you but I became suspicious, you know, just paid extra attention to him. He didn't go out much but the next thing I knew I saw him outside Molly and Joe's school one day. He was just standing there, glaring, looking around, taking notes. It seemed strange.

I don't know if you have children, Mr Simmons?'

'Yes, I do.' Bill nods his head solemnly, swallows.

'Well, then you know, you'd do *anything* to keep them safe. Anything. This man oozed danger. A few days after that, I noticed him go out during the day and this was so rare by then that I knew I couldn't pass up the opportunity. I garnered the courage to go round to see if I could look through his windows, see if everything looked as it should, just to put my mind at ease. Well, it didn't do that. Quite the opposite.' I explain what I saw, what I felt.

Bill writes lots of things down in a notepad as I'm talking. It's the type that flips open, so I can make out his handwriting as he turns onto each new page. He writes neatly, the letters looping, softer than I would have expected from this effectual man. He nods a few times while looking down at the notepad.

'Did you contact the police with this information?' he asks, looking at me.

'Of course!' My fist clenches tighter beneath the tabletop until my nails feel like they might pierce my palm. 'I called the police station after finding the receipt. Then when I saw him at the school, I went into the local station. After I looked through his window,

I Googled helplines to call and phoned with all the information. I chased it up time and time again. No one would help me. You all wrote it down, slowly, and told me you'd look into it. Nothing ever happened, nobody came, not even one police officer came to visit to see for themselves. You left us alone. And here we are.'

My hands are sore, the skin red and dry from me wringing them all evening, yet I can't quash the compulsion to keep doing it.

Bill's lips have thinned into a straight line, his chin tilts down a fraction. He has stopped writing.

'That's all for now.' His tone has changed, become curt, and it seems that he deliberately avoids looking at me. I can understand his repulsion. He pushes his chair back and it grates across the floor. The noise amplified in the small space. He covers the distance to the door in two long strides and starts to pull it shut behind him. As if something compels him to, he pauses then, and looks right into my eyes until the last crack of light disappears around the doorframe. I see all sorts in those two blue pools. I expect he sees all sorts in mine.

Sitting across from a member of the police force again brings the memories rushing back. It's a different voice, but it triggers the helplessness. The first time I called the police, after the receipt, I was confident.

I was perched on the edge of the coffee table when I dialled. Nine, nine, nine.

'Police please.'

I felt my seat bones crunching against the wood each time I shifted my weight to dissipate the discomfort. I couldn't take my eyes off the wall behind the sofa, the bright wall-paper cheerful when I'd chosen it, garish now. Almost comically distasteful given it was the wall that connected us to James and, thank God, separated us from him. Although unease raced through my veins chauffeured by rushing blood, I was calm, for I knew exactly what to do, how to solve the problem, or at least who would. Only the fast tapping of my left toes against the rug betrayed my buried nerves. As soon as I heard the line connect, I launched straight into describing the receipt, and the man it belonged to. I had a clear vision of what I was expecting to happen – a voice, kept proficiently level but with rising pitch and accelerating speed would respond with threads of reassurance and promise. It would tell me someone would be sent immediately. The danger would be fully assessed and neutralised. They would keep me and my family safe. I was shocked by the exhausted dismissal I actually heard from the voice thickened by a nasal note, fattened by an accent that misshaped words, broken by rattles of ill health.

'We'll look into it.' I felt like my tyre had just blown out on the outside lane of a motorway.

Then I heard the monotone humming of a cut line. Desertion. I sat silently for a few minutes, stupefied. Disbelief blew across the embers of unease until they were roaring, burning me up, not flickering but violent. I felt so truly alone, but I also felt the fervour of the irony – that if only I was alone this would all be okay. Instead, I'm alone in a cage *with* this sinister stranger, who breathes and builds his fertiliser, five hundred nails and electrical wiring into God knows what, a few feet away from me, from my children.

I spoke to Neil that night once I'd got the children to bed, hoping this might be the catalyst for him to grow back into his original silhouette, to fill his half of us the way he used to before Joe was born, before he started shrinking and didn't stop. I was disappointed for a second time that day. At least this disappointment I knew deep down was coming.

'I'm scared, Neil. The way he looked at me, at Molly, the blackness of his eyes,

I can't even put into words how awful it made me feel. Something's very wrong, I just know it. Look, I've got goose-bumps and shivers even now.' I pushed my blouse sleeve up my arm and showed him the pale flesh, newly landscaped by the pimples of fear. I glanced from my arm to his face and thought I caught the dart of his eyebrows back from a rise.

'Right.' He had that tone. The empty one, not exactly trivialising, but on the way. Indifferent, I suppose. 'I guess the only thing you can do is call the police?' He turned it into a question by lifting the last few words tighter, stretching them out, exactly what this day has done to me.

'I've done that, Neil,' I couldn't help but flick a flash of frustration towards him. Maybe it was sharper than I intended. He held his hands up in a mock surrender at me. How patronising. This was not working. 'I suppose I was hoping for a bit of support and help working out what to do.' I sighed and felt defeat drop my shoulders.

'If you're honestly asking what I think, then I don't see there's anything else to do. If there's something to find, you've given them the heads up, so the police will get him. When you think about it, I bet if we knew what happens in any house on this street behind closed doors, we'd be a bit disturbed, but that doesn't mean it's harming anyone. You just happened to see a receipt that I admit seems mildly alarming out of context, but for which I think there's more likely than not a reasonable explanation.'

Try and relax, I tell myself. Though it's a challenge when a man's bought fertiliser for a garden without a single blade of grass.

'We'll keep an eye out, alright?'

Alright? I thought. As bloody if.

I gave him the strained smile I'd worn far too often lately, my face presumably distorting into a caricature of raised eyebrows and stretched thin smile. The mask of exasperated disconnection. We're married, we love each other, but we don't recognise each other. We're trying to raise the same children but we're reading from different manuals, and they don't even seem to be in the same language anymore.

Then it struck me – that I'd finally unearthed the core of the difference: I felt let down by his apparent apathy for his own children. I couldn't love them any bigger; he couldn't love them any smaller. *Why wasn't he consumed by protectiveness in that moment, knowing what I'd just told him.* I felt I was parenting alone, in every way that matters – the ones to do with love; and isn't it all to do with love?

SEVEN

ANEESA

Jane Bell is the story of my lifetime. My head knows this, yet in a startling but familiar way I feel my heart being abducted by fear – at the overwhelming intensity of motherhood this story feels borne by. I'm a writer who uses currents as my compass – the pulls and pulses, not the isolated facts and technical landscape. Jane's decision is the riptide sweeping me away in this case. A mother's love. Situations where that is the headline repel me, for I know my professional objectivity tries to flee. Even twenty-five years on, the feelings are as raw and atrocious as the first moment I understood.

I was six years old. My world was my father, my mother, and me, in our terraced house with our cat. My mum stayed at home and my dad didn't do much apart from work, so my mum and I were... inseparable. My auntie walked me home from school each day, and Mum always watched from the front window for us. By the time we reached the gate, she would have the door flung open and arms spread wide ready to welcome me into her hug. It smelt of cinnamon and cloves and I always saw a kaleidoscope of colour through my eyelashes – Mum loved brightness. It's how I first knew – there was no flash of colour from the front window when we turned the corner and it came into view. It was the first day in my life where I came home to a closed, black door. As we drew before it, I felt my auntie stiffen beside me, her arm reaching out across my chest to hold me back: the gentle thump of it. My gut hollowed out. Auntie used her key to let us in. As she fumbled with it, I watched the curtains my mum had sewn, desperate for them to suddenly twitch with her movement. They stayed glacier still. I strained to hear beyond the scratching of the key against the lock as it tried and failed to slip home. I tried and failed too. I was longing to hear the sliding of my mum's slippers along the hall floor. They never came. When my auntie swung the door cautiously open, she tried to hold me back but I darted under her arm. I remember that chemical floral scent of strong cleaning products Mum used, which hung in the rooms, but it wasn't a Tuesday or Friday – her big cleaning days. Everything that didn't matter about my house was perfectly in order – it was pristine, nothing was out of place. Yet everything that did matter was in carnage – my mum wasn't there.

My auntie called my dad. I barely registered the urgent tone, the sharp words, I was too busy searching high and low. I realise now that my auntie must have already known by that point – my mum never broke her routine and rarely left the house alone – so Auntie covered the chasms in her voice with barking for my dad to come home immediately.

I peered round the door as she hung up, the phone lying on her open, face-up palm, laid flat on the kitchen table. She sat there silently for a few moments, not registering my presence, her shoulders juddering; like gunshots were hitting her sternum. A few minutes passed like this, stretching into infinity. I felt it physically – the shattering of my old life, the arrival of my new one, like a chick being born – the surface fracturing, the cracks opening, the new life forcing the shell apart completely, before leaving it behind. Just like the egg, I was never whole again. Then, my auntie lifted the phone up, as though it were as heavy as our oven, and pressed three digits, their synthesised beeping sounding as loud as cannon fire. A beat later she spoke one word, quietly, solemnly:

'Police.'

I never saw my mum again. We didn't get answers – we got no contact from her, or news that she'd been found... in any form. She disappeared from my life without a trace and I have never understood why, or how, or what happened to her. It has feasted on me for ever, leaving craters of damage in its wake. She is a mystery which has been the headline of my life ever since, one I could never write the ending to. Being in the dark, in any of its guises, is a destructive thing. The right piece of news has the power to flood people with light. I am still searching for my light switch, but I went into journalism to try to turn it on for everyone else I can.

When I arrived at the crime scene yesterday evening yellow tape was whipping in the wind. There was a tree at the centre of the action and its bare branches were swaying, bending, like fingers playing a grand piano. As I opened my car door and stepped out, a wall of noise hit my eardrums – notes of radio static, voices, car engines and fast, heavy footsteps making up the melody. The street was buzzing. I was lucky that the Birmingham suburb in which the Bells and the victim lived is on the *Gazette*'s doorstep, so I got there within twenty minutes of Eliza's instruction. I used the drive to attempt to process the feelings this story brought up – the sting of rejection that felt a foot long – my mum *abandoned* me, never mind killed for me; jealousy that there were children out there so loved by their mother that she would do that for them. I quashed the feeling quickly, focussing my thoughts on the professional magnitude of the story instead – just how big it felt, how important it could be, how much attention it would command. The thing about having a history like mine is that you grow strong, you learn how to reinforce weak places, not give in to them. I saw the road sign for Wesley Street and I roughed up my grit.

The police officers at the scene were clammed up tightly – I couldn't get comments from any of them. Unsurprising, but the wound to my professional pride still smarted. There was a tension in the air. It felt like gravity was a little more powerful in the metres surrounding those semi-detached houses. I've always recognised this as the sign something very serious is occurring.

The faces of the police were grave underneath the peaked hats, lips pinched together, shoulders shored up around ears. It wasn't just from the cold. The perpetrator and her husband had already been bustled into the back of police cars to be kept out of the way. I arrived just after the bomb squad in their armoured vehicles, their movements precise, chartered, a dance choreographed to perfection. They were awe-inspiring. They were considered and never faltered as they stepped into the unknown.

The *Gazette*'s photographer was by my side and he got a photograph of the bomb squad swarming into the house, dressed head to toe in black, visors covering their faces, their only identity being that of faceless saviours.

Once the activity settles, I look up one of the early photographs circulating online of Jane Bell – head bowed as she ducks into the police car. I see the sorrow in her eyes which have clearly landed on something. I turn my head to find the spot she must have been seeing based on the angle and where she was. There is a purple scooter propped up against the inside of their slightly crooked clean white garden-path gate. Parked beside it is one of the push-along tricycles toddlers ride. My heart twangs – phenomenal love beats in the heart of this and I'm reporting on a heroine. I'll make sure the country knows Jane as that. It might not be much but it's the least she deserves.

EIGHT

JANE

It was a long night. I didn't sleep at all. The bed is narrow and firmer than I'm used to. I couldn't get comfy, I still can't, just sitting on it. Even if I could, I don't think I would feel safe sleeping with strangers' eyes on me. I am alone in the cell, yet a police officer watches me constantly. I shudder each time I catch the penetration of their gaze upon me. I haven't slept without the comforting warmth of Neil's body beside me since the day we got married. We haven't spent a night apart in eleven years. I wonder if we'll ever spend one together again.

There is a frothing quiet to this place at night. A constant stream of buzz disrupts the silence; and low-level lights force out the reassurance of darkness. Every so often there is a burst of chatter from the police officers; I strain to hear what they're saying, and am frustrated that the distance swallows the words into a jumble. I've sensed a commotion outside, building ever greater, even through the night. There has been an atmosphere of rising pressure. The first raindrops of a perfect storm. Do they hate me? Is everyone outside there because of me?

The moment my foot hit the accelerator every particle of my awareness was focussed on that action. All I see now is this future: four walls, jumpsuits, plastic trays holding processed food, and photographs being the only way I'll document Molly and Joe growing up. At least they'll grow up. At least all the children will.

I close my eyes, breathe deeply, and fill my mind with them.

I don't have a window to see out of but I sense from the changing rhythms of activity that it must now be early morning. I feel the hint of sleep tickling the edges of my consciousness and I long for the welcome respite it could bring – the chance to be freed from the fear, the questions, the shock, for a short while. I don't quite make it, I feel my thoughts racing behind the cloud that dozing brings, when I see it. Him. James. I see his body there. The blood, the sinister way it appeared from beneath him like an oil slick, the way it spread... unstoppable. I see his open eyes. Emptied. By me. I bolt to standing, shaking my head as if that could clear it. No. I feel ligaments jumping in my neck, my arms, my legs, lifted tight beneath my skin, newly awakened by tension. For an instant they make me feel strong, but the haunting of James' body reminds me how fragile even the most dangerous things are, if only you find the right weapon.

Then I feel even stronger.

My adrenaline must wane for I am blindsided by a wave of nausea and the aching stab of my ribs. I realise my breath has grown ragged; responding to the memory I can't shake. I lower myself tentatively to the edge of the bed, force my breathing steadier, smoother. I see James' body lose its clarity, blurring at the edges, ebbing away like a piece of driftwood on a tide going out. Unexpectedly I panic. I need to sleep but I can't release that image of James' body. It's the proof I have that it's over; that Molly, Joe and the children are safe. If my punishment is being haunted by sleepless nights then I'll gladly become an insomniac. I hate being haunted by that image of James dead; but I love what haunts me – that his death means he can't hurt anyone anymore.

NINE

ANEESA

*BIRMINGHAM SAVIOUR PROTECTS ST OLIVER'S CE
PRIMARY SCHOOL FROM KILLER*

*NATIONAL HEROINE BIRMINGHAM MUM FOILS
TERROR PLOT*

*THE EVERYDAY HEROINE THAT JUST SAVED
HUNDREDS OF CHILDREN*

*TERRORIST BROUGHT DOWN IN THE NICK OF
TIME BY BIRMINGHAM HEROINE*

Jane's story has exploded across the media exactly as predicted – from headlining every national newspaper to being shouted from an array of news stations, Jane Bell's face is everywhere I turn. Television news crews are camping out in front of Jane and Neil's house, hoping for a shot of the husband and his children, or better yet, a quote or interview. There are journalists too, me and my photographer included, a complete melee. We are almost frozen, bundled scarves doing little to fend off the frost, chapped lips stark on faces tinged damson. Waiting. Neil Bell has understandably shut himself down inside, a fox bolting underground on hunt day, so I have no useful updates to give Eliza. Just as I start to expect a call pulling me away, my phone rings.

'Hey, Aneesa. You must be fucking freezing. Come back to the office, I don't think you'll get any more there now that the circus has come to town. I've got another way forward for you. Come and see me as soon as you get here.'

'Okay, I'll be with you in twenty.'

'Good.'

I'm sitting opposite Eliza twenty-five minutes later in her black, white, and fuchsia pink office. Eliza never usually seems to have much use for facial expressions, but her eyebrows are lifted, and the corners of her mouth are marginally tugged up, so I know she is excited.

'Aneesa, I want you to dedicate yourself to our local heroine for the duration of this initial flurry surrounding the case and then to take it forward with a weekly profile or investigative piece until it's over. Do you sense what I'm envisioning?'

I nod furiously and take notes in the notepad that seems permanently glued to my left hand.

'It's all yours, Aneesa, if you think you can handle it? Come to me with questions, or for guidance if you need it, but you have free rein to run with this series and make it sensational. This is journalistic gold dust, make sure you use it wisely.'

'Thank you, Eliza. I won't let you down.'

I stand up and hurry to the door. As I start to turn the handle Eliza adds, 'There is one thing I want you to remember, one rule to work under. Jane Bell is a hero. I don't ever want that to be called into question. Do we understand each other?'

I give a single nod and shut the door quietly behind me.

I arrive home at six-thirty that evening and as I shrug my thick woollen coat off my shoulders and kick off my boots, Bertie melts himself against my legs, threading through them so closely that he creates a trip hazard every time. His purrs sound like they've been fed through an amplifier. I pick him up for a quick cuddle before pulling on my bootee slippers and I make my way around the living space of my third-floor flat, lighting the candles and turning on the glowing table lamps, a little black and white shadow trailing me all the way.

I know I have a big task ahead of me tonight, and that rest will be a thing of the past for the foreseeable future, so I pad into the kitchen, flick the switch on the kettle and carefully grab my favourite mug out of the cupboard overhead. The mug has two chips in it, and is getting old, stained and ragged, but tea tastes so much richer when mixed with its inspiring message. It was a gift from my dad the day I left for university.

'The only thing necessary for the triumph of evil is for good people to do nothing.' Edmund Burke.

That is the quote I've grown up listening to, it being the last thing my father used to say to me as he kissed me goodnight and switched off the snow globe light on my bedside table. Finally, I might be in a position to tell a story that would make him proud.

Those are the words that keep my tea safe, written on the mug. They will help me tonight. It crosses my mind that Jane Bell would appreciate the sentiment; and that's as good a place to start as any with my planning.

Bertie curls up on the sofa beside me and I make lists: of the people I want to interview; of the order of the series; of the research I'll need to do; of the perspectives on this situation. I work hard to get excited rather than overwhelmed.

As I scribble my plans, Eliza's words ring through my ears, her one rule. It is a contradiction of how we usually work, too prescriptive and one-dimensional. It doesn't allow for exploration and grey-areas, which are two of the most important aspects of the type of writing I try to pen. I also hold in my heart my one rule – truth; always the truth.

I need to find out what's going on with Eliza. I spread today's newspapers out before me on the low slung, rustic oak coffee table that takes up most of the floorspace in the lounge. One thing is startlingly obvious, and surprising, to me. Jane Bell is glorified in every single one; she is named a heroine; a saviour; 'Birmingham's angel'. Not once is the word 'murderer' used. In the court of public opinion, the media is testifying, and it stands tall, proud, and certain that Jane Bell is a hero.

TEN

NEIL

Joe cries all the time. So do I; though that's between you and me. He wailed through last night and Molly led him into her bed and cuddled him. I sat beside them both on the comfy chair I moved from the living room. He asked for Mummy constantly. He's three and isn't a big talker but he's said that word hundreds of times in the past day. I want her too, I tell him.

Molly seems to be coping a bit better, thank goodness. She doesn't understand, I think, so confusion haunts her more than loss. Things get so complicated, don't they, as an adult? What do I tell my five-year-old daughter without scaring her? I don't know what to do, I just know that I can't do this alone. It was never meant to be like this. Things change so fast.

I hate the way the media are hounding us, a sea of colour and noise outside our front gate. Jane worked so hard making our three-metre patch nice – planting pansies for colour – to welcome us home, and the reporters have trampled them. Police hold them back, stop them knocking on the door at all hours, and I've pulled the curtains tightly closed in every room so that the children don't see. Molly peeks through when I'm not looking though, and she asks, 'How will Mummy get through when she comes home?'

'I'll push them all apart, don't you worry about that.'

'Will you carry Mummy, like in the films?'

'Your mummy likes to stand on her own feet, but if she wants to be carried, I will carry her.'

'Is she coming home soon?'

'I'm not sure yet. But she loves you, she misses you, and she wishes she could be with us.'

'Then why isn't she?'

'She has to help answer some questions to stop some bad people.'

'She does always tell us that being good and being kind is the most important thing in the whole world.' Molly paused. 'So, she's busy being a good people, and then she's coming home?' She pauses thoughtfully.

'I hope so.'

We have had this conversation several times, and every time we've finished, I've seen that it wasn't enough. I wasn't enough.

The police warned me that the media presence will continue for a while.

Anger often bubbles out of me, when tears aren't leaking, and the mask of 'everything's fine' for the children slips. Last night I got overwhelmed and threw my mug against the kitchen wall, smashing it, the tea trailing down the yellow paintwork. It woke the children up. I made up a story for Molly this morning – that the brown lines were caterpillar trails, and I told her she should look out for butterflies. *The*

Hungry Caterpillar has been her favourite bedtime story for a while, so I know every single word. I thought it would cheer her up to think we have our own caterpillars and butterflies in our home. She looked up at me and smiled for a moment, and then her bottom lip trembled, and she said, 'Butterflies are Mummy's most favourite.'

'Yes, they are, so think how happy she'd be that some are looking after you.'

Tears pooled in Molly's eyes and then rolled down her cheeks. I felt wetness on my cheeks too.

'You never cry, Daddy. Does it hurt?' she said, placing her tiny hand on my chest, over my broken heart.

I nodded, mutely. She trotted off to the cupboard next to the washing machine and fumbled in a small box. She came back over and carefully peeled a Mr Bump plaster, her face an adorable knot of concentration. She stuck it on my two-day worn T-shirt, right in the middle of my chest. Then she climbed into my lap, cuddled me tight, and we cried.

It shouldn't be like this. Jane told the police, I told them too. We did everything we were supposed to do.

After Jane called them and they rejected her I saw my chance to finally achieve something for my family and gain back some ground with my wife. I pulled into a car park on my way back from the office and called the police. Despite the reassurances I'd tried to calm Jane with, I was panicky. Fertiliser, nails and wires... on Wesley Street. A lone man barricading himself into a semi, I shuddered every time I let my mind dwell on it. The hairs stood up all the way down my arms as I dialed.

'He's making bombs, I'm telling you. We have a receipt he

dropped – for fertiliser and nails. He hardly ever comes out; he has no friends or visitors.'

'Could you give me his full name please, sir?'

'It's James Foster. He lives at 44 Wesley Street.'

'There's not much we can do, sir. It's not a crime to purchase nails and fertiliser, in fact many individuals would buy those things for DIY or gardening projects. If you have any more concrete proof, though, do let us know.'

'Can't you send someone to have a look? I'm telling you, I'm sure about this.'

'I don't expect so, sir. We just don't have the manpower for that.'

I felt my shoulders crumple forward and defeat howled its brash braying into my eardrums. Another failure. *How could I possibly get concrete evidence without putting my family in graver danger?* The pickaxe of impotence chipped another chunk from me. I never mentioned it to Jane, imagining the way she would wrinkle her nose in accepting disdain, my inadequacy a given formality in her day.

When Jane saw the maps and bomb supplies, and called again, we had a bit more of a positive response, but it was still slow and unproductive in the end.

'We'll look into it, thank you for being in touch.'

No one ever came.

Plenty of manpower appeared for Jane, after what she did to him – they managed to mobilise instantly. Funny that. People need to know that Jane would never have chosen this. She was distraught. We were on our way to bed one night after she'd seen the maps, standing at the children's bedroom door.

'What shall we do?' Jane asked me, her voice shaking. 'I

can't bear the thought that they're sleeping here, just metres away from someone who's planning to... do that.'

'Why don't we check into a cheap bed-and-breakfast for a few nights while we give the police a few more days to come? I'm sure they'll protect us, monsters like him are their top priority these days.'

'I don't know, Neil, I hate this.'

'Me too, babe, but I'm sure it'll be okay.'

It clearly wasn't. We tried to make it an adventure for the children, a mini holiday, since we wouldn't be able to afford a real one this year now. We returned a few days later when our spare money had run out. I went to chat to our neighbour in number forty. He said the street had been as quiet as a desert – not even the local lads from the next street over making a racket on their way home from the pub late at night like usual. I was at my wits' end, I had no idea what to do, how to get help. We piled the kids into the car and drove around endlessly to pass the night, them sleeping silently and peacefully in their car seats – we were too anxious to be at home, next to him overnight. The following day was bin day. Then it was all over, anyway.

I felt helpless. I was as worried as Jane had been about living next door to a bomber, I guess I just had more faith in the system to protect my family. I never thought it would let us down this badly. I expect Jane thought the same things about me; and I hate myself for failing her like that.

Rachel lives a few streets away. She has children of a similar age to Molly and Joe.

I hear the doorbell ring, and through the frosted glass I see her shape. I couldn't be more relieved and grateful. I know I've been floundering, not even strong enough for the children, and I'm desperate to try to see Jane and find out what is happening. I've kept the phones switched off since it happened, unable to face speaking to the people we know.

I haven't even been able to bring myself to call my mum, who might have wanted to help, I wouldn't be able to cope with her. Rachel marches into the kitchen where Molly and Joe are colouring, and she draws them straight into her arms for a three-way hug. She holds them for a few minutes, making sure she holds on until they let go, which in Molly's case is quite a while. Rachel strokes Molly's back and murmurs to her in a motherly way. However hard I try, a mother is one thing I will never be.

'I've emptied my diary for the next two-weeks so think of me as your daytime nanny,' Rachel says. She doesn't smile, thank goodness, but her eyes meet mine with understanding. 'I can hold the fort here this evening too, I'll take care of the bedtime routine so you can get a visit in now. Jane needs you.'

Joe walks to her side then, and wraps his little arms around her leg, clinging on.

I nod after a beat, knowing they'll be okay, better even than with me. Rachel looks me straight in the eyes and says, 'Tell Jane I love her, and I'm here for her all the way. Also, thank her for me. It would have been my three, you know.' She pauses. 'There are no words.' Tears flow down Rachel's cheeks and I pull her in for a hug. A moment later she pulls back, visibly steels herself, and looks to the children. 'Even though it's late let's bake butterfly cakes. How about it, hey?'

Molly grins, her first proper one since Jane was taken away.

'Can we make purple icing? Purple's my favourite.'

'We can do some purple, and what colour do you want, Joe?'

Joe looks up at Rachel from beneath a low brow. She smiles gently at him and takes his hand. After a few moments he says quietly, 'I like green.'

'Green it is then.'

I walk over to give the children a cuddle and tell them I'm going out for a while, but I'll be back later. I expect more fuss from them, but Rachel has already got them tootling off to wash their hands ready for their baking frenzy.

'I don't even know where to start,' I say to her, over-whelmed now by the task ahead and by everything I don't know.

'Well, that one's easy. Start with Jane.'

ELEVEN

BILL

This case is the toughest of my career, and comes at the worst time. At any other point in my thirty-plus years on the force I would have relished this. Resentment swings in for a visit most days, that I'm being pulled so fiercely in two directions – Becky and Jane – trying to give my whole self to both and therefore neither getting enough of me. There's a media firestorm gathering momentum every second. My job has become as much a matter of calming the press, strategising about protocol, and covering our own asses as it is about justice. That doesn't sit well with me. There's a woman sitting in a cell who has a husband and children and has lived a good life; and there is a man in the morgue who had three bombs in his house and maps taped onto his walls with circles around a school; *that* is what matters here.

I anchor myself deeply in the process – investigating the crime, gathering evidence, and preparing the case for passing to the Crown Prosecution Service who will determine the final charges and bring the case to court. I've worked unofficially through the night.

It is just past seven o'clock in the evening now, on the day after the incident, and I'm sitting across from Jane in the same dingy interview room we were in yesterday. Jane has a solicitor with her today, a squirrelly woman with a thin blonde bob and a nervous smile who strikes me as being thoroughly out of her depth. I hope that Jane gets herself stronger counsel going forward. She'll need all the help she can get. I take us through the formalities of the interview process, and with the tape recorder running we begin.

'Let's pick up where we left off yesterday, Mrs Bell. Can you tell me what happened that led to you driving into Mr Foster?'

Jane looks exhausted today, puffy black bags sitting below her slightly bloodshot eyeballs. Her hair is lank, and her skin has a grey tinge, her hands look sore and her clothes are crumpled.

'I realised what James was planning when I spotted him surveying the school and then saw what I did through his window. I knew that he had the physical means of carrying out a bomb attack – I saw the receipt from before for the nails and things. I knew that you weren't coming.' Jane scrunched her eyes shut and paused for a moment. 'I knew that my children, and potentially hundreds of other children, would lose their lives.' Jane's intensity deepened further. 'I'm sure you must have seen, sitting across from some of the people you sit opposite, Detective Inspector Simmons, that a person's eyes show you their soul. James's eyes were blacker than coal, and *dead*.' I catch myself, my breath hitching. 'Even before they actually were, you know.' I have to look away from her searching stare. 'Anyway, I dropped Molly and Joe off at my friend Rachel's for an hour – for a playdate – and I arrived home and saw James outside with his wheelie bin. In that split second, I knew. I knew that this was my one chance to do something, an opportunity I might never get again. And I took it. I drove into him.'

'Did you intend to kill him, Jane?'

'Well, I wanted my children to be safe. I wanted to protect them.'

'Did you mean to end James's life when you hit him?'

I look over at Jane's solicitor here, surprised at her lack of intervention, however futile. She is just scribbling notes down with darting eyes.

'Well, I never thought of it like that, about after, but I suppose somewhere inside me I must have realised that he wasn't going to fare well, being crushed between my car and the wall.'

'Is that what you wanted? For him to be dead?'

'I wanted him to be gone, I wanted my family to be safe, I wanted the hundreds of children to be safe, that's what I wanted.'

I end the interview here, satisfied that, along with all the other evidence, the Crown Prosecution Service has enough to determine Jane's charge. Putting the facts aside, I have an aching in my gut that nags at me to listen. I succumb. It tells me that there's a strong chance Jane intended James to die when she saw her opportunity; not just to injure him enough to stop him from carrying out the attack, but to ensure end of life. I'm too fatigued to work out whether I agree with it.

Just when I'm finally ready to leave, Jane's husband arrives for a visit... at last. It's far outside normal hours. I make an exception – it's hard not to for someone so soft, so harmless. He has a round face on top of a body never hardened by weights or athletic endeavour. His slightly curly hair bounces as he nods hello. I guide him into an interview room to have a moment with Jane. I stand there while he holds her and watch as he falls apart around her. Somehow, she pieces him back together. Then I guide her by the elbow and walk her back into her cell. I slide the door shut and I turn the key in the lock. I feel like a coward.

I close the door softly behind me as I arrive home that evening, my mind on not waking Becky if she's had to go to bed early. I look to check where she is when I feel my foot trip on something, my body pitching forwards, right hand stretching out, smacking the wall just in time to break my fall.

'Shit!' Anger flares, I look down and see a mud-crusted trainer. Scott. I kick it to the side, and stalk up the stairs, pulling open his bedroom door. I see his head jerk up from where it is bent over his body, curled over itself at the head of his bed, knees pulled into chest. And just like that he seems five again, hurting from being ridiculed in his first football match for being too small to do any good. I'm proud that he proved them so spectacularly wrong. He was in the local talent academy until Becky's cancer diagnosis. His choice to leave to be at home with Becky every minute possible, but also his mistake... or not... to make. My lecture evaporates, a distant memory that doesn't matter anymore.

'Oh, son.' I close the gap to his bed, sit beside him and pull him under my left arm. Still a sparrow. *How on earth do you keep them safe?* There are too many monsters – human and cellular. I feel Jane enter my mind, show me her truth, leave me with my boy.

'Dad,' his voice, still that of a child, not broken into manhood, is pleading. I don't let him see me notice the shine down his cheeks and the damp pattern at the neckline of his

T-shirt that give away the tears that have fallen. 'I want to start taking the bus, if you can't pick us up anymore.' Confusion lingers only a moment before regret forces it out.

I know the answer but still ask the question – you learn more that way.

'Why? Because of your mum?' Scott's lower lip trembles, I can see words behind it, but he can't let them loose on their own; and can't handle what they travel with.

He gives a single nod while his eyes swim... drown. My heart breaks for his courage.

'Son, you can't be coming home on the bus yet. You know why. It's just not safe.

I know some of the other boys use it, and I know that makes it hard to understand why you can't, but I'm not prepared to put you in harm's way, not with Amal on it.'

'I can handle Amal now, Dad.' He's bluster and indignation. It's gone too soon. 'Mum can't manage to get us.' His voice is struggling to break out of a whisper. 'I think if she keeps making herself, we'll get less time, you know. The nurse told Sean who told me that it's a bit like a phone battery when you've lost the charger – it runs out one day and then that's it, so you have to use it sparingly.' I feel devastated by what he's having to understand, far too young, far too soon. It's another rock added to the pile of guilt I already can hardly move beneath – that Sean had to hear that without my hand on his shoulder, my strength to lean against. Scott finishes: 'I don't want to use it like this, not on something so unimportant.' His voice grows certain, confident, betrayed by the fear in his eyes. 'I'd rather take my chances with Amal.'

'Not an option, Son, but I've heard you.' I look into his eyes and nod, reassuring, until he knows I mean it. 'I'll find another way that means we don't use any more of the battery on that. I promise.'

'Okay, Dad.' The trust in his voice is the hardest part. Vital but terrifying. I used to know it was well placed. Lately, I can't seem to be who I promised I was – I can't seem to keep the people I'm responsible for safe.

I think I hear the faintest of shuffles behind Scott's bedroom door, which I left ajar. Scott and I lock gazes and the corners of his lips turn up in a knowing smile.

'Sean, are you there, bud?' I call out, still looking into Scott's eyes. There's a moment of silence, during which I can almost hear indecision from the hallway. Fifteen, the age of constant pushing and pulling, even without a dying parent. I'm relieved when I see the door start to swing open and a shock of dark hair appear, lifting to reveal burning eyes full of questions and anarchy.

'What's so important about this case, Dad, that you can't just be here more, like before?' Sean's shoulders are locked up underneath his ears, his arms folded tightly high up on his chest. He is rigidity and rebellion, the showy bluff of vulnerability. His eyes bore into mine, relentless until they strike what they're drilling for. My chest swells with respect for my articulate son, slowing my answer to give it the thought it deserves. My soul deflates with sadness that I haven't delivered what they need.

'That's a fair question, Son,' I pause, scrabbling for the right words. 'I think what's so important about this case is Jane Bell. You'll know the details from the news, right?' They both nod solemnly. 'Well, I feel guilty. She came to the police, my people, for help. We rejected her. She should never have been faced with the choice she had to make.'

I glance up and see Sean's shoulders lower an inch or two

to the floor, his arms loosened into a comfortable folding. 'She's going to be charged with murder. I don't think she deserves to be. My heart tells me she deserves a statue; my training tells me she needs a cell. Plus the thought that it could just have easily been your school streaks across my mind at all hours. I know without any doubt I'd have wanted her to do the same thing – stop him at all costs – to protect you two. Which makes all this really complicated.' I'm baring my soul to them, and it doesn't even register that maybe this isn't what fathers are supposed to do, or that I've obliterated my professional boundary. I feel a sucking in my chest. 'I think I'm still trying to work out what's right, what should happen now, and I feel like the more I find out the less I know. Does that make sense?' I look properly at Sean first, take in the way he's opened the shutters to his face and I can actually see my son again, the boy before Jane and the diagnosis. I reach my hand out to him and something lets go inside me when I feel his cool palm in mine. I tug him to sit on the end of the bed opposite Scott and me and the feeling of his yielding, the dip of the bed beneath his weight, feels like coming home after a month away.

I twist to look at Scott, still settled beneath my left arm. He gives me a tight smile, which I look away from when Sean starts to speak.

'I get that, Dad, but you surely know it's not on you. You didn't build those bombs and it wasn't you sat at that station turning her away. Shit happens. You have to get this, Dad, or it'll destroy you.' I see fear fill his eyes slowly, 'And we need you too much for that.'

I nod, reaching my hand out to squeeze his shoulder the way I should have done when he heard his mum's battery is running out. 'What will happen to Jane Bell, then?' Scott enquires.

'I don't know yet. That's what I'm working on. I know all this is tough but I need you to know that our stuff is what matters most to me and that I've heard you both. Nothing, absolutely *nothing*, is more important to me than you guys, so we keep talking, okay?'

I want to say more, afraid that they don't understand this – how much I love them, how hard I'm finding this, how terrified I am at how out of control life seems to be slipping. We all hear the sounds of movement from mine and Becky's room. Becky stirring, trying to get up. Remorse fills me once more. I should have been home to make tea, to see her into the bath, take care of her. It shouldn't have fallen to our two boys... again; ever. Suddenly the room is filled with scrabbling, the boys unable to get to her fast enough – every 'good' moment with Becky at her fullest too precious to miss now they are becoming so rare. I feel the breeze across my forearms as they rush out and hear the thundering of their feet across the landing.

Unease has made itself at home in me, turning my stomach into a deep pit, as though the bottom of it has dropped out. I'm not a doctor, I can't fix Becky, even they can't. I'm not a psychologist, I don't know how to help my boys cope with this thing that breaks people. Even the only thing I am – a policeman – I can't seem to do properly anymore. It makes me a fraud. It's my worst nightmare in every area of my universe – bombs destined for a school in my city... that I don't stop; my wife given a terminal diagnosis, not enough time left for my boys or me; my two sons, heading for something impossible to emerge from unscathed, when they are still far too young, too fragile to possibly be okay. Impossibly worse than that, they've all been spawned into reality at the exact same time. My head feels like a squash court and there are these three balls, being smashed into the walls, bouncing around almost too fast to see. I am exhausted from the confusion, from trying to follow them, return them... and never succeeding.

I leave work at three the next day to collect the boys from school and drop them off at home, before I head back to put another few hours into the final reports for Jane's case. I'm surprised to notice a slight jaunt in my step, fully able to propel myself forward easily and freely rather than the feeling that I'm walking underwater that I've had the past few days – limbs dragging against pressured resistance. Perhaps it's because I've finally been able to achieve something positive, albeit as small as a school pick-up.

My brain snaps out of wherever it was lost and into the place it was beckoned. The conversation wouldn't even have registered had my boss not spoken my name exactly as I was passing his office door. Vincent's voice is low, suppressed. I wouldn't even need to be a member of the police force to recognise the furtiveness.

'Bill's got some personal matters that I can only surmise are affecting his judgement.' I pull myself up short, bending low over my shoe on the pretence of tying the lace. 'His wife is gravely ill; he's got two teenage sons. Skewing his judgement, I think. What you need to focus on are the hard facts. Jane Bell was alone in her car without the children she could apparently hardly bear to be without. She had dropped them at her best friend's for tea. Why wouldn't she have stayed for the tea with them? Why was she returning home?'

'And from the transcripts I've read, Simmons never asked her that in interview.'

I recognise the voice of Bethany Rigby, a prosecutor for the Crown Prosecution Service. My blood runs cold. Somehow, I start to sweat through it.

'The post-mortem shows horrific extensive injuries,' Vincent continues, momentum building in his snarling tone. 'She was driving like a bat out of hell. She never claimed to have lost control of the car, not that we'd believe that anyway given the forensics. There's no doubt whatsoever that she intended to hit him and it's farcical to claim she thought she'd only injure him in the circumstances. She was not "stopping him", the facts show it was fully intentional killing.'

'In Simmons' interview Bell did admit she "wanted him to be gone". He didn't push but that sounds like a case for pre-meditation to me. Certainly, more than enough to justify a murder charge.'

I glance both ways down the corridor. Nobody is in sight but I'm so exposed.

I take my shoe off, ready to start shaking it if anyone appears – as if something is stuck in it.

'It would be irresponsible not to go for murder, with the evidence and the context. Bell drove at high acceleration into the pedestrian victim while they were presenting no immediate threat. The fact she'd taken her kids away, but returned herself, at such an opportune moment is the key that tells us it was pre-meditated. The force was excessive. It must be murder. Can't be seen to let someone off who clearly needs to stand trial for such. That could open us up to people thinking they can take the law into their own hands like she did – we'd be overrun with vigilantes for Chrissakes.'

Loathing for Vincent rises up in me thick and foul in my

throat. 'Even taking away how it looks, the law is the law and must be upheld.'

'I'll prepare for the press conference.'

Hearing them wrapping up, I quietly drop my shoe, twist my foot into it forcefully and execute a half-hopping lope down the corridor into the fire exit stairwell. The wall has that dirty tinge of a forgotten area, tainted by human presence yet not cared for by it.

I don't care; I let my back slide down it until my seat bones hit the floor. Instantly damp cold hooks into them, spreading in that way that promises aching later. I drop my head into my hands, marvelling at its weight. The disease of self-doubt infects me, taking me over cell by cell. Are they right? Did I let empathy cloud my judgement? I am unaware of the passing of time, it is only the acknowledgement that if I don't stand now I never will that forces me, creaking and groaning up from the floor. Even then it is tempting to lie fully down and never get up. It is with the thought that if humility can't be found in policing then I shan't believe in it at all that I realise I haven't lost myself completely... yet.

TWELVE

ANEESA

I settle in at my desk for the morning, placing my chamomile tea on the cork coaster next to my keyboard. The steam delicately rising from it brings a strong musky scent to my nostrils. I've never acquired the taste for it fully but it's a ritual I have found calms my mornings and centres my mind.

'Morning, Aneesa. Nice evening?' Sian, Eliza's personal assistant, asks as she passes my desk.

'Nice enough thanks, unexciting but cosy, same as usual. How was yours?'

'Don't get me started,' Sian says with a flap of her hand and a roll of her eyes. 'Trouble with Tommy again.' I give a grimace of sympathy for her struggles with her wayward son. Sian's been working with Eliza since she was made editor, perhaps she knows what's going on with Eliza about Jane.

'Hey, Sian,' I ask just as she's walking away. She looks back over her shoulder.

'Yes?'

'Do you know what's going on with Eliza over the Jane Bell story? It's just she wants me to pursue a very specific

61

angle, even before either of us has gathered the full detail of the landscape. I'm wondering if there's something more behind it?'

Sian stills with the rigidity of someone trapped within an awkward decision.

'What's the angle she's asking for?'

'Jane is to be portrayed as a heroine, no matter what.' I lift my eyebrows as I say it. Her face instantly collapses into sympathetic understanding.

'Ah. Yep,' she starts, before pausing. 'I don't want to gossip, and it's very personal.' She pauses and I can see guilt stalking her. I hunt it down.

'I only want to know so that I can handle myself sensitively throughout this story. So that I can understand how much it's appropriate to push if I need to, you know?'

She gives me a motherly smile before her brows pull down into a chevron as she explains. 'Her sister died when she was a child, some kind of accident none of us know the details of. Eliza gets even more intense than usual when anything comes in to do with children passing. Jane Bell stopped three hundred children being killed, each of whom had a family that'd have lost them like she lost her sister. I think it's as simple, and heart-breaking, as that.' Sian gives me a single nod accompanied by a tight smile and leaves me.

I mull over what Sian's told me before opening my Facebook account to ease into the day by checking the *Gazette*'s page while I sip my tea. Social media is a hotbed of secrets leaking out from their locks and cages. Even with tight privacy settings the odd comment on a public page's post can be the breadcrumbs on a trail all the way to the gingerbread cottage for someone like me.

I find our page, and the links to my initial articles about

Jane. I glance through the comments, knowing the value of understanding opinion's current roost. There are comments as extreme as you'd expect for something like this. I feel a shudder rack through me and I close the tab down. I have my limits. I lean back in my desk chair, finding the moment of spring back, as the thought pings against the edges of my mind like a pinball: I have to find him. Somewhere out there is someone who knew James Foster; most likely someone who loved him. It's awful hearing nasty things about someone you love, however bad a thing they've done. I know how they feel. At least it never got as gruesome with mum as suggestions that she 'burn in hell' as is being said about James. That 'he's lucky it was Jane that got to him... I wouldn't have let him off so lightly'.

I'm still thinking about those articles and their comments later that evening, when I'm home and pacing my kitchen waiting for the microwave to ping with my tea. We live in a culture of taking sides. The media do it, groups do it, individuals do it: they take a position and defend it to the death. Yet that's not real, is it? Situations aren't two dimensional like that. There is texture and depth to everything we encounter. Just because we aren't open to its existence doesn't mean it's not there.

I finally hear the ping and fumble for cutlery and crockery to plate up the re-heated meal my Auntie's left for me. She does this every week – five meals left with my neighbour, each in a small Tupperware. As I slide a bite of food off the fork with my teeth, not even tasting whatever it is I'm eating, I gaze at the print hung above the little desk crammed into the corner of my lounge space – it's of two painted hand prints – one little and one large. It tugs my mind to my mum and how her disappearing taught me to never be so focussed on the puzzle piece you're holding that you lose sight of the fullness of the picture it belongs to.

I hate that people are so rash and insistent with having opinions about other people and situations they're not part of. I've come to the conclusion that if they must be so then my mission is to give them the best information possible so that maybe they can form more accurate and balanced opinions. Perhaps that way there will be a bit less hurt driving the world.

That conclusion brings a niggling successor: how does this translate to my approach to Jane Bell's story? It hits me with the familiarity of something always known but recently forgotten: the whole landscape. Everyone has been so busy building an encampment on the tiny puzzle piece of Jane's hero worship that we have lost sight of the context.

James Foster was about to bomb a school. A thirty-three-year-old who had grown up amongst us, who must have been known to people, and at some time loved by someone had slipped through every safety net the nation has. Who was he? How did he get to having built three bombs, ready to detonate them? Why were his chosen victims three hundred children? How do we stop the next James Foster from being successful if they don't live next door to a Jane Bell? Did we do anything to push him there?

My mind ricochets to Jane herself. She killed a man bringing his wheelie bin in. Not a man standing outside a school with his thumb over a detonator switch. Would he actually have gone through with it? However strong the evidence, none of us was in his head or heart so we can never *truly* know. Can we? Does that even matter in the end though – was it too big a risk to take when the stakes were three hundred children's lives?

My eyes dart to the photo wedged into the side of the pinboard above my desk that slipped from Neil's wallet as he pulled out a business card to write my number on. I must remember to return that. Molly and Joe. Sitting right now, no doubt scared and lost, inside a house without their mum. The memories sear through my gut like a welding gun being slashed back and forth across me. I connect the dots. The world is on fire with her act of protecting them, but in the ashes lies the fact that she left them. They might grow up with their mum locked behind bars. If she knew James was going to use the bombs on the school – the very justification for what she did – even in a worst-case scenario where she couldn't take her children away from Wesley Street she must have known they'd be safe *as long as they weren't at the school*. Therefore, because of a choice she made, however justified, to save other people's children, she has potentially condemned her own to what I can vouch is a cruel fate – growing up without a mum. If she was willing to do that, is she quite who we've judged her to be? Not worse, but different – putting the lives of nearly three hundred other children before being at home to raise her own. Selfish, selfless, where do you draw the line in this?

I wish I knew.

I pull out a new notebook. A red, fabric-covered hardback. Texture to run my fingers over. I open the front cover, feeling the tingling of excitement at hearing that first crack of a beginning. I make a note, which isn't for now but can't be forgotten: Find James Foster. Understand. Don't ignore the man beneath the bonnet.

THIRTEEN

BILL

Time is running out and my nerves are in its rucksack. I want to somehow do more, but I can't work out how to. I need to talk about this with the one person I know I can trust completely, Becky. I know everyone says 'my other half' so casually, but Becky truly is mine. She knows me better than I know myself, so her opinion is more valuable to me than my own. We met when we were both eighteen. We fell in love to the backdrop of her gruelling time at nursing school alongside my time at the Academy. We were both grafters, determined to make a difference in our little piece of the world. She's so unwell now that I try to burden her with my work less often – concentrating saps her energy and I can tell she tries to save every last flicker of it for the boys. In ways like this the losses are already well underway. That's the thing with terminal illness. It's not just the big loss at the end, it's all the little losses, which aren't so small at all really, that you have to survive on the way. We used to share everything and she helped me navigate the hardest parts. Now I'm lost on every journey. Though I hate taking any of her reserves for myself, I need her now, she'll know what I should do. I can't do this without her.

'It's so good to be home. Thanks for staying up. You didn't need to, but I'm glad you did.' I say to Becky as I arrive back at the house.

I wrap my arms gently around her and pull her into a tight hug. I savour the feeling of her heartbeat next to mine.

'Becks, you know the Jane Bell case, the one I mentioned last night?' She nods.

'I need your advice.' We sit down on the sofa and I take her hand.

'Sure, Bill, tell me about her.'

'She's done this terrible thing. She killed a man. He had three bombs inside his house, and plans to blow up the local primary school. She saved countless innocent children's lives. She was desperate. She'd asked time and again for police help. We didn't provide any. She thought her kids would die. The thing is, Becks, I think you'd have done the same thing – for our boys. I hope you would. And I wouldn't want you to pay with a life behind bars for it.

'I wanted a *defence of others* release for Jane, but I overheard a conversation today between Vincent and the CPS and they're going for murder. It's been spoken about before in high-level meetings that defence of others releases must be watertight – so that vigilante killers aren't given the keys to the city. There's also some weighty evidence against her. Should I try to get them to only pursue manslaughter as a compromise, futile though it seems, given it's the eleventh hour and they've already decided the charge? Or better yet, keep pushing a defence of others release, even though in reality I have no say? It might be that even if I can't change anything now, my testimony at trial will be critical.'

Becky sits up straight and is pensive for a few minutes before she answers.

'I think you know in your heart what you can live with. I know you believe in the law with every fibre of your being and your role within it is to enforce it. Justice and fairness have always been out of your hands between the judges and the juries in the courtrooms. But, from what you've said and how I can tell you feel, this is a case that has the power to haunt you if it's given the wrong outcome. I also think this in an imperfect situation and when I've faced them, they never leave you. They're the moments that I most hope there is a God – to put right those wrongs in the long term.'

I was right to ask.

The next day, I settle into my desk chair even earlier than the previous morning. The office is quiet, the shell of our team is pitiful without the life everyone brings in – the permanent smell of half-day-old food pervading the air; the artificial lights casting everything sallow. I've never been a morning person but I've been struggling to sleep since 16th January, and I seem to be disturbing Becky with my restless tension in the mornings around the house. She needs those hours of stillness before the boys get up to let her medication take effect and to mobilise her body. I think it's feeding into my sleep issues that her deterioration is getting faster. It's such a cruelty – for her, and for us who love her. The helplessness; the powerlessness; the stretching, grinding loss. I don't even know how to *be* at home now. Do I need to stay strong for Becky and the boys or do they need to see my pain in order to process their own? It's a minefield and we're already falling apart too much to survive even the breeze from a distant blast. It's ironic beyond belief that it's the prevention of a real detonation that has loosened me. I feel like a rope half cut through. I appear strong, seem stable, but threads are fraying below, and with each tug and pull of pressure, they are unfurling, weakening, until there will be nothing useful left of me at all.

I rest my head in my hands while I wait for that gratingly cheery Windows start-up tone to sound. It is only the mechanics of stacked bones that keeps my forehead from smashing into the desk. I open my inbox to the red 'urgent' exclamation mark beside the terror task force leader's name and my spine suddenly stiffens. I click the link to the attached report with no liquid left in my mouth. I type in the password to access it and start reading. Further plans have been found that illustrate James Foster's detonation schedule – notebooks with timelines and diagrams. Details of the ignition methods, which were all in place, ready to press. Two names, written over and over again, an obsession: Leo and Lilia. I pause, the fibres of my mind wrapping themselves around the facts, digesting them to their fundamental parts to release the consequences of their message – those bombs were live in the house next to Jane, Neil, Molly and Joe. If anything had spooked James, he could have detonated them instantly, undoubtedly killing himself and the Bell family. I feel a thought trying to penetrate the others – the fleeting, ethereal whisper that it's hard to conceive that, given the state Jane was apparently in, she wouldn't have given any hint to a neighbour who was also on edge and *so close*. It's gone before I can grasp it, or am even fully aware it was ever there. The rest of the report is forgotten while I chase feelings through my brain, wrestling down remorse, self-contempt and shame from where they taunt me: that this happened under me. I sit, shifting in my seat as if it were as easy to release emotional discomfort as physical. I read on.

It has been confirmed that his intended primary targets were his two children, twins who are pupils at St Oliver's. A murder-suicide. Intelligence has discovered James Foster had two children who one month prior to the planned bomb attack had been matched with an adoptive family. His phone and computer have been searched and it seems he was targeted via an online chatroom for family rights, from which an individual had radicalised him into this violent plan as part of their own agenda. They are now being searched for.

Pieces tear through my chest, my gut splintering. They swim around in there, nicking each other, crashing, grating along. I am unaware of the day building itself around me until a colleague lays a hand softly on my shoulder.

'Bill. You okay?' I turn my head slowly towards him. I feel myself blink once, involuntary but requiring great effort.

'No.' I push my chair away with the motion of standing. I pick my jacket up from the back of it. I feel the friction of the hem of it dragging along the carpet beside me as I stride out. I don't have the spare energy to lift it higher. I ignore the half-shouted questions that follow me, get into my car, drive to two streets away from my home, park up, and lose the rest of the day to a numb shutting down.

The following day I find out that Jane will appear before a magistrates' court for an initial hearing, where her plea will be entered, and bail will be determined. Her case will be referred to the Crown Court either for sentencing, if she pleads guilty, or to start the process of a trial by jury, if she pleads not guilty. I don't get to decide what happens to individuals. The police system exists to make sure that laws are followed. Black and white. Black and white Bill Simmons is who *I* am. I look at Jane Bell, and at the bars she stands behind. A few minutes later I look at the photos spread out on my desk of the bombs waiting on Foster's kitchen table, of his maps of the school, of his bleak eyes. I feel lost.

I feel like maybe black and white don't even exist after all.

If I did get to decide, Jane would be at home right now reading a story to her children, one tucked beneath each arm. And I would have been the man to lock James Foster behind bars for the rest of his life.

My boss, Vincent, calls a press conference the following day. The CPS has given us its charge decision and it's ready to be announced to the world. After I introduce and hand over to my boss, I stand on the sidelines, watching, waiting, far away. I listen vaguely to his preamble – giving the outline of the case. I focus more on the differing expressions on the faces of the staff who are present – they range from panic to smugness. I couldn't tell you the mask I'm wearing.

The cameras click and flash in the dusk light. Phones are held aloft in a sea of glinting screens to record every word.

'Following the incident that occurred on Wesley Street we have concluded our extensive investigations. The outcome of which is: we are charging Mrs Jane Bell with murder...'

My heart meets my stomach and together they drop through the soles of my smart black shoes.

FOURTEEN
ANEESA

Yesterday, on 18th January, I attended a press conference held by the Birmingham Police Department. Jane's charge was given. Murder. Even though I knew this was coming, I still felt a python tighten around my ribs when I heard it. This world is fast blurring from a sharp charcoal line drawing into a water-colour abstract.

I'm seated at my desk again, it's just gone 7 a.m. and I'm the only person here apart from our cover receptionist, Leila. I snap out of a reverie when a commotion in the entryway catches my attention. I hastily push myself out of my chair to find out what's causing such turmoil.

'Is everything alright?' I raise my left eyebrow meaning-fully at a young man with ruffled shaggy hair and a bicycle helmet swinging from his forearm. He has the branding of the city's most reliable courier service on his polo shirt.

'You're not Miss Khan are you, by any chance?' He asks me, almost pleadingly.

'I am indeed.'

His shoulders drop and his head rolls to one side with relief.

'Oh, thank goodness.' His words tumble out in an exhale. 'I have a letter for you, Miss Khan. It's an extremely important one I believe. My boss was fuming when I took it back with me last night. Apparently, we were urged that it absolutely had to be delivered yesterday. Not a day early or a day late. And that it had to be placed into your hands and yours only. No middlemen.' He gives an apologetic half-smile and nod to Leila. 'I'm so sorry it's late. I did try twice yesterday, but you were out. The other receptionist said I'd have to come back today.' He trails off, an expectant lilt to the end of the sentence, I can only guess hoping for an acceptance of his apology.

'Don't worry. I have no idea what you actually have for me.' I hold my hand out to take this mysterious letter from him. He glances down at it.

'Ah, sorry, I need to see I.D. please, Miss Khan. Specified for by the sender.'

I reach into my inner jacket pocket for the card wallet I keep tucked in there.

I present my driver's licence. He scans it, gives me a single nod, hands the letter over and leaves, calling out a 'thank you' over his shoulder as he does. Leila gives me a grateful smile before settling back down behind the desk.

I look at the letter. A5 brown paper envelope, thin. My name and our address written directly onto the envelope, leaving score lines in the paper. Handwriting uneven, angular and slightly shaky. I turn it over and slip my thumb underneath the sealed flap. It unsticks easily, ready for me. It turns out I was not ready for it.

Dear Ms. Khan,

My name is James Foster. By the time you are reading this, you will know that name as belonging to the man who blew up the school.

I have sent this letter to arrive the day after it happens. I need everyone to know why I did something so awful. I need them to know how deeply sorry I am. That it was a hopeless man's very last resort.

I have chosen you to take this message to the world because of an article you wrote years ago now. I can't remember exactly what it was about, I could yesterday and no doubt I will again tomorrow, but my memory is a bit funny like that these days. Anyway, I could tell from it that you are a person who understands that parenting isn't like the Hollywood films. That not all families have 2.4 kids, two perfect parents and a picket fence. That parenting is love. Love, graft and showing up.

I am an imperfect man, flaws and mistakes sewn together make up this rough silhouette I live inside. Despite all that I created two miracles. Perfect and flawless. They made me better. I would do anything for them. Anything.

They arrived into a mess but they were always loved. I met their mother when we were both on the streets. She got clean for the pregnancy, so they were protected, but she OD'd when they were six months old. I was all they had. I tried everything Children's Services asked. I got clean in rehab. I found jobs labouring so I could rent the house Children's Services said I needed to provide. It's nice, with other kids about the same age next door. Wesley Street would be a decent place to grow up. I decorated my daughter's bedroom with unicorns and fairies because when I last saw her, she was wearing wings and talked twelve times about unicorns. I counted. I papered my son's bedroom pink because it is his favourite colour and I put lava lamps in it so that he'd be able to see one wherever he looked as they were the only thing that calmed him when he was a colicky baby. Still my children were kept from me. I was only allowed to see them in a supervised centre every six weeks. For them to come home to me apparently I needed a sign-off from a psychiatrist that I was mentally stable, yet they wouldn't give me the counselling I needed to become stable, no matter how much I begged.

Three months ago, I was informed that my children were going to be placed up for adoption. Since then they have been matched. The only way I will know them is through letters sent by their adopters once a year.

No.

I need to be the one to see all their moments. The big ones like teaching them to ride bikes and being their tooth fairy, but also the small ones, like knowing their favourite chocolate bars and the way they fall asleep. I need to raise them. I need to know them. I need to love them.

They are my reasons for living. I can't live without them. I won't. Nothing in this life would be able to soothe the oblivion of this pain. So, I've done what I did. It would be too long to wait for them to grow up. Even if I did, they would be someone else's kids by then, not mine. But they are mine. I need us to be together now. So, I have made sure we are, for eternity.

I am truly sorry for all those who have been lost alongside. I know my apology won't matter though, when their parents are where I am now – facing a lifetime with their kids having been taken from them. I wish there had been *another way but I don't know which classrooms my kids are in and I couldn't risk my son or daughter being left behind.*

It might not seem like it, but I did it for love, I promise.

James Foster

I finish reading and only then do I notice the way my hands are trembling. I can't get enough air into my lungs. I don't know whether to try and heave more in or retch. I can feel adrenaline coursing through my veins.

Is this monster a monster at all? Or is he a desperate father who made a heinous mistake? The way we all can. Monster or mere mortal, he chose *me*. How can I possibly be responsible for somehow conveying his message to the world, when more than anything right now I feel a connection to him. He loved his children so much he couldn't live a life without them. He couldn't leave them behind. I was lived without. I was left behind. So, however abominable his choice was, I can't hate him for it right now. A tiny part of me understands it. Which leaves me with more questions about myself than about James Foster.

FIFTEEN

SIMON

I hear the ping of a notification on my phone and my heart jumps. I loathe being chained to that small rectangular cuboid. Not enough to do anything about it, of course – they save so much time, an area in which I am most impoverished. My phone is lying face down next to my glass of whisky, buried beneath sheafs of typed court documents and my messy scribbled notes on that yellow lined paper that rustles deliciously. I snatch my phone up, unlock it, and see it's an alert for one of Annie's articles. I flick my eyes along the lines of it – a profile piece on a Jane Bell – the headliner these past few days. I've been in London, winning a case which has consumed me night and day. When I read what Annie has to say about her, the details of what happened, her current legal representation, I feel a universe form in my chest – stars burning, black holes lurking, suns blazing, planets turning, and endless yawning space, sucking me into it. Thoughts no longer flow, they pop in my synapses. *This is what I've been waiting my whole life for.* I take a huge slug of whisky, relish the feel of it burning down my throat. Then I reach out to pick up my telephone.

I trained for five years to become the barrister of standing I am today, amassing experience after experience to get where I am. If you ask my friends, they'll say, firstly, 'who's Simon?', and then once reminded of my existence they'll say I'm a workaholic and a sharp, intense bastard. If you ask my previous boss – which I have – he'd say I'm a barrister who's too in love with my own ideas about the philosophy at the heart of justice to ever be strategic and political enough to realise my unlimited potential. He says this job is about dirt under the fingernails of small print and my head is in the clouds of concepts and theories. Well, I'm about to get my knuckles bloody and my face bruised up here in the heavens in taking my concept all the way to the words 'Not Guilty' being pronounced when the jury returns. I'm thirty-four years old, my name is Simon Rafferty, and I'm about to change the course of legal history.

I don't sleep, too fired up for such an inconvenience. In the small hours, I come down enough to see how the stars aligned to bring me to this moment I was made for. She always did shine. Aneesa is my... something. We began as two strangers in the same city starting jobs a bit beyond us at the same time, both breaking for lunch at noon on the dot, buying baguettes from the same tiny sandwich bar. We grew into eating them together in the park next door when the weather was fine. I knew I'd got my job through showy flair and was arrogant enough to think they were lucky to have me. She'd got her position through raw talent and quiet grit but was worried she couldn't live up to the pressure. I lent her confidence, she showed me the value of humility. We're friends, though somehow that pinches, ill-fitting. We get together now whenever I'm in Birmingham for a case, sharing lunch like the old days. If I wasn't me, and she wasn't Annie, I wonder what we'd become.

I know the answer really, I just shove it angrily into my attic along with everything else that is in an inextricable but troublesome part of me. She's the only lens through which I ever see myself clearly. I wrap myself up in my ego and most of the time it convinces me of the things I need to feel. It builds me up to the point of hands shaking as my fingers hover over my keyboard, an email being drafted with Annie's name in the recipient box and the title 'meet me for dinner?'. It's in the precise moment that I'm hovering over the send button that I actually see myself beneath all the smoke and mirrors. I see that the 'special occasions' for which I pour myself a whisky have become entirely un-special and who the hell has three 'special occasions' every evening? I see that I'm sharp edges and have a work addiction that covers up the fact that I was never taught how to love. I see what someone like me would do to someone like her. With that image seared into my mind like a calf being branded, I shut the email draft down and return to the beginning – my ego ready to step back in and start building the new clothes around the emperor once again.

If you're doubting whether it would really be so bad if I was with her, the very fact that she is 'Annie' to me, not 'Aneesa' tells the only story that matters. I gave her that nickname after she told me she didn't have her mum around growing up and that her dad died just after she got to university – Annie, you know, 'tomorrow, tomorrow', the orphan.

Who the fuck comes up with that? I wonder if she has ever connected the dots as to where her nickname came from. I'm too ashamed of myself and too much of a coward to tell her. Which is why I feel like a beast when I allow myself thoughts of us as an us – she's already been through too much. The last thing she deserves is to have to go through me too.

SIXTEEN

ANEESA

After I read James' letter, I folded it carefully, slid it back into its envelope and tucked it between the pages of the novel I carry in my bag. I haven't breathed a word of it to anyone. I have things I need to work out first. I know it's not what James intended for his message – to be kept silent, buried in a handbag, but alas here we are. I need more time to work out what on earth to do with James. Eliza has been pressing me to get the next piece related to Jane published as quickly as possible, and it's been too much to splice my mind between Jane and James. They are opposing stories really, it feels impossible to write them both in a way each of the characters deserves, and Jane's story is my job.

I decide, for maximum impact on the readers and to achieve the highest possible level of connection between them and this story, that it's the right time to interview some of the parents of children who attend St Oliver's CE Primary School – James's would-be victims. I arrange my first meeting with a father eager to tell his story – Carl Wickham – for this afternoon.

I meet him at a quiet, cheap, practical coffee shop fifteen-minutes' walk from the school. It is popular with tradesmen and the hungry, being famous in the area for its greasy fry-ups. It is a place that most locals feel comfortable and at ease in. That is essential in getting the conversational gems; I've conducted many interviews sitting at similar Formica tables.

Carl Wickham is a well-built man who looks to be in his late thirties, and beneath his frown he has an open face.

'Miss Khan?' he asks as I approach the table. There is nobody else in the café. He stands and extends his hand for me to shake.

'Yes. It's a pleasure to meet you, Mr Wickham. Please, call me Aneesa.' We sit down opposite each other.

'Carl.'

'Are you happy for me to record our conversation? Just for my reference later, it saves me writing notes as we go,' I ask with a smile.

'Sure, whatever you need.'

I press the record button on my Dictaphone and place it on the tabletop between us.

'So, Carl, why don't you just start by telling me a bit about your little boy, if you don't mind, and how you're feeling about all this?'

'Aww, that's an easy one. My little lad is called Jason, he just turned five last month. He had a Power Rangers party. Molly came, actually – she's Jane's girl. Jason's in the same class as her. She came proper dressed up an' all, no tutu for that firecracker, she was as good a Power Ranger as any of the lads.' He chuckles softly, his eyes full of warmth. 'Jason's the best kid, he's a cheeky monkey too, but he's amazing.' Then Carl pauses and his eyes dim. 'I can't believe what I've heard on the grapevine and on the news – is it true, do you know? Was that creep really going to blow up the school?'

'Based on the information the police have released, yes, he had three nail bombs in his house, packed into rucksacks, with mobile phone detonators. It appears that he had children who attended St Oliver's, who he had been denied any access to and there were maps on his walls suggesting that his target was the school.'

'Well, fuck me. What a monster. I wouldn't have survived it, let me tell you, if my lad had gone. He's my whole world.' Carl lets a moment pass quietly, tears pooling in his eyes.

I swallow the lump in my throat. I was my mum's whole world, and then my dad's. Worlds end. I'm grateful that Carl's didn't have to, just yet.

'Why didn't the police stop the bastard? How did it ever get to this point? He shouldn't have been allowed to have bombs sitting in his house, with Jane and her kids right next door. Why would he even have gone after littluns – how sick and twisted can you get?'

Although James is an angle I'm going to pursue later on, Carl isn't my vehicle there. This piece is about Jane. I shift in my seat, which I know will unconsciously represent a matching shift in conversation direction. Ironically, for a journalist whose whole career is words in isolation, far more of my job lies in the unsaid than the spoken.

'Did you know Jane Bell well?'

'Well enough.' Carl nods. 'Saw her on the playground most days. I finish work in time to pick Jase up, perk of being my own boss now and having the lads to keep everything running.' His language has grown briefer, curter, I detect his desire to lead the conversation so I make it about him again, teasing him back.

'What do you do for work, Carl?'

'I'm a plumber, fifteen years now, I was an idiot at sixteen, made a lot of mistakes, but the one good decision I did make was learning a trade. Dad strong armed me into it, of course, but there you go. The old man knew what was best for me, even if I didn't.'

I give the chuckle I know he's expecting before casually adding: 'So, what is Jane like?'

'The loveliest woman you could hope to meet. Salt of the earth. She isn't like some of the mums, with their bright lipstick and blonde highlights and not much else. She is a lady with substance. You can tell most by the kids, like, and Molly's a lovely little thing – bright as a button, always smiling, kind to Jase. Raised right, you know, unlike most around here these days. Jane is always so friendly, and if you ever need anything she'll be the first to help – I got held up on a job one day, no one could get to Jase for an hour, and I turned up to find him playing with Molly and Joe, with Jane sat on a bench, half an eye on the three of them and half an eye on a book. Soon as she saw me, she said, "He's such a sweetie," and just took herself home. She does the right thing, straight off the bat, not for the thanks or for how it looks, just because it's right.

'Not all the parents are like her, though; bit cliquey it is, that place. Jane's busy, you see, she works every morning I think, so like me she can't always go in to help with reading, or join the PTA. I see them looking down their noses at us. Ironic, given we struggle to earn our living while they draw theirs from the dole office.

'I can't believe what she did, like. I'd take a bullet for her, and you can print that.' He nods down at my Dictaphone. 'To have sacrificed what she has, to save our littluns; if there's ever anything I can do for her, you tell her to let me know, okay? I still can't get my head around it – hundreds of children he was trying to blow apart, one of them my little Jase. He wrote his whole name for the first time yesterday, you know? Want to see?'

I nod encouragingly, and Carl reaches into his wallet for a scrap of paper with big, scratchy letters on it.

Jason Wickham, I'm sure it says, if you squint just right.

I look up at Carl as I hand it back. I see his smile, his pride, his devotion, his love.

I think to myself: James Foster may have had his reasons. But, Jane Bell, we can never repay you.

SEVENTEEN

JANE

I'm not entirely sure how time has passed over the days and nights that have followed my move into prison. I've never really slept, adopting a fitful pattern of napping when my tired mind shuts down and waking to restless thoughts. I'm in constant turmoil.

I can't eat, I can only sip water. Even something so pure and natural tastes rancid. I can tell the officers have gone from frustrated to concerned, but I can't help it, I'm doing my best. Every noise is alien, everything I know is absent. Waking up is so lonely, and I do that so many more times in a night. I'm used to feeling the warm squirming bodies of Molly and Joe arriving next to me in the darkness, wedged into the bed with us. They have their own smell, a perfume of softness, and floral washing powder, and love. Here, my nostrils are filled with the smell of urine, bleach, and cabbage. My skin only touches hard blankets and a cold wall. My heart is in agony.

Neil's first visit here was a precious hour. He folded me against him, and I got a slice of home for a short while. He has assured me that Molly and Joe are doing okay, and that Rachel is helping, which is a relief – they're in loving hands. I told him I answered all the inspector's questions as best I could and that I felt that he was being kind to me, given the gravity of what has happened. Disappointingly, Neil said he doesn't know any details of what the police have found out about James. I suppose I'll be privy to those facts when they're relevant to the court proceedings. I just hope that what I've done, and all the attention it's got, changes things. That it makes the people who are supposed to protect us actually do that in the future.

A few weeks after seeing the receipt my unease ratcheted up further, winding me tighter. I was walking to the school to drop Molly off, Joe in his buggy, Molly holding onto the handle, trundling along. It was overcast, drizzle curling our edges, pressing damp into my bones. I kissed Molly goodbye and watched as she skipped towards her friends when we arrived and Joe started trying to get out of his buggy to go to nursery, but it wasn't one of his days for that. Joe never does well in wet weather, perhaps it not suiting his lungs, and he was grizzling, crotchety. With a wave to Rachel, who was engrossed with her youngest's teacher, I turned him from the school and hurried away, hoping movement would settle him. As we were emerging from the school gates, he threw his juice cup out in a surprisingly large arc for one so small. I sighed, gritted my teeth, and bent down to pick it up. It had rolled behind the school sign which meant I had to angle myself specifically to reach it. My fingers touched the gently pitted grippy surface and I felt a tiny flash of relief at this small victory. I used to think that seemed to be the essence of motherhood – the swelling sense of achievement at ridiculously

minuscule things. I remember being a bit disappointed sometimes. Now, I have moments of longing for such simplicity, for
that version of motherhood that I slightly resented. As I
glanced up, I saw something that stilled my heart. A shock of
dirty blond hair poking out the front of a black hoodie. The
distinctive blond beard. My neighbour furiously scribbling in
a notepad, bright brow slung low over angry eyes. I felt the
bite of alarmed intrigue. I noticed the drumbeat of my heart
against my chest wall, speeding faster and louder. I realised I
needed to appear natural, for him to not recognise that I'd
seen him, yet I needed a few extra minutes to work out what
was going on. Why on earth was he here?

I let the juice cup slip out of my fingers and I nudged it
further out of reach so that if James saw me, it looked like I
was just retrieving it. Normal. I willed Joe to keep quiet, and
used my spare hand to tickle his leg softly through his
corduroy dungarees just the way he likes. I was mostly hidden
by a wall on the other side of the gates, and James was tucked
behind a bush just enough to be guarded from mainstream
view but not enough to be suspicious. I tracked thoughts
through my mind, desperately trying to keep a fingertip hold
on logic, grappling with the wind of emotion that was trying to
snatch it from me – *what does this mean? Why would he be
taking notes outside our school?* It was drop off time – was he
making notes on children walking in alone, was he planning to
take a child? My breath hitched and my resolve hardened. I
was close enough to make out the focus of his gaze, and I saw
that it wasn't trained on the children at all, it was scanning the
building. That didn't add up then. The movement of his hand
looked disorganised, moving all around the page rather than
across it. Drawing, I realised, not writing. I kept the fight up –
trying to maintain the flow of sensible possibilities; though

somewhere beyond my conscious thoughts already the dreadful, terrifying truth had made a home. Was he a parent, estranged from his child, trying to catch a glimpse of them? Why would he be making drawings of the school then? He stopped drawing and cast darting looks down the street both sides of him. I could tell one would land on me within seconds, and I moved my body around just in time, so that it looked as though I'd been facing away from him. I let my fingers find the juice cup again, plucking it out this time, and stood up, giving Joe a smile. When I looked over at where he was, I saw the back of his figure swiftly disappearing, striding away, in the opposite direction to Wesley Street. I didn't even have to think, I knew the opportunity I had been given, I felt in my gut that something was horribly wrong in this situation, and Molly was inside. I tightened my grip around the buggy's handle, noticing the white peaks to my knuckles – snow dusting a mountain range. I followed.

James was agile, unmarred by the ravage of carbs and childbirth. I knew I couldn't jog to keep up in case he saw me, which is how I almost missed him. He had been turning down the street that run parallel to the school's perimeter and I nearly shot past the little staff and service road, narrow and shaded as it was by a wall and a tree. Looking back, that shows how much this has changed me – I can chuckle mirthlessly now at that inept woman, playing detective. *Of course* he went down the service entrance – you should have realised that the moment he took off, foolish Jane. It was only that blond hair that gave him away, that caught my attention as he jumped up onto the large bin. Even that was silent, like a panther stalking prey. Which I suppose is literally what he was doing. Bile rose in the back of my throat, scorching its path. He crouched down once he was up there, peering through the railings that topped the six-foot high wall. He reached slowly into his back pocket, pulling his notepad and pen out again, before flicking it open and recommencing his plotting. I stayed tucked round the corner, peeping at him, until I was sure there were no mistakes in what I was seeing. Danger. Threat to Molly. Something deeply wrong. I can remember the exact moment I realised it, standing with my fingers chalk-white in their grip around Joe's buggy handles, breath shallow and panting like at pre-natal class: *James Foster was going to do something terrible and St Oliver's was the target.* I remember the surface calm I showed – the way I walked home with Joe as if nothing was amiss.

I remember the storm that was raging beneath – the fear, the pulsing drive to understand this, the clamouring need to get help, the disbelief and hints of denial, the sense of going mad, the certainty that life had changed for ever, that James was bringing something dark, darker than I'd ever known, and that I found myself at the heart of it.

The initial hearing at the magistrates' court passed in a blur. My solicitor had been in to speak to me beforehand. I think she is someone who hears but doesn't listen, so I kept very quiet. I've learned to choose people for how they make me feel rather than the uniform they wear or the job title they spout. I actually trust Detective Inspector Simmons far more than my solicitor, ironic as that is, given that his team are the ones holding the keys to my cage, and the ones who put me in it.

The part of the hearing I know I'll remember most is the charge – that huge word that was proclaimed as if it was nothing when to me it remains everything: murder. Another part of the hearing that left me reeling was my bail being rejected. As we'd parted ways beforehand, I'd asked Detective Inspector Simmons if it was possible, if I might get to go home to my children, however briefly.

'Off the record, you have a cat in hell's chance, I'm sorry. I wish it could be different,' he replied. He was right, and even though I knew it could be coming I have never understood the expression 'soul-destroying' so truly.

I know my case is now referred to the Crown Court and Neil tells me that a very high-level barrister has come forward – a member of something called the Queen's Counsel – which means that he's one of the very best. Neil says that he wants to help me, for free, but that he can only take over after the bail hearing. I ask Neil if this barrister has said why they want to do such a thing – I've never clicked well with huge egos and limelight lovers – and apparently this man said, 'I want to represent Jane because her life is now in the hands of the justice system, and very sadly, in my experience, that system doesn't seem to know too much about justice. I, however, worship that bastard.' I think we'll get along just fine.

I'm meeting Simon Rafferty on Thursday.

EIGHTEEN

SIMON

I meet Jane for the first time in the prison, three days after the magistrates' hearing. I've only managed to get access to her and be appointed to her case now the magistrates' hearing has been held, with that fuckwit of a lawyer representing Jane during it. Sorry, you'll have to excuse my language. Don't worry, you'll get used to me, my heart's in the right place.

When I catch sight of Jane for the first time in person – her flesh, blood, and essence before me rather than just digital pixels on a screen – she is seated at a round table in a bare private visitor room, with hunched shoulders and panda eyes. Prisons aren't big on interior design, let me tell you. They also aren't big on comfort. I stride over to Jane and she stands to greet me with a handshake.

With bail having been denied at the hearing, Jane will remain locked up here until the main trial. I'm mortified. If I'd been representing Jane, I'd have fought a bloody hard battle for bail to be granted. I think I'd have won too. I'll make sure I win the big one instead – her freedom.

Until you've stood in these shiny black brogues that we

criminal defence barristers favour, you don't see freedom for what it is, or the law for what it is. You might think you do, but you don't. If justice is the goal, then the legal system is a farce – it's more a system of *order* now. Order and justice are different beasts.

The courtroom is such a contradictory place – it's a stadium of both drama and tedium. It can vault from electric performances worthy of acting accolades to the mind-numbing dreariness of hearing for the thousandth time the list of every social media platform in existence that jurors are forbidden from discussing trial details on. In the modern world that list takes a while. It feels like a stage, set with comic fancy dressed figures from a period drama; yet at its most sensitive moments it moves with the bite and ferocity of a spy thriller.

Although we can work our way out of ever admitting it, we barristers are at times liars, schemers, manipulators, and the worst of us are even cheats. However, we are also knights in shining armour, freedom-fighters, defenders of the defence-less, and individuals who have committed our lives to justice. Paradoxical, aren't we? The last important thing to note is that we are neither judge nor jury.

Jane has slightly chapped skin and a steady grip as she clasps my hand in hers for a brief handshake.

'Hello, Mrs Bell, I'm Simon Rafferty, your new defence barrister. I'm delighted that you have agreed to let me represent you, and I'm deeply honoured to be doing so.

I promise you that your life is my life now... until I've got yours back for you.'

'It's a pleasure to meet you, Mr Rafferty, thank you for all this.'

We both sit down. I never get comfortable being in a

prison – the inmates may be locked away, but I'm locked in here right along with them. I sit on the edge of my seat rather than settling back into it.

'I just have to ask though... well, I can't afford any expensive fees – ends only just meet for us as it is. My husband said you wanted to help me free of charge, but seeing you in that fancy suit, I'm worried he's made a mistake?' Jane gives me a small, embarrassed smile.

'There was no mistake, Mrs Be—'

'Jane, please,' she interrupts softly.

I give a single nod of acceptance.

'Well then, Simon too,' I reply. I see her give an almost imperceptible shake of her head. Hmm, she's an interesting one.

'I'm going to represent you pro bono, which means one hundred percent free of charge. You will be my top priority until you step out of those courtroom doors and get knocked flying by your two gorgeous children.'

Tears pool in Jane's eyes as I speak.

'I don't understand... why would you do that for me?'

'You're a heroine, Jane. An inspiration. You represent hope. Hope for anyone who feels powerless or abandoned; for anyone who needs courage to stand up for what's right. I'm a man who lives to stand up for what is right, but I think most people can't even tell what that is anymore. We need to show them, to remind them what that looks like, and that every single human being must shoulder responsibility for their fraction of doing the right thing if we want any moral integrity at all to remain here on this earth with us.' Jane is nodding slowly, but also frowning. 'I'm a straight shooter, Jane, so I'll tell you off the bat that obviously there'll be a huge media following for your case. There is a lot of publicity available for my chambers. That's why they've gone for it. But for me, well, this is the chance to stand on the right side, the chance to make a real difference, to actually assist true justice in being done.'

Jane looks overwhelmed and confused. Perhaps I've grown too fond of the drama and eloquence of closing arguments – I've gone full scale soliloquy on us both.

'I'm not sure I understand, Mr Rafferty, I'm sorry. Would you mind explaining again for me? It's just that the lawyer I had before you – for my first hearing, at the magistrates' court –said that it would be a fairly quick and simple process. That it is a case of determining my sentence at the next trial at the Crown Court – that there would be no jury, none of the spectacle. But that sounds very different from what you're describing.'

'Ah. Yes. That's the big question we need to address – your plea. The next hearing is the plea and directions hearing at the Crown Court. It will take place within the next four weeks. During that hearing all the charges against you will be read out in open court and you will plead "guilty" or "not guilty". If you plead "guilty" the judge will sentence you quickly. However, if you plead "not guilty" then the case will go to trial. That involves a jury being convened and the trial being organised.

'Jane, I *know* that you have to do it... you have to plead "not guilty". It's your proclamation. It's your sign held up to the world in huge, stark print, that says "I stand". It's our event of taking back ground, of rejecting the misleading narrative that will otherwise go out in the world. It's another day of courage.'

'How can I? I am guilty, Mr Rafferty. I killed James. I couldn't let him take those bombs to the children.'

'You acted in defence of hundreds of innocent children's lives, Jane, including the defence of your own. They were in imminent danger. They are an extension of you. Therefore, we have substantial grounds for a self-defence case. I'm not going to lie to you, Jane, ever – it would by no means be a cut and dried win, but I truly believe we stand a jolly good chance – especially with a jury being involved. Outcomes of trials by jury rarely follow the letter of the law, rather, they follow the letter of human nature. Yours is a case that's all about what makes us human.'

'I'm not one for the spotlight, Mr Rafferty, and I'm not a liar. I don't think I could stand up in front of the judge and say that I'm not guilty.'

'I understand, Jane, really I do. However, it's my job to help you navigate this system and I need to impress upon you that what you would be pleading "not guilty"' to is not to *killing* James, which isn't in dispute, but rather *murdering* him. This is a *murder* charge. Did you honestly believe that your, or other, children's lives would be taken by James imminently?'

'Yes, I did.'

'And did you truly believe that there was no other way to stop that from happening?'

'Yes, absolutely, I tried to get help from the police several times. James was going to do it. The police weren't coming.'

'So, you acted in defence of your, and other's, children, believing this to be the only way?'

'Yes.'

'Then you did not murder James Foster, Jane, you acted in defence of others, which falls under the self-defence clause. You have to plead "not guilty".'

Jane is thoughtful for a few moments, staring down at her folded hands.

'Won't I get a longer sentence if we try this and I lose? Be away from my children and Neil for longer?'

'It's a possibility, yes, but I wouldn't be suggesting this if I didn't believe we stood a very good chance of winning. I can do this, Jane; and so can you.'

'It'll be awful for Neil and the children, though – the media and attention. We live a quiet life, Mr Rafferty, we like it that way.'

'Jane, I'm sorry, but that quiet life ended the moment your foot pressed down on that accelerator. It's gone, either way. Besides, isn't that a price they would happily pay to get you home? If we win, you could see them grow up – Joe's first day of primary school, Molly's first day of secondary school; she could cuddle up with you to tell you about her first crush, her first kiss, you could go prom dress shopping together; you could see Joe score his first goal, get his first A. Those things have to matter more than anything, don't they?'

Jane looks me levelly in the eye for a minute, then she says simply and strongly, 'Yes. Let's do it. "Not guilty".'

NINETEEN

JANE

Meeting my new barrister, Simon Rafferty, is a great experience. He is radiant. Never has a suit looked so modern, so sharp – he makes dapper seem old-fashioned – but he's warm and has deep dimples when he smiles. Most importantly, he feels synonymous with hope, something I've felt precious little of throughout this whole process, and for quite a while. My soul has grown so weary, so broken, carrying the fight against James alone for so long. Knowing Simon has taken up the fight for *me* has restored something in me. Even as the solidarity bolsters me, I feel the burning of shame – I don't deserve this, do I – given I killed a man? Simon even believes that there's a chance I can get out of here. He explains that his defence strategy will rest on the grounds that my killing of James should be deemed defence of others– which is given the same legal standing as self-defence – rather than murder.

My children are without a shadow of a doubt a part of me. I am them. For months after Molly was born, I remember she was an excellent sleeper (we weren't so lucky with Joe), and I couldn't believe she would sleep so soundly given how restless babies are reputed to be. So, every night, when Neil drifted off to sleep, I would go into Molly's room, pluck her gently out of her cot and sit with her. She lay on my chest. Beating heart above beating heart. I was mesmerised with the feel of her tiny chest rising and falling.

I spent those nights for months settling with an awakening knowledge that my life was no longer just *my* life; rather it extended out and around this tiny person who I'd made; then grown inside me, a part of my body, until she was safe to face the world; who I now, until my dying breath, am responsible for loving and protecting. I knew from that moment on that my life belonged to her – that in any nanosecond of any day I would give my life up for hers.

I think I just did.

Hearing how Simon talked about what happened, what he named it, has changed something for me – like a switch flicking to make a circuit whole again. It sits right within me, like sliding tired feet into hearth-warmed, well-worn slippers. Simon has taken something sullied and made it wholesome. *A rose by any other name would smell as sweet?* Equally, it was exactly what happened – I, myself, defended others. It brings to mind what happened in the wake of seeing James lurking outside St Oliver's. I felt rattled, like James had his hand wrapped around my throat and was choking me, a sadistic giggle escaping his lips as he felt my fear and heard my desperation. I raced to the local police station the next day and filed a report with yet another bored desk sergeant who couldn't care less about me. He looked at me through a vacant haze as though I was crazy and peered with distaste over the rim of the desk at Joe grizzling in his buggy.

'You wouldn't believe how bizarre some of the reports we field here are that turn out to be false starts, love. I'll file it for you, and I'll make sure someone puts eyes over it, but I wouldn't be alarmed. There are lots of systems in place that flag up suspicious activity.'

I felt my temper flare. 'There can't be a better "system" than the person who lives next door to him who's seen things no computer could ever find?!' I was conscious of my voice starting to fly, but I couldn't quite get hold of it enough to bring it down. My brain was telling it: *they're not listening, again, try louder*. The policeman had raised his eyebrows and tilted his chin up in an authoritative show of disapproval, whilst flapping a limp hand up and down slowly, gesturing at me to calm down. It incensed me more. 'What happened to community police work, boots on the ground, *protecting* people?' The emotion of that word floored me, laying upon my shoulders the weight of the burden I felt – of being the only person who seemed to understand what was happening with James and of being unable to get anyone to listen, to believe me, to help. I was exhausted by my desperation to feel safe again, of reaching out and always having my hand slapped away. My voice dropped to an agonised whisper as my chin fell forward, even the weight of my head being too much to hold up anymore. 'Why don't you believe me?'

I felt his gaze washing me with his judgements. When he answered, his voice had softened, and he sounded like a *person* for the first time.

'I do believe you, love, and I miss the old days of policing too. But cuts, you know.' He lifted his hands and twisted his mouth in apology. 'I wish I could do more, but being straight with you, we don't have the personnel to follow up every single report we get. We have to triage, decide which ones have merit, or grounds, that justify a share of the time. Your information will get its chance. If there is enough in it, we will proceed. That's all I can tell you.' My time was up. I felt the strong current of air created by someone pumping the door open and then closed against the wind. As I turned to leave, I found myself eye to eye with someone covered in lacerations; bruises blooming beneath skin that looked somehow too thin. I saw them limp forward, the pain shuttering their face closed every time their weight transferred over that leg. I saw the trauma in their haunted eyes. I understood two things: firstly, the police don't stop bad things happening, they just try to catch people once they're already too late; hence, secondly, no one in blue from that building was coming to Wesley Street.

Once I got over the feeling of rejection, and the smarting anger at the state of the world that meant the police weren't coming, I felt my resolve harden. It was like my emotions were heat and all I had around me since the receipt day was petrol and bone-dry firewood.

I was on my own. I could not accept the future it appeared was destined for me – that there was no stopping James, only picking up the pieces once he'd done whatever he came here to do. Those pieces would be my children. I would do anything to change that ending. *I delivered.*

The first step on that journey had to be to work out exactly what was going on.

I couldn't stop what I didn't know. I had my ideas, but that wasn't enough. If I got some proof together, maybe I had a chance with the police, perhaps I could go straight to the top of the right specialist unit. It came to me like a flash seared across my brain. That unit would be the terror division. I felt my chest hollow out, shatter, and combust simultaneously. That understanding, as fundamental as how to breathe and how to give birth, galvanised me.

The door of the station banged shut behind me and with a flinty determination I marched to Rita's house. As I glanced at her front window, I saw her there, bones all joined at sharper angles than the rest of us. Her house is not the best kept on the street, but her heart is, which is what I was there for, what we should all be here for. If there was any information about James to be had, it would have been hiding in number forty-three.

I lifted a hand to wave at her and before I even had chance to lower it, she had gone from sight. My foot hadn't landed from its next stride before I saw a pair of those funny croc shoes as her door opened. It is a shade of red that matches her perfectly – dramatic, loud, yet warm in every speck.

'Hiya, duck, how have you been keeping?' She made her way down her doorstep slowly, pulling the door ajar behind her, and smiled kindly at me. 'And this little fella? My, he's a cutie.' She bent down to give him a fuss and I felt a peace try and fail to penetrate the incessant humming of my frazzled stress.

'I'm having some difficulty actually, Rita, to do with our new neighbour.' I inclined my head towards James' house, and I saw her glance that way and knot her brow into a tight frown.

'Doesn't seem the best sort, not that I've actually met 'im mind, or even seen 'im come to think of it. What's the trouble been? I suppose you'll have more to do with it, being 'is semi.'

I nod and give a troubled sigh. 'I've got a bad feeling about him. I don't want to start anything, speaking badly of a new neighbour before people have a chance to meet him,' I let genuine strain jump into my voice even as I played the political game, 'but I've seen some things that have left me... afraid, if I'm honest.' I let Rita see me, dripping distress. 'I feel like I'm going mad half the time – Neil seems to think I'm overreacting, I've been to the police, and they aren't taking it seriously, but I *feel it*, Rita. Something bad is... in there.' I gestured to James' house and shuddered. Rita noticed, and she looked long and deep into my eyes as she nodded.

'Do you want to come inside, have a cup of tea, talk about it properly? You look like you're about to collapse.' She put a motherly hand on my shoulder and I almost cracked. I longed to accept, felt a visceral pull from my middle, but I knew I would break down if I did, if I was mothered, and might not have been able to put myself back together, so I shook my head, hoping she could read the regret seeping out of me. 'What can I do for you then? Let me help?' she implored, gently yet with conviction. Gratitude overwhelmed me. I didn't speak for a long moment while I swallowed down the lump choking me from the back of my throat.

'I don't know that there's anything you can do right now, though would you mind keeping an eye on his place? Seeing if you notice anything... anything at all, and if you do, call me straight away. Though stay safe, please, don't give him any reason to suspect you're watching – I saw a receipt of his, for nails, fertiliser, wiring, that's what started all this.'

I saw her visibly draw back, alarm stretching her eyes wider. Relief flooded me, like a waterboarding – painful, sudden, too much. She *got it*. I was not ridiculous. How I felt was real. It spurred me on into a gallop, my words muddling together with the rush to validate the rest. 'Then I saw him at Molly and Joe's school, St Oliver's, you know?' I didn't wait for a response. 'He was making notes. It looked like drawings to me, from the way his hands were moving all around, not in straight lines, if you see what I mean? So I think he's targeting the kids.' Rita was artificially still and all I could hear were my panting breaths, working overtime after my onslaught of words. To fill the silence, once I got my breath back, I said, 'So be careful, okay?' Rita nodded absently a few times. I felt the grip of panic at her expression, that maybe I'd said too much, scared her unnecessarily, but then I saw her jolt back into that space with me, lock eyes, and the solidarity told me I was right to share.

'You've said all this to the police? Exactly like you've told me, all the details from the receipt, that he was at the school, making drawings?' She spoke sharper and faster than I had ever heard her, like someone else entirely.

'Yes. Plus, even more, how angry he is, the way he's boarded up the garden, all of it. They said it's not enough to go on, basically.'

Rita shook her head in disgust.

'You couldn't make it up. Leave it with me, duck, I'll think on it, work out if there's anything else we can do.' She seemed to space out then and she started opening her door. As an afterthought she added, 'Anytime you need somewhere to park the kids, you hightail straight here, you hear?' I nodded and she looked straight at Joe. Something I couldn't read passed strongly across her features. I couldn't bear to acknowledge what it was... and what it meant.

TWENTY

ANEESA

I'm sitting in my flat trying to unwind by watching some train wreck reality TV, which is my guilty pleasure, and trust me I feel *very* guilty about it. My feet are curled beneath me; Bertie, lying in the nest he's formed behind my knees, is purring. A text comes through. I reach forward to pick my phone up off the coffee table, stretching my torso to discomfort to avoid disturbing Bertie. I can't ever make myself leave my phone alone when I hear a text arrive as my mind jumps straight to: *what if it's news about Mum?*

Simon's name on my screen brings a volt of pleasure. My breath hitches into an aborted gasp. I hate how hard I have to work to not let him in.

> *Annie, saw your stunning profile piece. Taken the case. Met Jane today, love her already. Thanks for the heads up, not... and also, you're welcome – now you'll have so much more to write about! Si*

I roll my eyes at his text manner which truly represents his in-the-flesh personality. Simon calls me Annie, because of my almost-orphan status, and it was the first moment he cracked my shell – people usually skirt around it, clam up, get awkward, and that makes me feel like there's shame in what happened to me. By cutting straight to it, and calling it out from the shadows into the open, Simon showed me his bravery. He made it okay, into a nickname said with affection and a smile, which showed me there's nothing to be ashamed of, it's just out there in the world like red hair, or glasses – something outside you, not inside. Which is how *he* went from being outside my walls, to the only person who's ever made it in. Simon taking Jane's case is an exciting development. It's so *him*. I'll bet anything that he's helping Jane pro bono, though he'll pass it off as somehow advantageous to him. He's an enigma – projecting cockiness and acting audaciously, as though they could hide his heart of gold. He has an insatiable lust for goodness, for true absolute justice. He stands with people who can't protect themselves. It's who he is, not just what he does when he's on the clock. Back when we spent more time together dissecting our days over lunchtime sandwiches, he saw a woman getting assaulted behind a tree in the park we were in. He approached, filming it on the camera he always has in his beaten-up leather satchel, the same one he still carries into the courtroom, stopped it progressing further, took the lady and the film to the police, represented her and supported her through the case, won, blew the top off the human trafficking it was connected to and then gave me the scoop on the story.

I think about how much closer we'll grow again both working in the same metaphorical space and my heart sings as it sinks. My head tries to take control by sending minions to the drawbridge. Meanwhile my heart is a maverick and it flutters almost tauntingly at the thought of what could be... and when have you ever heard of a maverick surrender?

Simon and I have grown tantalisingly close several times now, always spitting sparks meeting corny punchlines. Then, when we're right on the cusp of the freefall one of us hauls us both back from the edge, pushes away, and flees. It's how it has to be; for both of us, I think. It's just never been in our stars. Imagining a different ending is a happy thought because somewhere inside myself I desperately want love's infectious warmth, the way it shines light into dark spaces, the scaffold it lends to allow you to build. Yet, I also know the darkness that engulfs you when love's taken away. I know the agony.

I have a good life now, one that feels satisfying. I've known times where I never thought it would be possible to feel this okay. I don't think I'd survive another detonation, so I shut love down, whenever it shines its beam across me, though that doesn't mean I don't enjoy the splash of sunshine on my face while it passes over.

I'm at my desk in the office the next afternoon when a withheld number rings through on my landline. Given it's come directly to me rather than through the switchboard I briefly consider ignoring it, not in the mood for a cold caller, but curiosity gets the better of me along with my rule: never ignore a call that could be the one related to mum.

'Hello,' I state; my name too personal to give to an anonymous silence. A few beats pass. I start lifting the phone away from my ear to hang up when I hear a gruff response.

'Who am I speaking too?' It's sharp and fierce. My guard fires up, quickening my breathing.

'A member of the reporting team at the *Birmingham Gazette*. Who am *I* speaking to?'

'I'm trying to reach Aneesa Khan.' There's something about how rushed the words are, combined with their roughness that arouses my investigative attention.

'You've reached her.' I reply, pausing before asking, 'how can I help?'

'I think... I think I want to talk. About the main story you've been covering.' There are wars in his voice. Reluctance, force. 'I need to... let people know.' I can feel him teetering on the edge of withdrawal or freefall. I try to ease him forward.

'I can help with that. Would you like to chat about it over the phone now or would you prefer to share face to face?' I don't usually offer this without knowing how useful a person's information or story is, but the timing of the call combined with the caller's tone leaves me buzzing with the certainty that this is big. I barricade out the musings of who this man is, what he needs to tell me, to focus on ensuring I actually manage to get him to.

'You know what, I'm going to call back. Sorry.'

'Wait–' I start, but he's gone.

I thump my clenched fist onto the desk, my pinky finger snarling with the cracking impact. I needed that lead. I'm losing momentum. The lengthy wait for Jane's trial will be slow and boring for our readers unless I find something more to keep them engaged; and I'm desperate to avoid having to use James' letter for that purpose. My gut tells me I need to know more before taking it to Eliza. I'm scouring every avenue I can for clues about James Foster's connections, but even the police haven't found anyone yet. None of the intellectual angles have enough draw to them – I know my readers won't be engaged by lectures from priests or judges hypothesising.

Rather, they want startling insights into the mystic modern real world they move within every day but which is ever changing and full of guerilla warfare booby traps.

I jump at the sound of my phone ringing. I can feel the mass of my heart in my throat, a taste like bile coating my tongue and my hand sprints to the handset. My fingers slip over it to begin with as I take in the withheld number again. My voice feels unsteady, as though it is legs trying to get purchase after an earthquake.

'Aneesa Khan, *Birmingham Gazette*.' I give my name this time, hoping it's him, trying to take charge of this conversation even though my voice is threaded with tremors and notches.

'I, spoke to you-' It is him. My fingers are cramping from how tightly they're gripping the phone.

'A few minutes ago. Can we meet? Before I change my mind.' His voice is low, a soldier alone in a bunker deep behind enemy lines.

'Yes. Just name a time and place.'

'Six a.m., the park just west of Wesley Street.'

'I'll be there.'

There's a pause so long I wonder if he's walked away and forgotten to hang up. Then it comes, a vessel carried in on a tide of resignation.

'So will I.'

TWENTY-ONE

NEIL

It is time. Time to kick myself into action and turn from a flailing sap into the man Jane, Molly, and Joe need me to be. I need to captain my ship.

I treasure the time I visit Jane, though it has been bleak and heart-wrenching to see her under lock and key. I've at least been lucky that they've let me hold her to me once, and I felt my stress fade as she comforted me. I know that means I've failed her again – being the one to be comforted not the comforter – but that's the way we've always been: Jane the strong one, the brave heart; me quiet, steady, and gently following.

Back near the beginning of our relationship I worried over it every single night – that it was only a matter of time before she realised I wasn't much of a 'man' in the way so many of the people we grew up with were. I've never thrown a punch or yelled profanities at a football referee, I've never drunk endless pints in one night or shown off scars in the pub. Someone like Jane, who's always been gutsy and stood up for what she believes in, she'd want someone who'd match her, I thought, someone tough.

When we'd been together just less than a year, I managed to save up enough to get us out of Birmingham for a couple of nights. We went to a tiny cottage in the Peak District. We went for walks, just soaking up the natural wilderness, the peace, and the space stretching out. On one of the long walks, we stopped for a while at the bottom of a hill so big it looked like a mountain. I had to tell her:

'Jane, I love you. With all my heart and soul, I love you, but I'm not a mountain of a man – I'm not hard and strong like that.'

I lifted my arm to point straight at that behemoth. 'I'm not tough and impressive and bold. You deserve a mountain, and I'll never be one, and I'd rather know now if you think that one day you'll wake up and say you could never have a future with me, because, you know, you want a mountain for that.'

The corners of her eyes crinkled up then, followed by her mouth stretching wide into a smile, and a chuckle bubbled up from her stomach. She wrapped her fingers around my forearm and squeezed it.

With the smile still lighting up her face, she replied, 'I love you, Neil, just the way you are. I love you for your huge heart – I don't think mountains have them. I love you for how much compassion and sweetness you give the world – mountains are too hard to show that. I love you for your gentle care, your tenderness, all that soft warmth you have inside you, and mountains seem to me to be cold. Those are what matter to me in my partner in life, I don't want some great hunk of rock. I never will.'

I remember that conversation as I step across the threshold

of the prison to visit my wife today. It gives me a lightness of spirit as my heart grows heavier. My breath catches painfully as I set eyes on her. She looks like she's shrunk down inside her body, like there are some empty spaces in it, instead of her spirit spilling out and into the room all around her like it usually does.

Things are clearly different here – there is such a sense of regimentation. Everything is functional only, beauty never allowed to permeate, even when it would have been equally easy to make it so. This is also a place filled with tension. There is no peace here... it's no place for Jane.

Although all I want is to wrap Jane's spirit and love around me like a blanket, the new captain in me knows there is so much to organise at home now that Jane's bail has been refused, decisions to be made, so I force these to the front of my mind: past the longing, past the loneliness, and past the fear.

She speaks urgently. 'How are the children?'

'They're doing okay. Rachel keeps them busy and distracted during the days and we pull together as best we can at night. I won't lie to you, we're struggling without you, of course we are, but I'm trying to hold it all together. Mum's offered to come and stay for a while so that there's two of us in there, to keep on top of things. I said I'd ask you.'

'You need to do what *you* think is right now, Neil. We can't know when, or even if, I'll be coming home to you all. I know it's a heavy burden to carry but you're going to have to forge ahead, whatever's right for you and them, you do it, never mind me.'

I feel whiplash at this sudden U-turn and resentment slices through me, that she's chosen this moment to hand the reins of our family back. Her words feel hard and unloving. I don't recognise the woman I love; the dynamic has changed... again. I feel cast away.

'We're not there yet, Jane.' Her eyes flare open at my anguish. 'We're nowhere near there.'

'We're very near there indeed, Neil, just a hair's breadth away, and it'd be better if we started a transition process with decisions and things, don't you think?' I can see from the tightness in her face and the sorrow in her eyes how hard it is to say these words. She finds a way to continue, 'It would be wildly unfair of me to expect you to try to include me in every tiny decision when it's you out there dealing with everything and living with the consequences.'

'Whatever has gone before, we're still a team, Jane,' I sigh, 'we always will be, even if we're not inside the same four walls. Don't put me there yet, out on my own. Please, don't quit our team, not when we're still in the game.' I suck in a desperate breath and my voice breaks on the next statement. 'I'm not ready.'

Jane is silent, her eyes turning to the table for a few moments. I work on slowing my breathing, then I reach across to wrap my fingers around hers. Her eyes lift as our digits connect, flashing straight into mine. We both look to the prison officers, to check if we'll be allowed this contact.

'It's Maggie. We've become a strange sort of friends. She'll give us a minute.' Jane pauses, her voice graver when she speaks again. 'I won't quit our team, Neil. Bring your mum in, if she's kind enough to do it, but only if it's stable – indefinite.' She gives a firm nod then, 'They can't lose someone else; you know?'

I nod, the most confident I've been since I arrived.

Thoughts already on sofa beds and school collections. It helps, having something to do, to hold on to. Jane breaks into my reverie though, speaking quietly but surely, as if to herself more than me.

'Let's play to our strengths. Your mum's a mountain. The kids need all your love and heart, but with such a vicious storm swirling around them, they need a mountain too.'

I feel my chest squeezing – my ribs feeling several sizes too small for what they hold. That's all it takes for my confidence to belch a farewell as it's sucked down a plughole.

I think the first hairline fracture formed when Molly was born. I could see how natural Jane was, holding this fragile thing she loved more than either of us knew it was possible to love someone and hers to protect. Jane was maternal perfection, which meant there were never any discussions about roles, they were pre-ordained by the hand that bestowed that instinct on Jane. I was the support vehicle; Jane was the headliner. Then Joe came along, and the crack became a chasm; by settling for being Jane's support I hadn't learned how to warm the bottle up just right, how to soothe Molly from a bad dream, how to talk her down from a tantrum. The only piece of fatherhood I claimed for my own was a bedtime story every night. I feel it now as I did back then – that agitated swallowing hollow that is regret.

When Joe came, chaos joined him, not because of anything he did, but because two kids is a different game. Molly was at a completely different stage with completely different needs and the energy that took was overwhelming. What Jane needed from me was a break. However, being away all day working, I didn't have the same level of bond with them as Jane did... how could I possibly have? I hadn't built the efficiency, I still needed to think about every step of a task with them. I tried so hard, but I was slow, one of them always seemed to be crying or stropping. The house was too small for Jane to pretend she didn't know. It became easier for her just to do it all. I tried to insist, to explain that I just needed to learn, but she was too exhausted to have that sort of patience. I saw how the kids used up more of that than any human has. There was none left for me. She got frustrated when I didn't get it right, nudging me out of the way with a smile or a sigh depending on the day. I was pushed out – literally and metaphorically. I didn't open my harbour to resentment or frustration of that – I understood. It wasn't her fault, it wasn't even mine fully, it lay within the misfortune of timing and circumstance. We didn't see the point of no return until it was in the rear-view mirror. I was okay with that whilst I had the pride of earning enough to support us all, to allow Jane to be the stay-at-home mum she had always been open about wanting to be. We thought we knew how expensive children would be. We were wrong.

It was mind-blowing, even with taking hand-me-downs and never spending an unnecessary penny. They have two parents who love them with all their hearts, that's what that really matters, I thought. That's not all Jane wanted for them. She wanted more – for Molly and Joe to do all the things they wanted to, the chance to take opportunities, to be able to go to the fancy baby music class after Joe banged on the pans a few times. So, she went to work for a few hours a week to pay for that tuned-up-tots thing and for Molly to get a karate uniform and weekly classes. I'm proud of her for that now, but back then I was lost in growing self-loathing. She'd had to do it because I hadn't been given that promotion I'd been going for.

I was failing in every area of my life while she was thriving. I shut down to her while I tried to get past that.

When James came, I couldn't even keep my kids safe. I shut down on another level. I see now how much my mistake cost us; how much all of them did. I pray it isn't too late to make amends.

TWENTY-TWO

SIMON

'Murder' is legally defined as someone of sound mind unlawfully killing a human being with the intent to kill or cause grievous bodily harm. Self-defence is one of the criteria that qualifies for 'lawful killing' under certain circumstances. My first task is to go over every piece of evidence provided, to try to disprove Jane's intent to kill. My best guess is that the case is watertight on the forensics, given the speed and confidence with which the CPS made their decision for the murder charge.

Nearly a week after the plea and directions hearing at the Crown Court I meet with Jane. The hearing was a good day. It was a day that deceived with its simplicity, its calm. Jane entered, she stated, she left.

Today, appears to be a bad day. The first thing I see is the defeat in her eyes. She holds herself tall, her shoulders aren't curling downwards, but the light in her eyes has dimmed.

'How are you doing... really doing?' I ask her.

'I'm coping,' Jane replies, her mouth set into a thin line.

'Are you though? I wouldn't be.'

'There's nothing to say, Mr Rafferty, it is what it is.'

'Simon, I insist. And there's everything to say, Jane. What we have here together is a safe place. It's one of the few safe spaces you have right now. You can share with me what you're going through. No one will be closer to you than me in the coming weeks. We're facing this together, as partners in a sense. Sound away. Get it out, or it'll consume you.'

Jane lets the silence sit between us for a few moments. I've learned that silence can be a master persuader, negotiator, and interrogator so I let it join us, knowing that Jane needs to keep the weight on her shoulders as light as possible. The mere task of enduring this trial will be more than most could bear.

'It's the helplessness, Simon.' She looks up from under her dipped brow as she says my name, and her mouth and eyes soften for a moment. 'It's the idleness and the emptiness and the locks. It's time passing and me sitting. It's the hole of my children not understanding why I've left them. It's slowly suffocating me.'

'I get that, Jane, really I do. I'd be gasping for air too. I'm an action man' – I chuckle – 'if I don't like something, I change it. I know the world is tight fisted. I graft for the things I want. I fight for the things I believe in. So, I wouldn't be coping at all on my own in here. But hang on in there, Jane, the thing is, you're not in it alone. You might feel helpless, but we're not hopeless. And it's hope that fuels the spirit, it's hope that lends us courage; hope is warmth and a future, it can strengthen and nourish. These bars might hold you now, but they won't for ever; your heart burns for your kids, but soon you'll be together. Hope is yours, Jane, and hope is life.'

The room feels thick with a palpable tension. Jane breaks it with a joke.

'You're a poet and you didn't know it.' She smiles softly.

'Oh, I knew it... it's my secret weapon. Law is contracts and rules. Humans are emotions and language – it's words, Jane, words build connection, and connection grants freedom.' I pause and force myself to calm down a fraction from yet another soliloquy.

'I can do the contracts and the rules for the judges, but the juries hold the verdicts. The jury is twelve human beings. Twelve human beings with a big decision to make.'

'You're like no one I've ever known, Mr Rafferty.'

I roll my eyes and throw my hands up in a gesture of indignation. 'It's Simon!'

I shout, with a smile.

TWENTY-THREE

ANEESA

I've been vibrating with anticipation about the interview. Sleep stood me up last night, sending me the apology gift of puffy bags under my eyes and a strange pallor too stubborn for make-up to tame. It's dusk and foreboding crawls through my veins, making rats of wind-carried crisp packets and monsters of lamp posts on my walk to the park.

I feel an undertow of fear, at the danger I could be putting myself into – a park in the dark with a strong-sounding stranger. It snaps at my heels, a sheepdog trying to turn the flock from the cliff, but I am too obsessed to take heed. Joggers ahead, encased in rainbows of neon and bouncing headtorches reassure me as I approach the park. The clear air starts hissing with rain, falling as if the sky had tripped and a full bucket it was carrying had sloshed over. The noise of the drops torrenting onto the pavement mask other sounds, which worsens the straining headache tightening at my temples from my jaw being a clamped vice. One foot in front of the other.

Just when I begin to feel the last of my determination leaking out through a puncture, I see a figure sitting on a bench, eyes scanning the two approaches professionally. He stands when he sees me, a coiled spring. He lifts a hand in greeting and something in his movement shouts out gently: friend, not foe. He gestures to the other end of the bench as he sits. I notice a crumpled sodden towel on the ground next to his feet and a glance at the bench shows he's wiped it dry for me; he must have seen me before I him. A smile tugs the corners of my mouth up as I sit. Suddenly I'm aware of a hand shooting towards me and he must notice my panic for he bobs his outstretched palm up and down with a wry smile, indicating he was just offering a handshake. I smile an embarrassed apology and grip his fingers. A handshake so tight it might bruise greets me, along with his first words:

'I'm Officer Briggs – a member of the highest level British Anti-Terror Task Force. Pleased to meet you.' I slide my arm surreptitiously behind my back as I shake my hand out. My head is spinning at the possibilities. What on earth is he here to share? For an instant I feel overwhelming thankfulness that I followed my driving urge to come here.

I take Officer Briggs in. He has several tattoos over his forearms, which are the only large patches of skin I can see, as the rest of him is covered with practical looking black fatigues.

'You guarantee my identity will be protected?' are his next words to me.

'Iron-clad,' I reply, mirroring his economy with words.

'Can I trust you?'

'Yes. I promise.'

His eyebrows shoot up as if they've been electrified, and he stares me down for a long moment before jutting his chin in what looks like satisfaction.

'Very well. Let's proceed. You can turn on your recorder.' I slip the Dictaphone out of my pocket and place it on the bench between us, clicking it on to capture his words. He looks at the Tarmac path just beyond his knees, seemingly reflecting. I assume he'll want to set our conversation in motion, carve out its context and purpose, rather than me pummelling him with questions, so I share the silence. I take a deep breath in an attempt to settle my charging pulse, to ground myself from the frenetic adrenaline high. The air in my nostrils brings with it the scent of wet grass and vegetation. I decide to grasp the hand of the story, give it the comforting encouragement to step forward with me.

'Thank you, Officer Briggs. Are you here to talk to me about something related to Jane Bell or James Foster?' I ask tentatively. It's the only thing that fits. His eyes snap onto mine, a jack in the box erupting. My inbreath hitches sharply, catching on the intensity of his stare.

'Yes.' There's another pause. I have to stoke my patience. 'I'm here for some... corrections. To fill in some dubious gaps in the narrative.' Excitement is a wave rolling into my stomach, building up to its foamy climaxing crash. 'The entire thing is an atrocity on more levels than I can count. The threat was more real than dirt. Those bombs Foster had in the house on Wesley Street were designed for maximum death. Fucking morbid. As sinister as I've ever known. You don't get bombs to that stage without following through – they were ready to detonate.' The pedant in me lurches – whatever we think, we'll never *actually* know if James would have gone through with it since he never got chance to flick the switch. Yet I know Briggs's perspective deserves to be heard without argument. 'The plans were so thorough, the exact points identified in the school are where there would have been the densest concentration of children. This was evil incarnate, and nothing would have changed its course. Well, nothing, except Jane Bell.'

This has the bones of a ground-breaking news piece, but it's still just opinion on facts already shared. I need more, much more. I go after it.

'Why did you miss it?' I push, knowing this is likely a trigger to the heart of the truth he is here for. I wait to check he doesn't explode and judge his drooped shoulders and fractionally hung head as defeat I can lean on. 'What broke down in the system – surely this is something your team should have prevented?'

His face tightens and twists into a grimace of regret. 'Yes, definitely. The trouble nowadays is that we get so many tips daily that it's impossible to attend to each one. There are protocols and criteria linked to local police departments and this just slipped through the cracks with the local station not escalating it correctly. There was no chatter in our surveillance systems about anything going on in the area, so we'd not raised any alerts or paid extra attention to tips from the Wesley Street locale.' I can see some muscles on the story's skeleton now – a failing policing system, under-resourced, the schoolchildren in our cities having to foot the bill. It's not enough.

'What's changed to bring us here? More terrorists, or funding cuts by the government?' Readers need figures to blame. The Salem Witch Trials didn't end, they got less discriminatory.

'Both.' His eyes have narrowed with what I'd be forgiven for interpreting as respect and he's looking at me, instead of the chewing gum and leaf mosaic at his feet. 'We have a huge problem as a task force – the threats we face are snowballing faster than we can keep pace with. People are spending more time on the internet, on social media, than ever before. Connections, dangerous ones, are being forged across all sorts of previous divides. Master manipulators with dark agendas have a perfect pool of vulnerable individuals to trawl their nets through. People reveal so fucking much about themselves without realising just who might be watching. They paint themselves with fluorescent targets totally unaware until it's far too late. Take James Foster, this whole shitshow started because he posted in an online open forum for family rights asking for advice on how to deal with Children's Services. He revealed details in that post, and I'm just talking about turns of phrase and words he chose, that highlighted his desperation, his ability to be influenced. We know that someone with a far bigger social agenda targeted him, having found that. They masqueraded as a friend, found a reason to send him a private message and from there drip fed him exploitative information, under the guise of helping him navigate the "tyrannical" system.' Officer Briggs raises his eyebrows in exasperated anger before shaking his head and letting loose a humourless single laugh. 'They then positioned the outcome of the appeal in such a way as to condition and manipulate him into a frenzy in which he believed a large-scale murder-suicide bombing of St Oliver's was the right path of action.'

He pauses, searching my face for impact. Shock is an echo within me. I'm speechless, floundering around, fumbling any appropriate response. He places an envelope on the bench between us. 'The forum messages – you found them yourself, okay? And you absolutely *cannot* use them,' he says with a meaningful nod of discretion, his hand guarding the envelope until I nod my agreement.

As soon as he lifts his hand clear, I take the envelope and tuck it safely into the zipped pocket of my bag. Satisfied that

I've absorbed what he's saying, he continues. 'Don't misunderstand me, it takes something wrong in the head to make a choice to kill hundreds of children, no matter how much someone influences you. But I'm saying monsters are more often made than born, and with the state of the online world and how we live our lives now, frankly it was only a matter of time before something like this happened.'

I've recovered enough to ask, albeit slowly, 'So, by extension, it's a matter of time before it happens again... only next time there won't be a Jane Bell?'

'Well, I hope next time there won't need to be, because we'll have caught the bastards ourselves... but yes. I just thank God that Jane managed to save the kids. We'd have fucking killed Foster if he'd gone through with it and we'd then got the chance, so the ending is the same. Jane Bell just made it happier because three hundred kids didn't have to die before we could deal with him.'

'What about the person behind James then, the one who made the monster, have you caught him?'

Regret abducts Briggs's features, taking a hammer to his shoulders and switching off his spark. He looks me straight in the eyes, something like fear lurking behind his as he says, 'Not yet, but I promise you we're working on it.'

I squash a gasp and force my next question past my teeth. 'So, do you think this is just the *beginning*, that a bigger threat is on the horizon? In general, I mean, beyond this case.' My headline is hostage to his answer.

His answer waits on the other side of long moments stretched agonisingly ahead, where my mind is whirring like a laptop overheating – noisily trying to keep up with the demands on it. He picks at a hangnail, while I hold my breath and listen to my heartbeat – a bird the wrong side of a windowpane. Eventually my headline is freed, and gosh was it worth the wait.

'No, not on the horizon, I think it's like James Foster and the man who made him – here already. In our neighbours; in our streets; in our towns; in our cities. It's right here, just dormant. Darkness. At least Jane Bell has put us in the fight.'

Later, once I'm home and have fed Bertie, I perch myself on the edge of my sofa to read the posts Officer Briggs gave me.

Justwantmykidsback
Posts: 1
Joined: September 2018
Post date: 2nd September 2018

Thread title: What more do I have to do to get my twins home?

Hello users of Family Rights Services Forum. Please can you help me? I'm at my wit's end.

I am the father of twins who are four years old in foster care. They were taken when they were six months old after their mum died of an OD and I couldn't get a permanent home for us as well as the food and things they needed just off the benefits I could draw. The social worker told me it was temporary foster care until I sorted things out. But because I couldn't cope with the stress and pain of them being gone I relapsed into drug use. I went straight into rehab and got clean and Children's Services have been helping me to get the twins home. That's what I thought at least. They said I had to show changes, like getting a steady job, providing a house and equipment, all obvious father things. I did every single one. I've got a job now, I'm renting a house in a good area and I've got it set up right for the kids. They are starting school very soon which will allow me to keep working my job while they're there. I see them every six weeks supervised and we're really close. I need them home with me. They want to come home. Every time I see them they ask me "Daddy, when can we go home with you?" At the start of this I promised them we'd all be living together soon, it's been years now and I am wondering if Children's Services were ever on my side after all.

I've been told by my social worker that there is a big multi-disciplinary case conference coming up in a few weeks to decide what to do. They've done these before regularly but I have been told this one is especially important, with doctors going as well as my social worker, the twins' social worker, their foster carer and one other person who I can't remember. I have a psychological evaluation tomorrow which she says is my "final hurdle". Because of my repeated substance abuse history I have some issues which I've been working on that are "of concern" and I need to prove to the psychologist that they're gone.

Is there anything else I can do or show before the case conference that will help me get my twins back?

downonhisluckchuck
Posts: 1109
Joined: April 2016
Post date: 2nd September 2018

Thread title: What more do I have to do to get my twins home?

Hey mate, so sorry to hear you're going through such hard times. I wish I could say I can't imagine how awful and cruel it is to have your kids taken from you when you're working so hard to be a good father, but I've been there, sadly they did it to me too, there are loads of us. It's shit, isn't it?

I bet you feel hopeless right now, but you have done so much. Show me a father who claims he hasn't made mistakes and I'll show you a fraud. It just seems such an unfair system doesn't it, having to prove your right to the most fundamental part of life – being a father to your own children?

I hope to God CS see sense and don't do to you what they've done to us and steal your kids from you permanently. It sounds as though they'll be deciding whether to put your twins under a placement order to adopt them out. If I'm right, come back here to update us, won't you, and I'll do anything I can to help you?

Good luck at the case conference. Bet they've said you can't even be there, right?

Justwantmykidsback
Posts: 5
Joined: September 2018
Post date: 3rd September 2018

Thread title: What more do I have to do to get my twins home?

Hi Chuck, thanks for replying with that advice. You're right, they said I can't be there. Feels beyond strange knowing so much will be decided about my twins without me even being able to contribute. Though I've got used to that.

What?! I had no idea they could be placed up for adoption at the meeting. I'm reeling a bit from that now.

I'll let you know how it goes.

downonhisluckchuck
Posts: 1117
Joined: March 2018
Post date: 3rd September 2018

Thread title: What more do I have to do to get my twins home?

No problem, mate. I'm here for you 100%. It's so important to have people behind you who understand your fight.

I am so sorry I had to be the one to break the news, Children's Services should have told you themselves, but yes, it is likely they are already planning a placement order which allows them to put your twins up for adoption, without your consent.

Based on the timeline you detailed in your first post, your twins are at an age where CS will be looking to get a permanent and stable home secured for them. Starting school, becoming little people rather than infants, it's a time when they need to establish their forever family.
I know that should be you.

They'll say they've allowed you over three years to prove changes. Because you have done so much to provide them an amazing life and future, if CS take your twins away from you and give them new parents, it'll be because of the psych eval. What are the changes you experienced from the substance abuse? If I know that, I can advise you further on what to do at the evaluation. PM is probably best – if you click on my user-name at the top of the post then it'll show a link to private message me. Best way for friends to do things anyway.

Justwantmykidsback
Posts: 9
Joined: March 2018
Post date: 1st October 2018

Thread title: What more do I have to do to get my twins home?

Update for all you who answered, thank you for doing it.

The psychological evaluation came back against me. They found my issues caused by the substance abuse to be perma-nent and impossible to reverse. I know I've improved so I paid for a second opinion but this was mostly the same – still saying my deficits are too big for me to be a safe single father.

The case conference results were exactly what *@downonhis-luckchuck* said – a placement order has been granted which is basically the state forcing an adoption on me and my twins, against all of our wills and permission. My social worker says there is nothing I can do, it's because of my deficits from the past drug use and that my twins can't wait any longer to get the life they need.

I feel hopeless. Like Chuck says, I was doomed from the start but they still led me on for three years while they slowly ran the clock out and then stole my children. They've started school now, 4 years old. I've never seen them in their uniforms or waved them off from the gates.

I hate it. I hate everyone who did this to them, and to me. I hate myself for this being my life. Chuck says loads of you have experienced this too, I am so sorry for all of us. I'd wish you all luck in the fight, but I know now luck is useless against so powerful and merciless an enemy. So I'll just send best wishes that you survive the pain. Please pray I do, for right now I feel
I can't possibly.

I fall back against the sofa cushions. This 'chuck' is a monster who looks and sounds just like a man. If monsters like him masquerade as men, and can make men such as James look like monsters, what hope do any of us have?

TWENTY-FOUR

JANE

They let me see Rachel, and they let her bring Molly and Joe. As soon as they see me their anxious frowns are replaced by face-splitting grins, and they detach themselves from Rachel's legs to charge over to me, or in Joe's case, toddle. We form a human pile-on, and although I can hardly pull air into my lungs with how tightly I'm being squeezed, it's the first time since that moment on bin day that I can breathe. I glance up through the tangle of limbs and Molly's loose hair to find Rachel's gaze, and see tears streaking down her cheeks – best friends, always matching.

I know the prison visiting rules shouldn't allow us this close contact, but through my haze of emotions at being together again I see Maggie, the prison officer I have grown close to, turn away from the scene for a few extra moments before she intervenes. Rachel has to pull Molly and Joe off me, but I keep a tight hold of their hands, so the connection doesn't have to be broken yet. All of our tops are damp, our tears mixed together into a cocktail of the bedfellows love and suffering. I hate seeing them crying but I never want to be dry again, since the moisture means they're *here*. I can see their faces full of beauty and new shadows; I can touch their soft skin, feel their sticky fingers, and a dried paint mark on Molly's arm; I can smell their strawberry shampoo and the lavender fabric softener I use on their clothes. They are *here* – flesh and blood, not just firing neurones and imagination figments.

'Tell me what you've been doing, Mol?' I push the tremor out of my voice for her. Joe is whimpering; my heart breaks all over again. Fresh tears sprout from Molly like a fountain switched back on.

'Mummy, why can't you come home?' she replies. I pull her onto my lap again, to a stern look but no further discipline from Maggie. I'll pay any price I have to later, though I doubt Maggie will call in the debt.

'It's like at school, Mol, you can't just choose when you leave, you have to be dismissed at the end of the day, when the bell goes and the learning is finished. The people in charge, like your teachers, they still need me here.'

'*We* need you more, Mummy!' Molly is getting extremely agitated, her sobs hiccupping through her whole spindly body. 'Daddy can't even make nice chicken nuggets, and he doesn't tie my shoes right with the rabbits, and he never tucks me in properly.'

She is clinging round my neck, her feet scraping at my thighs as she tries to push herself impossibly closer into me.

'I promise you, Molly, that I will come home to you the very first second that I'm allowed to. More than anything in the whole world I wish I could be there with you, but sometimes we have to do things that are hard, or that we don't really want to do, because it's the right thing. And the right thing is bigger than just you or just Joe or just Mummy.'

I squeeze her tightly to me, and then I pick her hand up, and place it over her heart. 'Can you feel that, Mol, that bumping?' She nods. 'That's your heartbeat.' I move her palm to cover my heart. 'And can you feel that – can you feel *my* heartbeat?' She nods again, with a frown pulling her soft, downy eyebrows together. 'They match, our heartbeats, because my heartbeat made your heartbeat. So, whenever you miss me, or I miss you, we can each put our hands right over our hearts and remember that we are always together in that rhythm. Do you think you can do that?' She puts her thumb in her mouth – a habit we'd as good as broken just before Christmas. This was just another tell of our undoing. But she gives a single nod.

Maggie comes in then, and ushers them away, with not even a moment for a proper goodbye – it hurts like nothing I've ever felt, but I know she knows what she's doing – it is a blessing – the goodbye would have hurt a million times more. Rachel carries a wailing Joe and has to tug Molly away. It's like daggers plunged through my heart over and over to see the way Molly's head strains back in an arch to keep looking at me until the last possible moment, her face scrunched up tightly and red with crying. But with every step Molly takes away from me, her free hand is pressed over her heart.

Rachel comes back on the next visiting occasion, and we agree the pain and setback for the children was too high to do that again before the main trial – if we have to make a new life thereafter where that is my only way to be with them then we'll deal with it when that future actually becomes mine.

Rachel is a pillar of strength and the definition of friendship in these days for me. She gives me so much more than childcare and physical support. She believes in me, she is proud of me, she picks up my slack, and pushes me on. She has faith. Faith, the sister of hope. It gives me life.

In the way that best friends so often are, Rachel is threaded through this so deeply. It was Rachel who believed me instantly and whole-heartedly when I arrived sobbing on her doorstep the day that I saw the maps. I felt like I was having a heart-attack, my heartbeat was so turbulent and wild. I couldn't breathe. She held me, tightly, and then she made me a tea with three sugars – always our best-kept secret – and she held space for me to tell her. About the receipt, the police, seeing James at the school, the police again, and then: that day.

I was walking back from dropping Molly off at school and Joe at nursery, their first day for weeks – we'd kept them out of there since I saw James outside St Oliver's, but the school was threatening legal action over Molly which would mean Joe losing his nursery place and funding. I was rushing to get home in time to get changed before work when I saw James. His neck was buried low between his shoulder blades but his hair was sticking out of his hood again so I couldn't mistake him. I froze. My breath grew sticky, hard to pull in and push out. I felt heat spilling across my cheeks. The proximity to him, half a street away, drove me to flee, but I resisted – the old me (before being a mum and certainly before James) stirring. The woman I thought I'd always be – a confident, self-assured, resilient, high-risk-project manager. Someone who loved pressure for the results it teased out of her.

While my body was firing every muscle to get away from James, my brain was whirring, realising the opportunity – he was dropping his bin at the curb, late, the bin had usually appeared overnight. Was he on his way out? Leaving his house empty, where the clues I needed could undoubtedly be seen?

My fists clenched, my nails biting into the soft flesh across the centre of my palms, giving me something to focus on as I stepped forward, overcoming my screaming instincts to do the opposite. I forced my legs forward, whilst allowing myself a novel dawdle in the hope that I wouldn't have to cross his path. As he turned towards me, I sucked my lips between my teeth and bit down on them – the only way to avoid the audible gasp I felt rushing into my nose. He walked with a long, loping stride that was somehow also choppy – as though his body was designed for someone else, someone without so much to hide. He was heading towards me too fast for me to cross the street or find a reason to leave the pavement. I tilted my chin down and swallowed away the excess saliva flooding my tongue. I filled my thoughts with the knowledge that this could be my one chance to work out his plan, to then be able to stop him, and that if I did anything whatsoever to alert his suspicion, I was certain he would return home, hunker down like he had been, and I would lose my chance, most likely until it was too late. Not an option. As he passed me, I couldn't stop my eyes snapping to his face. He must have sensed it, for his met mine. I felt iced water flowing down my spine, chills to my fingertips. I could hear my pulse in my ears. I couldn't drag my eyes away. His eyes were inkwells glinting in darkness – blacker than black. Then his eyes flicked away and felt I a dam in my chest burst, air torrenting into my lungs. I sped up, hearing my steps falling faster, the baseline to a soundtrack of an escape scene. Fear was a rabid wolf snarling at my heels, propelling me forwards. Even though there was nothing on the path I was struggling not to stumble, as my body was thrusting forward unwilling to wait for my feet. I was counting their beat, forcing myself to hold it steady, knowing there were two ears under a hood trained on that rhythm.

I reached home and lost precious seconds to my trembling hand not able to hold the key flush to the lock. My second hand had to join the effort, which only made the shaking twice as fast and in different directions. Luck alone meant the key tip caught in the snag of the slit eventually. I locked it behind me, relief chasing the dull clunk, sliding the chain home too, and I ran up the stairs, chest heaving. I folded myself flush against the wall of Molly's room, at the front of the house, where I could watch James round the corner out of sight. I rubbed my palm across my back pocket, feeling for the solid shape of my phone and I plucked it out and called my boss, eyes fixated on the spot where James' black hoodie disappeared from sight.

'Mina,' it's only when I had to form a word that I heard the tremors cutting my voice apart, 'it's Jane speaking, I'm so sorry to let you down at the last minute like this, but I can't make it in.'

'What on earth's happened, I can barely understand you, are you okay?'

'I can't talk now, I'll explain tomorrow. I should be fine by then.' I listened to a beat of silence in reply, decided I didn't have any more time, and hung up.

I shrugged my chunky knitted jumper off over my head, so I at least looked slightly different, and pulled on a darker sweatshirt of Neil's. Then I did a final scan from Molly's window; satisfied myself that James wasn't returning, and slipped back out the front door. James' high fence and solid wooden gates were kept bolted from the inside usually – top and bottom, but he'd had to leave them unlocked so that he could get back in. As I pulled the looming panel shut behind me, I logged the vulnerability of my position – I wouldn't be able to see him approaching if he came back quickly and there was no escape other than the gate he would come in through. I pushed this aside, feeling my senses lighting up, sharpening themselves. I allowed myself to enjoy the deliciousness – the thrill licking up my fingers, the pressure firing me up, the high boosting the chemistry of my brain. I slunk across the narrow front garden, noting the sodden cardboard boxes piled haphazardly up, the dirty plastic barrel rolling on its side in the breeze, the dusting of wood shavings from the new fencing that hadn't been cleared up. The smell of the chemicals from the preservative was overpowering, caustic in the back of my nostrils. The occasional low hum and the rattle of the plastic drum knocking against the wall and the rising and falling hum of a car passing left room for that faint rushing in my ears that came with adrenaline coursing.

I took a split second to think it through: it would obviously be far too dangerous to try to get inside so I'd have to do what I could from through the windows. Fortunately, these were bare, with some grey netting hanging limply at the edges. I let myself shudder.

I lifted my hand up to the glass to shield my eyes from the glare, enjoying its refreshing coolness against the side of my damp and prickling palm. My eyes were drawn first to the detritus spread all over the floor, in three piles. There was the wiring, tubs of nails, all sorts of other things I couldn't fully identify. It was spread out, messy, yet clearly also organised. I felt like cement had been poured into my lungs, rendering them useless, unable to pull air in or push it out. I couldn't breathe. Seeing them all together like that, confirmation clicked: there was only one thing these could be – bombs.

I saw big sheets of paper taped up across the far wall, mottled with a pattern, like the wide calves of an old lady – spider webs of stark veins wrapping through skin. Maps.

I squinted to see more details, twisting my eyelids around my eyeballs like a photographer's fingers twitching around a camera lens. It was hard to distinguish anything except three thick vermillion circles drawn on clumsily yet specifically. I kept focussing, and I saw the sprawling Asda supermarket and then the park a few streets up from here. I was a tracker, knowing the pawprints I was following belonged to a big cat, yet still entirely unprepared for the feeling of confronting its huge amber eyes. Of staring into the jaws of death. Of the power and the predation. I came here to find evidence, but it turns out I was not ready to see it. Not when the three bombs matched these three red circles, which closed around three points within St Oliver's CE Primary School. They contained my children.

My throat closed up and my stomach contracted. I recoiled back, spine curving as I curled around a heaving retch. The pain stripped my throat, as I longed for the purge, for the release of this terror, to be able to leave it there in a thick, innards-coloured puddle in front of what it belonged to. I was not that foolish. I pressed my left hand into my stomach, begging it to wait. My right hand fumbled across my back pocket for my phone.

I found it, and lifted it up to the window, on a wrist that felt like it would snap under the weight of it. I snapped photos, tilting the phone, shielding it with my other hand, but nothing I did made the maps clear, or the story they told. Despair took ownership of me, hollowing me out, but my self-preservation bargained for control just long enough to get me through the gate, making sure everything looked exactly as I found it – no smudging on the windowpane, no footprints on the littered concrete, the gate shut exactly right.

I slid back inside my home and dragged my exhausted

form up the stairs to the toilet, where my body tried its best to rid me of the poison of what I now knew. If only it were so simple. I crumpled, arms cradling the porcelain, head lying on the seat, while I waited for the numbness in my limbs to recede. As soon as I was confident my legs could hold me up, I made the same journey that I had before or after so many of the big moments of my life. To Rachel's, where I looked into eyes that made me feel then as they do now – safe.

Today she stays visiting me in the prison as long as she is allowed to – nowhere near long enough – and she focusses not even for a moment on her needs. Rather, the conversation is all about how to make nice chicken nuggets, how to tie shoelaces with the rabbit through the burrow, and how to tuck a little girl in just right.

TWENTY-FIVE

BILL

Now that Jane has been officially charged with murder and is deep within the bowels of the justice system, I should have let the case go. However, my mind continually binds itself up in knots. A sucking in my chest reminds me of the anxiousness I feel about my confusion. I'm a Detective Inspector, I can't bumble around, adrift between stances, drowning in dismay. I also don't want to have sympathy for a killer. Yet in just a few weeks I have developed it for two. My feelings about Jane are stable. It's James I yoyo about.

I need answers. There are so many questions I have about his situation – what led a father to such a precipice? I wonder whether my contact in Children's Services has access to anything he can share. I open up my emails and begin typing.

To: Josh McCormack, Children's Services
From: Bill Simmons
Subject: James Foster Case History

Dear Josh,

As I expect you're aware, I was leading Jane Bell's case before it was passed to the CPS. The information given to me about James Foster focussed on the plans and bombs found in his home as well as his radicalisation. I have questions in my heart though, which remain unanswered by police investigative angles and centre more around his fatherhood. I wondered whether there is any background information you could share with me from his case history? I guarantee as always it will be for my eyes only, to be destroyed as soon as it's read. I greatly appreciate whatever you can offer.

Regards,
Bill

I let out a sigh and flex my knuckles after I have hit send, occupying myself with other paperwork for the rest of the morning, keeping half an eye on my inbox. The reply is waiting for me when I return from my walk around the block with my sandwich at midday.

To: Bill Simmons
From: Josh McCormack, Children's Services
Subject: James Foster Case History

Bill,

So sorry to hear of the sad news for Becky.

As you know, I'm limited in what I can share without due

procedure, but given the circumstances please find below a
summary of the most pertinent details:

Children's Services first became involved with Mr Foster's
twins upon pregnancy acknowledgement in 2013. Mr Foster
and the mother of the children were not in a relationship and
were both homeless, living between the streets and shelters. We
supported them through the pregnancy as the drug taking that
they both admitted to previously had ceased and a housing
placement was provided by a charity. The twins' mother died
six months after the twins' birth, from an overdose. It was Mr
Foster who appeared to be the primary caregiver on the visits
made by our team between the birth and that time. Upon the
death of the mother, the housing placement was revoked, as it
was only for homeless mothers. We tried to intervene and allow
it to be extended to Mr Foster, but it was out of our control and
was denied. Mr Foster could not work to gain the financial
position needed to access adequate housing for the twins whilst
caring for them, as such we had to take the twins into foster care
as the shelters Mr Foster could access were entirely unsuitable.

We worked with Mr Foster to facilitate his regaining of
custody, signposting him to services that could help him find
employment. However, shortly into the twins' foster placement,
it became apparent Mr Foster had relapsed. There were
circumstances preceding this that I cannot discuss. Mr Foster
was supported into a rehabilitation facility by a charity and he
successfully completed the programme there, at which time he
underwent a psychological evaluation. Sadly, this showed up
permanent damage from his years of substance abuse. This
extended to: hyper-activity, violent outbursts, obsessive behav-
iours and decline in cognitive function. There were also motor

issues that would impact his ability to carry out care tasks for infants.

Mr Foster found employment. He asked to be given support to become stable enough to be granted custody back. However, it was the professional opinion of two psychologists, one of whom he paid for as a second opinion, that he would never be able to recover fully enough from the methamphetamine damage to be a responsible and safe, single father. Additionally, he had no support network. You know it is never an easy decision for us to permanently remove children from the care of a willing parent, yet first and foremost we must always act to protect children, and in this case, it served their best interests to be placed into an adoptive family. Mr Foster did not respond well to this new development and shortly after he attempted to kidnap the children from the supervised visitation centre. Given the security measures we have in place this was never a real threat, yet his intention was clear. At this point, it was decided that visitation rights would be removed.

As promised, I know you will keep the above information confidential in the manner it requires.

All the best Bill.

Regards,
Josh

The mention of Becky thrashes my chest like a bullet. I can't succumb, not here in the frigidity of a work afternoon in a police office, so I use the feelings to build a new, more fitting emotion: anger. I feel the blooming sting of my fist bouncing off the desk beside me. The moment I first learned his name, I checked 'James Foster' through all our systems and there were no hits. Why the bloody hell hadn't Children's Services logged that supposed kidnap attempt with us. It might have been the red flag we needed to initiate an investigation. That single obvious act might have saved Jane. Saved James.

I have always been proud to have a badge number within the British police force, to be part of a system that protects the innocent, that tries in every moment of every day to keep them safe. I click the email closed and as I press my finger onto the mouse I wonder why it is only when it's too late that we realise something is breaking.

James.

Jane.

Me.

TWENTY-SIX

NEIL

My phone call to my mum is a strained one – she remains hurt that I haven't fallen at her feet in gratitude the moment she offered her help days previously. She and Jane are too alike in their strength for my mum to have ever warmed to her. It's funny how that works. Okay, not funny, but you know what I mean.

She picks up on the third ring – it's a point of pride for her to never let it go longer than four.

'Mum, I've met with Jane—' I begin, once the greetings are done with. I still catch myself using odd choices of words to keep reality out of all but the forced moments.

'Visited her, you mean,' Mum interrupts me, pointedly, ever direct. I choose to ignore it.

'We would appreciate the help, if your offer of coming to stay still stands?'

'Of course, it does, son, family pulls together in crisis.' It's hard to tell whether she's being genuine or making a slight about Jane's father's absence – it's not the first time she's made a similar comment. Either way, needs must – my bosses have been very generous so far with time off, but I work in advertising and my clients can only be managed by someone else for so long, given I've had no chance to do a handover as I would have done before annual leave.

'Thank you, Mum. The only thing is, with everything being so unstable for the kids right now, we want to make sure they've got as much security as possible. So, if you do come and stay, will you be able to stick around for a while – you know, so that we can build routines with you in them, and I can get back to work and stay there? As much as temporary relief would be kind, it's help in the long haul we most need, and that will take some staying power.'

There's a silence on the line, I presume because Mum is used to being the director not the directed.

'That will be fine, I'll bring enough of my things. Can you make sure I have my own room so I can bring the things I want and unpack properly?' This is a command in disguise, not a question. 'I'll be with you by 5 p.m.'

'Great, see you later, Mum. Thanks again.'

'You're welcome, Neil, really, I truly want to help you all as much as I can. Bye for now.'

When you become a parent, I think you have a 'what if' moment – you ask yourself the question: what's our plan for if the shit hits the fan? However, I think that you imagine 'the shit hitting the fan' will be one of you getting ill, or the main earner losing their job, or something happening to one of your parents; not that your children's mum is locked behind bars and on trial for murder.

I'm sure dealing with any of those things takes a similar emotional toll, yet with this it's the invasion I didn't know to prepare for, the violation by the public's interest. It's the cameras snapping photos of your children when you drag them to the corner shop for a pint of milk, and it's the questions you don't know how to answer, like 'Daddy, why is everyone staring at us?'. That's what strips away the structure – not being able to do a supermarket shop without worrying that something will happen; not being able to even walk your kids to school without being mobbed by the other parents at the gates; and walking past a news-stand and seeing your wife's face in grey on the front page.

Rachel has been a godsend. People don't recognise her, so she's done the food shops and the school runs, but she too has a job to get back to tomorrow. My mother has her straight spine and her few words, but she is structure and discipline and strength.

I never thought I'd be so relieved to open my front door and see her, with suitcases spilling down the path, even though I'll be the one on the sofa bed in the lounge. As she reaches forward for a rare embrace, I see her lip curl in disgust at the lone camera flashing. They don't know what's about to hit them, I think, though neither do we.

TWENTY-SEVEN

SIMON

I'm appealing the court's bail decision. Jane is legally allowed to be remanded in custody for one-hundred-and-eighty-two days – six months – before her trial, and usually with big cases the trial is scheduled toward the end of that. With bail having been refused, these are numbers that Jane has been horrified by. Six months is the difference between... well, all sorts, I'm sure, in a child's life – I don't know any kids.

Jane has agreed to appeal the court's decision, though I've told her the chances are slim just so I don't get her hopes up. Her morale is fragile right now and I need her focussed on the big win, so we can't afford for her to feel the blow of her soul being ripped out all over again – it's a kindness to her to ensure she never believes bail could be real. But it is.

The appeal will take place any minute. I'm sitting in the atrium of the Birmingham Crown Court, which is where the showdown between Mrs Rigby and myself will occur. The courtroom will be emptied as a clerk announces, 'Court as chambers', and it will be just the judge, and both of us advocates, and two possible outcomes for Jane that will become one real one. At the very least it will be extremely useful for me to understand Mrs Rigby – how she operates, her style, how she treats the judge, how she reacts when she's on the front foot and the back foot – any one of those scraps of knowledge could end up being a piece of the jigsaw that will be my trial strategy. It is imperative I remember that the law is not the enemy, rather it's the arsenal we share; the prosecutor is the foe.

Bail hearings and appeals are usually very quick affairs, and this is no exception. Mrs Rigby dispenses no courtesies or niceties before she gets launched into the crux.

'This is a woman who ploughed a neighbour down, in their quiet street, killing him immediately. There is clearly a very real danger presented to the community if she is released on bail.'

Here I go, the battle commences.

'She felt the victim was threatening her children's lives, and we now know she was entirely correct in her perception of that threat. She tried to be law abiding in her way of handling the threat, but was unsupported, then desperate, and alone. Clearly the circumstances were entirely unique. We both know she poses no danger whatsoever to anyone else.'

'I disagree, Mr Rafferty, as far as we know, anyone she perceives as threatening her children is unsafe. What if an innocent man slows down at a crossing and looks at her daughter a moment longer than usual? What if the parents of one of her son's friends lets her son play unattended with a dog that's known to be rough? Is she entitled to just kill them? No. Do we know for certain she knows that, and so wouldn't do it? Based on history, also no. Just because someone is desperate does not mean it's valid to *kill* another, otherwise the whole of the country would be a bloodbath. Until we know the full situation underlying this case, it would be irresponsible to grant bail,' Mrs Rigby counters.

'Oh, for goodness' sake, what preposterous suggestions, Mrs Rigby – you must be struggling,' I retaliate.

I catch the flicker of a tight-lipped smile on the judge's face before he shoots me a mock-stern look and instructions.

'I think you would do to settle down there, Mr Rafferty. Now, is that the only basis on which you are proposing refusing bail, Mrs Rigby?'

'No, though I maintain it is quite reason enough, especially as we have witness statements that attest to the zeal with which Mrs Bell committed the act,' Mrs Rigby asserts.

'Noted,' the judge responds, his eyes narrowed a fraction. I share his sentiment – some people are just *so* hard to like.

Mrs Rigby continues, 'There is additionally a significant danger that Mrs Bell would interfere with key witnesses – her neighbours have given statements and agreed to testify as to the events. It is almost impossible to believe that, if released and mixing freely with them for the next few months, Mrs Bell will not attempt to alter their testimonies.'

'As you have seen in the application, we have an alternative address established, where Mrs Bell could be well away from any prosecution witnesses.'

The judge glances down at the papers in front of him and gives a single nod of satisfaction. My hopes swell, Mrs Rigby's shoulders rise.

'It cannot be in the best interests of the eldest child to be removed from her school.' Into the fray Mrs Rigby enters again.

'That is hardly our concern, Mrs Rigby, and I think it's blindingly obvious that it is far better for the child to move schools temporarily than to have her mother in prison,' I state, unable to resist an eye-roll of exasperation while the judge eyeballs Mrs Rigby.

'Once again, Mr Rafferty, I believe common sense is evidence enough here, and Mrs Bell has friends on the street that she would no doubt attempt to visit, during which time she could easily seek out the witnesses. We all know this case is too important for us to allow even a tiny risk to prevail.' Mrs Rigby lets out a barely stifled sigh before she continues quickly yet with a trace of weariness now audible in her speech. 'We also have the matter of Mrs Bell's safety. It is believed that by killing James Foster she successfully prevented a terror attack. It has been revealed to me that there is suspicion of others involved beyond the victim, James Foster. By killing him and preventing the attack and whatever its intended message was, it's possible that, Mrs Bell has drawn a rather enormous cross on her own back. Police intelligence units have picked up references to very serious death threats being waged against Mrs Bell. We believe she'll only be safe enough to stand trial by being remanded in custody.'

'She cannot be forced into such conditions when there are other viable options' – I think on my feet – 'a police protection detail could remain in place for her at her home, she could enter protective custody with her family.' I look long and hard at the judge, hoping he receives my imploring with kindness and understanding for Jane.

'That's as maybe, Mr Rafferty, but when added to the other factors I've presented, it is abundantly clear that the easiest, safest, and most responsible decision for everybody is for Mrs Bell to be remanded in custody until her trial.'

I shake my head fervently enough to feel the tickle of my slight fringe as it swishes against my forehead. I can feel the slight ache of tension in my frown. I see the judge take me in, take Mrs Rigby in, with her erect back, raised eyebrows, and forefinger tapping hard on her crossed forearm.

'While it is not a decision I make lightly, I have to deny Mrs Bell's bail – it is clear from the summary of facts about the case that this is a violent offence, though my decision is based on the fact that with such significant risk to Mrs Bell's safety, the conditions cannot be satisfactorily met for granting bail in a murder case.'

'Thank you, Your Honour,' I manage to grind out, before I spin and march out of the courtroom, not able to withstand Mrs Rigby's smug pug face a single moment longer without locating something sticky and messy to mush into it. They take away law licences for such things; and I've got far too much to do to settle for that outcome – Mrs Rigby may have won this battle, which I'm devastated about for Jane, but I'm far more concerned about winning the war.

Today has cemented what I'd previously anticipated – I expect Jane's main trial to be carnage. I also expect it to follow due process in such a stringent way that whole days will be lost to details. For other souls in other courtrooms in the country the details that make the difference to outcomes won't even be presented. There are so many who slip through the cracks of this decaying institution. I'm heartened that Jane won't be one of them, even though the glaring imbalance of 'justice' hurts every time I breathe – as if it's striking my physical ribcage, not just my professional passion.

Back to Jane. I know I set her expectations that bail was about as likely as snow on Christmas Day in California, but I still harboured a very real hope that I'd be her Jack Frost. I don't know what makes me feel worse, that I have to tell Jane her captivity will rage on for another six months, or the niggling doubt I have burrowing through my gut that this could be a foreshadowing of the trial to come. I'm unused to failure. I've set myself up as Jane's knight in shining armour. I forgot that sometimes knights in shining armour die gruesome deaths on bloody battlefields; and that the people they're protecting fall behind them.

TWENTY-EIGHT

ANEESA

I spend the day after meeting Officer Briggs typing up the interview into an article. Writing is woven through with reflection – snapping excitement, shivering chills, and nibbling anxiety. This piece will be phenomenal. Truly taking something hidden that people deserve to know, and revealing it – the very reason I wrangle words for a living. However, the *Gazette* has had to pull articles far tamer than this due to pressure from external powers. The ramifications of taking this to press could be widespread and Eliza will bear the brunt. If I'm to ask her to publish this, which I certainly am, then I need some advice. I pick up my phone before I can think myself out of it, and feel my heart lurch into my mouth as my fingers comply, typing out the text:

> *Si, could do with some advice – half legal, half friendly!*
> *Don't suppose you have time for baguettes tomorrow like old*
> *times? Annie x*

I cast my phone to one side, refusing to sit waiting for it to ping with a reply. Most likely he'll be in court in London for hours anyway. My shallow breathing gives my anticipation away though and I chastise myself. I jump with the vibration of my phone on the desk.

Annie! What have you gotten yourself into now? You know I'll always help bail you out... do I need to bring a thimble or a barrel? 12 noon? Can't wait, Si x

I feel impending panic at just how giddy this makes me, the need to pull back, escape the inevitable pain that comes with feeling anything close to this. Something else pushes up too this time, and it's steadier and stiller. Solid ground that I want to stand on as opposed to the flimsy, fragile, fragmented platform my past pulls me onto. It's the feeling of being in it with someone. With Simon.

I lift my thumbs over my phone, two message options rolling through my mind, like fruit machines. Chance, luck, fortune, fate. I choose one and I press send.

I'm hoping a thimble will do but bring the barrel just in case! 12 noon is perfect, can't wait either. X

Now I've got my coverage of Jane onto this level, I'm desperate to keep the momentum building, to find a side to the story that peels back another layer. I know what I want, I just can't get a hold on it – on James Foster. I've got his letter but I don't feel I can do anything with it until I have that grip. I've spent plenty of time over the past days making calls, following rabbit warrens on the internet, trying to find someone who knew him and is willing to talk to me, anyone with some light to shed on who he was. I've drawn blanks. He's the dark side of the moon in this and you know how I am about bringing the darkness to light. I rub the fatigue out of my eyes, roll my head and neck around to set the tension free, and pick up my phone again, to make another call.

Once I've hung up, and have let my heart rate slow, my breathing settle, I realise how obsessed I've become with finding a lead on James. Although I'm sure there are more truths to know within the letters of his name, ultimately, he was there in that house with his bombs and his plans. I try to clear my head – the story I need to focus on telling is about the woman who stopped the tragedy. I have so much to do, to make sure that, whatever the courts decide, Jane Bell is remembered authentically, that her life and her choice leave the mark they deserve to. After all, it's like Peter Scrople said, 'Legacy is not leaving something *for* people, it's leaving something *in* people', and whatever your view is of what Jane did, she's built mountains in all of us.

TWENTY-NINE

BILL

I pick up my ringing phone handset, positioned on my desk beside the M&Ms and the cellophane wrapped card I've yet to write for Becky's birthday tomorrow, with trepidation. I have answered all phone calls over the past three days with the same heaviness in my greeting.

'Detective Inspector Simmons speaking.' This time the sigh of relief never expelled.

'Hello, Detective Inspector, Bethany Rigby speaking, prosecution barrister in the case against Mrs Jane Bell. Could we meet to discuss the particulars of your report please?'

This is standard procedure. Although this time it means the clock has run out and I must decide what I'll stand for, who I am.

'Of course, when and where?' Such conversations are always perfunctory.

'I can be at your station tomorrow morning at eleven, if you can secure us a room?'

'Yes, I can, I'll see you tomorrow then, Mrs Rigby.'

I hang up the phone and, in that moment, the last vestiges of doubt disappear.

I know what I have to do.

Mrs Rigby arrives in a cloud of perfume and wearing glasses of the severe and conspicuous variety that, in my experience, show she wishes to be taken more seriously than she probably often is. I suspect the overpowering scent of a department store beauty counter blasting all who meet her might be why she is not always respected as much as she might hope.

I stand and shake her hand before showing her to the interview room I've reserved for our meeting. I wonder why she has chosen to come to me here rather than have this discussion on Crown Prosecution Service ground. I decide any tactics she is employing don't matter – I shall overcome them.

Formalities are quickly danced through and the meat of the interview begins.

'Detective Inspector, can you talk me through what your testimony will include, please?'

'Certainly. I expect it to include details of what the situation was when I arrived at the scene, what Jane's behaviour was post detention, and details of my subsequent interviews with her. All the facts and transcripts of which, you have in the file. I will remain consistent with them. My memory of the event is clear. Will you be calling the first responding officers as witnesses too?'

'I plan to.' There is a long pause that drags into discomfort painfully slowly. After shifting in her seat, Mrs Rigby's eyes flick up to meet mine with the steel of a decision made. 'Can I rely on you to confirm the likelihood of a pre-meditated act?' I hold my gaze steady and strong as I grip her eye contact.

'No, Mrs Rigby, you cannot.'

Her eyes widen a fraction and her lips slacken into a faint oval. Then they snap shut into a clamp.

'How will you respond to any questions on that subject then?' she asks, terse and rigid.

'I shall respond with my professional opinion, with truth and openness: that Mrs Bell displayed the range of symptoms associated with deep, genuine shock both upon my arrival at the scene, and through her first night of detention; such that I had to conclude her act was far more likely to have been unplanned and opportunistic than coming from an intent to kill. If given the question, I will also state that with the maximum speed Jane could have hoped to attain, she could only have had certainty that Foster would sustain severe lower body injury, not that he would have died. If anyone from the Crown had cared to ask my opinion about charges, I would have suggested at the most manslaughter, at the least no charges and releasing Jane on the grounds of defence of others.'

'You can't be serious?' A slight stutter is now evident in Mrs Rigby's voice, if you listen just right, as I'm trained to do. You learn the tells are more often in the small inflections than the big statements. 'Neither the defendant nor her children were in any immediate danger. Mr Foster could have changed his mind about the attack at any moment. You know as well as anyone, Detective Inspector Simmons, that we cannot let civilians start deciding to mete out their own warped versions of justice on the streets any way they want – society would fall apart in seconds.'

'I do know that, Mrs Rigby, but I also know we are not

dealing with someone who has killed someone for treading on her flowerbed. Foster had built bombs that he was storing, *live*, in the house next to where her children slept, bombs he was planning to detonate at a bloody primary school.' I cringe internally at the awful double entendre of my cursing. She doesn't appear to notice it. 'Hundreds of children would have been blown apart, Mrs Rigby. She asked for help. If a civilian can't defend themselves against that, when we've failed to step in and protect them when they asked for help, then I think society has *already* fallen apart.'

There is another long silence. This time it's anger that pulses through the room, inflaming the air, streaking it invisibly crimson.

'If that's the testimony you're going to provide, it will confuse the jury, it will give them the impression that this case has no grounds for a murder charge.' This seems like a statement, but the way Bethany leans forward towards me, exuding the body language of a threat, makes me believe she is challenging me and wants a response.

'I've been a witness for the prosecution enough times to know that only the jury members themselves ever know what dots they'll connect. All I can do to assist justice is to tell the truth as I believe it, based on my professional training, experience, and knowledge. I've never pretended to predict the future, Mrs Rigby, other than that my future involves telling those truths as I see them to the jury when it's my turn on the witness stand.'

'Don't count on getting to that witness stand now, Inspector,' Bethany hisses at me, spittle and all, as she erupts to her feet. 'Your superior will be hearing about your plan to derail this case, to go against your own force's work.'

'That's as maybe, Mrs Rigby, though I'd be surprised if

you could manage to avoid me being called, given I was the lead on Jane Bell's case, that I conducted the interviews, that I wrote the report. My name is all over the paperwork, my face on the videotapes, my words in the transcripts. I would expect to hear my voice in the courtroom too.' I let the words soak into a break. 'I'll find someone to see you out.'

THIRTY

SIMON

My mind keeps pinging to my lunch with Annie. The second I read her text inviting me, I cancelled my long-standing lunch plans with a fellow barrister I trade war stories with each month and felt a fool for the way my stomach felt fuzzy. If she hadn't mentioned she needed my help, I'd have cancelled lunch with her ten different times overnight – I realise the danger of proximity to her during a period when I am emotionally strung out by Jane, exhausted by my passion for this case, opened up by weakness.

As it was, in anticipation of her arrival, I had bought her old favourite – a baguette filled with the strange combination of egg, mayo, tomato and cheese. I shared consternation through eye-rolls and banter with the 'sandwich artist'. I loathed my heart for the way it flipped when a smile split her face and blood rushed to her cheeks as she bent over the paper, unfolded it carefully and saw that I'd got it right.

'You remembered.' It was barely more than a whisper, her eyes giving it volume, firing sparks as they turned to meet mine.

She told me all about her incredible interview and I read the sensational – in the best way – article she's written about it. I advised her that it would undoubtedly hurt the police but that, as she had Briggs' full permission to print his words, then it was the right thing to do to go to press, even with the ramifications for the paper that would ensue. Annie wanted to go through the legality, so I explained why it was green-lighted all the way and to call her legal representative – me – if anyone had anything negative to say about it. She laughed at that, but quickly stopped when she saw my set jaw and flinty eyes. They made her reach out and squeeze my hand. I pulled it away, hating myself even as it happened for hurting her, but comforted by the resolve that this hurt far less than the alternative would. Didn't she understand, she was too precious?

It's late that same night. I try and get my head back into work. There is a chill threaded through the air in my office. I like the warmth, but this late at night I need the cool to keep me sharp. My junior, Marco, brings me espressos every half-hour like clockwork. If I weren't so consumed by the mechanics of the case, I might spare a thought for sending him home, try to let him maintain the semblance of a life outside of the law in a way I've never managed. Then again, maybe I wouldn't be so generous-hearted – it's a choice we make the day we first wrap the black gown around our shoulders. Or maybe it chooses us. Either way, the sacrifice is as much a part of the job as the creepy wig and the caffeine addiction.

I holler through the thin, grey wall to Marco. There is a canvas on it that I didn't pick, that I would never pick, of a pier leading into an ocean. Meaningless to me; yet sometimes I see my clients give the smallest hint of a smile when their eyes land on it.

I often wonder what they see in something so plain, depicting somewhere they've never been. I have frequently yo-yoed between being envious of their ability to feel such lateral things and being relieved that I'm not encumbered with so wild and loose a brain – I imagine it would rather hinder actually getting things done. Still, now as I glimpse the pier out of the corner of my eye, I think, *it must be nice*.

Marco appears in my doorway, his eyes bright in a drawn and grey face.

'Can you give me a hand with the strategy brainstorm?' I cut straight to the chase.

'Of course, Si.' Despite the hour he sounds eager. I remember the days of my pupillage, and the moments of inclusion, being so precious, so exciting. I would never tell him, but I like having Marco around, it reminds me of those feelings, stops me getting too jaded. Maybe that's partly why I let him get away with calling me 'Si'; that and the fact that somewhere inside my heart is a pitiful joy that someone cares enough to give me a nickname.

'Where can we go with this?' I ask him. I know what I think our options are, but I always like to give him the chance to take the journey himself too.

'Well, we'd usually start with identification, but we can't do much with that,' Marco launches in, and I feel a flash of pride at how thoroughly he must have already thought this through. 'The witnessing neighbours, Jane's own confession, and the lack of any other suspects mean that's watertight – we'd never get reasonable doubt out of that.' Although Marco delivers this as a statement the rising pitch at the end of his sentence reveals his questioning lack of confidence. I bolster it.

'Absolutely right, I agree completely. Where to next?' He knows this, it's defence strategy basics, but a fundamental part of what I've taught him is never skip the foundations, always build them anew in each case. No complacency, no corners cut – discrepancies and clues that are case winners can be hidden in the simplest of places.

'Intent to cause serious harm is a dead end too, I reckon,' Marco continues, 'given the pathologist's report and that the photos of James's body have been included and are so grisly. Although I reckon it would be nigh on impossible to convince a full jury that Jane's intent was anything other than to kill him or cause grievous bodily harm. I think there's room to work with it, make the point that vehicular attacks can be hard to predict, that no one except Jane could know what her intentions were. I'd get her on the stand and address it. But while it could help get us over the finish line, I doubt there's anywhere near enough fuel in it for the entire race.'

'That's my feeling too – we use it, but as a side show, not the main event.' I nod, thoughtfully, chewing the lid of my very expensive fountain pen. 'I like your point about vehicular attacks being less predictable in outcome, we can use that as a lever, make a stronger case that it *was* only reasonable force. Good work, Marco.'

He flushes, still young enough that he hasn't mastered professional detachment. Then again, given how Jane's gotten under my skin, maybe neither have I.

A few other points are bandied between us, though they're all ultimately rejected as being neither useful nor usable. The foundations are firmly in place. Then I move on to outlining the task I'd had in mind for him.

'I'd like you to prepare the case as if you were the prosecutor. I will defend, using the counter attack we discussed, acquittal by way of defence of others. We are looking for any holes that Mrs Rigby can snake her way into.' I prime Marco for his task, it will be a useful training exercise for him. Given his shining brilliance, cherry picked as he was from hundreds of young, blundering graduates, followed by years of tutelage by me, I know he'll present a stronger case for Jane's guilt than Mrs Rigby ever would. Marco's eyes light up, he pushes his papers together hastily, and as he dynamically gets up to leave, he says,

'I'll see you in court, Mr Rafferty.'

I laugh, his boyish enthusiasm sparking something long lost inside me. I feel myself soften a fraction. I like his style.

'Go home, rest, start in the morning.' I glance at my Rolex, unsurprised but tired to see it's already 'tomorrow'.

'Is that how you became the best, Si? I think not.' He gives a small grin, and a single nod. Moments later I hear the door to his office shut and see the flash of light spilling into the hallway from his desk lamp. He reminds me of someone I vaguely recognise; someone who breathes for this work, who lives on espressos and whisky, someone who was reckless and passionate and didn't know what it would cost him. I don't know whether to be proud or mortified.

My most important task today is to instruct an expert witness to persuade a jury into something very different from what they'll be hearing from the prosecution – someone who wholeheartedly believes in Jane, and is just convincing enough, to win Jane back her life.

The thing with 'experts', from the perspective of a barrister, is that while there are undoubtedly a few for every field, in most cases you can find two people who are supposedly at the forefront of their specialism, yet who disagree entirely on a matter at the centre of their remit, and who are prepared to stand up in court to explain why. This is problematic because they tend to just undermine each other, confuse the jury, and therefore both end up being discounted. So, I need my expert to be qualified and educated beyond compare, but also with an authenticity and humanity to win my jury's hearts and minds. I believe I've found her – the formidable Dr Melanie McCulloch – Professor of Psychiatry at Cambridge Medical School.

Melanie is someone it takes courage to meet – she is Sherlock Holmes crossed with Gok Wan – the fiercest intellect housed in a sharply decorated body. I suspect that's all part of her method – distract you with the colours and oddities on her, while she picks through your mind for your every secret and button. She pulls no punches either – the first time she met me, while I thought we were still on handshakes and pleasantries, she'd detected the childhood loss of my father; my rebellious streak; and my complete disregard for authority (only when I can't respect it) that I mostly successfully wrestle into a straightjacket for the sake of my law licence – her words, not mine, immediately after she'd passed her judgement on the sunshine that Wednesday.

Juries love Melanie. However, she has been very reluctant to serve as an expert witness lately. She has been involved in several miscarriage of justice cases that have destroyed her faith in the judicial system, and she refuses to participate in its 'stacked deck circus' any longer. I can understand that – the cases of Eddie Gilfoyle, Sally Clark, and Michael Shirley broke my legal heart too. Yet I had to try to change her stance – Jane needed her. She can lend our case reasonable doubt. She is irreplaceable in my strategy – no one else I know in the psychiatric field can be so convincing from a well of such extensive knowledge. I need a maverick, and I know Melanie is one.

It has been a minor battle just persuading Melanie to meet with me. The first phone call we had was full of thinly veiled contempt for the justice system, until the last moment.

'I want no part of it, Simon, I love my job and I can do more good here than in these cases where the fight is fixed before it sees a single wig.'

'Please, Melanie, you know me, you know what, and who, I stand for. This is a special case, it's one of those that gives you tingles, where you know that finally it's up to you to make a difference. And the fight will have to be fair – there'll never have been a more viewed trial, never a more attentive public. But I need you, Melanie, you're the only one who can clinch it for Jane. Please, just meet with me, let me explain.'

There was a short silence, where I think Melanie must have been holding her breath for I couldn't even hear air moving. It was a silence heavy with a future. Eventually there was a long sigh.

'You said "Jane". You don't mean Jane Bell do you, Simon?'

'I do indeed.'

This time there wasn't even a moment of pause.

'I'll meet with you, Mr Rafferty. Tomorrow.'

THIRTY-ONE

BILL

After my meeting with the prosecution barrister I know the CPS will be unhappy with me, but I don't imagine my own force will turn against me. Therefore, I feel a jolt of surprise when Vincent arrives at my desk within half an hour of the termination of the meeting, his shoulders dead square, his eyes flinty.

'To what do I owe this pleasure?' I greet him unassumingly.

'Oh, it won't be a pleasure, Bill, I can assure you. You're a top man, Simmons, one of my best. But you've gone and messed up big with this one. You know as well as I do that the police and the Crown can't be seen to be at odds – we'll look like flaming imbeciles if you take the stand and say you think she should be let off on self-defence. She was not under imminent threat. People can't just go around killing each other and walking free.'

'The delightful Mrs Rigby called you, did she? That was quick.'

'I'd hardly be standing here if she hadn't. Now, you need to stop this nonsense and get in line with the Crown's stance.'

'I'm an officer of the law. I will not perjure myself by telling a lie to the court. I also won't dishonour myself or my life's work by misleading a jury. Self-defence and defence of others are written into our laws for a reason. This reason.'

'No, *not* this reason. The spirit of those laws is to protect people whose lives are under immediate threat, for whom the only way to protect themselves is to use force against an attacker.'

'Yes, exactly like Jane did.'

'No! She could have done many other things before resorting to that, and as such her actions do not fall within the intention of those laws.'

'Like what, what could she have done?'

'Remove her kids from the school.'

'She'd done that for a while, and they'd served her notice of prosecution if she didn't return her daughter to school immediately. Plus, there were still nearly three hundred other children in danger. I know I couldn't have lived with myself if I'd just left them to die, I'm sure Jane felt the same way.'

'Okay, she could have explained and asked the school to close.'

'What, when the police refused to take her seriously? She could never expect a school to believe her and take such significant formal action without police support and encouragement.'

'Okay, she could have tried to restrain him, or called the police under the guise of another complaint so they would discover his bombs.'

'A small lady, try to take on a young, strong man, who she knows has live bombs metres away – only a fool would try that

– it'd nearly be suicide. And why would she trust the police to assist after she'd tried so many times before?'

My livid boss lets out a heavy sigh, laced with barely constrained contempt. His breath from the exhaling puff reaches me and it reeks of staleness and stress.

'Still, this is too high profile, the message we send if you go up there and say what you clearly intend to will be: the legal system is weak – the courts and the police can't even agree and work together; there are loopholes in the law that mean you can take liberties; and that the police are the soft ones. What that would do to the country doesn't bear thinking about.'

'I'd say that an innocent woman going to prison for the rest of her life doesn't bear thinking about.'

'This is bigger than just one woman, Simmons, surely you aren't so bloody blind as to miss that? This is about the greatest good for the greatest number.'

'On the contrary, I agree entirely – this *is* bigger than just one woman. This is so big as to challenge the integrity of the entire justice system. It's so big as to call into question the willingness of the people entrusted to serve and protect to do what's right, no matter what. It's so big as to highlight the reality of the ridiculously and unfairly hypocritical society we live in – where every single day humans decide about the lives of other humans. Soldiers are trained, at great cost to the country, to kill people; fire fighters have to make heart-breaking choices of lives to save and lives to lose; even certain units of the police will take human life if it meets a specific set of criteria under the exact same circumstances as Jane did – defence of others, self-defence, or, as you said, the greatest good for the greatest number. Some of those people are celebrated – the soldiers, the fire fighters, and the police; but some are punished – Jane. Jane is fighting the *same fight* we fight, and that soldiers fight – good versus evil. She shouldn't lose the rest of her life while those others line up to collect their medals, not when all of us just did exactly the same thing – the *right* thing.'

My boss's eyes narrow to pudgy slits. His tone deepens, menace kidnapping his voice.

'If you continue down this track, Simmons, your job is on the line. I won't tolerate rebellion and dissent in my force. We need unity. I demand accord within my team. You're starting a shitstorm here and it won't go unnoticed.'

'That's as maybe, sir, but I have to be able to live with myself. I believe in doing what's right more than I'm inclined to be scared by threats. Some things are worth fighting for. To me justice is one of them.'

He never responds. All I see is his expensively clad, wide form as he stalks out the room, wearing thunder as a cloak.

I'm fortunate that I have loyal colleagues – good men and women who have spent their days walking alongside me. We've all given our careers to this same drive to protect. In an effort to break my will over Jane, men far higher up the police food chain have exerted pressure on my men in arms to rally against me, to leave me truly alone in the sea of blue. Somehow, they've all retained their allegiance to me, and I'm tremendously grateful.

Rumours sliced through the Birmingham police stations – that I wouldn't be called to trial as the prosecution witness. These were swiftly followed by the confirmation that I will, because it is believed Jane's new barrister, the spectacularly impassioned Simon Rafferty, would uncover in a heartbeat that there was something the prosecution was trying to keep secret. So now my superiors have decided they'll hide me in plain sight. I'm not planning to launch a rebellious crusade, just to answer questions I get asked honestly and with integrity. I'm seeking to honour the justice system by trusting it to do as it promises – to deliver justice. That's not to say I'm without worry – because after all, the law is enforced and decided by humans – it's a human system, and humans are nothing if not inherently flawed. A life in this job teaches you that with certainty – all I've seen my whole career are human flaws.

I'm lacking confidence, but we all have to believe in something, right? The robes and wigs that make up the courtroom costumes, they are my dog collars and clerical shirt. The courtroom is my church. And Jane Bell is my hill to die on.

THIRTY-TWO

ANEESA

I'm passing half an hour before I leave for my next interview combing through the latest online references to Jane. Social media is saturated with the hashtags #Birmingham'sHeroine, #NationalHeroine, #BeMoreJane, #LetHerGo and #I'mWith-Jane. It's hard to find a comment, tweet or post representing opposition to what she did. The ugly head of the internet is reared only to spew hate about terror and James Foster, rather than questions over whether Jane did the right thing. Laid bare is an overpowering feeling of unity and passion for Jane's cause. Having poked around Twitter and Facebook I turn to Instagram and quickly come across photos of James' would-be victims – the children attending St Oliver's – connected by the same hashtags. They are for a protest being organised, campaigning for Jane's release, due to happen outside the Crown Court starting two days before her trial. These photos are emotive enough to fill me with the overwhelming conviction that this is the story to start her trial with when the time comes. I pull my attention back to my interview today.

. . .

The gentleman I'm meeting shortly, Rosh, can show readers the road not travelled, the path not taken, the opposite choice made to Jane's... he could be the public's Angel Clarence from *It's A Wonderful Life* – showing everyone what life would look like *without* Jane. Rosh approached me asking if he could tell his story as part of the series around the Jane Bell case. Once he explained why, I was delighted to agree to meet him. He had the opportunity to make Jane's choice, albeit on a smaller scale.

He chose not to.

I'm standing outside a chain coffee shop, reading a text that says simply, '*I'm in the back left-hand corner – we have full privacy so I'm ready to meet you*'. My interviewee warned me when setting this up that if anyone could overhear us, then he would cancel. I'd suggested meeting in the *Gazette* offices to ensure complete seclusion, but anonymity was apparently the highest priority – even other staff members seeing him and being able to identify him there, or him being caught on our CCTV, would be more risk than he was willing to accept.

The coffee shop has a low ceiling, giving it a darkness that creeps in from the sides of your eyes. I look to the back left-hand corner and see a man dressed in a smart-type checked shirt, shoulders curled over, bulk slight, head tipped down, unruly too-long hair flopping over his face. I see sadness, and a soft, gentle guilt in the way he holds himself as though he's trying to be invisible.

I walk over to him, shortening my stride to bring me to him from a quieter, slower approach. His eyes hold a question as they look up to me, and I smile with my full warmth.

'Thank you,' I say earnestly, by way of greeting. He gives a single nod in response, with a hint of a smile in his eyes. 'Can I get you a drink?'

'I would love a coffee.' His voice has a beautiful lilt to it, full of gentle melody.

'So, what can I tempt you with today – a latte, americano, something else?'

'If you're sure, I'd love a cappuccino, please?'

'Coming right up,' I say cheerfully, paired with a smile.

I wander over to stand in the queue that's a few people deep. I spend a fair amount of time meeting people in coffee shops and I find them the most fascinating places – there aren't many spaces that are so filled with words, with conversations about lives being lived. They are full of mundanities about water companies overcharging to life-changing declarations of overseas moves.

It was in a coffee shop that my dad asked me if I'd go with him to a hospital appointment for some tests, some years ago. I could have found it odd that he hadn't asked me at home, but I knew his motive. Our local coffee shop made the biggest, most decadent milkshakes you could imagine, and, as a child, these were my biggest treat in life. For all the big stuff, good or bad, we'd be found in there guzzling those humongous milkshakes – I got an A on a test: huge milkshake trip; I recovered from a bout of the flu: huge milkshake trip; Dad told me he'd lost his job: huge milkshake trip. He always said, '*Everything* is nicer with a side of sweetness.' No milkshake in the world could mask the bitterness of the moment he told me about the diagnosis, though. Or stop the foreboding that crept through my whole body, head to toe, covering me in goosebumps. Nothing was sweet enough to hide the fear in my dad's eyes – fear of something inside himself. As I always do now, when there is something big to face, I head to a coffee shop, look at the menu board on the wall behind the counter and decide on the biggest, sweetest-sounding milkshake (or frappé as these coffee chains like to call them) and know that I could suck up some of Dad's wisdom and love through the straw. It's never stopped stinging that I can't look into his eyes to feel his affection, or hear his voice giving me his advice anymore, but a sting is far better than letting him be lost to me completely.

There are many places that are full of certain types of life – maternity wards spring to mind for new life, airports for journeys beginning or ending – but there are few places that appear so commonplace but that hold so much of humanity inside, as coffee shops. Secrets are told here; joys, and tribulations, shared. I wonder what secrets will be spilled into my ears today, to be polished and then whispered to thousands through the rustling of the *Gazette's* pages.

I look over to where Rosh is sitting. He has his elbows on his knees and his skin looks a slightly wrong shade – tinged with grey – as though even it is trying to fade away on Rosh's behalf. He looks haunted, but not as though he holds a fear of anything around him. No, I know, the only thing he fears is inside himself, and that's the scariest thing of all.

I place the tray down on the low-slung table between the two once-plush, now-tatty, chairs. I want to start by honouring Rosh's bravery in talking to me today – wounds are so painful to knowingly re-open.

'Thank you again, Rosh, for meeting me today, telling me your story, it takes a lot of courage, and I'm very grateful – I really believe it will help people see another dimension to what Jane did.'

Tears have sprung in Rosh's eyes, quicker than a gunshot, and they climb over his eyelids to drop down his cheeks like abseilers over a cliff edge.

'Courage isn't something you'll find in me, Aneesa, much to my regret.' Rosh's voice trembles, as does his hand when he reaches down to pick up his drink, the porcelain mug rattling against its saucer.

'I beg to differ. Everyone has made a choice they don't like, it comes with the territory of being human. What you're doing today is choosing to use that to help someone else, even though to do so is causing you great pain. That's bravery itself right there – in *that* choice.'

He doesn't nod, but his eyes do connect with mine – a proper, true contact, and that's better. That means he's taken back his place in the world, for now.

We sip our drinks for a few moments, both preparing for what we know is coming next.

'Can I just tell you what happened first, get it out of the way, then you can ask me whatever else you want to know?' Rosh asks me suddenly, his words tumbling over each other in a rush to escape his mouth.

'Absolutely. Are you okay with me using my Dictaphone to record it? Your anonymity is guaranteed, and I'll delete it as soon as I submit the article?'

He nods, and then begins, his suffering diffusing out of every pore.

'I was young. I thought I knew how to be a good man. But I was living within myself – only doing what was easy for *me*, or in *my* best interests. When things fell inside those lines – of helping me too in some way, – then I was a "good man". But anything that risked me, or didn't hold any benefit to me, I turned away from it, even if I shouldn't have.

'I had a neighbour, older than me. He scared my girlfriend at the time – he shouted at nothing late at night, his front garden was a mess – piled high with sharp and dangerous rubble and junk. He seemed like a man with nothing left to try for.

'He was an alcoholic, I always knew he was, though I tried to tell myself in the weeks after what happened that I had no proof. I did, though, really – his nose was redder than Rudolph's, his breath was a fug of alcohol no matter the hour of the day, his eyes were always glassy, his hands never stopped shaking.

'I told myself it was none of my business, what he did with himself. My girlfriend urged me not to get involved – not to risk angering him, in case it made our lives difficult. But I *knew* he wasn't safe. I must have been one of only a handful of people who knew that, and I did nothing to stop it.

'When I first moved into that house, he didn't go out in his car – every time I saw him coming or going, he was walking. Later, when he did start driving, he always appeared sober – he walked straight, acted like anyone else. Then one night he got home late, loudly, engine roaring. I looked out of my bedroom window to see what was causing the noise and I noticed him stagger out of his car and crash into some piece of junk lying in his front garden, swearing into the darkness. That was the start of a repeating pattern. No one could have doubted he was unsafe to be behind the wheel. I certainly didn't doubt it, but I didn't do anything – why put my neck on the line, I thought – not my business. I shrugged it off – a one-off, everyone's allowed a bad day or two, right? I used to do anything to let myself off the hook back then, tell myself whatever I needed to hear to convince myself I was doing the right thing.

'The police came to our door after the big crash happened – as part of an investigation into the deaths of the children. I went to court to testify, even then I didn't want to – a coward despite everything – I was too ashamed; but I got subpoenaed and was forced to go. I had to stand facing the elderly lady in her maroon skirt and teal blouse – they clashed nearly as badly with each other as they did with her scarlet, raw eyes from all the crying – as she held the hand of a sobbing man like a vice, or a lifeline, while I spoke the words out loud. Yes, I'd seen indicators that the man on trial for death by dangerous driving was regularly drunk. Yes, I'd previously seen him drive while displaying signs of intoxication.

'The worst part was, when the photos got put up of the kids, dead in their seats in the back of the car, their mother mashed up in front, her car door a crumpled mess; the eyes of their father, her husband, and their grandma, her mother, they didn't hold blame or accusation or hatred – there was no room for that through the pain and horror in them instead.

'While I know it wasn't directly my fault – I didn't choose to get in a car drunk, drive at sixty miles per hour in the dark on a country lane and then crash into a car holding a young family on their way home from tea with relatives; killing two beautiful young children and their mum... I know I could have stopped it – I could have phoned the police and urged them to try to catch him driving drunk. It wouldn't have been hard – wait at the corner of our road late on a Friday night. I could have parked my car across his driveway to stop him leaving in it that fateful night, but I couldn't face up to his wrath. So, every day I carry their deaths in my heart – indirectly my doing, my responsibility, my fault. It's not enough to say "it's none of my business" when you know that's not the right thing, when you know the price could be innocent lives lost. Protection of innocent lives should be *everyone's* business. We're all here together and we need to step up to that, or else we'll have to accept a world where terrible, cruel, wrong things happen to innocent people, *all the time*. And I don't know anyone who wants that. I don't think we can call ourselves human, if we let that become normal.

'I haven't told anyone this, but I tried to end things twice in the years afterwards – because I thought I was a burden to the world. I thought I didn't deserve to share in it since I'd been willing to stand by and let children die because I was too selfish to stand up for what I knew was right. And I can't pretend that's not the truth – drunk drivers kill and harm people – that's why it's against the law.

'Jane faced a deeply hateful thing all alone, and whatever her judgement at court, I truly hope she knows, deep inside, that she did the right thing, and that in doing so she helped to save the world, for that's the only way to save it. One right thing at a time.'

THIRTY-THREE

JANE

Life in prison is worse than I could ever have imagined. Not because I'm being treated badly; quite the opposite is true in fact – everyone else in here, prison officers and inmates alike, treat me with kindness and respect – but because of the helplessness, and the separation. To have been removed from everything I know, from the people I love, and to have no ability to change anything, is draining me away down an existential plughole. The one thing I'm holding onto is the hope I'm lucky enough to have burning inside me. Some days it's so powerful it rages into an inferno that consumes me, it's all I think about, all I focus on. I can't help but sink deeply into it. Other days it's an ember, barely glowing; but it never dies. Not yet, anyway, not while there's a chance I can still get home. I have to keep the embers fanned on my lowest days, for my children need me, Neil needs me. While I might have simultaneously saved them and let them down in the same moment, they need me to stay *me*, for when we are reunited. However much I sense the shadows of doubt about that outcome flickering at the edges of my conviction, I cannot allow myself to acknowledge them, for that would be the undoing of me, and I cannot possibly accept that, not when it would mean Molly and Joe losing the only piece of their mum they have left.

I cannot resent being here, I feel no hatred – I killed a man, and I understand the need to clarify in court the fairness of that. I still wonder whether what I did was fair in the fight – was my force justified by his threat? The pounding of my heart that creates a drumbeat in my ears, tells me 'yes'; as does the iceberg in my gut. Yet there is a yawning vacuum, pulling at my skin, sucking my soul, that laughs at me and tells me mockingly 'as if'.

From what Simon has said though, I am concerned that fairness won't feature in my trial for even a second. Six months ago, I would never have believed him – I felt the comfort of a world-leading justice system wrapped around me, the safety of a strong and authoritative police force protecting me. Now, I feel fear – if it is as Simon says, it was all smoke and mirrors to cover cracks and crumbles.

Today, the hope is a gently popping and hopping flame – I'll be meeting with someone who Simon says could be the key to the lock of the cage around me – an expert witness he believes has the ability to rouse the jury to my self-defence position in an uprising of conviction.

The prison officers are at my door now, to take me to an interview room so that she can meet me, so that she can pore over my life with a microscope and see into me. I've never met a psychiatrist before, but I know what is said about them – they see right inside you in a second, they know the secrets of your soul in minutes. I hope they're right –

I could do with someone seeing into mine; seeing and saving me.

. . .

When my gaze first lands on Dr Melanie McCulloch, seated as she is in the dull and lifeless interview room in the prison, I'm startled. There is no colour in here – everything that was once vibrant has now faded pathetically – but Dr McCulloch is vivid. It's as if she has been digitally brightened or filtered – like the adverts on television for 4K– all the colours richer, the images clearer, than it seemed they could ever possibly be in real life. I've never seen a red as scarlet and glowing as her scarf, nor a yellow as lively as her blouse. Her smile matches them too – full of spark. I warm up inside instantly.

'You must be the extraordinary Mrs Bell?' This vision of a woman asks me, as she stands and reaches for my hand. I'm a little awestruck as I raise my hand to hers, and it's the squeeze she gives it that breaks my reverie and brings me back fully into the moment.

'I'm not sure about *that*, but I'm Jane, yes... and please do call me Jane.'

'I'm Mel. I trust Mr Rafferty has explained why I'm here?'

'Thank you, very much... Mel,' I stutter. Using such a casual name for someone I know is so esteemed and high-flying feels caustic on my tongue. I feel clumsy and awkward, which I desperately don't want to be in front of her, so I feel heat bloom in my cheeks. I look down at my cracking hands and rush on to try to cover it all up, even though I can't. 'Yes, Simon said that today you're going to ask me questions so you can prepare fully for the trial, and that you will be our expert witness. Is that right? I'm still having to work hard to keep up with the format and proceedings of everything.'

'That's absolutely right. I'm here today to discuss with you the run-up to the events of 16th January and the events themselves. There will also be questions about your life in general, all for the purpose of allowing me the deepest psychiatric insight into why everything happened the way it did, so that I can speak with the most specificity and certainty possible at the trial. That's what the jury need to be filled with – *certainty* – we need *beyond* a reasonable doubt.'

I nod. 'I'm ready,' I say, quietly but solidly.

'Okay, let's start at the beginning, please, with the first moment you suspected something was wrong.'

'Of course,' I respond, dutifully. I've recited the facts so many times that I can do it fairly shut down now. This actually helps – the feelings overpower me otherwise, make everyone uncomfortable, slow me down, hurt me. 'We got a new neighbour about six months ago. He appeared to live alone, which seemed slightly unusual as our street is all three-bedroomed semis, but that didn't really catch my attention at the time. It was nice to have the quiet was all we thought – in our area neighbours can be a nightmare with noise and mess and nastiness, though we're lucky on Wesley Street itself. You wouldn't even have known he was there most of the time, other than he put his bins out and back in every week like clockwork, like we all did.

'The moment I wondered if something was amiss was when he made the changes to the house – boarding the fence up so high and the like. My first idea was that maybe he was dealing drugs. The whole thing was weird, it rang alarm bells for me. Neil said it could just be a lifestyle difference – a young bachelor.

'Then there was the receipt. That's when I *knew* something wasn't right, but I didn't realise then just how fully wrong it was. I called the police; they wouldn't help based only on a receipt for DIY and garden products, they said.

'Then, on one of the rare occasions that I saw him leave his house, I looked in his window and I saw the maps, saw the bomb parts. Lots of materials, strewn all over the room. *Lots*. Then I knew.'

'Thank you, Jane, you're doing so well. I can tell you're used to reeling off the facts for the law enforcement officials who have interviewed you but I need to understand what you were *thinking and feeling* as all this unfolded – they are what will most help me– knowing *you*.'

'Okay.' I pause. This is a heavy door, with hinges that are beginning to rust, to a very dark room. I need to keep a tight hold of my composure to face it. My fists clench in symbolism. Mel's eyes flick down to them. She misses nothing. I take a deep breath and begin. 'I felt what I think any mother would feel... terror.' I suck in a sharp breath then, as I realise exactly what I've said. 'Well, you know what I mean... petrified. I feel like I haven't been able to breathe properly since that moment, like there are scaly, scratching fingers clawing at and crushing my heart.

'Initially, when I thought that I could tell the police and they would come and fix it all and the nightmare would be over in the nick of time I felt a weird, frenzied relief. When they didn't come, I felt all-consuming panic that didn't leave me until James was dead. Neil and I took the kids away for a few nights, stayed in a bed-and-breakfast, but our spare money for that ran out quickly – we don't have much at the best of times. We don't have family that can accommodate us, so we had to go back to the house. We swapped the kids into our room though, moved the bed to the farthest wall from his house, so that if something went wrong, they had the... best chance. We couldn't rest in the end though, so we drove around with them sleeping in the car until the morning. That next day is when *it* happened.

'We had taken Molly and Joe out of school and nursery, but soon enough I was phoned and told that because Molly was absent without permission, prosecution proceedings would have to be started if we couldn't get a doctor's note for her and that the local authority would be informed about Joe, meaning he would lose his free nursery place. I needed that to be able to work the little I do. I hate leaving him, but there are things we need that extra income for. I couldn't afford to fight the school about Molly either. I felt full of horror and despair. I knew it, deep in my bones – embedded in my gut – that they would die. That there would be my children and all these other beautiful children in a bloody massacre if I did nothing. I felt like I was going insane because no one was believing me. I was telling these terrible things to these important people, who promise us so much, who have all the power, and they just ignored them. I was all alone. They ignored me, my children, and all the others. I felt like we were targets, left to die, left to be slaughtered.'

I'm struggling to get my words out now, my tongue feeling too big and clumsy in my mouth. I can feel the skin on my cheeks tightening with the soaking of silent tears. But I have to finish.

'So, when I got the chance, I took it. I did what I had to do to make it stop, to save Molly and Joe and all those children. What choice did I have? How could I have lived with myself if I had made a different one? If I have to pay with the rest of my life, then I won't be okay, but I also won't regret anything, because Molly, Joe and all those children will *live* now. They won't have to scream... they won't have to be ripped apart... they won't have to *die*.'

I stumble to a stop here. I feel like I'm going to retch. I can't go on. I can no longer get my words out, they've been getting harder and slower with every moment, but Mel's eyes locked into mine had kept me going until now.

She leans forward, wraps my clasped hands in hers, holds onto them tightly and says, 'Thank you, Jane. Thank you.'

It is only as she lets silence settle around us, and keeps a tight but comforting hold of my hands, that I realise how much I'm shuddering, that I can hear my teeth clashing together, can taste the blood in my mouth from where I must have bitten my tongue. Eventually, I still, feeling frozen for a while. Then I feel like me again and am able to attempt a joke.

'Was that enough "feelings" for you?' I manage a small smile.

'Just about,' Mel responds, in a voice full of warmth. 'I will help defend you Jane, as vehemently and strongly as I can.'

Mel saw my soul and I hope she'll try to save it.

THIRTY-FOUR

ANEESA

I'm sitting on a scratchy fabric train seat trying to work out how to use Rosh's interview for greatest impact while battling motion sickness. Looking out of my window at wild countryside I feel a flash of impatient fatigue and wonder how much farther it is back to Birmingham New Street when my mobile rings. I glance around the carriage as I unzip the front pocket on my handbag to reach my phone and note everyone seems to be plugged in to their devices so I shouldn't disturb anyone by answering. I look at the name lit up on the screen and anticipation fizzes through the nerves down my spine to my fingertips as I see it's my private investigator calling. I rush to press earbuds into my ears and plug them into my phone before sliding my thumb across the cool screen to answer.

'Hi Charlie. I'm travelling home from an interview and I'm in the back of beyond so if I lose you don't go anywhere, I'll call back as soon as my signal lets me.' My voice has ended up being that loud whisper that always sounds angry as I try to retain privacy whilst ensuring Charlie can hear me.

He gives a gruff grunt in response. He's too busy for social niceties, though he's always humoured mine. He's a scalpel cutting cleanly and efficiently straight to everything, as he does next.

'I've found the brother.' I'm stunned into silence. He can't mean...

'Whose brother?' I ask cautiously – I daren't believe it.

'Foster's.' Now I can't help but gasp loudly and dart my eyes around the carriage to see some dirty looks and irritated sighs of admonishment. I'm too excited to care.

'How, where?'

'Skills and sources.' He never gives anything away, though there's a shade of pride in his usually unmovable voice. 'He's bunking with a friend in Leeds.'

'Have you made contact?'

'No, just got you the address, didn't want to spook him. Looks like he's been on the move these past few weeks, never staying anywhere for more than a few nights, so I'd hightail it over there if you want to catch him.'

'Thanks, Charlie. Personal best this one, hey?' He chuckles – there's a first time for everything. He hangs up. I sink backwards, jellified, melding with the grimy seat.

I can comprehend his words but not absorb their impact yet. A minute passes while my mouth is boneless, slack. Slowly the information begins to assimilate. *James Foster has a brother*. Charlie's found him, which means the lead's mine. This could blow the whole story wide open. Dynamite in a sponge. James Foster's brother, before anyone else has found him, that's a king-maker of a story. An image of Eliza rises into my line of thought. *No matter what, Jane must be a heroine*. If he'll talk, James Foster's brother will make him a human, not just an anonymous monster. Depending on what he says, every bit of humanity his brother gives James will take a piece away from Jane. Eliza won't like that. I don't know whether or not I do. Nevertheless, the truth must be told. I'm sure Eliza'll come around, given this truth will be so good for readership.

My phone vibrates with a text from Charlie. I hastily open it to find a name – Luke Foster – and a Leeds address. I feel a pang of fleeting sadness, for all the years I've been waiting to see the same message from Charlie but containing my mum's name instead.

Charlie and I go back a long way. I was fourteen when he entered my life. My dad agreed to let me start sewing for my auntie's business and when I got my first envelope of wages I phoned round some private investigators to help me find my mum. The idea had come to me when I was ten and was introduced to Sherlock Holmes books – my mind had been blown by what he could do and it was a lightning bolt of hope that mine and mum's story could have a different ending. Charlie was the first one who didn't hang up on me when they heard how young I sounded.

'What's the job?' he asked me. I was so flustered to be actually having this conversation that I flush recalling it.

'To find my mum.' My voice was so heavy with its load that I could barely lift it above a whisper.

'Ah. What happened?' he asked, a hint of gentle kindness beneath the quick professional tone.

'She left, years ago. One day when I was at school she went and never came back. She didn't leave a note or a message.' I was gabbling, desperate to get him to understand. 'She's never got in touch since. My mum wouldn't have done that willingly, I know everyone says that, but it's actually true. We were inseparable. She never really left the house on her own. My dad and I were her whole world. I need to know what happened... whatever the truth is.' I waited for a response but it was slow coming and I heard a sigh down the line, so I added a plea. 'Help me, please. I *need* this.'

'Do you know my charges?'

'Not specifically. But I can pay. I earn thirty pounds a week from sewing for my auntie. You can have it all. However much of your time that gets me each week, for however long it takes.'

'Okay. That'll only get you an hour a week, but I'll make a start and see if it's worth pursuing.' He asked me to send him a letter with all the information I had about mum, as well as the first week's payment, which I did the moment I hung up.

I kept it a secret from my dad and auntie for as long as I could – my auntie hated any talk about what happened to mum, they were the only times she ever got really cross with me. Over time, I became suspicious of that, unable to understand why she shut down so much about something so important. I still wonder what she's hiding. About two months after Charlie started investigating, she found out all my wages were gone and when I refused to tell her why she was so furious that, in an attempt to get answers, she opened one of the reports Charlie posted to me. I was instantly fired from any more sewing work and forbidden from ever contacting 'that man' again. I called Charlie to explain that we'd have to take a break from searching until I could get another job and he asked me to hold the line for a few minutes. Charlie came back on to say he wasn't far from exhausting all avenues and that he'd finish for free.

'No one should have to live with such questions haunting them,' was his explanation. I remember the heat of the tears as they wore trails into my cheeks. He came up with a coded report style – a letter from a supposed pen-pal with our agreed phrases in it. It injected a morsel of fun into something heart-breaking. Of every case I've ever given him since, Mum's is the only one he's still yet to solve. I feel the familiar stinging behind my eyes and the powerlessness to stop the trails being worn again. I just need to *know*. After everything I've had taken away, why can't I even be given that?

THIRTY-FIVE

NEIL

There hasn't been much that I've felt useful doing but I've certainly been busy. I've coordinated all sorts, managed the children, got back to work, undertaken huge amounts of legal research, fended off the press constantly, and continue to cope – with Mum's unique brand of help. To be fair, though, I couldn't have done this without her. I've met every request of Simon's for the provision of documents and details of our history. It has all been time-consuming, and no doubt necessary, but I haven't felt useful in the bigger sense of helping Jane get out of this dark hole. What really matters to my Jane is getting home and at least in Simon we've got the best we could ever have hoped for to help get her here.

Simon has asked to meet me this morning, to update me about Jane's defence.

My doorbell rings one minute before Simon is due to arrive. I'm ready, but I feel a flutter of nerves. Simon is brilliant, everything about him is *just right*, and I feel inferior when I've spent time in his company – frumpy, small.

I open the front door to see him filling the frame. This

defies logic, as he is a slim man, but somehow, who he is is not limited in dimension by his physical body. He's like Jane in that. He looks startlingly out of place – never before has Wesley Street seen a suit so sharp, brogues so shiny, nor eyes so fiercely intelligent. I try to stop myself shrinking, my children are around, and if they see us, I want them to be inspired by Simon, not to learn from me to be intimidated.

'Neil, good to see you.' Simon extends a hand for a warm handshake – his customary greeting.

'Welcome. Sorry about...' I tail off, gesturing behind me. Mum's kept the place much straighter than I managed, so I'm not ashamed, but it just feels so inadequate. Simon and our home don't belong together.

'You have a lovely home.' Simon sweeps my insecurities aside with his smile. 'Thank you for having me here – I thought that since I've asked for the meeting, the least I could do was save you the trip. Besides, a slice of me is curious, I realised it would be lovely to see Jane's home. I've driven past before, of course, to understand the scene of the incident, but much like us humans, exteriors and interiors should never be assumed to epitomise each other. I grew up in a house that was stunning to look at, but I never felt like I was at home when I stepped through the door. You've got that here – a heart for your family.'

I let a moment pass, slightly taken aback by this deeper, softer side to Simon. Perhaps sensing his own vulnerability, he glosses over it instantly. 'A table would be best for this meeting, if you would be so kind?' Simon asks, raising his perfectly shaped eyebrows in question. I haven't looked in a mirror for weeks. Next to Simon I must look like a yeti.

Once I brush aside Molly's latest drawing of the puppy

she so desperately wants, we sit down. Simon steeples his fingers together and leans towards me.

'Before we get down to business, how are you, Neil? How are you actually coping?' The humble genuineness of his question catches me unawares.

'I'm how I think anyone would be – struggling but getting each day done for my kids.' I can feel the desolation choking me, wrapping around my throat, looking into my eyes and whispering, *he can't help you, don't waste his time, you're alone with this*. I almost succumb to it, can feel a shrug starting to form, words finding their way together to put Simon off this topic. Then, he reaches for me. Simon's hand finds my forearm and he softly squeezes it.

'Tell me, Neil.' There's a voice telling me this is weird – men don't go around touching other men's forearms and getting emotional, but something stronger inside me silences it. The physical connection is a lifeline, and my loneliness grabs onto it. I look into Simon's eyes and he meets me there, his gaze kind and urging.

'I'm...' I start, and then I realise there are no words big enough for these feelings, nothing that could ever convey their magnitude, how they've swallowed me as hugely as a blue whale would an anchovy. Still, I can feel a yearning to try to continue, that it will help. 'I'm lonelier than I ever imagined possible,' I begin, my head now bowed down, a defeated man. 'I feel like every moment is an eternity, every single part of my body feels like cement. I feel numb and yet even air hurts my skin. I feel like I'm drowning.'

'I am so, so sorry, Neil. Truly. I can't even begin to imagine how horrific this is for you, but I offer my support – not just with Jane's legal case, but to you, for whatever you need. The reason I'm here today might not help with all of what you're feeling, or indeed any of it, but I'm hoping there's a chance it will fight the loneliness... because it's come from Jane. She asked me to have this conversation with you, to make sure you understood this element, although she didn't enlighten me as to why, maybe you'll know, since she was very insistent about it. Maybe there's a thread in it to link you. Shall I start?'

I nod, feeling a greater sturdiness now I've opened the door to air out my feelings. No one can help me, but I feel cared for and that can make all the difference.

'Eyewitness testimony. A living nightmare for any barrister. Unreliable, inconsistent, sometimes pure make-believe, yet capable of winning jurors over and deciding cases. A particularly vehement or likable eyewitness with total confidence in their story, even if it's wrong, can be enough to swing a jury member – and often there are key jurors who influence all the others to the verdict. There have also been cases where a false eyewitness testimony has led to a miscarriage of justice. Entire cases have been lost on the evidence of a single, completely wrong, eyewitness.' Simon pauses for a moment; a thought having clearly just struck him. 'Do you have any training in psychology, Neil?' Simon asks. 'I remember you're in marketing and elements of that can be pure psychology. I wouldn't want to patronise you.'

'None at all. I don't even work in the creative part of marketing, I'm the nuts-and-bolts implementer so I know nothing about that side of things.'

'Okay, that's no problem, it means I get the excitement of introducing you to something incredible.' Simon gives an infectious grin brimming with delight.

'In my estimation, almost every single eyewitness testimony has a detail or more, said on the stand under oath, that's not remembered from the event in question. The brain can only store in memory what it has attended to in each moment – that is, what its attention is directly on. As that leaves so many details not stored, when recalling a past event, the brain uses its historical experiences and other memories to fill in the gaps. This could pull from all sorts of sources – even, say, from films you remember. However, you fervently believe you have a memory of that detail, with absolutely no clue that it's false. Does that make sense so far?'

'Yes,' I say slowly. 'It seems logical.'

'Brilliant. Now, there are countless studies which prove, beyond doubt, that eyewitness testimonies are extremely unreliable. Given how many court cases pivot around them, futures in the balance, it's shocking that every single juror is not given a thorough education of the findings of these studies before they take their place in the courtroom. Anyway, you should be warned, there is one key eyewitness in Jane's case, who has given a lengthy and very damning statement. She says that she saw the whole incident occur and describes Jane's actions as being very determined and brutal. The prosecution is likely to bring it out early, get some black marks against Jane at the start. It will undoubtedly damage our case. I'll do what I can to undermine it in my cross-examination but the impact of it on the jury could be very difficult to overcome.'

'Who is it?' I interrupt, not having previously realised anyone was doing this to us.

'Your neighbour across the road – Rita Smith.'

I zone out here, floating through the rest of the meeting, the goodbye, trying to process the implications of what Simon has explained, and knowing deep in my gut that they aren't good. I spend every spare moment of the next few days lost on the internet, following links Simon has sent me, travelling deeper into this new world – one that lives inside our skulls our whole lives, but which we understand so unbelievably little about. My laptop and phone are a mess of open tabs, downloaded PDFs, and videos watched.

The more I absorb, and the deeper the implications sink, the clearer I hear Jane's message to me. I realise she must have asked Simon to explain it to me so that I finally come through for her. I know what I need to do, who I need to visit.

It leads me to Rita's doorstep.

I knock on the peeling, Merlot-coloured door, the doorbell hanging off on a wire. The sun is reaching down through the cold air so that my forehead feels warm, my back icy. She opens the door a crack with eyes narrowed to slits, shoulders around her ears. The door slams shut and a few seconds later I hear the scratch of the chain being slid, the door opens wide, and I'm ushered in.

Cat hairs bathe the mud brown hallway rug and, with not enough room for Rita to pass, she gestures toward the kitchen. I wander through, past a plastic bowl overflowing with wet, smelly cat food.

Rita flicks the switch on the kettle, and I sit down at the breakfast bar as invited. The room is a mirror reflection of our kitchen but feels more spacious with the breakfast bar rather than the kitchen table we've squeezed into ours to allow for art projects and sit-down family meals. There is only Rita and her husband, Nev, living here.

'You've been a hard man to pin down since it 'appened, Neil, you 'ave. I've been starting to feel like a stalker I 'ave. Chasing after you every time I get a glimpse of you coming or going. I know you've got the weight of the world on your shoulders, but bleeding months without sight nor sound of you – getting to take it personal I am.' I can see there is a mask of hurt on Rita's face. With Rita being the street's maternal busybody, I know I'll have insulted her avoiding her the way I have. I just couldn't take it all.

'I'm truly sorry, Rita, I've gone to ground with almost everyone – it's been such an ordeal. I've barely got from one day to the next. I just haven't been able to handle chat, even with your biscuits – the best on Wesley Street.' I see her soften.

'Understandable, that is.' She pauses and stretches up to lift a tin down from above the cupboards. 'Got to make up for lost time then,' she says with a sympathetic smile, pushing biscuits towards me. 'How's she holding up, duck?' Rita asks.

'Good days and bad days I think, Rita. She's being treated kindly enough in there I think, at least, and she has a great defence barrister who seems to be keeping hope alive for us.'

She nods keenly. 'Terrible business, the whole thing. What an animal. Happening right across the street an' all; I told my Nev you just can't believe it.'

'You saw the incident happen, Rita?'

'Right before my eyes, duckie. Saw the car, saw the disgusting body.' She makes the sign of the cross over her chest. 'Your poor Jane, what a burden to carry, but what a brave heart she has. And you and those two lovely little-uns without her now. Do let me know if I can do anything to help.'

'Well,' I say hesitantly.

'Ask away.' Her back is still to me as she bustles about plucking mugs off the draining board and pulling a battered box of Yorkshire Tea out of the cupboard above the kettle.

'It's about your statement to the police, and your testimony at the trial.'

'Gosh, yes, what a palaver that'll be. Still don't know how I'm going to find something to wear.' Rita brings the mugs of tea over and sits down, her brows knotted in either mock or real consternation – I can't tell how much of this is dramatically enhanced.

'What do you know about eyewitness testimonies in general?'

Rita's eyes have narrowed, a question born from suspicion in them and in the set of her jaw. 'Only what the police have told me.'

'They should have gone through the official information with you, but I'm talking about the stuff everyone can find out if they look, things they teach in A level psychology for crying out loud. This is our Jane, Rita, so obviously I've looked into everything. I just want to help her as much as I can.' I can hear earnestness in my voice now, laced with emotion. Rita clearly hears it too, for she softens once more.

'Oki doki, duck, tell me what you've found.'

'It'd be easier if I showed you – is that okay?'

'Of course. This is getting a bit exciting now, hey?' I don't respond, thinking my wife's potential prison future is hardly 'exciting'. Instead, I busy myself with setting up.

I pull out my tablet and load up the video that's commonly used to demonstrate the holes in eyewitness testimony – the same one Simon showed me.

It shows six people, three wearing white T-shirts, three wearing black T-shirts, passing basketballs between them. As is standard in this selective attention test, I ask Rita to count how many times the white T-shirt team pass the basketball between them. Less than a minute passes as she does this. At the end I ask her, 'How many passes?'

'Fourteen, I think, but I got a bit muddled in the middle.'

'Close, Rita, there were fifteen.'

'I've never been the best at puzzles,' she says with a disappointed shrug.

'Did you see anything unusual in the video?' I ask nonchalantly.

'No, just the players passing the balls.'

'So, no gorilla?' I enquire with a smile.

'Oh, don't be daft, duckie, a gorilla, as if!' she exclaims, laughing.

'You're sure?'

'A hundred percent.'

'And you'd say that under oath on the witness stand?'

'You've lost the plot, you have, Neil, of course I would. A gorilla, as if I could have missed that!' She's still clucking away to herself.

I rewind the video to the beginning and hit play. When the person in a gorilla suit comes onto the screen, I point to it. Rita's hands fly to cover her now open mouth. She watches in bewildered silence for a few moments. I watch her process the information. 'Well, I never,' she says at last, faintly. 'I can't believe my eyes.' Her expression transitions to shock. She's silent for a few moments, her eyes glassy. She looks very anxious now. 'Oh, my goodness.'

'The thing is, Rita, this test just proves that *everyone's* brains are made to focus only on the thing they're giving attention to – in this case, the white team passing the ball. For everything beyond that, our brain fills in the gaps based on its experiences and memories. But it doesn't mean everything you think you see is wrong – the white team *were* passing the basketball.'

'Thanks for trying to make me feel better, but I didn't even get the blasted number of passes right, did I?' She looks down, staring at a spot in front of her. 'There are so many things I think I know about because I keep an eye on things.' She looks up at me here and shoots a cheeky wink my way. 'But what if I'm missing things and don't see the real picture. What if I've not remembered it all right - it was very exciting? I was certain there was no gorilla,' she finishes with quietly.

'Usually, we can put it right or make amends. If we're fortunate,' I pause here, hoping she'll connect the dots or fill in the gaps. I pray I'm not being too optimistic.

Rita nods.

'I will never forgive myself if I say the wrong thing and hurt our lovely Jane.'

'Thank you, Rita, for taking the time to listen, and for being open-minded.' She nods, eyes still full of sorrow, as I put my empty mug in the sink and make my way to the door, ready to do it all over again with Raj – the neighbour two doors down. The process and outcome are nearly exactly the same there, just with no 'ducks' thrown in, and not nearly such nice biscuits.

I hope that, finally, I've done something today that Jane would be proud of.

THIRTY-SIX

ANEESA

The moment I got home from the station last night I booked my train ticket to Leeds. The times were best with a late morning departure which has worked brilliantly in allowing me to get the article about Rosh's interview written and submitted to Eliza. It was a struggle to focus, my mind making urgent pleas to divert to thoughts about what lay waiting for me in Leeds, but I managed to restrain it enough to do Rosh justice – I hope. At 11 a.m. I pack my notebooks and laptop up from my desk at the office and email Eliza to tell her I'll be working from home this afternoon. While I'm staring at my inbox, I double check my train time to Leeds, glance at my watch, and realise I need to hurry.

I arrive at my flat panting and with sweat cooling on my forehead. I rush to get Bertie fed and give him a quick cuddle before getting changed and grabbing my satchel.

I scoop Bertie up and kiss his head as I plop him back through the door with a final nudge when he tries to follow me out.

'See you on the other side, best buddy,' I whisper to him as

I turn the key in the lock. I have a compulsive feeling that I've forgotten something important as I half-jog to the train station, though mentally running through everything I need and patting their locations to find them in place, I reassure myself that it's my customary show of extreme nerves.

Having made my way to two wrong platforms, such is the muddled puddle my brain has become amongst this, I squeeze through the train doors at the last moment.

I lower myself gratefully into the seat, this time forgiving of the harsh fabric and cramped space as I appreciate its support. I'm so overstimulated that I zone out for most of the journey and operate on autopilot all the way to Leeds.

I step off the train at the other end and follow the signs to the taxis. I give the address to my driver; a check on Google maps before I left revealed the location is deep in a residential area. I don't take in the city beyond my windows, I spend the time reading over the notes I have – carefully memorising the small number of details the police and Jane have provided about James Foster as well as all potential avenues to question his brother on. Mainly though, I try and conjure up the words that will convince him to speak to me at all. My fingernails show how deep my worry runs, that in this pressure climax I will crumble and be found wanting.

My driver clears her throat and points to a house squashed in a brick terrace just beyond the taxi door.

'That's it.' She points a finger. 'Ten pounds ninety.'

I pass her eleven and then take my first proper look around. It's strangely deserted, certainly not a street I'll happen across an empty taxi.

'If I pay the meter charge for your time, will you wait? I don't expect it will be a long visit – at most half an hour.' Her eyes scan me, narrowed with assessment.

'Okay. If you leave a tenner as a deposit, I'll wait for your half-hour. She pulls the car a bit closer into the curb and then reaches up to click the meter back on with a pointed look at me through the rear-view mirror. As I step out the door, I see her cracking open a Maeve Binchy novel and I hear the start of a contented sigh. I feel a longing to be able to enjoy a simple pleasure like that. To switch off.

The air bites its greeting, wind smarting against my cheeks. I hear a crunch under my boot as I step forwards and look down to see green broken glass shards. I hope no cats roam this street.

Fast, hard footsteps attract my attention. I see a man walking quickly down the street from my left, head down, hood tight around his ears, just a tuft of startlingly bright blond hair sneaking out from beneath it. A plain white carrier bag swings from his hand, bulging with the outlines of a pizza box, the scent of grease and melted cheese around him hitting me. When he's a couple of strides away he looks up suddenly, noticing me for the first time. His gaze snaps from me to the house I am clearly standing squarely in front of. His whole body tenses, his head snaps back, taught atop newly strained shoulders. He jerks to a stop and seems to freeze, mirroring me, two strangers in a street, trapped in a moment of adrenaline and indecision. His mouth slackens and then almost instantly tightens into a knot. Before I can react, he has spun around. It breaks my state.

'Luke Foster?' I call out, quietly. He hesitates almost imperceptibly, an unconscious reaction only possible if that were his name. I sprint to close the gap he's made. He doesn't turn, he begins to stride longer, more frantically. 'Please, I mean no harm. I just want to find out who he was, your brother. I'm a features writer for the *Birmingham Gazette*. I want to tell the truth about James. I want to understand, to help everyone else understand.'

I could swear he slows slightly. 'I know this must be terrifying but if I've found you others will follow. You can't run for ever.' I say this softly, no hint of confrontation or accusation within miles of me. His shoulders drop and he stops before slowly turning, looking me dead in the eyes. I stand, unwavering, not pressing. A drowning man, about to go under, he whispers: 'I want people to understand too.'

The friend of his who owns this narrow, terraced house looks wide-eyed from Luke to me and back again comically before slapping his palms to his thighs and stating.

'Need a few things from the Tesco Express. I'll be back later.' Luke gives him a grateful nod and watches him leave.

'Can I get you a tea, coffee, water, anything?' He asks.

'No, no. I'm good thank you.'

Luke gestures to the low, dark faux-leather settee and I perch myself on the edge of it, arranging myself to look poised but natural. He's staring into space, and I feel like a hunter – the exact type of journalist I've never wanted to be. My conscience nags words from me, I'm grateful to it.

'Are you okay?' I ask softly. 'Or at least as okay as you could possibly be?' He merely shrugs. 'I don't want to pressure you, Luke. I found you, I do believe the police and other reporters will follow but I only want you to tell me what you're comfortable with. I'll maintain your anonymity for now, keep back your first name if you do let me share the truth of your brother with the world.'

'It's been hell. I've been scared, wanted to escape it, flee, but I realise now that's unsustainable. The world needs answers and I get that. I'm so angry. But, God, I'm *so sorry.*' He looks up at me for the first time, his eyes plaintive, full of sorrow, his face split open with pain. I surreptitiously click my Dictaphone on. I'll make sure I get retrospective permission later. 'James was actually my twin, though we weren't like the twins from movies, we were yin and yang. I was a sport fiend, competitive, driven, all energy and laughs. James was quiet, studious, lost in his own head. Our father left when we were nine and before then he only had eyes for me – the son he understood. James was always on the outside, ridiculed by Dad for not wanting to join in with our rough and tumble and sports at the park. I could see how he wanted to and there was a time when we were, I don't know, five, that James built up enough courage to try. Football just wasn't his thing, and Dad got angry with him, called him a wimp, a wuss, a girl. He never came again, and I didn't blame him. It was toxic for a child like him. I wish now that I'd tried to find ways to include him in things, get him out of his room and mixing with people, but I didn't, I was too wrapped up in my own world.'

'You were just a child,' I interject, 'that wasn't for you.'

'He was my twin. It *was* for me. I guess he embarrassed me, is the truth of it, and so I let him down. Mum was on her own with us from then on, which meant she had to work long hours to keep us fed and housed. James retreated into himself... and his computer. He was pretty much a genuine genius with books and studying and he poured himself into that, I think to try and be good at something, to have a place to belong. But we didn't live in the kind of area where that was valued. The kids at school picked on him more than ever, singling him out as a "nerd" and pushing him around for that. He was alone, the teachers never helped him, or seemed to recognise his ability, they were too busy trying to tame the kids like me filling the classrooms.' Luke pauses, seems to get lost in a reverie, a frown knotting his eyebrows in a low, tortured sling. I feel one of my legs starting to cramp because of the angle I'm sitting so I shift and wince internally when the settee material squeaks and groans.

'How traumatic for any child. What happened to him from there?' I speak steadily, but encouragingly, trying to draw Luke back out from the cave he's shuttered himself into.

'It's my fault. All of this. He wasn't evil, everything he turned into was because of what happened to him.' He stops again, the silence charged with emotion, feeling like a heavy fog wrapping around our shoulders – dense, and concealing everything important.

'What do you mean? Did something happen?'

His eyes pounce on mine and then scuttle away.

'He loved the skies. He was constantly going on about planets and star stuff. He pleaded with Mum to get him a tele-scope one Christmas and said he'd go without birthday presents for the rest of his life if she could find the money to buy him one. She did somehow, and he sat as sweet as anything the next birthday when all he got was a card and a chocolate bar. He was excited for me when I got football boots and a cricket bat, never complaining.

'He worked so hard to get out of there, to find his place to belong, to change things for the better. James wanted to be some kind of engineer to do with space and he worked so hard to achieve that. He had identified a course at university and had the prospectus on his desk all through exams and sixth form college. He applied on his own and managed to get top grades in his first exams, essentially teaching himself. The kids had never stopped bullying him. They would take his books and rip them up, they would lie in wait for him, spit on him, laugh in his face, shove him down every day, verbally abuse him constantly. He never retaliated, he plugged on. He changed to a different, better, college for his A-levels, to try and get away from them, but they were still around. Having dropped out of education themselves and unemployed, they had nothing better to do than lie in wait for him. I was at a sports college, working to get qualified as a personal trainer, still playing sports every chance I got and hanging out with my girlfriend. I guess I left him behind and never looked back.'

Luke jumps up from the chair with a start and starts pacing the room. It's intimidating – he has the physique of someone fit and athletic. He drags his hands down the sides of his face, stretching the skin down as he goes. Then he links his fingers and stretches them out backwards in front of himself, his body taking up all the space in the room. I want to draw myself back but resist, not wanting to be any more vulnerable.

I sense he's the only person he wants to attack, but I can't stop my body's response to the changed energy in the room, the body language I'm looking at.

'He never asked me for anything, you understand?' He looks at me then and I nod quickly. 'But he asked me to walk with him to his final exams. "I need these, Luke," he said, "I know I can do it, but I have to be able to get there to sit them." I still remember the fear in his eyes, the desperation. I walked with him for the first two, nothing happened. I had a football game on during the next one. It wasn't even important – just a Wednesday afternoon inter-college one. I told James I couldn't walk with him. I told him he'd be fine, that there had been no trouble. I remember the way his face drained of colour, went grey. He opened his mouth to respond and then clearly thought better of it.' There's another pause, Luke's chest rising and falling like a racehorse's flanks after the Grand National.

'He never made it there.' Luke suddenly punches the wall next to him. Not hard enough to do any damage but enough to scare us both. I leap up, knowing I should leave but enthralled by the story. *This is real journalism*, I chastise myself, *people need to know this*. He shakes out his hand as he lowers his shoulders, takes a deep breath and turns to me. 'Sorry.' He's sheepish.

I know from when Mum left, feelings get far too big for our bodies to hold sometimes. He lowers himself immediately back onto the seat.

'What stopped him getting there – the bullies?' I urge him on.

'Yeah. They beat him up, badly. Played with him like he was a ragdoll. The college called Mum. Apparently, he'd dragged himself there barely conscious, begging to be allowed to sit the exam. They couldn't let him; he was too late. He'd have had to wait another year to be able to sit it again. He gave up. Couldn't even get a job stacking shelves – nobody wanted to take on a broken man, which is what he was. Bitterness sealed the cracks the bullies had left him with. He withdrew, I could feel us losing him, but we couldn't reach him. Neither Mum nor I could really comprehend what he'd lost, how ill-suited he was for the life he was trapped in. He got a job online, I don't know what exactly, and then he moved out into a bedsit in Birmingham. He started using, we tried to help him but nothing worked. We lost touch completely. That was four years ago now.' He drops his head into his palms, covering his face, his shoulders shaking.

'So, how do you think he got from where you left him to where he ended up on Wesley Street?'

'Honestly, I don't know. Children's Services informed me that he'd had two kids since then, that they were having to take them into care. Mum's passed now, and I wasn't in a position to take them, so I think they were due to be placed up for adoption. I couldn't reach James on the old phone numbers I had for him, and he'd long moved out of the bedsit. I'd have liked to help, you know, support him. Get to know his kids. Just not raise them.' He gives me a look of regret and sorrow. 'I know I'm his family, and everyone will think I just want to see the good in him, but I truly believe he wasn't inherently evil.

I reckon he loved those kids of his; maybe being a father showed James the good he had in him; maybe they were a way for him to do something important with his life.'

'If they meant that much to him, do you think he'd have gone through with it? Detonated the bombs at the school?'

'I honestly don't know. I want to say no, but that's hard to do in the face of the evidence.' He lifts his head from his palms, and the downturned set of his mouth with the lifting of his eyebrows at the middle speak of his regret, his defeat.

'Final question. What do you think of Jane Bell, his killer?' His face twists into anger and agony. I don't feel any remorse, just fizzing in the pit of my stomach, the way bubbles of champagne look. Luke explodes from his chair and storms to the door. He flings it open wide and throws his arm out of it, his finger pointing with vibrating fury.

'Leave! Now!' he shouts. I begin clambering up, clumsy in my movements. Then he tilts his head slightly to one side atop a rigid neck, popping with risen veins and tendons straining against skin. His voice is low and thick as he asks: 'How the fuck do you *think* I feel? Yes, James made some horrific mistakes, had issues, but he was still my *brother*. Who was *murdered*.' He pauses and a grimace of pain squeezes his cheeks, making his eyes squint. It does nothing to hide the anguish in them. 'I *loved* him. How would you react if I came to you with questions about how you *"feel"* about the murderer of someone you love?' He pauses again, long enough for me to process his question. As I do, I feel winded by the realisation that I could so easily have been in his place, with a faceless journalist in mine – there are countless times I've wondered if this is what happened to Mum. Tears build behind my eyes, making my eyeballs ache with the pressure of restraining them. James isn't finished. 'Have you forgotten what love is – the ferocity of it, the consumption by it, the way it supersedes anything and everything else?'

Yes, I think I have. I'm startled by my thought, but feel it deeply, the way profound truths leach into every cell. Luke hauls me back again. 'I loved my brother, whatever he was planning to do. Use your fucking head... and your heart for that matter, when you talk to people about their dead loved ones, whose name and life you have blackened, tarred and set alight in a spectacle of sales figures, okay?'

I nod rapidly and dip my head down low as I inch towards the door. It means I can't stop the tears falling. I notice one lands on my left shoe as I step forward, creating a darker patch on the canvas – art more often coming from pain than pleasure.

His voice drops to a low growl, wrapped around steel. 'Don't print anything I've said to you, you hear?'

Every cell in my body is driving me to flee now, but he's half-blocking the doorway and I don't want to get close enough that he could grab me.

'Okay,' I force out in a stutter.

He changes, then, his tone shifting into disdain.

'It'll never get through to you, will it, the power you have to create so much pain or do such good, the way you walk away once you've lit the fuse wire and squander your power so abominably.' I edge even closer to the door. His eyes follow me. He steps back. 'Just go.' He sneeringly hisses. I run.

I don't stop running, not in the taxi or on the train, until I'm home, with Bertie clutched to my chest. My heart rate is still challenging a hummingbird's hover and a concert drummer's volume. My hands remain clammy, every commonplace sound causing my body to spin round to face my attacker. Sometimes you have to cross the line to find it.

I slip into bed with the lights on and the dimmer switch twisted to maximum brightness. I close the bedroom door so that Bertie remains with me, not that he minds, purring away at my feet. I open my laptop and type through cramp in my fingers, exhaustion in my bones, and from the darkness into the light of dawn.

I can feel it lurking though, a shark beneath the surface, the stalking fin the only clue: that I don't want to be alone, empty, writing my only way through the feelings and to fill the yawning, sucking hole my life has left in me.

THIRTY-SEVEN

JANE

It is 11th July 2019. We are a week away from the trial. Almost every waking moment I feel anxious, which is most unlike the old me, but I understand it, here, now.

I'm so exhausted. I don't often use that word – I think there's a bigger gap between tiredness and exhaustion than most people seem to think – a gap that stretches from an hour extra at work to the ravaging poison of chemotherapy – but today I feel it's appropriate. It's so much more than that though. It's desolation. A deep guttural misery stemming from the grief. I have lost so much.

It has been nearly six months since I last slept in my own bed, since I snuggled my children into my sides as I read them *Guess How Much I Love You?*, since I chatted over coffee with Rachel, and since I heard the door close behind Neil when he arrived home at night. Those months have been filled with learning a whole new language in the form of endless legal jargon (not ideal for someone who failed GCSE Spanish), within a totally alien environment made up of bars and locks, and more plaguing thoughts haunting me with darkness

216

than I've ever known. I've tangled myself into knots so tight in my mind that I wonder if I'll ever be able to think straight again. And yet it's barely begun.

I have spent another night snatching minutes of rest from the nightmares and memories that are sleep's keeper. Threads of daylight dance through the bars on my window showing me a new day is dawning. I stagger from my bed to the sink, my body seized and stiff from far too many minutes of stillness in each day. My muscles remember the school run and they too are angry at what's been taken from them... by me. My fingers clutch the sink, gripping it so hard that the sinews strain starkly against skin almost translucent. My eyes meet their reflection in the speckled mirror that is hung a few inches too high for me, but they wouldn't recognise the image staring back, regardless. I scan over the sickly pallor, the new wrinkles and dark roots, the faintest hint of shadow over the upper lip that used to be waxed. All of these I am used to now though, so my reflection is a cellmate, not a stranger. The set of the eyes, though, is what shocks me afresh each morning – the guarding in them, like a hand being wrenched back from a hotplate, newly wounded and afraid.

I feel like a fraud. What will the world make of me when they see me in the dock? They are expecting the hero they've fabricated from the facts and the embellishment. That hero is vibrant and empowered; gutsy and unabashed. They will be so disappointed when they see this new Jane: plain and ravaged.

I am so disappointed.

THIRTY-EIGHT

ANEESA

It's sunk in, what Luke said, the realisation I made that I've lost love from my life completely. That I can't be the person I want to be without it. I've come to know that often big dawning moments come to us in ugliness and mess. Phoenixes from ashes.

I went too far with Luke, I asked an insensitive and unacceptable question. Perhaps it was of divine purpose though, for the severity of Luke's reaction forced me open, and that space allowed an arrow in, which had Simon's name carved into the flint and love flying the shaft. Fear has led me to denial of something imperative: love. I allow myself to acknowledge that it's Simon I want to share this with. I can't be the best, fullest version of myself without love. I tried so hard to be, but I can't. I'm scared of it. I'll use that to create courage. Not right now as both Simon and I are too absorbed by Jane, but afterwards, when the timing's right, I'll finally invite him in.

I'm wrecked by the emotions of the past twenty-four hours and I'm yearning for comfort, so I detour on my way to work via a café that does the fabulous frappés my dad and I loved sharing together. I'm sipping the remnants of one through its straw as I duck my head to the cold breeze that nips my ears. I feel like now my nerves have the first sliver of a chance to regenerate from the burned down stumps they became last night.

I toy with the options as to how to approach Eliza about what I've put together on Luke. I can feel myself starting to assume and overthink myself into chaos so I decide to just talk it through in person.

As I arrive back at work, I knock on her door.

'Come in.' It's curt but civil – which is Eliza's version of a balmy tropical beach.

I curl my head around the door.

'Do you have a few minutes to talk?'

She flicks a quick look to the clock above my head and then nods. I step into the room, shut the door behind me and fold myself onto the edge of the chair opposite her.

I notice a bunch of roses in the corner of her desk and when I look up at her, I see she's got a lingering blush on her cheek. She must have clocked me looking. I take a deep breath to ready myself and it brings with it the faint sickly-sweet smell of chemical strawberries. Eliza must have been vaping – her form of stress self-medication. I steel myself. She invented taking it out on other people.

'To cut a long story short, Eliza,' I launch straight in, 'I found James Foster's brother, in Leeds.'

Eliza's mouth flaps open and she stretches her head and neck forward in shock.

'How the hell did you manage that?' she exclaims.

I take a fraction of a second to weigh up whether I admit I used Charlie. I decide I have to – I can't explain it without and this is so big she'll want every infinitesimal detail.

'The private investigator I know tracked him down for me.' She pulls her jaw up and tightens it in displeasure. I hold my hands up in surrender. 'Don't worry, out of my own pay cheque.' She gives a single nod of satisfaction. 'I got an interview, of sorts. The whole backstory of their childhood and teenage years. The multitude of ways James got lost. I want to run it.'

Eliza narrows one eye and purses her lips for a moment.

'What is the angle? Sympathetic or cold-blooded monster?'

'Victim of a broken system, bullied, isolated, dreams stolen, lost his way, turned to drugs when he lost everything else. Children's Services took his kids away, were placing them up for adoption against his wishes. Nothing definite on the people behind it.'

'This brother wants it out there? Now?'

'Not exactly. He was willing right to the end, then I asked what he thought about Jane. And he flipped.'

Eliza sighs, long and hard – for show.

'That's your blind spot, Aneesa. You look for things beyond what are there. You go too far.' She pauses, and just when I open my mouth to respond, she continues, 'Anyway. I don't think it's the right piece for us. We're so close to the trial. We need to keep the focus tight around Jane. I don't want our narrative to get confused by a messy red herring flung in at the last moment as a distraction without true value to what's at hand – the trial. Besides, it sounds as though your article will humanise a monster, which I refuse to endorse.' I feel my fists clenching, my nostrils flaring. I was considering whether to tell Eliza about the article today. Not anymore. I bite down hard on my tongue for a few moments to quash my frustration before defending my story and fighting to get the truth out in its entirety.

'I disagree. Nothing could be more relevant or important and the timing is perfect.' I can't let such an illuminating piece of this puzzle be snuffed out, hidden, buried. 'What James Foster did is the reason we're having a trial at all and it's up to us to report on the truth, not manufacture the narrative–'

'Not true.' Eliza cuts in matter-of-factly. 'What *Jane* did is the reason we're having a trial. If she *hadn't* done what she did, rather than a trial we'd be having a mass funeral. For *three-hundred* fucking *children!*' Eliza's open palm bangs down on the desk next to her computer and her lips are quivering with rage. 'So, stop. Don't even think about coming back at me with your doe-eyes and over-principled self-important pouting because I decide it's not right to run a puff piece based on the brother selling some spiel about the sorry bullied childhood of a *fucking child-murdering terrorist!*' The palm slams down again. I jump, along with everything on her desk. I have never seen Eliza like this.

'Okay.' Realising there is nowhere to go with this, I acquiesce, and stand up to leave. As I turn at the door, I see her leaning right back in her chair, her chin tipped up high, blinking rapidly – the way women do to stop themselves crying through their mascara.

THIRTY-NINE

JANE

Simon, who has been a cherished gift to me in these heavy days, says that the trial is likely to be long and gruelling, that I'll be under examination every second of every day in the courtroom – whether it be by the press, the jury, or the legal teams. Every reaction I make to every statement, even down to a tightening of my lips, could be noted by someone important. Essentially, I'll be judged constantly for an indeterminate period of time, before all those mini judgements are woven together to reveal a huge, screaming judgement that will change the course of my life – for ever. And I'm so exhausted, I just don't think I can face it. Yet I know time stops for no man, so there's no way it'll stop for a woman.

I don't even have the ability to make my own choices anymore, my freedom is gone in every way – I'll be in that courtroom tomorrow whether I walk there myself or am dragged, knees being grated, shoes getting scuffed, shoulder joints sprained. I will be judged. I will be for ever changed.

Simon has coached me to focus on the positives. Neil is taking the time off work so all day, every day that the trial is on, although I'll be enduring the trial, I can at least look for him in the courtroom.

Simon will be beside me every step of the way and I've never met anyone I would rather have on my side through an intellectual ordeal.

Simon says I have hundreds of thousands of people across the country praying for me, wishing freedom for me, believing in me. He says all that energy directed to my greater good will matter, somehow.

Most importantly, I still have hope. There is a chance that I'll walk free, that by a miracle I'll leave and be able to put this system behind me one day. I'll never 'move on' from this, never forget James Foster's eyes, never lose the feeling of terrified hopelessness I felt living next to him, never fail to recall the moment I stepped out of my car and the knowing hit me, of what I'd done.

But for now, there's a chance that I can live again, taste freedom again; never the same, but again. It's all I have.

FORTY

ANEESA

17TH JULY 2019, *Birmingham Gazette*, Aneesa Khan

Tomorrow, at Birmingham Crown Court, begins the trial of Jane Bell for the murder of James Foster. This high-profile case is one that has gathered a huge following and has united many in a passionate campaign for Jane Bell's release. Protests to that end are ongoing outside the Crown Court, with numbers swelling daily. A march has been organised for 9 a.m. tomorrow morning, to coincide with Jane Bell's trial beginning. Delays are expected in the area around the courthouse tomorrow morning from 7 a.m. onwards, as marchers converge.

Support for Jane Bell has been overwhelming since the events of 16th January 2019, which culminated in the death of James Foster. Upon his death, police found three nail bombs inside his home, along with plans for their detonation the following day at St Oliver's CE Primary School. He died due to injuries sustained when Jane Bell struck him with her car. Jane Bell's defence so far is that she acted to prevent the terror attack in the absence of any police assistance.

A "Gratitude Movement" has been formed for Jane Bell. Individuals from across the nation have been donating money to the "Jane Bell Gratitude Fund" to ensure that the futures of Jane Bell's two young children are secure financially whatever the outcome of Jane Bell's trial in the coming weeks.

Both of Jane Bell's children attend St Oliver's CE Primary School and Nursery. Hundreds of thousands of pounds have been donated already. Jane Bell's husband, Neil Bell, spoke to the Gazette in response to this kindness:

"Speaking on behalf of Jane and our children, I cannot find the words to adequately thank you all for what you have done for us – not just every penny donated to the Gratitude Fund, but also every single person who has turned up to protest, or who has said a prayer, or sent a message of support for Jane. As everything was unfolding leading up to 16th January, the most awful thing we felt was not the fear but the knowledge that we were completely alone – that no one would help us or stand with us. So, your help now, your unity with Jane, showing up and standing up for her, that's the greatest gift we could have received – no longer being alone in this. Thank you. A million times, thank you."

The murder trial of Jane Bell is expected to be the most followed trial in the United Kingdom for decades. The Birmingham Gazette will continue to report on it, bringing you daily updates as the case progresses.

Yesterday, I went to Birmingham Crown Court to get what I needed for my article on the protest. The area was bursting at its seams, figures spilling outwards in all directions, like a writhing spider, growing bigger every day.

There were swathes of people there, protesting against Jane's incarceration and murder charge, and the trial hadn't even begun. Some carried heavy placards, some held banners aloft, others wore t-shirts emblazoned with Jane's picture. All shared one message – their support for Jane. The feelings were so powerful – waves of anger, frustration, helplessness, sympathy – so strong that I felt every single one heavy in my gut. They connected me to every person present – their eyes mirrored the feelings in my own. Connection forges relating, relating leads to openness, and openness writes my pieces.

One particularly vehement and fizzing man, whose face was a map of the human condition, led the pulse with a chipboard square that he punched above his head to the rhythm of the song 'Stayin' Alive' – it caught attention. It read, in rough scarlet paint that had dripped down like blood, 'HOW DARE YOU? SHE DID WHAT YOU COULD NOT'.

He was among a large group of protestors radiating energy, always moving, constantly shouting, overflowing from their space completely. Most had a spirited glint in their eyes and a hoarseness in their tired shouts. Organised chanting happened for ten minutes every hour, the yells changed, and the words could be hard to make out but the intent shone through. The rest of the time, individual outrage spilt forth and claimed the air of the courthouse entrance. There was a passion there, bright and vital against the dull grey monotony of the inner city. They were pinned back by police so that they didn't swarm the steps and block people's movement into the courthouse. The police presence was large, although the individual members looked small, all identical in their uniforms, covered completely by their protective and offensive equipment, so that they were themselves marooned inside the oceans of their own gear.

Across the way stood a row of nearly three hundred individuals. These were people wearing pain like capes, and grief like make-up. Each one held an A3 picture of a child. Each child was different, each one was smiling, each picture told its own story – party time, bedtime, dressing-up time, dance recital, sports day and tooth fairy visit.

I counted them. There were two hundred and eighty-nine. They were silent, unless spoken to directly, but they stood shoulder to shoulder forming a human chain that reached as far as the eye could see. These mute figures, clothed in hurt, were the representatives of the children of St Oliver's CE Primary School – each person a parent, aunt, grandparent, or a stand-in who cared immensely.

The sight of these photos, held across the heart of each person, took my breath away, like a punch in the stomach, winding me, stealing my balance, hazing my mind with the pain of what so nearly was.

I sent my photographer to take photos, to capture every pixel of this space, to hold in the camera's memory not just the colours and the shapes but the feelings too – every single link in the chain of saved children, every pair of eyes that gazed out of a body stood there in testimony.

My photographer moved like a fairy, the camera's eye capturing more than the brain saw – for when you took each frame away from the chaos, you saw it – the reality. The big picture there was power and laws, morals and anger, war and justice; but the hundreds of little pictures that made up the pieces of the big picture were gap grins and tooth fairies, nativity plays and mud pies, lit up eyes, Down's Syndrome and an unfortunate bowl haircut. It was nearly three hundred slightly different shades of skin and entirely different finger-prints. The little pieces were two hundred and eighty-nine real children who deserved to grow up. Jane Bell ensured they can.

Support for Jane was, and is, overwhelming in the biggest sense of the word. Even having inserted myself into fraught, frenetic, and at times dangerous situations throughout my career, I had to take a big gulp, breathe right down into my stomach, and steel myself for what stood before me. Pain is more powerful than peril.

As I crumpled against a wall with a view of the protests, I soaked it all up for a while. I was a witness, and I felt it deserved to be seared into my soul so that I will remember for ever how many people came forward for who and what they believed in; how deeply feelings formed in support of a single act; so that I will always know there can still be hope in humanity, however tenuous it might sometimes feel.

I didn't end up writing a standalone piece on the protest – for the first time in my career, words simply couldn't convey what was happening there. I published the photos online instead and the reaction has been astounding. I went yesterday for a story with supporting pictures that painted a thousand words, though I have to admit, much as it pains me to do so as a writer, the images of the protestors paint millions.

I am sunk deep into my squishy sofa this evening, Bertie curled into a ball forming a grounding weight on my thighs; I feel drained. The toll of sifting through the emotion I've been pummelled with over the past few months has reached its peak, and yet I know the journey has barely begun. What I face over the next months will be far tougher – sitting in the courtroom all day every day hearing every detail of the prosecution and defence cases, returning home and having to sift through it all to unearth the pertinent details, and then wrap them all up into an article, carefully ensuring I don't suggest progress or outcomes that aren't accurate.

I'm still processing Eliza's stance on the Luke Foster piece, and what it means for the piece I'm working on using James' letter. I've been a cyclone of emotions, so many different feelings creating pressure in my chest. Ultimately, I'm consumed by disappointment. I've believed Eliza to have integrity in what she prints, running an honest and progressive newspaper. I'm forced to reconsider. I will see Jane's trial through to the end with the *Gazette*. Then, who knows.

So, tonight I'm focussing on cuddling Bertie, letting a bubble bath soak away my tension, and listening to the silence. I need to find peace. I also need to call upon the spirit of my dad I carry in my heart – he'll guide me through this. Whatever justice is or isn't handed out in Birmingham Crown Court, there needs to be justice at my hand, on the pages of the *Birmingham Gazette*.

PART 2

THE TRIAL

FORTY-ONE

MARY

It started with an envelope, sitting one day on my doormat like a spoiled cat – entitled and smug. I felt its officiality heavy in my gut from the moment I plucked it up. My heart rate sped up a fraction, my palms grew clammy. I read my name stretched across the front in solid capitals, with the feeling of a noose put in place around my neck.

I stood silently and paralysed at the breakfast bar as my juxtaposed offspring arrived in the kitchen – Lottie quiet, scowling, and hunched, Ollie's booming voice barging ahead of him through every door. I hastily tucked the envelope under a cereal box as I set to, bustling about the small space, pulling bowls, bran flakes, and bananas out for their breakfasts, not wanting to give Lottie's searching gaze even the slightest notch to grip on to. They need their mum to be secure and solid, not worried over an unopened envelope.

That day was months ago now, and I received the specific details ten days ago. Since I first laid eyes on the word 'summoned ' I've had a small gnawing in my chest. I've thought it all through – the possibilities of what this responsibility entails. I've spent hours researching on my laptop late at night or early in the morning when the whole house is sleeping and dark. I know the following facts now. One: a jury is only summoned for criminal cases in the Crown Court where the offence is an indictable offence or an offence triable either way. Two: a trial with a jury is used when the defendant pleads 'not guilty' but the police and Crown Prosecution Service are as certain as they can be that the defendant has done it. Three: while the judge guides and the lawyers are responsible for presenting all the evidence, it's the jury which decides, the jury which determines the course of the rest of an individual's life. Four: I will be on such a jury – that will be my decision to make. Starting today.

I've made it to the Birmingham Crown Court now, and someone here has explained to me that jurors' names are chosen at random by the court ushers – the trial I'm part of will be determined by chance – a cut and dried assault, a fraud, or a drawn out and fragile child's murder, at the hands only of fate.

It is a strange experience waiting in the courthouse – I'm in the jury assembly area with lots of other individuals – we are a varied group, of nearly the full adult age spectrum, dressed in all manner of attire, from a sullen-looking young woman dressed in only black, with colourful tattoos forming her sleeves, to an elderly gentleman in corduroy trousers the exact same colour as his polished wooden walking cane. I'm feeling fluttery inside, unsure how to act in here. I never enjoy being among strangers – I'm constantly trying to work out what I should say, what the right level of friendliness is – not wanting to be cold and aloof but also worried about being too intrusive. I find it easier when there's a purpose to a gathering, some kind of organisation that I can draw boundaries from... finding security in having a starting point with everyone. Yet, while there is purpose in all of us here for jury duty, there is no one to explain how we can interact, if there are things we're not allowed to discuss.

The woman in black has huge headphones over her ears, creating a wall to keep out conversation, the elderly man looks glassy-eyed and vacant, and the man next to me, who looks about my age, and appears as normal as anyone can look – in jeans and a collared shirt – seems engrossed in a Kindle. Even such a simple device unsettles me – not knowing what someone is reading, where they're up to in the story. It kills any chance of knowing what sort of conversation you'd be getting into. I like conversation. But I need to know things, and I find that lately I feel so little is known, so much is uncertain, which makes me feel fluttery inside.

My tangled and spiralling thoughts are broken by a figure stepping right in front of me. My feet dart backwards underneath my chair as the toes of the shiny black loafers stop close to mine.

'Mrs Bates, would you follow me please?' says a uniformed man, his face still and empty of clues. Clearly fate has decided what I am to face. I hope she's been kind to me.

FORTY-TWO

SIMON

The jury is being brought in. This is always a slightly painful stage for the barristers – as we scan them and realise just who is given the ultimate power of a future. It's a depressing moment. They troop into the courtroom and huddle in a pack ready to have their name called or not called. With it the fate of their coming weeks is decided. They look unanimously petrified, as if they're the ones being led up to the gallows rather than Jane. They should be scared – this will be the most disillusioning trial I can imagine it being possible to be a juror for. They will be under scrutiny more barbed and intense than actors; they will be required to have more stamina in their focus than brain surgeons; their decision will have more influence and the consequences will be more far-reaching than the prime minister's. Not only did they never ask for this, they could never be ready, they're not in any way qualified or nominated for this responsibility. They are random and unfiltered. They are not the carefully curated, most able of the jurors available at this time, rather they're just meaningless names on a roll. Well, they were. Their names are full of meaning now. The twelve individuals holding Jane's life in their hands. Many would wish to be sitting where they are – with the illusion of power and the blade of justice at their disposal. Many could think of nothing worse than facing what they now do. These twelve look shocked, like they haven't even begun to process what lies ahead, what has happened, that this is the courtroom that they've ended up in, on this day, with that woman sitting across the room from them in the defendant's dock, and the public gallery bursting at its barriers.

'I swear by almighty God...' shakes out across the room, almost swallowed up by the vacuum of foreboding in this space. I'm surprised this fellow can read his oath card with how much his hand is jerking it around.

'...That I will faithfully try the defendant and give a true verdict according to the evidence.' His shoulders are hunched and he's more mutterer than thespian – I conclude his greatest wish right now is that the ground swallow him up whole. He is first – a challenging role – and in this case yet another difficulty in his day that's the result of random chance. The remaining jurors mostly swear the Judeo-Christian oath and affirmation, with one Muslim oath recited. This may seem interesting and informative for the prosecution and defence. However, much as in life, what people claim religiously all too often has limited bearing on how they live and the choices they make.

I consult my computer screen as the judge begins her monologue about jury requirements, life, and so on – there are information sheets to be distributed and, as I'm sure you can imagine, it's rather a case for me of doing whatever prevents me nodding off for a nap. Besides, every minute is now crucial, every moment a chance to refresh a fact before the judge sets the treadmill of this trial to sprint speed.

FORTY-THREE

JANE

The judge is telling the jury all about the sanctity of the courtroom – the confidentiality they must maintain, even from their husbands, parents and children. Before all this started, I never dreamed how divisive the court process is... for everyone, not just me behind my bars.

I try to focus on every word, but my mind wanders. It's still so new and, sitting here on what could be a throne in different circumstances but feels to me like gallows. I can't help but remember the beginning of all this – when I first realised what breathed next door to us. Back then, in my naïve daydreams, I imagined that I would be sitting in a very different place in this courtroom – in the witness box. I imagined that I would reject the offers of screens around me as I gave my testimony – just so I could look right into James' black pits of eyes as I told the jury, in a voice as strong as it is now trembly, exactly who he was. I imagined my relief at seeing the monster in his rightful place – flanked by a white-shirt-wearing security official – isolated in the courtroom gallows. Me waiting for the moment when I watched him being led down the stairs into the cells, never to emerge again. All I can think now, in this spot, flanked as I am by white-shirt-wearing security officials, who make me feel anything but secure, is that I must now be the monster I so feared; and I wonder will those twelve strangers be any kinder to me than my imaginings were to James; will *I* ever emerge?

FORTY-FOUR

MARY

I'm paralysed here, halfway along the back row of the jury box; trapped inside my own wild and turbulent thoughts. I know the judge is speaking to us all, but I can't hear it right now, all I hear is whooshing through my ears. White noise bouncing around my skull.

I'm ashamed to admit how many things I'm afraid of. I'm terrified to think of how scared I am even of my fear – of the way it grips my heart in its icy iron hands and squeezes so hard that sometimes I can't breathe anymore, can't speak, can't move, can't do anything except feel fear consume me. I'm horrified by how much of my life it has taken over, how many things in me it rules. I fight so hard against it, though I know it doesn't look like it to most people. Sometimes I even win, for a minute or two; I might hold it back enough to reclaim a decision or a moment and make it how I truly want it. But not often. One of the fears that occupies my mind most hours of the day is my fear of failing my beautiful children. I didn't used to be like this – when they were young, I was full of joy and freedom. I was so proud of what I'd somehow created, and I loved nurturing them and making them smile. Now, though, I'm afraid of this most core part of me – that I'm a mother.

One day something happened with Ollie, back when he was four – I got caught up chatting to our elderly neighbour out on our street as Ollie and I were setting off to collect Lottie from school. I didn't notice until I heard the screech of tyres and then everything slowed down. I felt my head whip round, my neck has never felt quite as secure since, frantically searching. I felt my heart cave in as I realised what that sound must mean. I felt myself flail as I lurched towards the sound – as attracted as I was repulsed. I didn't feel Ollie's hand find mine and I didn't realise what that meant – that he was safe. I didn't hear my elderly neighbour telling me it was the blind cat from two doors down that had caused the commotion. Even when I did come down enough to understand, I was still consumed by the could-have-been. It could have been Ollie. It could have been him beneath the tyres – I didn't have my eyes on him, I didn't have hold of him, I didn't have my attention with him. Ever since then I've known... every single second is vital; could be the difference between my precious and incredible creations being okay and... not. And the only controlling factor standing between those two outcomes is me, their mother. I don't think I have ever fully switched off since then, never been the same as I was before.

Thank goodness I haven't, because it's kept them safe. As I look at Jane, and I think about what she did and why she did it, I feel the swell of something sure and steady inside me – and I'm never certain of anything much anymore. What I feel is a deep reverence, for a fellow mother who identified danger in time, who then did what was necessary to keep her children safe. I've heard tyres screeching, I've felt the heart-shredding horror of believing someone is beneath them. I've been reactive when I should have been proactive. So, I can feel nothing but awe for this woman who is everything I've hoped I could one day be.

FORTY-FIVE
ANEESA

I manage to wedge myself into a seat in the press area of the public gallery, squashed and uncomfortable but triumphant just to have this precious foot of space. The court staff have had to apply strict rules of priority for admission to all areas of the public gallery today, with the number of people trying to get into the trial reaching an unprecedented high. I'm fortunate that my *Birmingham Gazette* press badge guarantees me one of the highest priority spots, but there are countless journalists who've had to be turned away. It's strange to think that across the country, for hundreds of hearings every day, usually the public galleries are as populated as a ghost town. Jane and James' story sucks people in. It's like the snowflake that causes an avalanche, making gatekeepers out of court staff and protestors out of grandparents and plumbers.

If you've ever visited a courthouse, you'll know that inside the courtrooms there is an underlying silence – when the judge or barristers aren't talking, you'll never have noticed your breathing sound so loud or your skirt scratch so audibly against the fabric of the seat. Yet in Birmingham Crown Court today, unlike for every other trial that has ever been heard here, silence has scarpered, fleeing from the force of will that sustains the swelling protestors outside who refuse to leave. The avalanche.

Police are now involved in growing numbers. They try to hold back the hordes who overwhelm the surrounding streets. The protestors roar. The shouting voices meld together into a symphony of support that penetrates even these thick walls. The roar may have been muted to a buzz by the metres and barriers and soundproofing, but it's unmissable. I can see its impact worn on the faces of everyone in here. The prosecuting barrister looks agitated; the judge resigned; Simon has excitement hanging onto his robes; and Jane has the shadow of a smile dancing on her lips. I can see one of the jurors – the sweet looking, soft-edged, permanently wide eyed one on the back row – straining to hear what's being said out there. I doubt she'll be able to make anything out; but I hope she hears victory.

FORTY-SIX

MARY

We've only been in the courtroom for an hour and I already feel drained. I can move again though, and hear, so I've made progress. My eyelids feel like they're pressing into my eyeballs, making it hard work just to blink, or keep focussed on anything visual.

I can feel so many other sets of eyes on me, from the packed-out public gallery, the judge, the barristers. Eyes are darting everywhere, all the time, and when any pause over me it feels like their gazes burn me. To begin with, I try to follow where everyone's looking, so that I don't miss anything important. I feel my palms prickle with sweat when I realise that's impossible. Next, I try to watch for whose eyes are on me – that's a bare minimum thing I always need to know. I feel my shirt start to stick to the hollow of my back when I realise that too is beyond my capabilities. I feel my breath shorten, shallow pants all that emerge, and then my gaze finds Jane Bell's form. She's up there, in the middle of all of this both figuratively and now literally, sitting in her own box bang in the middle of the courtroom on the back wall. I realise that she is completely alone – her team are nowhere near her – Mr Rafferty is sitting in front and consumed with his evidence and process, her husband is in the public gallery where he is contained by court staff, forced into silence.

I have eleven other people surrounding me who are sharing this burden. We are protected by the minds of each other – we must become one verdict, and that gives us safety. Jane faces this entirely alone.

I look at Jane Bell's eyes and I see they're calm. I search harder, so used to examining people – mining for the important unsaid. I see her gaze rests steady on Mr Rafferty, which is unexpected – I imagined she would have been feeling even more anxious than me. I have to know why, so I look harder. I see that her shoulders are held too softly for there to be arrogance in her. I see that her mouth is too tight for there to be insolence behind her stillness. I see that her eyes are widened ever so slightly which shows me indifference is not there either.

Maybe her peace comes from hope. Maybe it comes from faith. Maybe it comes from trust. Whichever it is, its goodness, and I feel my frazzled mind reaching for it, connecting to it. I feel it begin to refill me. I feel inspired by it. I hope Jane knows she's not alone at all.

FORTY-SEVEN

SIMON

Having prepared everything I can for this instalment of the trial, I focus for a few moments on the jury. While there is so much you could never know about someone from their appearance, which is why I work hard to shy away from stereotypes, how we choose to present ourselves to the world is a big part of our identity, and there are clues to who we are within the artwork of our external choices.

I see a true mixture of people in the jury box, sitting in two rows of six. I see seven women and five men. I see one head of white hair, ten heads of natural looking hair, and one head of brash dying – a jet black with that greeny sheen that tells you genetics didn't gift the shade. I see twelve different skin tones – some fractionally different, others markedly, some changed entirely by make-up. I see lots of neutral clothes – many different beiges, white, caramel, mocha – and two pops of colour – a red blouse, an alarming blue scarf. I see some shirts that grip every muscle so tightly I don't imagine there is movement beyond ten degrees, I see tops so baggy anything could be masked under there – exactly as is the intention. I see bouncing knees and hair touched once every minute; I see manspreading and hands pulling elbows tightly into an abdomen; I see thin lips and a chin tilted tensely upwards. I see insecurity and vulnerability; I see faux confidence and, most importantly, nothing to alarm me.

It's time for the prosecution barrister, Mrs Rigby, to give the opening statement. I'm relieved the judge has been the first person these shaky-legged jurors have heard. She generates calmness and exudes control – in stark contrast to Mrs Rigby with her bullish intensity. Mrs Rigby stands up, smooths her gown, and directs herself to the jury box. After some initial transparent babble that anyone with half a brain-cell can tell is patronising sucking up to the jury, she begins the thrust of the case.

'At four forty-five in the afternoon of the 16th January this year, Mr James Foster walked out of his driveway onto the pavement outside his home on Wesley Street, Birmingham, to bring his wheelie bin in. As he was taking hold of his bin, the defendant, Jane Bell, drove into him. She was in her car, had dropped her two children off with friends and, as she arrived home, rather than pulling into her driveway, she accelerated and drove directly into James Foster. She did this with such force that he was crushed against the wall outside his property. The degree of internal injury he sustained from this act meant he died at the scene.

'I put to you that given Jane Bell was in no immediate danger, that she was, according to witnesses, completely purposeful in her driving beforehand, and given the degree of acceleration she used, that this is a simple case of murder.

'I expect you will hear from the defence advocate, Mr Rafferty, that Jane Bell was acting in defence of others – namely her children and the children who were their fellow pupils of St Oliver's Church of England Primary School and Nursery. He will base this on the fact that Jane Bell believed the school was under threat of being bombed by James Foster. Yet, Mrs Bell did not act to restrain Mr Foster. She did not carry out her attack when he was actually implementing his plan. These would have been reasonable reactions to the situation. For all we know, he never would have carried out his plan. For all we know, even if he did attempt to, he could have been restrained, and then dealt with in a fair and legal manner.

'I will present to you a number of pieces of evidence, all of which will show you that Jane Bell murdered James Foster. I will show you clear CCTV footage of the incident which will show that Jane Bell drove at great acceleration directly into the victim while he was collecting his wheelie bin – demonstrating no immediate threat to the defendant or anyone else. I will also bring an eyewitness who was watching to give testimony that concurs. We cannot know the future or what James Foster may have done, just as we cannot know what anyone may do in the future. We can only know that at the moment the defendant killed Mr Foster, he'd done nothing to immediately threaten or harm the defendant, her family, or anyone else. This was an act in which the defendant made the first move. It was an act where far more force was used than necessary. This was murder.

'I will also bring the pathologist to the witness stand, who will present his findings to you from the examination of James Foster's body. The pathologist's evidence tells us that Jane Bell's attack on James Foster could only ever have ended in his death. Could only ever have ended in his death,' she repeats with brazen great emphasis. 'The defendant made an active choice to do this. There is no way she could have believed such an act of extreme violence could end in any way other than the killing it did.

'I will bring to the witness stand the detective who led the police investigation. He will testify as to the scene of the crime and the context of the death.

'You will hear from the forensic director of the case who will show you diagrams and graphics that demonstrate how the combination of acceleration and angle the defendant used were chosen to cause the maximum harm possible within the parameters of the environment.

'All of this will give you more than enough evidence to determine that the degree of force used was unreasonable, and the defendant acted with the full intent to kill Mr Foster. The defendant, Jane Bell, is unequivocally guilty of murder.'

I subtly turn to glance at Jane, aware that it isn't wise to be seen looking at her for too long – it tends to lead the jury to think there's disallowed or underhand communication going on. I know, it feels like you can't even care anymore without people's cynicism rewriting the caring's goodness. Jane appears calm – our training having worked: her head at just the right angle – no defiant chin raise or defeated head dip; her hands cupping each other in her lap to avoid the fiddling that can suggest culpability; her eyes never looking too long at the judge, barristers, or any juror, to ensure no one can accuse us of trying to influence or intimidate the jury. Those accusations and interpretations can lose cases.

The rest of the afternoon drags on, with various legal questions being asked, mainly by Mrs Rigby, surprise, surprise. It means the jury have to file in and out. This takes a lot of time. The judge tells the jury it is vital; in reality it just pisses the rest of us off.

At four-thirty in the afternoon, on the dot, the judge addresses the jury.

'I'm aware of the impact that being on a jury for a murder trial can have on you jurors, so we'll adjourn for today. If I may be so bold, I suggest that you all try to get a good rest this evening and allow yourselves some time and space to process today's information and events. It will be a long and tiring few weeks for you all. Thank you for your service thus far.'

After her unusual speech, which shows her heart, the judge waits for the court staff to guide the jury out of the courtroom before disappearing through the door to her private chambers, her personal clerk holding it open for her as she sweeps out.

I make my retreat too, though it is to an evening of desk lamps casting warm lights over cold papers in the vaporous dark; lots of strong black coffee that I'll feel the scorching of in my throat tomorrow morning from where I've gulped it down too desperately; and trepidation. There will be none of the rest and processing the judge has kindly advised for the twelve jurors.

No, I have a life to fight for.

FORTY-EIGHT

BILL

I'm standing in the corner of an interview room at the station, sweat soaking through my shirt, heat ready to combust me. I am taking the statement of a young man with a turquoise stripe through his hair, who has been raped.

'I'm sorry, could you repeat that for me?'

Concentration pinches the corner of his left eye together. I understand, I'd be struggling to focus too. I want to do better for him, I just can't. Weariness owns me, slowing my hand, making even writing down the information challenging. All day I've been making careless mistakes, struggling to concentrate on anything. Jane is sitting in court today on the opening day of her trial and everything I'm doing feels futile in comparison, even something with this much gravity. I'm not allowed to be in there until after my testimony, which will be in the second half. I've been checking the *Birmingham Gazette*'s website and Twitter feed all day, desperate for any crumb of insight.

'Please just tell me, do you think you'll catch him?' I barely register the question and my neurons feel like there's treacle in the synapses, so slow is my brain to connect and create a response. I can't bring myself to give him the usual spiel – honest but reassuring, inspiring confidence.

'We'll try our very best but ultimately I don't know.'

His eyes widen incredulously and I watch him turn questioningly to my colleague.

I hope to God they take over, stop deferring to me, so I can check out. My colleague just shrugs. I let out a tired sigh, try and summon an explanation. 'I couldn't see any cameras in there where it happened, and your description doesn't give us much to go on in an identification process. We'll check any CCTV footage from businesses on the street, but we'd have to get lucky to find anything solid enough to pursue. Beyond that it'll come down to the rape kit.' I pause and then find it in myself to give him a moment of connection. 'I really am sorry this has happened to you, and we'll truly do our best.' My voice drops, almost too heavy for my lungs and mouth to carry, 'Though it appears that hasn't been bloody good enough lately.' My colleague finally steps in and I give in to the urge to blank my mind.

Presumably a few minutes later, certainly after the victim has left, my colleague nudges me.

'Bill, are you okay?'

'I don't think so, not really,' I reply. 'How can any of us be? It's all so pointless. Like that chap. Some scumbag has hurt him, scared him, left damage no doubt in his head, *taken* so much from him. We've spent all day dealing with a string of similar hurts. Each one genuinely awful despite how commonplace they are, and we'll be able to do... nothing. We both know we'll never find the rapist, not with how careful he was. People get away with atrocities every day.' I see his eyes widening more with every sentence I'm uttering, see his body language closing up, not knowing how to handle this, wanting me to stop. I can't. Like vomit, it needs to come out and it shall – something else on the long list of things outside my control.

'Come on, Bill,' he interrupts, 'it's not that bad.'

'It really is though. You know today is the start of Jane Bell's trial? I want to be in that court room or in the protests outside, where I feel I belong. We let her down, she did the right thing, unlike most people nowadays, and she's being punished for it. Everything is so bloody messed up. I can't stand it.'

I'm disconnected from myself. I don't recognise this man, his disillusionment and his terrible policing. I reach into my pocket, pull out a Mars Bar and unwrap it. I see a look of distaste pass across the face of my colleague... I forget his name. I don't care – about what he thinks of me or what he's called. As I bite through the nougat, chocolate and caramel, I feel my teeth react to the sugar – they can't take it anymore. It's the reason I broke this habit when I was newly pacing the streets – a few too many fillings. It doesn't matter anymore. I need the lift of being absorbed by the sweetness for a moment. That was my last one. I'll need another for the drive to collect the boys. That must be coming up now. I start walking back to the car.

An hour later I unlock the door to the house and the boys rush past me, eager to find Becky. Anger blasts through me at getting knocked into the door.

'Watch where you're bloody going, boys!' I shout after them, trailing off half-way through, giving up. I *never* swear at the boys. *What's happening to me?*

I pad slowly through to the kitchen and take in the dishes and pans piled high in the sink. The ones I couldn't face after tea last night or breakfast this morning. Obviously Becks wasn't up to sorting them. I'm glad she didn't spend any of her energy on that but I can't ignore the worm of frustration that wriggles through me – how am I supposed to manage all this? I can't keep up.

I sink into one of the chairs at the kitchen table, folding myself down onto my crossed arms – just for a minute to rest my head. I can hear chatter through the wall, the boys telling Becky about their day. I think back to how it used to be easier to get confessions from conmen than details from Sean about his life and now he can't tell her enough. *It's okay, Son, she knows you.* I want to tell him, bring him that peace. Maybe I will... later.

My phone vibrates in my pocket, a call incoming. Just five bloody minutes I needed! I want to scream. I ignore the buzzing. I take a deep breath of relief when it's over. Then it starts again. I picture flinging it against the wall, imagining the satisfaction it would bring me. I think I'd find the energy for that if it wouldn't scare the boys and Becky. Instead, resigned, I take it out. Vincent. Fan-bloody-tastic. I answer, knowing it's rare for him to call when I'm off the clock and there are no big cases ongoing.

I don't get the chance to even speak before Vincent starts barking.

'Bill. I heard you had an incident today.' Staccato. 'It's unacceptable. You know that. Talking to a victim like that. To a colleague like that, frankly.'

'Oh fuck off, Vincent. That was nothing compared to what half the force does every minute of every day. When you've fired the guy behind the desk the day Jane Bell went in, then you can start talking to me about this.' I can hear the shock in his silence. Fair response. I've never spoken to him with anything other than respect for his authority before. I suspect it's the only reason he let me climb so high.

'Can you clean up your act or do we need to have a more serious conversation?' Where is his compassion? I've given three decades of service to the police, the best of myself, missed Sean's first steps and too many of Scott's football games – the thing he loves most. I have left Becky to parent alone through nights of the boys being sick, I have lost so much, thinking it was for the greater good, that it would make a difference to something important. Yet this is what I get in return. An unpleasant phone call because of my only slip up. No empathy, no seeking to understand what drove my responses today, no caring and no kindness. I can't take any more. I hang up on Vincent and switch off my phone as everything that truly matters is just beyond my fingertips. *So why can't I reach them?*

I hear murmurs building around me. The boys whispering to each other. The noise of the water running into the sink, the clanking of dishes being done. I want to tell them to stop, to focus on their homework, have the fun they so desperately need as a pressure-release valve amongst this nightmare; but I can't. I sit, unmoving, staring in an unfocussed blur at the window, while it happens around me. While they make sandwiches for tea, then tidy up, then get Becky upstairs. Every single second I want to jump up, help them, but my mind and body have disconnected, a sailor thrown by a storm into the lethal crashing waves, unable to re-unite with his vessel no matter how hard he swims. *Is this my life now? A never-ending procession of letting everyone down? How on earth do I get back?*

FORTY-NINE

JANE

At the end of the day I'm loaded back into the transport van and driven to the prison. I'm trapped in a tiny cubicle – two foot by two foot at my best guess – and even when it's cold outside it's sweltering in here. The other prisoners call them sweatboxes and now I understand why. I get so hot and stuffy that I fear I'll pass out. It's a unique discomfort that comes from stifling heat, as though your body will combust from the pressure of it.

I arrive back at the prison and am subjected to a strip search as I re-enter. The indignity of these is something I've never grown accustomed to. The unwelcome invasion. I'm not comfortable with the way I look downstairs, and only Neil and two other men had ever seen it prior to all this. Now strangers who I don't even know the names of could tell you the details of my personal grooming regime and the specifics of my anatomy. Even my body is no longer my own. As always, my cheeks burn with my mortification as I pull my uniform prison clothes on.

It's such a stark contrast, being back in here, that it hits me anew, making my knees wobble and my head spin. I'm only a few geographical miles away from the jurors, who will all have returned home to their lives, their loved ones, or their sports, or their solitude. They will probably in turn be a few miles away from the judge and barristers who I doubt any of us would recognise out of their gowns and wigs – maybe they wear jogging bottoms, maybe chinos; maybe they prefer flannel shirts, maybe worn and tattered band T-shirts with hundreds of memories between the threads. Who knows who they really are? Here in the prison, we are all made the same by our identical clothes, our identical routines, our bars on our cages – a million metaphorical miles away from the freedom of every single other person I spent the day with in that court-room today.

The scrape of my wicket being drawn open makes me jump.

'Bell, time to wash,' is commanded through to me. In the strip of her that I can see through the wicket I register brown eyes, black hair, dark skin. That means it could be Maggie. I hope it is as I know she'll let me have an extra minute or two to feel the streaming of water soak away the day – a small but relished pleasure. What a day to wash off, too.

Once I'm back in my cell, I spend hours thinking. Usually I pass my evenings in here reading books – escaping to count-less other worlds far away from this box. I've lived a life beside a hobbit, searching for a ring. I've re-lived romance on a deso-late moor with a brooding Heathcliff. I've lived the thrill of driverless cars being hacked and taken over among a public rage against a wrong society. All those worlds were so much better than the one inside these four walls; but none of those adventures I've lived fill even a fraction of the hole that fills my body – my longing for the simple but perfect world that's inside 42 Wesley Street, where the main characters are a loving and steady toast burner who answers to the name 'Neil', and two glorious, cheeky, once-joyous children who have sunshine in their smiles and share my heart between them.

My thinking leads me into a rabbit warren of connections. I ponder how the day went, what the jurors are thinking, whether they saw any good or bad in me, whether I did everything right that Simon told me to and, mostly, whether Neil could still see *me* inside this exhausted body. Even if I get out of here one day, will my children be able to recognise me?

FIFTY

MARY

By the time the judge releases us all for the day, with her instructions not to discuss the trial with anyone apart from our fellow jury members repeated vehemently and earnestly, I'm exhausted in a way that makes me feel as though my body will cave in on itself like a sinkhole, disappearing into oblivion completely. Therefore, it's a challenge to navigate my way home through city traffic in the car. I play a classical music CD to help calm me. I'm too tired to try to decide if it worked, but I arrive home in one piece. I trudge slowly to the front door and am startled when it's opened with a whoosh before I can manage to lift my key to the lock. Two questioning faces peer out at me, jostling for shoulders to be in front. I feel like I can barely lift my arms so I expect the hugs I give them are rather a disappointment, but I feel nourished and renewed spending a few moments in the arms of the two most important and special people in the world to me.

I realise that my feelings aren't the only ones heightened and tangled tonight when it's Lottie who speaks up, chattering, and Ollie who stays quiet while picking at a nail, roles reversed completely.

'We made you tea, Mum, just spaghetti Bolognese. We couldn't get the sauce like you do it – it's all runny and thin, but it tastes okay. We've grated the rest of the block of the parmesan for on top which should fix it, anyway.'

My heart sinks as much as it rises – uncharitably I feel doubtful about how nice the tea will actually be, given Lottie and Ollie struggle to boil an egg between them. Once, when I was almost comatose with the flu, they made spaghetti hoops on toast for tea, with the toast essentially bread and the hoops stone cold. I forced it down, a smile on my crusty lips. I'll force their spaghetti Bolognese down too, even if I would have given a week's wages for an Indian takeaway tonight. Instead, it's all gone on parmesan. I'm touched by, and inordinately grateful for, their effort, though. Really.

'How kind of you both to do that so I don't have to think about cooking – it means a lot, you guys. How were your days?' I'm so tired that I don't even realise my mistake – asking Lottie anything about her life – until the moment her eyes harden and her arms cross her chest in a physical barrier going up to match the mental one.

'I've got to keep stirring the sauce,' she mutters, huffing as she stalks back to the oven. Ollie takes my arm and pulls me through to the kitchen. He drags out a chair for me, sits opposite and, with a now captive audience, launches into a blow-by-blow account of his lunchtime football match. We're back to their usual characters now at least, maybe they are okay after all. I catch Lottie glaring at Ollie out the corner of her eye every minute or so, between stirring sessions. It's been like this all the time lately and I feel the concern rise through my chest – what am I missing with Lottie? Is it better for me to let her come to me to open up when she's ready or could that be too late? Should I be firmer about getting her to tell me what's going on or will that scare her off and shut her down even more? I try to focus on the positive – that this evening they've worked together on the meal and that's progress, but my nerves don't stop prickling at what I'm doing wrong with my daughter, and what the consequences could be.

Lottie serves the spaghetti – definitely *al dente* – and the sauce – definitely thin – spooning about ten pounds worth of parmesan on top, and we sit down. My husband pads in silently from wherever he's been seeking refuge, he gives me a peck on the cheek, and we eat.

Lottie looks up from underneath her curtain of dark hair and shyly asks, 'How was it, Mum?'

'It was a tough day, Lots, with so much to take in, so many instructions.'

'Did you see a killer, though?' Ollie jumps in, excitedly. Lottie rolls her eyes.

'I'm not allowed to talk about the details of the case, Ols, I'm sorry.' I pause, taking in his crestfallen look of dejection. 'But I suppose I can tell you that the charge is murder,' I add conspiratorially, even though I know I shouldn't really have given such a hint of the courtroom happenings.

Lottie looks up sharply. Her eyes sparkle with the passion of a fifteen-year-old full of opinions, just discovering the wide world.

'Is it *her*, Mum?' she asks tightly. Her eyes stay trained on mine, as intense as a fireball, and I see how much this answer means to her.

'I can't say, Lottie,' I say in little more than a whisper, while nodding my head slowly.

The colour drains from my husband's face, his hand stilling over his rubbery spaghetti. Lottie is oblivious.

'Oh my God. No way, this is awesome.' She speaks so fast her words blur into one and I see more energy and vibrancy radiating off her than I have for years. 'You'll be a part of history, Mum; this is so exciting. Make sure you remember every detail, okay, so you can tell me after?'

I nod vigorously, overwhelmed that my aloof daughter cares so much about this thing I've got caught up in by chance, and delighted that maybe we can finally reconnect. 'Just don't do the wrong thing, will you?' she adds acerbically at the end, scowl now back in place.

'I'll try my best.' I give her a strained smile. 'I've just got to work out what the right thing is first,' I add, but I think it comes out too softly for either of them to hear over the scraping of cutlery against crockery.

Later, when I'm working my way through loading the dishwasher with the mountain of washing-up that two teenagers trying to cook creates, I think back over the day yet again. The events play over in my mind and I try to find my way to the other side of my confusion, but I only manage to get lost deeper within it.

FIFTY-ONE

SIMON

We're on day two of the trial now, the jury has been brought back in and the prosecution's evidence is about to start being heard. The CCTV evidence will be first up, followed by the neighbour's eyewitness testimony. Mrs Rigby is starting at the beginning, telling her skewed story.

Finding the CCTV footage is one of the prosecution's biggest strokes of luck – usually even if CCTV evidence exists, which is in itself rare, it's so grainy that it's useless. Unfortunately for the defence, one of Jane's more 'community-minded' neighbours had a camera fitted at the top end of the street to catch any 'hooligan' activity. Retired as he is, he fastidiously checks and maintains his camera and I can just imagine how smug he looked when he produced the tapes for the police. I expect he felt his accomplishment was on a par with ending world hunger.

The footage shows the whole incident with nearly cinematic clarity. It is not easy watching. It's about to be played to the jury, and I know this is a big moment.

The court usher presses play, and Wesley Street appears

on the plasma screens in front of the jury box. It is the first time they've seen the image of James Foster during the trial and I see some of the jurors take him deeply in. He is wearing black jogging bottoms and a dark grey sweatshirt, the hood of which is pulled up so far that it falls over his forehead. He's stooped. The footage shows him come onto the screen – from the direction of his drive – and stalk to his wheelie bin which is just round the wall. The one way in which the CCTV footage does help Jane's defence is that it shows the jury exactly what those two houses on Wesley Street are like, which I hope will lead them to conclusions about who their inhabitants are. James has erected what looks on the tape like a very new solid wooden fence above the existing four-foot-high wall. It looks aggressive. The new fence and wall mean that to six-feet-plus the garden and ground floor levels of his property are entirely invisible to the rest of the street, except the Bells' house. Their dormer-style windows protrude; so from their first-floor windows they can overlook his whole house-front and garden. This is useful in establishing that the Bells, from their beautifully kept, warm, inviting, colourful home, were the only people on the street capable of observing his movements within that boundary fence.

The jury will see that James Foster's home looks hostile. They will see that he has worked hard to remain sequestered – I hope they will take that as meaning he had something big to hide. They might conclude that living next door to that would feel threatening and intimidating. They flaming well need to, given what they will see next.

James' gate has no lock on it though, just a bolt from the inside, and the camera shows him slip through his fortress access and move to his wheelie bin. What happens next plays out quickly.

A car appears as a flash of movement. It moves so fast it's hard to make out details. There wouldn't be time anyway – James has vanished behind its bonnet before you can blink. After the impact, Jane's car bounces back off the wall a fraction. The camera angle shows a crushed body fall down the gap between Jane's car bonnet and the wall, hood thrown off, a shock of blond hair visible. There is a lot of blood, smeared over the crumpled silver car bonnet and slowly trickling out from beneath the front tyre. There is complete stillness for ninety seconds (I've counted), which only serves to increase the horror of the scene. Then, Jane opens her car door and stumbles around it, walking slowly to the front of the vehicle. She inches closer to James and, shying as far away from him as she can physically hold herself, she nudges his shoulder away from her. This serves to rock his head back and the viewers see his wide open, cloudy, lifeless eyes. Jane recoils, as if shot. She staggers backwards until she hits the one tree on Wesley Street – right outside her house – and there she falls to her knees.

Suddenly, there is chaotic activity – several people arriving at the same time, surrounding Jane, blocking the view of the car and James. The tape ends, the screen going blank. I look at each juror and I see more emotion there than I've seen since the moment they stepped into this courtroom. I see revulsion. I see blanched faces. I see set jaws. I see twitching mouth corners and bouncing knees. The trial has finally begun, and my heart sinks at how.

FIFTY-TWO

NEIL

It's startling to see the actual moment playing out on the screen in front of me.

A war of emotions rages through my chest so fast that I don't even have a chance to identify them all. I think fear is the ultimate victor though. My chest feels like a black hole that sucks in all of me so that all I am is *afraid*. This is the first time I've thought the jury might actually find Jane guilty, that I might lose her all over again, this time for a life sentence. I'll get one too, in a different way; just as painful a punishment.

It will take a lot of explaining from Simon to convey what we felt, what we knew, how alone we were, how desperate in the end when no one would help. If Simon can't show them, and all they have is this picture seared into their minds as deeply as it will now be permanently branded into mine, then I'm not sure they'll be able to get past the conviction with which Jane appears to have operated. However well it's explained, the jury can never know the full story, never actually feel what we felt. We will always be the only two who share it. That's beautiful and terrifying.

Rita is in the witness box now. I hope I've changed her narrative; I realise now what a crucial thing it will be – this is the first impression that no one ever gets a second chance to make; this is the jury meeting someone who knew Jane, who was there in this other world of wheelie bins and death; who is human rather than pixels on a screen, and who therefore can connect to them.

'Can you state your name and your relationship to the defendant, please?' the court clerk asks Rita.

'Mrs Rita Jones, I'm Jane's neighbour, across the way, our houses look at each other.'

'Thank you, Mrs Jones.' Mrs Rigby turns to face the jury. 'Mrs Jones' house is marked on the map of the street you have in your jury packs.' She's back to Rita. 'Can you tell us where you were when the events from that CCTV clip happened?'

'I was in my front room, watering the spider plant I have on the windowsill.'

'Can you describe in your own words what you saw?'

I feel far more nervous than Rita looks. I can't tell if that's a good thing or a bad sign. The court usher has made sure I have a seat in the front row of the public gallery so I'm close enough to the witness box to see Rita take a big gulp. Perhaps we're all better than we think at keeping our inside and outside detached. Until we're not. I'm close enough to see her slowly reddening ever closer to the scarlet of her blouse. I see her look straight at me and I give her a tight-lipped smile of sympathy and encouragement.

'I remember looking out of the window as I set the plant down in its watering dish and I remember double taking as I saw, James—' she falters, stumbling over his name, 'Foster. He hadn't been about outside for months. I remember I kept looking at him because, like I said, we hadn't set eyes on him for a while. He was pacing out to the wheelie bin, leaving that huge solid gate of his only open wide enough to get the wheelie bin back through. I remember that because I'd have liked to have seen what he'd done with the front garden and I thought that might have been my chance, but he'd been careful to keep the gate mostly shut. Everything then happened so fast – Jane had come home, and her car was crumpled up against his wall.' She pauses, swallows audibly. 'He was gone.'

'Could you give some more detail about that part please, Mrs Jones – when the defendant appeared?'

'Not really. I've played it over so many times in my head and it's gotten confusing.

'I can't be sure of what I remember, not now. I couldn't swear to what was real and what I've imagined or added in myself – you know, my brain filling in the picture for me.'

Mrs Rigby's shoulders stiffen, and she gives a less than subtle glare to poor Rita. It's me Rita glances at, though, and I try to show her my appreciation through a quick twitch of my mouth's corners, without the judge getting suspicious.

'Perhaps I can refresh your memory with the statement you gave to the police, Mrs Jones. Could you please read it aloud to the jury?'

Mrs Rigby thrusts a sheet of paper out and the court usher scrambles as elegantly as he can to collect it and pass it to the witness. A nod from the judge appears to give him permission.

'I saw my neighbour, Jane Bell, come around the corner. She was driving at a normal, slow speed. She's always a very careful driver, aware of the children often playing in the street. Next, I noticed her speed up, as if she was standing on the accelerator, and she turned a bit so that she was pointed at Mr Foster. She never slowed down or used the brake; she went into him so fast that the engine was roaring, and the car bounced back a bit from the wall when it hit. It looked like a scene from a film. The car started smoking from the bonnet – it was badly misshapen. I rushed outside then; Jane had stayed in the car, so I was worried she was badly hurt. By the time I got outside, though, she was out of the car and standing over our neighbour at the front. I arrived a fraction before the other neighbours who'd heard the noise. Jane said to me "he's not breathing". He looked disgusting – there was blood all over the pavement and covering lots of his body. His tummy was caved in and mangled, his legs at awful angles.'

A long pause falls on the courtroom when Rita finishes, before Mrs Rigby speaks again – I assume it's left for impact. If so, it works – I think I see the twisted mouths of distaste on some of the jurors' faces.

'That's your signature at the bottom, Mrs Jones, can you confirm please?'

'Yes, it is.'

'So, that is your account of what happened?'

'That's what I told the police right after, yes, but I definitely can't say for certain now, though, that I remember all of that, or that I'm sure of it. My memory's not great at the best of times – it drives my Nev mad.'

Mrs Rigby looks angry and confused, as well she would be – a key witness has gone rogue and the jury will now have to disregard her police statement somewhat – Simon has explained to me that what's said under oath in the courtroom overrides anything that's been said prior without an oath being taken.

'Do you have any further questions for the witness, Mrs Rigby?' the judge enquires, after a minute of silence has passed.

'My Lady,' Mrs Rigby directs to the judge, 'may I request a short recess to allow me to adapt my questioning to the testimony of the witness, which I'm sure you can tell has differed from the previous statement unexpectedly?'

'Very well, we will adjourn early for lunch and sit again at one forty-five.'

'I'm grateful, My Lady,' Mrs Rigby says with a bowed head.

Bloody hell, so am I.

FIFTY-THREE

SIMON

After a behemoth of a jacket potato, drowned in butter and covered in a mountain of cheese, just how I requested it, I'm ready for the afternoon session. It's great to have the on-site café with its smiling staff – most days those warm jackets are the closest thing to a home-cooked meal I get. Cholesterol be damned. Most of the barristers sit down to catch-up over lunch, I usually take mine into the kitchen to chat with Monty who runs the place. I'd rather be working, but I make sure I find the discipline to give my mind a break, and my body a fuel up. I've learned the 'guilty' way that it's my clients who pay the price otherwise. I know the name of Monty's kid in college, though I forget where it is, and I guess he's the closest thing I have to a friend. Let's just forget that he literally can't escape my company, hey?

During the last day and a half, it has crossed my mind often that I wish I could be spending some of my lunches with Aneesa. I've found myself imagining grabbing two jacket potatoes, having found out exactly how she likes hers, no doubt just as funny a mix of toppings as her baguettes, and taking them out to eat on the wall outside, some early summer sunshine lighting up her face. Hopefully I'd bring a little sunshine to her day too. However much I try to suppress it, she does *something* to me – my eyes narrow when I see her and my heart lurches. If Jane teaches us one thing, surely it is the immense capacity and power of love and how much bigger that is than anything else. I don't want to miss out on something so important. I'm finding myself settling down ever more often with the thought that maybe rather than fighting so hard against the possibility of love, I should use that effort fighting for it. Annie seems so pure and I worry about her getting sullied by all my shades; but having seen her in action telling the world about Jane I'm beginning to believe I'm a drop in the ocean of what she can handle. That's it. When this is all over, I'll send that 'meet me for dinner ?' email.

I can't believe how well Neil did with the eyewitness neighbour. Her police statement was so dramatic that she would have caused some trouble for us if she'd gone on to embellish that further in court, as so often happens. Months to exaggerate it in their minds tends to lead witnesses to do that, and I feared never has there been such a drama queen in the making, thirsting for a big performance, as Rita Jones. As it turns out, Neil has neutralised that threat. We have the added win of making Mrs Rigby look mildly incompetent to the press, the judge and, hopefully, the jury – though they might not know how to tell at this stage. I confess, I'm somewhat surprised that the meek and gentle, slightly buffoonish, Neil managed to achieve such an overwhelmingly successful outcome from the task, but then I suppose that his quiet and docile sweetness engenders complete trust, even when unearned, and a propensity to want to support him in whatever he needs or asks for. They say the Lord works in mysterious ways.

'Court rise,' the clerk instructs with her customary commanding efficiency. The judge strides in, a vision in red, purple, and black. Not many women can pull that colour combination off. We couldn't have been more fortunate with the judge we ended up with. She is known for being extremely fair and calm, with a leaning towards being directive to the jury on points of law where some judges would be more objectively explanatory. This could work well for us if she believes in the defence of others case I make.

The jury troops in next, taking their seats. The witness, Rita Jones, is then brought back into the witness box.

'My Lady, I have no further questions for the witness at this time,' Mrs Rigby says, and even though I know her manner well by now, I'm still surprised that it's said with more irritation than embarrassment. I'm hoping that big pride of hers is about to give way to a big fall.

'Very well, Mrs Rigby. Mr Rafferty, would you like to cross?'

'Indeed, I would, My Lady.' It's my turn under the spotlight for the first time.

I draw a deep breath and put my invisible Oscar hat on over my archaic wig.

'Mrs Jones, you said earlier that you had not seen James Foster for several months before the incident on 16th January. Is that correct?'

'Yes, it is.'

'Was that normal on Wesley Street, were there other residents you didn't know?'

'Oh no, it was very unusual, everyone knows everyone. Not everyone is friendly, mind, but we all know each other well.'

'Did that make you feel suspicious of who he might be, because you'd never met him and he was elusive?'

'Yes, very. Quite a few of us had talked about how he must be up to no good, hiding away in there like he did, putting up that fence and all, like some kind of fortress.'

'That seemed strange to you too, did it, the high fence?'

'So strange. The only reason for someone to do something that major is if they've got something bad to hide, I reckon. What a way to live. Never mind what the landlady would have said when she saw it.'

'Did you ever speak to Jane about how you felt about James Foster? Or did she ever speak to you?'

'She did. Jane doesn't talk badly about other people. Even Darsh in number fifty, who's got dementia and sometimes scares the kiddies – shouting at them in his boxers on the street – she only ever says how awful it must be for Darsh, how she wishes there was something more she could do to help. She's no use for a gossip, you know, more's the pity. That meant that when she came to tell me how scared she was of James Foster I knew it must be bad. She'd been to the police, she said, told them everything – that she'd found his dropped receipt, that he'd been making drawings outside the school, that she thought he was targeting the kiddies there. She was out of her mind with worry.'

'So, would you say Jane seemed nervous to you in the weeks leading up to 16th January?'

'Oh, more than that; she was acting totally different to normal, she was deeply scared. I didn't do anything to help though, which I regret now, but I had my own stuff going on – everyone's got shit to deal with, haven't they?'

Mrs Jones went bright red then, I presume because of using a profanity in court, her face blending into her blouse that's brighter than most witnesses choose to wear in court. I suspect it will lead the jury to think she is bold and daring, which will imbue confidence in her and what she says. It's fortunate it's going our way. 'I'm so sorry, judge,' Rita splutters.

'That's quite alright, Mrs Jones, I've heard far worse I assure you.'

'I have no further questions, My Lady,' I add as soon as I can. I feel comfortable that I've sown some very useful seeds in my cross-examination.

If I was in Mrs Rigby's position now, I'd make sure I took advantage of the opportunity to ask some clarifying questions – namely, confirming that Rita never felt personally threatened by James or his presence on the street, and to state that she'd never actually seen him or anything connected to his house that aroused criminal suspicion or indicated any wrongdoing; both of which would be as damaging as they are true. Therefore, when Mrs Rigby indicates to the judge that she has nothing further for Rita Jones, I can only presume she's just taken in huge, salty gulps in her struggle to keep her head above water. I doff my Oscar hat to Neil Bell.

I had hope and I had belief already, but now I also have form.

FIFTY-FOUR

BILL

I'm waiting inside Birmingham Crown Court on day three of Jane's trial, ready to give my testimony. I haven't been back to work since that day, that call; they've put me on leave until today, a review to follow. No doubt my return is dependent on my cooperation in saying what they want me to on the stand. Someone else to let down. At least this time, I'll be coming through for someone too. Lots of people – not just Jane, but my boys, Becky, who all believe in my decision. Who love me for it.

Courthouses usually feel like places of stillness and quiet. However, today this courthouse feels chaotic. The hordes of protestors outside are chanting so loudly you couldn't hear yourself shout and the press pack bustles about, filling every spare nook and cranny.

I imagine the prosecution barrister is currently giving the final run-up to me being called to the witness box to give my evidence. My bosses have decided to throw the weight of pressure from their authoritarian numbers against me, and have brought a few stalwarts here too, who I know are now in the public gallery, presumably to intimidate me. They obviously don't share my thirst for doing what's ultimately right.

Doing what's right has such high intrinsic value, but it's certainly not as glorious as it is when actors depict it on screen. In reality it's scary, and underwhelming, and often leaves a mess behind. Doing what's right is laced with sacrifice, spreading out from it steadily yet slowly and almost imperceptibly like a child growing. I'll walk away from the trial with my career taken from me, or maybe I'm knowingly placing it on the altar. I'll be bundled away, covered up, treated like a stain on the highest ranks of the police – scrubbed at, then thrown away when it's realised I haven't faded. As I walk to the witness box, these thoughts make my steps falter, but I don't stop. We are imposters if we don't live our truths; if we spook when we are called to follow through on the beliefs we claim. The price I'll pay today is sky high, but it's not my freedom at stake. It is not my children. It is not my spouse. It is not my parent. Therefore, I am the lucky one. I will do what's right.

There are so many formalities to wade through, but I'm sworn in and begin the substance of my evidence by mid-morning.

'Can you describe the scene at Wesley Street when you first arrived, please, Detective Inspector Simmons?' Mrs Rigby begins her questioning. It's always a strange feeling being on the answering side of this dance.

'I arrived at 44 Wesley Street at just after five-thirty in the afternoon on 16th January. There were already lots of police personnel there, and official tape was used to cordon off the scene. Mrs Bell was being held in the back of a police car, and her husband, Mr Neil Bell, was also being held. There wasn't much chance to assess the body immediately because within two minutes of my arrival I was informed that there could be bombs inside the victim's home. I had to shift my focus to that matter and the safety of my colleagues and the other residents of Wesley Street before being able to proceed with investigations into the death of Mr Foster.'

'What was your initial impression of what had occurred, based on the state of Mrs Bell's vehicle and the body of Mr Foster?'

'I learned long ago in my career not to speculate prematurely on happenings as it can lead to detrimental prejudice in the case. I had been informed before my arrival that it was a serious situation and my first thoughts upon arrival were all related to how I would organise what appeared to be a high-intensity scenario whilst maintaining the integrity of the crime scene – no mean feat. The development that happened very quickly, regarding the presence of active bombs just metres away from the scene of the incident, is my predominant recollection of my early impression.'

'Were you treating the situation as a potential murder at that point?'

'A death had obviously occurred, with a clear, and openly admitting, perpetrator. That causes certain protocols to be enacted in how officers treat a case. However, it became apparent very quickly that there was a much more complicated situation underpinning the incident itself, so my conclusion at that point was not automatically murder, no.' I notice Mrs Rigby's nostrils flaring slightly with her frustration, and from all the shuffling going on in the public gallery I conclude I've already drawn outside the carefully constructed lines of the official narrative; and what the prosecutor had been promised.

'Mrs Bell was detained at the scene, though, wasn't she?'
'Yes.'

'So, you did have enough evidence of wrong-doing to proceed with a murder investigation?'

'We had questions, and protocols to follow, yes.'

'In your lengthy career, Mr Simmons, have you seen other comparable incidents?'

'Comparable in what regard?'

'Cases where the death of a pedestrian has resulted from being struck by a vehicle.'

'Yes, I have.'

'In those cases, have they been front on collisions?'

'Yes.'

'Of those, have the cases in which forensic analysis shows that the defendant accelerated before the hit, all resulted in arrests for murder?'

'Yes.'

'And have those cases all been won at trial?'

'I don't know, and I don't have the statistics to check.'

I'm surprised the judge has allowed this line of questioning to proceed as long as it has, since it's not related to Jane's actual case. I can tell from Mrs Rigby's slightly smug smile that she thinks she's scored a point there, and I'm unsurprised to hear her declare she has no further questions for me at this time.

The dazzling Mr Rafferty stands up, and from him a wave of proficiency spreads. Without being flashy he commands the whole courtroom. He has a quality about him that's rare in criminal barristers. Free from any evidence of domineering ego, full of conviction and passion for justice, and with an air of tranquil wisdom about him; I've never encountered a barrister I respect more. He stands and as his gaze piercingly meets mine,

I see his hunger for the not guilty verdict.

'You've described to the jury what you encountered when you first arrived at 44 Wesley Street, but I would like you to tell us now, please, what your professional thinking was when you first got the opportunity to study Jane Bell herself?'

I give a nod before I start, my body wanting to be a part of my testimony.

'I believe Jane Bell was in shock. Her behaviour showed the key characteristics of it. I see a fairly large number of people in some degree of shock – from witnesses at crime scenes to victims. Jane showed such similarities to them that my gut instinct, which I credit as being my most reliable professional tool, told me that she'd suffered greatly that day, that she'd been terrorised, and that her brain had shut down somewhat as a result of the events. The officers who detained her said her behaviour had been the same since the moment they arrived at the scene, though she'd been able to communicate, with much fear, the presence of the bombs inside Mr Foster's home. Based on her injuries – cracked ribs, extensive bruising and lacerations – I was in no doubt that she had put herself in harm's way, possibly risking her own life, in the name of stopping a terror attack.'

'We have the transcripts of your interviews with Jane, which members of the jury have a copy of in their jury bundle. From those interviews, was it your professional opinion that Mrs Bell felt that her children, and hundreds of other children, were under significant threat from Mr Foster?'

'Definitely.'

'In your professional capacity as a high-level police inspector, was that threat real and valid?'

'Absolutely.'

'In the jury bundle, there is a copy of Jane's phone records for the three-month period leading up to the incident. A copy of it can be provided for you now.' There is a pause while the court usher rises and hands me a sheet of paper with the promised evidence. I scan it quickly to check it's the same as I've seen before. 'Based on this, is it correct that in the ways Mrs Bell told you she'd tried to reach out for help to remove the threat Mr Foster posed to her children and the other children of St Oliver's, she was telling the truth and she did reach out, only to be rejected and left to fend for herself?'

I gulp down the shame in my throat.

'Yes, the phone call to the reporting help line and her visit to her local police station have been verified.'

'In such a situation where a member of the public fears a terror attack or plans being made for a terror attack, are there any other avenues available to them to receive help than the ones that Jane accessed?'

'No, Mrs Bell did everything that is recommended to pursue in such circumstances.'

'Thank you, Mr Simmons.'

I know there is as much Mr Rafferty wishes he could ask as there is that I wish I could implore the jury, but he has honourably respected the parameters set to him about admissible evidence.

I step down from the witness box and at once feel consumed by relief that I'm finished on the stand, alongside the putrid hollowness of helplessness and the yawn of regret that I can't do more.

All I know, now that my part here is played and the curtain has fallen on my career for ever, is that I haven't slept right since the day I met Jane. I doubt I ever will again.

FIFTY-FIVE

MARY

I'm not thriving at all during this trial, and it's only midday on day three. The policeman who was just in the witness box confused me more than he informed me. I'll be glad to discuss what he said with the other jurors later. I'm finding it a very difficult environment – I feel that there is far more loitering in the unsaid than visible in what's spoken out to us. It's also making me feel very uncomfortable that we're the only ones who so much is being kept from – I feel like I did at junior school when I got bullied for being different in ways I didn't know made me 'lesser'.

'You can't play with us anymore. You're so fat that you could never be a princess. And your clothes look ugly. And you never have nice clips in your hair. You make us look bad,' some of the other girls in my class said to me one day. I told my mum what they said, cheeks burning up, tears cascading down my cheeks, and I remember she told me.

'That was very mean of them. If that's what they're like then you're better off not playing with them, Mary, though I know it probably doesn't feel like it right now. That much nastiness inside them, it's like poison. But if you want, we can get you some clips for your hair; I know you've been wanting some for a while. We can go on a special trip to the shops and you can choose exactly which ones you want.' I nodded eagerly, and we went to a shop in town, where I chose some slides with daisies on them. I loved those slides and my mum clipped them into my hair the next morning.

'Chin up, my darling. You're beautiful, strong, clever, and, more important than anything, kind. Never let anyone else change that, okay?' I squeezed her tightly and nodded, only focussed on my excitement at showing off my new daisy clips.

I walked into my classroom with my head held high, hoping the sunlight through the window caught on the silver of the clips. The leader of the group of girls stared at me for a few moments before she pranced over and stood a few inches too close to me. My heart dropped into my stomach and I felt discomfort and fear tighten over my skin like clingfilm.

'Where are *they* from?' she spat at me, pointing at my clips aggressively.

'Um, a shop on the high street – Shelter,' I mumbled.

'Well, they look cheap and tacky. And yuck, that's a *charity* shop,' she sneered.

I didn't even know what tacky meant, and I'd always been taught cheap was a good thing, but I could tell from the venom in her voice that she was ridiculing me.

'I bet they're *plastic*,' the jibing continued.

'Maybe, but why does that matter?' I asked, muddled rather than indignant.

'Because it means you're *poor*.' Suddenly she jabbed her hand forward and snatched one of the clips out of my hair, pulling strands out painfully with it. Before I could react, she had snapped it in two.

'Ha, see, I told you so, they *are* plastic.' She looked around her, checking all the other girls were watching, holding the broken clip up for them to see.

'This is exactly why you can't come near us anymore, you cheap, dirty, fatty.' She turned on her heel and flounced off, a smirk smeared all over her face as obviously as a crimson lipstick snuck from a mother's make-up case messed all over a toddler's cheeks.

My embarrassment was made so much worse by the cloud of confusion I felt – I loved my clips, and my mum had told me how lovely they were, had taken me out on a shopping trip just to buy them – I had felt special. Was I the only one who didn't know the truth – that they weren't nice at all? That being plastic made them bad, that there was a whole other set of rules that no one had told me.

From that moment on I've felt at my most vulnerable when I know I'm being kept in the dark, when I'm a pawn in someone else's chess game but they've not told me the strategy. That's what I feel now, sitting in this courtroom with so many people who know so many things that I don't, but expecting me to stand up, in front of the whole country, and bear the weight of the final decision for the rest of my life.

The judge, who seems at times patronising, who sends us out so she can discuss matters of law with the barristers, makes me feel excluded.

The journalists, squeezed into the press area, writing things to whisper to the world that I'm banned from reading, make me feel pushed out.

That policeman, clearly wanting to tell us more than the questions were letting him, looking into our eyes and urging us to work out his coded message, makes me feel slow and behind.

The changing members of the public gallery, this morning being wide men all dressed the same; with their eyes shooting daggers across the courtroom, their shoulders rising, their sighs getting puffier, shorter, louder, angrier – make me feel intimidated.

It all comes together to make me feel like I'm standing back in that classroom, with my daisy clip broken in two and life as I knew it changed. It makes me feel like I'm an actor in a foreign film with no cue cards being held up for me to read and it all being gobbledegook to me, anyway. It makes me feel like I don't belong, that I'm an inconvenience, that I'm not good enough; and I'm devastated because I've worked so hard to never put myself in a position to feel this small ever again. Clearly, that's just something else I've failed at.

FIFTY-SIX

SIMON

Mrs Rigby stands ready to bring in her next witness with a look on her face like a politician the day after a successful election – smug, arrogant, and conceited.

'I have so far taken the court chronologically through the events we are concerned with, from the defendant's neighbour, Rita Jones, who saw the victim being killed by the defendant, to Detective Inspector Simmons who led the case, who told us what happened thereafter. Within the jury bundle there are the transcripts of his interview with the defendant which show her confession to killing James Foster. Next, I will bring evidence from the most indisputable source possible – the victim's body. The pathologist who carried out the postmortem was Dr Elkan Stein.'

There is a pause as the doctor is brought into the witness box, oath sworn, and the questioning proceeds.

'Could you state your name and role in this case to the jury please?'

'My name is Dr Elkan Stein, I am a forensic pathologist for the Home Office.

'I carried out the analysis of Mr James Foster's body after his death.'

'Can you talk us through your findings please, Dr Stein?' Mrs Rigby encourages, a non-too-subtle hint of glee in her voice. It defies understanding how she made it to be a QC – the Queen's Counsel are renowned for being the top of the barrister tree, with the brightest minds and the smoothest tongues. It is the pinnacle of achievement for a British barrister, yet Mrs Rigby is messy and unprofessional in her operations in the courtroom, possessing none of the usual QC traits. Somehow though, she seems to get results. Wonders astound.

'My examination of the body showed that the deceased was in optimal physical health prior to his death. There was no evidence of any prior disease or injury. I confirmed that he was in his early-thirties and five-feet-seven-inches tall. I deemed cause of death to be severe internal bleeding as a result of extensive crush injuries to the abdominal area – his liver, intestines, stomach, and bladder were all destroyed beyond recognition, his pelvis was smashed into many pieces and his lower spine had been crushed as well. The muscles in his upper thighs had been pulled off the bones, which had been snapped. It is my judgement that he died within two minutes of the impact.'

We had lengthily debated with the judge in chambers whether any or all of the photographs taken of James's body should be admissible and shown to the jury as part of the prosecution's evidence. The judge eventually agreed with Mrs Rigby that the photos showed the jury an important element of the case and were the only way for the jury to fully appreciate the extent and severity of the trauma to James' body. My concern was, and remains, that the photos are so grisly as to distract the jury from anything said in the following minutes, as they recover from the ordeal of seeing images so disturbing. The judge has agreed to pixelate out the worst of the gore. It won't help much.

'There are now some photos of the victim's body that need to be shown on the screens to the jury.' Mrs Rigby gives a nod to the court usher who promptly gets them displayed. There are a couple of audible gasps from the jury box, and I see the sweet looking uneasy woman visibly recoil, her hand clamped over her mouth, her face greying as I watch. I look over at the judge and I see her swallow, her eyebrows knitted a little tighter together than usual as she surveys the jurors. I suspect she realises her prejudicial mistake now.

'If we can get those taken down now, please?' the judge instructs the usher, a trace of urgency laced through her tone. She then turns to address the jury. 'I understand how troubling it can be to witness images such as those. It was decided by myself and counsel that it was necessary for you to see them briefly to understand the full extent of the case before us. However, I now believe it is also necessary to impress on you the context of this incident being vehicular, in which injuries are often very severe in nature. Your focus must remain on determining the legality of what occurred, rather than dwelling on the specific state of the deceased.'

I'm rather pleased with this unexpected addition from the judge, it should very subtly keep the jurors tuned into the key word 'legality' which my entire defence rests upon. Even that tiny reference to it could help me no end, spoken so early on as it was from the judge's lips.

I can see Mrs Rigby is as ruffled as I am pleased by the judge's interjection. She looks to be hurrying to get things back on track.

'So, Dr Stein, in your expert, professional opinion, what is the probability that the victim, Mr James Foster, died as a result of the defendant driving into him?'

'Oh, absolutely one hundred percent. That is definite.'

'Thank you. Have you seen other victims of vehicular incidents?'

'Yes, many.'

'How would you describe the severity of Mr Foster's injuries in comparison to other similar cases?'

'Mr Foster's injuries were extremely severe and extensive. It is unusual to see that degree of crushing in vehicular related incidents. I can only conclude that the level of acceleration must have been high, given it was in a residential, urban area. The victim being so close to the wall when it happened will have contributed massively to the injury severity – if that hadn't been there and he'd fallen backwards then the crush injuries would not have occurred to anywhere near the same extent.'

'What would you conclude from that about the nature of the attack on the victim?'

'Based on how tiny the probability is of Mrs Bell losing control of her vehicle at the precise moment that would have led to her making contact with Mr Foster, then I would have to conclude that the attack was purposeful and dedicated – the level and nature of the injuries I have found on the victim are consistent only with a high-acceleration collision, which I logically conclude must have originated from a *determined* collision – if the victim had been struck at 30 m.p.h. or less, away from the wall, as does happen accidentally in residential areas, the injuries would have been markedly different in type and pattern and only a fraction of the severity.'

'Thank you, Dr Stein,' Mrs Rigby addresses the witness

before turning to the judge. 'I have no further questions for Dr Stein at this time, My Lady.'

It's my turn now and I am relishing this opportunity – the evidence the pathologist has given is exactly as I anticipated and leads in smoothly to my point here. At the risk of coming off as complacent – which, trust me, couldn't be further from my current state of edgy and humble focus – I couldn't have set it up better myself.

'Dr Stein, the defence are not attempting to suggest that Mrs Bell did not kill Mr Foster. Rather, we are seeking to prove that it was not a murder; rather that it was a fully legal act of defence of others. Therefore, I ask you, is there anything in your examination that suggests that the means of death of Mr Foster was in any way planned or previously intended?'

'Well, no, but in such a vehicular collision as this, I think it would be very hard to determine that from my examination.'

'Oh, I see.' I pause lengthily and make eye contact with several of the jurors, in an effort to push home this admission.

'In that case, I won't waste too much of your time with any more irrelevant questioning.' I can see the judge giving me a warning look, but I suspect, based on the hint of irritation held in her elegantly arched eyebrow, that she too is frustrated by the less-than-helpful prosecution questioning that has occurred. 'You have indicated that you have vast experience in unnatural deaths?'

'Yes, that is the main area of my work.'

'Would it be correct to state that, in general, the greater the level of emotion felt by the individual instigating the death, the more extensive the injuries appear on the deceased?'

The pathologist takes a moment to furrow his brow and

contemplate. I can feel my held breath running out, my lungs starting to smart.

'Yes, in general I would say that there is a noticeable pattern and correlation between the circumstances of the death and the injuries presented. Premeditated murders tend to have a more calculated cause of death than crimes of passion in which it tends to be more abstract. Similarly, calculated murders usually have a more precise or minimal injury pattern whereas emotionally charged manslaughter tends to have a more extensive and uncontrolled injury pattern.'

'Do the self-defence cases you've been professionally involved in fit either pattern?'

'Yes, they do. I add the very important caveat that there are exceptions to all that I've said, I'm speaking directionally not absolutely, as I believe I have been questioned. That said, the injuries I see to the deceased in self-defence cases tend to be more wild, desperate, opportunistic in design or infliction.'

'Thank you, Dr Stein. How does Mr Foster's injury pattern fit into the correlation you've just outlined for us?'

Dr Stein lets out an almost imperceptible gasp, as though he never saw this question coming. It's surprising how witnesses often don't think ahead in a cross-examination. Here's me thinking I led him here very transparently, while he looks like he's just had a blindfold and handcuffs taken off.

When Dr Stein starts speaking again, he does so slowly, carefully, selecting every syllable delicately.

'I would have to say that, in my opinion, the injury pattern appears to suggest a more wild, desperate, opportunistic infliction.'

I give a single nod and look over to the jurors. One looks right back at me, solidly, curiously. Others are scribbling notes furiously onto their pads. There is a slack-jawed 'O' in the mouth of the goth, or do they call themselves 'emo's now? Narrow-eyed suspicion is scrawled into the troublemakers. I look over my shoulder at Jane and see her eyes are wide and filmed over with the beginning of tears. I can feel her disbelief. We're winning battles, but we're still a very long way from taking the war.

FIFTY-SEVEN

NEIL

It is agonising sitting in the courtroom watching the trial unfold. I manage to get a seat in the public gallery each day thanks to the court usher who makes sure I'm the top priority as family. Mum is beside me today; Rachel is looking after the kids. I am grateful for Mum's strength to lean against, to prop me up, especially warmed as it by the months of shared life, by the bonding crisis brings. It is exhausting trying to keep pace with everything in here – the judge, the jury, Simon, the prosecution, Jane. For a process that moves so drudgingly there is so much happening in every moment, and I can't afford to miss a single thing.

I haven't been able to see Jane since the trial started – I have to get home to the kids each evening, and she's whisked away into the prison van at the end of every day anyway, so quickly that I'm lucky to catch a glimpse of her. Simon is incredible in that he always makes sure he debriefs me quickly at the end of each day, despite all that he has to do through the nights.

My heart breaks to see Jane in the box she's in, so isolated and alone. It reminds me of a cage at the zoo, looking innocent and inclusive with modern glass panelling, but the locked doors and the zookeepers with their rings of keys give the truth away.

Joe is too young to know what's happening, though plenty old enough to make known his despair at Jane's absence. Molly, on the other hand, is a question machine, bombarding Rachel and me with endless curiosities about her mum. Rachel has been so selfless, looking after the children before and after school and nursery hours, to allow me to be in the courtroom with Jane. It has kept things as normal as possible for the children and has meant that my mum isn't overwhelmed (or scaring the kids too much).

'Daddy, did you see Mummy today?' I'm asked from a bear hug squashing my face as soon as I'm through the door today.

'I did, Mol, and she's staying strong.' She gives a nod of satisfaction, five going on twenty-five. It seems that she's come to terms with Jane's current absence, though refuses to accept that she won't be home in another few weeks.

'Why are your eyes all black, Daddy?' Molly asks now, rubbing her sticky thumbs across what must be bags-for-life.

'Because I'm a bit tired today.' Her eyes narrow with sass.

'Then why don't you sleep more?'

'Too much thinking, I reckon, and there's always something else to get done.'

'Like tea?'

'Yes, like tea,' I say with an exasperated smile.

'Fish fingers and smiles today?'

'Is that what you want... again?'

'Yes. Pleeease? Mummy always lets us have that when she's tired.'

'Okay then... for your mummy.'

She stands on her tiptoes and stage whispers into my two-feet-away ear, 'Will Gran make us eat thousands of peas again?'

I look over at where my mum's sitting rocking Joe and see her mouth tugged up into a smile.

'Maybe we can hide a few, hey?' I say to Molly, winking at my mum, who gives a jolly grin back. It's been heart-warming and surprising to see my mum blossom like this; she's a new woman. It makes me wonder if she just needed a place, a role, and in among art attacks and 'thousands of peas' and bath times, not just in 'best clothes' and dining room table meals and 'sit stills'. It's a new role I shall ensure she keeps; that I shall remain opened up to.

My heart sinks at every one of these happy moments, hating myself for letting us try to be normal, be joyful, while Jane is away from us, locked up. Then I make myself remember that the only thing keeping her going, and the only thing keeping me going, is the hope that one day she'll be back here with us once again. Then I know, the best thing I can focus on achieving right now is making sure she still has the home and family she remembers to come back to.

FIFTY-EIGHT

ANEESA

Simon and I keep meeting each other's eyes, and I know it's not accidentally in passing because the press are off to the side from the counsel. He's *searching* for me. The thought lands like an elephant on my chest, and breathing feels impossible. I have been searching for two decades – for my mum, for meaning, for answers. My focus has been so narrow that I have missed this profound discovery, hidden in the soft periphery. Someone is searching for *me*. Someone amazing, who makes me feel inspired, excited... full... and I'm ready. I don't get time to finish that thought's journey before I'm flicked like bait on the end of a fishing line, re-cast back into the courtroom by the throat-clearing of the journalist next to me.

Simon's been stealing points every day, turning the prosecution's witnesses to his advantage, but this one is fast turning into a nightmare for him – I can see it on the juror's faces. Standing up in front of the smarmy and utterly unlikable Mrs Rigby is a tall, reedy man with tortoiseshell square glasses, thinning hair badly combed over, a wristwatch just loose enough to scrape against the witness box as he over-gesticulates, and a well-deserved triumphant air about him. His name is Mr Burrows.

After much faffing and embarrassing examples of technophobia from the court staff, his evidence is now being played on screens to the jurors in the form of 3D graphics which he has devised to illustrate his 'careful formulas of alternative scenarios'. We've just seen the graphic showing the line, angle, and acceleration that Jane actually took, and if my expectation is correct, this will be the start of it all going wrong for her defence.

The next graphic starts playing, and Mr Burrows starts his explanation, his tone just nasal enough to be more-than-slightly grating.

'This graphic shows the difference in outcome if the defendant had chosen an angle altered by twenty degrees to each side. As you can see, the body of the victim would likely have sustained some crush injuries but would have been deflected sideways by the force of the impact. It has been deemed by the medical professionals that I work alongside, therefore, that the victim would have had at least a fifty percent chance of survival.

'Next you will see the effect of the defendant remaining on her course but reducing her acceleration by half, and so remaining at the same speed of twenty-five miles per hour that she was travelling at when she turned onto the street. This would have lessened the impact to the victim enough to reduce his crush injuries by about half, this time giving him a survival chance of over sixty percent.' The difference in speed as the animated car drives into the animated male body is stark.

Yet again the screen goes black as the graphic ends and the next animation appears.

'Now you will see the effect of both of those things combining – so a change of angle of approach by twenty-degrees, and a reduction of acceleration of approach by half.' This time Mr Burrows lets the graphic play out fully before finishing his description of events. He's added the rather frightful touch of James raising an arm in a wave of help once he's hit the floor. 'In these circumstances, the medical professionals have advised a survival chance of over ninety percent.'

A silence falls over the courtroom and I can see expressions of surprise on many faces, the jurors most of all. As I would have bet on, it's Mrs Rigby who first breaks it.

'So, are you saying, Mr Burrows, that if the defendant had made even very minor changes to her driving during this incident, then she most likely wouldn't have, in fact, killed him at all?'

'Yes, absolutely. Making even one of the aforementioned changes would have given the victim a greater chance of surviving than dying, and had she made both changes then he would almost definitely have survived.'

'And in your experience, would those changes have been difficult to make?'

'Not at all.'

'Would you in fact suggest that they would have been the more natural approaches to make?'

'From my calculations, yes. The defendant had to change from the more natural angle of approach onto the one she chose – it would have been the most difficult driving position to achieve the head-on angle that she did, given the street running parallel to the row of houses. She also sped up from her initial speed, which obviously required an active change to do so.'

'So, the defendant chose the exact set of circumstances that would cause the most extensive harm?'

'Yes. I obviously cannot say for definite whether the defendant intended to cause that maximum harm, but her choices in acceleration and angle of approach to the victim have ended up causing the most damage as was possible.'

'Just to ensure that I, and the jury, understand you correctly, Mr Burrows, can I clarify that you are stating that there was no possible way for the defendant to cause any greater harm to the victim than she did – she literally caused the maximum harm it was possible to cause within the boundaries of her circumstances?'

'That is correct, yes – based on the forensic analysis of the scene, she had accelerated to the maximum it was possible to do so, and she altered her line to one of head on to the victim, which was the only other factor in this situation which would have affected the severity of the outcome.'

'So, it would be appropriate to describe it as the most *violent* form of attack possible within the boundaries of the situation?'

'I suppose so, yes.'

'Thank you, Mr Burrows,' Mrs Rigby concludes, with as much flourish as one can achieve in a horsehair wig and black gown.

It's Simon's turn, and as someone who's studied his expressions for days now, perhaps with a little too much dedication, I'd say he has a hint of defeat in the angle of his chin, and a wariness in the wideness of his eyes. Though having also studied his attitude for years, I know he'll remain a warrior.

'Mr Burrows, you stated earlier that you couldn't know whether Mrs Bell intended to cause maximum harm to the victim. Can you know what *any* of Mrs Bell's intentions were in those moments?'

'No, but I can draw conclusions from the data that are usually accurate in suggesting what they were.'

'Perhaps, but suggestions are by no means *certain*, are they?'

'Obviously not, no.'

'And does the data you use include any way of measuring, or factoring in, human emotion?'

'No.' Mr Burrows' voice has grown more nasally – which I interpret with a shudder as his frustration mounting.

'So, really, if you don't actually *know* what Mrs Bell's intentions were, and your data includes nothing regarding emotions, then you are showing us the specifics of what happened, and what else could have happened, but not anything pertaining as to why or the deeper meanings of what occurred?'

'That is correct,' Mr Burrows grinds out.

Simon finishes his questions there, and Mr Burrows is moved out of the courtroom. I'm very impressed by Simon's handling of this dynamite, though let's be honest, I'm impressed by his everything. Despite all of his sharp and inspiring cross-examinations up to this point it is now that I most admire him. It would have been easier to try to labour Mr Burrows – to chip away at the impact he made by undermining little points. However, by landing that one significant blow and then dismissing him he minimised the air-time Mr Burrows had. His disinterested and dismissive air gave the very subtle impression to the jury that he was entirely unperturbed by the witness – the most effective way to limit the damage.

FIFTY-NINE

SIMON

Fuck. That was not good. I knew when I saw his name on the witness list that Mr Burrows would be the biggest threat to us, but I didn't imagine that his nerdiness would be so pronounced, or that his graphics would be quite so... creative. It's the first bit of actual skill and craftiness I've seen from Mrs Rigby. Selfishly, I'm actually glad she called Mr Burrows to the stand because now it feels like a fair fight. I'd be delighted for Jane if we'd got her freed without this, but from a purely professional perspective, there's not much satisfaction in winning an arm wrestle against an opponent with a broken wrist.

I'm hoping I've mitigated Bethany's progress slightly by getting rid of Mr Burrows as quickly as possible, and Bethany has helped us by bringing him to the stand last. I think that decision will prove to be the gamble she rues if we win this – her tactic will have been to deliver the biggest blow right at the end, as the crescendo. However, had it been my prosecution, I would have started with him to deliver a shocking first impression of the case, which could then have been built on with the other witnesses, even if they were less impactful. As it stands, the jury should have lost confidence in the prosecution, having heard so many ineffective witnesses, and now I can hopefully immediately undermine Mr Burrows' testimony with my blaze of glory.

That's not to say I'm sweating, though – my hands are clammy enough to set up a sauna, and I think I might have to throw away the shirt I'm wearing under my waistcoat – that type of fearful sweat has the tendency to linger beyond the capabilities of any Vanish.

Tonight, before I continue my preparation to take over in the morning and start the defence case, I will spend some time with my oldest and most reliable of friends, the one who never fails to steady my nerves and settle the shake in my right hand. Whisky. Neat. By the bottle. Rich, smoky, and bracing. My muse... or maybe, more accurately, my lifeline. Before that, though, I decide I don't want to wait any longer. I am on the brink of the biggest moment of my career, I have summitted the mountain I have been climbing my entire adult life, and I think not of my ambition, or my prospects, but rather only of Jane, of getting her home to her children and husband, of giving love the victory. That thought filling my head flicks me into action. I open my drafts, find 'Meet me for dinner?' and with a steady hand, press send.

SIXTY

JANE

I miss my family every single moment of the day and night – I'm never free of that yearning. Nor would I want to be, since it connects me to them. I dream of them. We're in a roller-coaster carriage. We're all together, having fun, and I hear their laughs, their excited screams but then, suddenly, the sounds turn to terrified wails. I turn around, and the part of the carriage they're in has broken away and starts travelling backwards. I twist round, leaning out of the carriage over the abyss now between us, but their fingertips are just out of reach. Then they speed up, away, away, away. I hear their shouts. 'Mummy, help us! Mummy, we need you! Mummy, save us!' And then I wake up.

I'm always damp with sweat every night after this night-mare; it prickles my skin like sharp needles everywhere, it runs like a stream down the indent of my spine, and I lie awake torturing myself with wondering: did I help you, did I do what you needed, did I save you? I thought I had... but did I really condemn you?

. . .

Not much is capable of breaking through that *missing them* wall. Simon does; and the one other thing that does is light. I search for it constantly.

Birmingham is not an easy place to raise a family, and it's not an easy world to bring children into either, not just because of the Jameses but also because of everything else – the destruction, the hate, the pain.

Somewhere deep inside me I believe in the power of light. I believe in fending off darkness at every chance you get. I believe there is safety and warmth and courage to be found in a candle flame. I wish I could have one in this cell, but I can't. I understand why – I wouldn't want some of my fellow inmates having a candle at their disposal. I just worry – have I lost the light from inside myself? Has my flame of goodness burned out? And how will I survive if it has?

SIXTY-ONE

ANEESA

I put my bag onto the table beside the metal detector arch and pat my pockets automatically to check that they're empty before being waved through it. Nothing goes off so I step forward and stretch my arms wide to be wanded by the security staff member standing between me and the trial. He gives me the nod and I sweep my bag off the table before skirting round the dividing panel and into the inner column of Birmingham Crown Court. It is not as imposing in structure here as in some of the grand older courthouses that I've set foot in, but the feeling it gives is one of gravity and sombreness nonetheless, and those things have a habit of sitting heavy on your chest until you step back outside and the air cleanses it all off.

After feeling like I was approaching a mental burnout yesterday, I decided to have a device-blackout evening, enjoying a quiet bath before curling up with Bertie and my oldest, favourite book, it's words as familiar to me as my palm. It worked wonders – leaving me the gift of feeling like a frosty field lying beneath a low-hanging sun this morning. I scurry up the stairs to wait in the melee outside courtroom eight. The usher mentioned to me a few days ago the idea of initiating a ballot for the press seats, given the scrum pressing to gain entry, but this doesn't seem to have been implemented yet. He seems to be attempting to mollify and calm the swarm around him. I manage to make eye contact with him, and I get the nod, so I push through the throng, utilising my sharp elbows, to stand a few people away from the door. I think his help is born of loyalty to the local paper, plus I've been one of the most thorough reporters of this case in the lead up to the trial, so maybe this administrator of justice wants to mete some out himself. I'm grateful. I feel like a knight at the round table. There is a live link set up that plays the courtroom events into another courtroom so that all press can watch, but a screen, even with full technicolour, gives nothing of the senses of the energy and atmosphere amidst the happenings themselves.

I have a takeaway cup of coffee in my hand that I was made to sip test at the security point, it's left me with that furry feeling on the roof of my mouth from a scalding. I blow on it furiously for a few minutes before gulping it down, conscious that I need every drop of caffeine I can get, and that no food or drinks are allowed in the press gallery, aside from the large bottles of water they lay out on the benches. It still scalds my throat slightly, but the burn is worth it – I can't afford to flatten. I'm surrounded by clues and details that I have to absorb and then regurgitate later. I feel the responsibility of my seat in the inner sanctum, the umbilical cord connecting one life to millions of others, telling a story that must be colourful yet entirely true.

I'm weighing up the challenges of my task when I feel the ground rumbling beneath my feet, and my thoughts vaporise as fear consumes me. There is only one thing this can be. Terror.

SIXTY-TWO

JANE

I hear the hum of the electric door whirring as it begins its climb up and over the prison transport entrance to the court-house. We pause here each day as we wait, and I always feel like my tummy turns to heavy lead during these moments – like it's the last chance to be spared before being swallowed into the mouth of the beast that's the court ordeal. I'm sat in the tiny compartment right behind the driver's cab today, and I've listened to the faint melodies of what must be the latest chart songs on the radio filtering through the wall all the way here. Initially, they lifted me, beautifully – the beats and lilting of melodies being a lost treasure to me. When I realised that I knew not a single one, though, I crashed so low. It sunk in that for every song that I didn't recognise there were hundreds of moments for each of my children I'd missed. Molly had just reached the stage of loving to perform songs to Neil and me. Most days we were blessed with persistent 'are you watching?' requests and then adorable exhibitions of mashed up songs, sung in her squeaky voice, accompanied by improvised dance moves, in her fireman costume. Maybe Neil would recognise each of these songs, because a version of them has come from Molly's lips every evening. My heart is squeezed.

I'm lost to my reverie, when suddenly I snap to, due to urgent shouts coming from the cab. It all happens so fast that I can't make out the words between 'man' and 'thrown under'. Then, for a split second, I feel like I rise up, the same feeling in my tummy as when you drive over a humpback bridge a little too fast. After that I see nothing. I feel nothing.

SIXTY-THREE

SIMON

I hear it long before the dots connect in my over-full brain - A boom that sounds so loud my ears start ringing before it has even finished. It is most odd, losing your hearing unexpectedly, in the midst of chaos. I can see that the windows of the courthouse have been blown inwards, spraying everyone close to them with shards of glass that glitter off their shoulders and in their hair. It could be beautiful, if there weren't flecks of red blood spotting faces like sequins.

Next, I smell it: burning; smoke; the acrid smell of melting rubber. I can taste the fumes clogging up my throat and I double over in a coughing fit, still mindless, saliva stringing down my chin. I reach up a hand to wipe it away, but it doesn't go where I wanted, it brushes across my neck instead, and I forget about it before I have a chance to correct it. There are open mouths everywhere, moving lips, so I know there must be screams and shouts. At this point, I'm perhaps relieved I can't hear all the pain.

I look around at the carnage to see if anyone's hurt. It must have been less than two minutes since the two booms, but time has slowed so it feels like much longer. I search around me, my head feeling distanced from my body, and I see *her*. *Annie*. The only person for years who has made my stomach feel all wobbly and jittery every time I glimpse her.

I see her lying on the ground in front of the chairs and she's not moving. Shockingly beautiful as ever, but with her mouth hung open, and although her eyes are shut, there is a stillness to her that breaks something inside me. I feel my abdomen tighten, my throat burn, and then I'm retching my breakfast of black coffee and a banana up over my shoes. The smell that usually horrifies me never gets the chance to hit my nostrils, swallowed up as it is by the thick, smarting smoke.

I push my way through the panicked and the distraught to where she is lying.

I can't understand why no one is helping her. As I reach her, I see a big gash on her temple, and I look at the metal frame of the chair next to her and see thick smears of blood over it. My mind is a muddle but is still clear enough for me to conclude that she must have been knocked over by the impact and struck her head on the chair as she fell. I try to lift her torso up, but she's limp and heavier than she should be in my arms, her head lolling back at an unpleasant angle and her shoulders rolled back too far. I think I must enter shock then, for I stay with her pulled to my chest, my mind blank, my body frozen.

A few minutes later, paramedics rush up the stairs and their green uniforms become a beacon of hope. I see people surrounding them, those few who haven't fled downstairs, trying to show them body parts that must be hurting. I finally click back into reality when I see one make eye contact with me, their mouth twisting slightly as they look down at her.

'Please help us!' I shout across to them, at least I hope it's a shout because I can't actually hear it, I can just feel it vibrate in my rattling chest.

The paramedics come over to us and move me away from her. I don't want to let her go. They try to ask me questions, but I can't hear them, and my eyes have become too sore to focus on reading their lips. Instead, I stagger backwards as they start compressions on her narrow chest. It's when police officers appear over the top step, mouthing the word 'bomb' that I finally understand what's happened. It then floods over me, like a monsoon rain that starts a flash flood in seconds: Jane.

SIXTY-FOUR

MARY

We all heard the thud, and then the commotion that followed beyond the wall from us, and then the next one, louder, closer, but we are ensconced in the jury room awaiting the start of the trial. I feel the tingling in my fingers and toes that used to be my anxiety scale. My body is not overreacting this time though, I take in the other jurors all showing their own tells. There is chatter at a much higher pitch than our usual voices, garbled questions:

'Should we try and get out of here?' I barely register who's saying what, it's enough to process their words amidst the sound of my stampeding heartbeat booming across my eardrums.

'What if that takes us into the heart of whatever the hell this is?'

'We seem safe here, let's wait it out until we're told otherwise?'

'It sounded close but not right on top of us. I think we're best to stay put too.'

Physically our surroundings and selves are unaffected, so

we all go with the consensus to stay. An usher appears and confirms that we're not in immediate danger and will be evacuated as soon as it's safe to do so. Someone makes more sweet teas and coffees, hands out the last of the biscuits, and we wait, lost in our own heads – those most labyrinthine of places.

It's half an hour later and many of us are beginning to get cranky and fed up with the clearly false pacifiers from the usher. He has now come in and sat with us, and all he'll say is, 'I don't have any information to give you regarding the delay, but we must all stay inside this room until we are advised otherwise.' He doesn't alter his statement by even a word, however many times he is forced to repeat it, though his irritation is certainly snowballing.

A sense of worry is a bubbling cauldron in the room. Every minute we are left to wait with nothing to do but strain to hear what is happening on the other side of the door is a flame licking the cauldron, building the bubbles into a roil, until they're in danger of frothing over the edges. Finally, a police officer bursts through the door and speaks to us all urgently. She wears a stern expression; lines of concern are trails across the landscape of a face weathered by hours filled with dread as she delivers the news I think we were all expecting but refusing to believe.

'The noise you heard was a bomb being detonated just outside the courthouse. I want to assure you all that you are safe, but we are evacuating the courts for the time being, so if you could all gather your possessions and prepare to leave, I will escort you out now.'

I feel a deep sense of dread settle over me, like a deep and dirty fog that I can't find my way out of. I do something that so rarely comes to me – I find my voice.

'What was the target of the bomb?' I ask once I've stepped

directly in front of the police officer. She is a few inches taller than me, so I push my shoulders back and tilt my chin up a fraction, determined to convince her to tell me. I don't know where this sudden need for answers has come from, nor this strength. I don't even recognise myself. But I like this Mary.

The police officer looks me dead in the eye for a few long moments, as if weighing up whether she can tell me or not, and just as I'm about to crack and dash away, she replies, 'There was a second smaller device that was brought in and detonated in the lobby during the commotion,' she pauses for a fraction of a second and her voice thickens with emotion. 'The main target though was a prison transport vehicle, bringing in one of the defendants.'

I feel darkness descend. I lose most of my voice so it's a quieter stammer, but I force my next question through.

'Which defendant? Please, I have to know.' I hate to be begging but the drive to know is so thrusting.

Her eyebrows dart down, knitting together – shutters on her face pulled closed.

'I'm afraid I can't give you that information at this time.' I see a flicker of sympathy in the police officer's eyes which lights a spark somewhere inside me. I feel my real self break the chains of the worry and anxiety that keep her bound up and locked away.

'We deserve to know. We have given up our daily lives for this place, and for our defendant, for weeks now. We are a part of this. Please don't do us the injustice of keeping from us something we have a right to know.' I speak with more confidence and presence than I could have dreamed was still within me. The police officer's head recoils slightly and her blue eyes widen. Then she suppresses me firmly.

'I wish I could answer that for you all, but I just can't, I'm sorry.' I feel the smarting of rejection and am about to turn away when I see her trying to catch my eye. She looks at me intensely and my question: *Jane Bell?* blooms in my eyes. She gives a single, almost imperceptible nod and understanding steals my breath in a violent armed robbery.

'Thank you.' I whisper, soft with shock.

We all move meekly into a line. The other jurors must have been watching our exchange intently for the room has fallen deathly silent, everyone suddenly speechless.

We are escorted to a nearby café, which has been sequestered by the police and all other customers removed, where we sit together quietly for a while. We are a diverse twelve, with very different stories, perspectives, and values; but we've been bonded together in a way that none of us will ever be able to sever. In those moments where I can see on every face that we all feel so much, we make a promise.

'If Jane makes it, if she's even alive right now,' I begin, hardly believing this is happening, and that I'm leading something, that my voice is ringing out strong, true, 'then shall we all swear that we will do what we have to do to see this through? Whenever Jane can continue, we will make it back here too, no matter the obstacles. We will make sure that on this horrendous and challenging journey, although we travel it entirely separately to Jane, we will walk beside her; together?'

Twenty-four hands join, twenty-four eyes meet, twelve hearts reach out.

SIXTY-FIVE

NEIL

There are no words to describe how I feel when I hear the bomb detonate. I just know in my bones that it's Jane – I feel like every cell in my body is splintering into shards. All around there is so much chaos that I can't even get to her – there are too many people fleeing, too much smoke to get my bearings. I try to pull out of the crowd but it's too strong, it sweeps me away. By the time I can break free and turn around to get back to her, there are police cordons everywhere, no way to get through. Helplessness screams through every fibre of my being. Panic consumes me. Terror strikes my soul. I am frozen, the world streaming past my eyes in slow motion and somehow also at warp speed. I feel elbows brushing my sides, shoulders shoving me, I'm aware of a melee, yet I can't move.

After goodness knows how long, I break through the surface and snap into action. One look at the mob surrounding each of the officers at the cordon line sends me running around the streets down the other sides of the courthouse, trying to find someone with answers, or for someone to find me. I'm clinging onto my mobile phone and its vibration against my palm pulls the trigger of hope. It's Rachel. It's hard to understand her through the noise here and the emotion choking her voice. I make out that police officers shocked mum at our front door, Mum called her as the kids were with her and the police officers wanted to set up a protection detail for them. The scariest seconds of my life are those waiting for her to give me news of Jane. Through the sobs, Rachel gasps,

'She's alive.'

I fall to the ground, my knees grazing badly but unfeeling. 'She's been taken to the hospital. Go to her, Neil, I'll make sure the kids settle with your mum later.' I can't even find words to answer with. A taxi driver pulls up to the curb then, drawn by the people who have surrounded me to help.

'Were you there?' they keep asking. I still have no voice to respond with. The taxi driver recognises me.

'You're 'im, aren't you, mate, the 'usband?'

I nod.

'Let me get you to 'er. They're saying on the radio she's been taken to the main hospital.'

'Thank you,' I gasp out, as he bundles me into the back-seat. He won't let me pay, and I find out later that taxi drivers from all over Birmingham have driven to the area around the Crown Court, taking anyone affected where they need to get to, free of charge. Just like all the emergency services personnel who run towards the carnage when everyone else is running away, I see a beautiful side to humanity in the wake of the ugliest side of it.

The taxi driver quickly hugs me goodbye at the hospital entrance and after stumbling in I finally pull myself together. I force my chin up, my shoulders back, and my brain into gear. I am needed.

As I'm waiting for the news that Jane will make it, I have

so many thoughts fighting for my headspace. I'd thought the situation was unbearable enough before, I never dreamed I would be longing for the days when Jane was only fighting for her freedom, not her life as well. I'm frantic with worry that since these people, whoever they are, have targeted Jane, they might target Molly and Joe too. Fortunately, the police have shared this thought and have taken them and Mum to a safer place for the night, with police protection. Molly will have endless questions; hopefully Mum will be living it as an adventure to spare Molly and Joe the fear.

I also realise that whatever the court verdict ends up being, our family has been given a life sentence no matter what.

SIXTY-SIX

ELIZA

25TH JULY 2019, *Birmingham Gazette*, Eliza Elliott

It is with deepest sadness that I announce the death of our exceptional reporter, Aneesa Khan. She was killed in a terror attack at the Birmingham Crown Court yesterday.

The attack was in the form of bombs thrown by an individual the police believe was behind the attack planned by James Foster on Birmingham's St Oliver's CE Primary School. One bomb was detonated underneath the transport vehicle bringing Mrs Jane Bell to the courthouse as it waited for the access door to be lifted; another smaller device was detonated in the courthouse lobby. Our beloved Aneesa died as a result of head injuries sustained during the bomb's blast.

The defence were due to begin giving evidence yesterday in Mrs Bell's trial for the murder of Mr James Foster. It is believed the bomb attack was a retaliation for Mrs Bell's actions in killing Mr Foster, timed to prevent her defence beginning. Mrs Bell survived the attack due to the enhanced security of the prison transport vehicles, though she is currently being treated for serious injuries at a Birmingham hospital. It has been disclosed that she has extensive burns to one side of her body as well as multiple broken bones. Her trial has been adjourned until she has recovered sufficiently to return to court. Extensive repairs will also be needed to the Birmingham Crown Court building before trials can resume there.

Aneesa Khan was a stunningly talented reporter for the Birmingham Gazette. She is best known for being the writer of the series on Mrs Bell that we have published in the newspaper for the past several months, as well as writing ongoing trial updates over the past weeks. It has been an honour to be her mentor and I will strive to keep her light shining in our philosophy and ethos for years to come.

SIXTY-SEVEN

NEIL

Jane has tubes and wires spilling out of her, but every few days there is one less and that is the only indicator of hope I have – that one day I will walk into this sterile hospital room and Jane will just be *Jane* again. I will see the brown of her eyes that is the colour of the Americanos she loves, rather than the blue spidering of faint veins scuttling over semi-translucent eyelids that veil those glimpses of her sparkling soul. That she will be unbound from these ties that keep her alive, finally free to be herself again... though that's about far more than oxygen tubes and drips feeding her.

I write everything down, everything she is missing, so I can tell her about it all when I go and sit with her each day, not letting myself forget a single detail she might want to hear. Molly now thrusts a pen at me every time anything changes – after every meal, at the end of each film, before she tells me what she did at school that day. She's developed a funny huffy sigh as she does it, a hint of the teenager we're yet to meet. That's in the notebook too.

. . .

I open my notebook and begin reading.

I got home from work to find Mum sitting at the kitchen table with Molly and Joe, all three bent over pieces of paper, backs curled into identical apostrophes. Mum draws with them, J, and she's flipping good too. She said she'd been taking watercolour classes, who'd have thought it?

Mum's come on massively in her role as grandmother but I know you won't be too surprised to hear that until yesterday I hadn't heard a single 'I love you'. However, I was hugging Molly goodbye yesterday morning when Rachel had arrived to collect them for the holiday club, and I told her I loved her, like always. From deep within the bear hug, Mols asked for the first time 'how much, Daddy?' I told her I loved her all the way to the moon and back, the way I know it goes in that book they love. She wriggled out of the hug and gave me a satisfied nod and her adorable new smile. With that front tooth missing that she lost last week - the pink swell of her tongue pushes proudly into the gap every time she grins. Super cute. I can't wait for you to see it. I've got photos on my phone ready for when you open your eyes, and so much video footage that you'll be watching for weeks on end.

Anyway, Molly marched over to Mum and asked her, in that inimitable way she does, 'Do you love me, Gran?' I swear I saw Mum well up, J, not that you'll believe it. She said it, though, she told Mols: 'I love you more than you can imagine, my dear, just like your daddy does, I love you all the way to the moon and stars and back again.' It was a breakthrough. She can't stop saying it now she's started. She said it again to both the kids at bedtime and then when they left for Rachel's today. It's almost comical. Mostly it's beau-

tiful though, the way Molly's face explodes with light each time. It's as though she's taking it as a personal victory; she's done what no human before her has ever managed – to make Mum mushy! It was a breakthrough for me too, well an epiphany.

I wish you could come back to us, J. I'm just the imposter with the easy job of looking to all the world like I'm holding us together. But anyone could do that, wrapped up within the safety you gave us with every newton of force you pressed your foot down on the accelerator. You kept them here for me to tuck one beneath each arm to read Guess How Much I Love You? *to, the way you used to every single night before sleep. I didn't want to, I know that book is your thing, but Molly insisted. She said in her very serious voice, you know the one, that you told her the night before it happened that it was a "very important book". So, I've kept it up for them, reading it every single night. But that's the thing, J.* Guess How Much I Love You? *I understand why it was so important.*

I hope you know that no matter what happens, after what you did for them they will never need to guess how much you love them again. No one will ever need to guess how much you loved them.'

SIXTY-EIGHT

JANE

When I regain consciousness, I feel the initial fog of confusion over where I am giving way to the deep fright of the unfamiliar. I'm surrounded by people I've never seen before, in a room I don't recognise, with all sorts of tubes and wires coming out of my body. Worse than all of this is how I feel – it feels like concrete must have been poured into my body, filling all of my limbs, because I know I couldn't move any of them. I feel my fear grow – my mouth opens slightly but I can't make words come out. I hear a beeping grow urgent, more rapid, as though it's an alarm sounding. That seems like the bare minimum for this situation – a siren call for help. It gets the attention of these strangers in matching pale blue outfits – the ones they wear in hospitals on TV medical dramas. It clicks. I must be in a hospital. Something bad happened to me. I can feel it edging closer to me through my mind – like a shadow growing as it moves nearer. Then one of the strangers breaks the connection as she looms over me.

'Mrs Bell, my name is Stacy. I'm taking care of you. I expect you aren't feeling too lively right now, but I'm going to do everything I can to keep you comfortable. You can ask me anything you want, but first, can you tell me how much pain you're in?'

I try to force out just two simple words: 'a lot', but they won't come, nothing will, not even a croak or a whisper. The beeping gets fast and noisy again. I see Stacy's eyes soften with understanding and she lifts a small paper cup of water to my lips. I feel the cool, pure liquid slide over my tongue and only then do I realise how dry my mouth is – scratching and rubbing itself sore. As I swallow, I feel the water cause a new wave of pain as it torrents down my throat – a searing, meeting stinging, meeting overstretching. I guess I haven't swallowed in a while.

It does lubricate my vocal cords though, for once I've stopped wincing, I finally manage to speak.

'What happened?' Joy floods me as I produce actual, audible words. It just shows that happiness is relative.

'You're in a hospital in Birmingham. You were involved in an incident that left you with some extensive injuries. You lost consciousness for several days. It's now four-thirty in the afternoon on 11th September.' Stacy's eyes are searching my face, I presume looking for clues as to how well I'm handling all the information. I manage to move my head in a fraction of a nod that I hope will encourage her – I need to know as much as I can take in.

'You're going to be okay, your injuries will all heal. You were severely concussed – your brain was very swollen – but that has now receded, and the critical period has passed. You have burns to one side of your body, but they've started healing nicely. You have a broken arm and leg on the same side, but they've been set in plaster and will be good as new in six weeks. I guess you just wanted to show us you are even more amazing than we'd already thought, hey?' Stacy asks with a kind smile.

'How are my children, do you know?'

'I do – they're doing just fine. Your husband comes in every day to sit with you for a few hours. He reads from a notepad he has, where he records every tiny detail of Molly and Joe's days. He reads it all out to you, to make sure you haven't missed anything.'

A smile bursts past my face's stagnation. It hurts. A lot. It's worth it.

There is a rapping on the door then, and as Stacy turns, I see my favourite prison officer, Maggie, march into the room. Through the open door I see a chair just to one side of it, used coffee cups, granola bar wrappers, and crisp packets strewn around it. I see Stacy's eyes follow mine and she jerks her head to Maggie.

'Been keeping a vigil sat on that chair out there, this one has. She's one of the hospital family now.'

'Oh, give over,' Maggie replies, flustered. 'Just doing my job.'

'First prison officer I've ever heard of who works every single hour God sends, and spends half their time out of uniform,' Stacy says with a wink at me. 'I'll leave you to it.' She places a remote-control type unit in my good hand. 'Press this button and I'll be with you in seconds. There is nothing too small to call me in for, okay, nothing.' She gives a firm nod and departs, pulling the door closed behind her. I should have known I wasn't free. This is just a different type of cell.

Maggie surprises me as she reaches in for a gentle hug. It feels like an age since anyone touched me with care and kindness. Tears roll gently down my cheeks.

'Had me flippin' petrified you did, my girl,' she says as a half scold, half endearment. It suits her. I soak it up.

'Thank you, Maggie, really,' I slowly say, still unused to my new stilted voice. There's a long pause, and lots of expressions pass across Maggie's face.

'You're most welcome, Jane, really.'

SIXTY-NINE

ELIZA

3RD AUGUST 2019, *Birmingham Gazette*, Eliza Elliott

ARRESTED: BOMBER BEHIND ST OLIVER'S TERROR PLAN AND JANE BELL ATTACK CAPTURED!

Yesterday, on August 2nd, police arrested the man responsible for the bombing of the Crown Courthouse on the date of the commencement of Jane Bell's defence. It has been confirmed that he is the individual behind James Foster's plans to detonate three nail bombs in Birmingham primary school St Oliver's last January. The police have not yet released the individual's identity, confirming only that he is a male, in his late forties, with extremist ideologies relating to "reclaiming stolen authority and demolishing the tyrannical system".

A statement released by the Birmingham police confirms that a search of his computer and devices revealed "hundreds of conversations with vulnerable individuals online, attempting to coerce them into subscribing to his ideology. If they showed inclination to do so he manipulated them toward taking violent action." James Foster was his first success.

The Gazette managed to get an exclusive interview with the detective leading the investigation, Seth Honour, who explained: "we now have the full communications between Foster and this individual. It is clear that Foster was very vulnerable at the time of contact, which was made via an online forum for family rights support. Foster posted, seeking advice regarding how to appeal adoption decisions. It has also been established that the bombs, and in fact any violence, were not Foster's idea. It required a great deal of emotional manipulation to convince him to take that action and he was spoon fed every single detail and step of the process. James Foster was the victim of a predator. We now have that predator behind bars."

Detective Honour went on to say: "Interviews with the individual in custody have revealed that his decision to bomb the courthouse was based on a fury that his plan using Foster had been foiled and that Jane Bell was being glorified and had stolen the attention from his message. It was an act of desperation to gain the attention back and promote his cause, as well as to exact revenge on Mrs Bell."

The police have assured they will be making contact with all of this individual's victims to offer them full psychological support and have also stated that he was working alone.

The further this situation unfolds, the more questions are raised. This new information paints Foster as much a victim as a perpetrator. We shall never know whether the hold over him mentally was strong enough that he would have gone through with the bombing. We do know that if he had done, he would have been a villain to the fullest extent. Equally, Jane Bell, the woman who stopped his plans by striking him down with her car whilst there were "live" bombs on his kitchen table, is being treated as a murderer. By becoming a killer, she also protected three hundred children. There is strong reason to believe she saved every single one of their lives from James Foster's bombs. Is there a hero and a villain in all of us? Is it only an accident of birth or a twist of fate that determine which one wins in us?

If you have been affected by the content of this article, please refer to the helpline numbers below:

- Supportline: confidential emotional support for a range of issues – 01708 765200

- The Police: if you are affected by online grooming or manipulation contact the police by calling 101

SEVENTY

SIMON

I went to a therapist after the detonations, after Annie. The psychologist told me I could let what happened to me become a cage or a wake-up call. I love my work, and this case, far too much to let trauma or grief ruin either. They advised I choose the wake-up call. So I have.

I don't have close friends. I don't have a loving girlfriend. I especially don't have Annie. I don't have a 'support network' of any kind. I've never fully worked out whether this is because of my intense, driven, idealistic yet righteous person-ality or whether it's because my job means I've never been able to be an attentive friend, a caring boyfriend, or a true family member. The nature of being a barrister means that days are so long that nights can become non-existent. I've known weeks where I've forgotten what colour the feature wall in my bedroom is. I've always been more committed to my clients' needs than I have to my friends' and family's needs – ignoring calls if I've been in the middle of trial preparation; not showing up to important occasions if I've had court. That's not been all callous choice, though; it's what's expected in this profession. A judge would think nothing of you missing a funeral to appear in court at their command. So, my training wasn't just in legal nuances, but in removing important personal connections. I'm fortunate that some of my oldest friends have stuck by me in a 'let's grab drinks' every few months way, during which we'll catch-up on everything that doesn't matter in life, skirting cautiously around anything of actual importance. They are in my life in a peripheral way, by name only, and I know that if they need a shoulder to cry on, or a lift to the hospital, or a place to retreat to, my name in their contact list won't be considered for even a millisecond.

My career is infinitely special, meaningful, and so important I've never regretted it... until now. Tonight, I crave that naff sounding 'support network'. I long for an old friend's shoulder to cry on, rather than an empty, cold, box of a flat that's bare of photos or memories. I yearn for a home-made meal cooked by a caring girlfriend, or wife, rather than this chewy takeaway in plastic tubs. I'd give an arm for a childhood bedroom in a family home to retreat to, with a huge, enveloping, soft hug as a welcome and the constant pestering of a hovering, doting mum. Tonight, I feel battered and wearied; by the world, and human-kind, and everything. Tonight, I wish I was more loved.

Don't worry about me, or maybe it's Jane you're worried about, and the impact me losing the plot will have on her. I'll have a drink, a strong drink, I'll sleep this off. I'll put my outfit back on tomorrow, consume mugs of strong black of coffee for breakfast, and I'll become the man the world needs me to be, under the black gown and the horsehair wig. I will set Jane free. But when all this is over, I might ask Jane if she has room in her life for one more friend, a real friend. And I might answer her calls even if I'm in trial preparation. And I might say no to the judge if they call me into court when she's invited me to a special occasion. I might give more love; and I might be more loved in return.

And that might be everything.

Jane's recovery takes what feels like an agonisingly long time. Not as agonising as the actual recovery for her though, I suppose. The judge granted an adjournment of the trial rather than declaring it a mistrial, which was a huge relief. That was enabled as much by the jury as by the judge. The jury would have been well within their rights to declare themselves unavailable for the new dates and liberate themselves from this heavy responsibility but united they've been, and they remain ready. I suspect they'll be a national phenomenon too when that story comes out after all this is over.

It's three months since the bomb went off and I'm standing once again outside courtroom eight, ready to continue. I feel wobbly, like all my organs are made of loose elastic bands. I look down and see my hands shaking, and I can feel my legs trembling. It seems my nervous system has gone rogue. I'll be launching straight into the defence and I'm feeling, for the very first time in my career, immensely vulnerable. These twelve jurors have had months to percolate on the prosecution's case. I've never come up against such a bias. I'm just praying there's some David in my DNA, against this Goliath.

I close my eyes and take five deep breaths, making sure I breathe out for longer than I breathe in each time. I focus on fuelling my fire. I think about the conversation I've just had with Jane, down in the cells. I remember how afraid she has been of making the journey in again, the hours of therapy I've

arranged for her to enable her to get back in the prisoner transport vehicle without having a panic attack. I see her skin – red,
angry, puckered still. I fan the flames with it. I think of her
words, her truth – that the most painful part of the recovery
was not the injuries, not the agonising redressing of the burns
that caused howls of despair, but rather the prolonging of her
not knowing whether she'd be living in a cage for the rest of
her life. I think of all that has led to this moment – my sacrifices, Jane's sacrifices. I hone in on my life's purpose. I snap my
eyes open. I take a step towards it: justice.

SEVENTY-ONE

MARY

I step back through the doors of Birmingham Crown Court with a different stride – longer, more level, more intentional. I feel like I've made a difference to something very important here. I know I'll meet all eleven of my fellow jurors again in just a few moments. I united them all. We stood for something bigger than us, and it made *us* bigger.

I'm through security quickly and I find my way with purpose to the right room. Once we've all arrived, we chatter about what happened, to us, to Jane; like a big excited family around the table at Christmas. The usher comes in fairly quickly, and after a fond smile at us all he proceeds to question us lengthily on whether we've discussed the trial with anyone, either in person or on social media. We look around at each other, all the feelings of nervousness from the first time we assembled like this, long gone.

I finally feel like a new woman. One who can travel somewhere new and not have to turn around halfway, back clammy with sweat. One who can pick an outfit straight out of the wardrobe without having to try ten others on too, for a simple coffee with a friend. One who can make small talk without fighting a desperate urge to flee. One who can go down a dress size because she doesn't comfort eat as often. One who can change things.

We file back into our seats and I feel a flicker of pride as I see the judge draw back slightly with surprise at the efficiency with which we remember our places and slip into them in the jury box.

My eyes settle on Mr Rafferty, the vision of a man, and I'm interested but saddened to see he looks like he's aged a decade in these last few months. He looks like a robin today – small and innocuous until you catch him at just the right angle, then you see his unbridled boldness revealed. It makes me feel even more in awe of Jane Bell – for her whole team to care this much about her.

The judge and barristers talk for a few minutes, but I only listen enough to deem it unimportant, focussing instead on taking everything in – the exact same pieces, each one not the same at all.

Then, even though I've known this was coming for weeks, I'm startled by Mr Rafferty stating he's bringing his first witness in. I thought I was ready for this, but I must have gotten wrapped up in myself, my progress, my growth; I'd forgotten how heavy the pressure felt.

Please, God, don't let me crack.

SEVENTY-TWO

BILL

I take a long breath. Five seconds in through the nose, six seconds out through the mouth. It's one of the many 'healthy' coping strategies I've been taught for stressors like this one: standing at the edge of the square outside Birmingham Crown Court on the first day Jane's trial resumes, Sean and Scott flanking me. I'm steeling myself to join the protests.

I am surprised at the volume of those who have returned, I had expected the bombs to have kept the place deserted, but no. The British rise above things. I feel a long-forgotten twinge of pride at the people I gave my career to. I've checked the security and it's much tighter. Hopefully the bombing of the court acted as a permanent warning to the police to up their game. They have today. I've learned all we really have is today.

I reach out to take the hands of my sons. Scott squeezes mine like a lifeline, and a glance at him reveals wide eyes and shrinking shoulders, tucked in behind me.

'Scott, how are you doing? It's a bit overwhelming, huh?'
He nods.

'Why don't you come into the middle?' Sean suggests, pulling his brother between us. Then he takes hold of his shoulder. 'We have to do this.' His voice is deep, full of strength and tenacity. Like I used to be.

'I know,' Scott confirms. Smaller, quieter, courageous because of the fear in the mix. Sean nods at him once, his mouth set by determination.

'Remember what Mum told us?' Sean is doing better than Scott at the moment. They seem to ebb and flow, each stepping into the breach when the other flounders. Scott drops his chin and shakes his head. 'Well I do. She said we should never let anything get in the way of doing what's right.' He looks up at me for a long moment, solidarity relaxing in his eyes. 'And it's right for us to be here to support Dad. Okay? We've got this.' He waits for Scott's nod before he lets go of his shoulder, but grabs hold of his hand.

I stand before them. Look at them each in turn long enough to really *see* them.

'Are you sure you want to do this? It's not too late to go back.'

Sean looks at Scott for confirmation before answering for both of them.

'We're not going back. We're heading forwards, together.' We share a look rich with the understanding that we're not talking about the protest anymore. Tears fill my eyes. I hate that my son had to become a man so soon. However, I'm bloody proud and in awe of the man he's become. It knits something back together in me – that I did something pretty right there; that Becky may be gone but she's still here, in them.

Scott steps behind me, unfastens my rucksack and tries to wrestle our placard out of it. Sean steps in when the frustration looks too much and gives it a tug without Scott noticing. A look of gleeful triumph spreads over Scott's face as he feels it free. We're getting more flashes of good each day. It's enough.

We're here because I couldn't get the closure I needed to move on into my new life. I was strong-armed into early retirement on medical grounds – a nervous breakdown – after my 'problematic' testimony, but I'd have left anyway because the most important things I'll ever do are standing right beside me. I've felt a chewing unease though, at how I left things with the case – suddenly, on the stand, when there was so much more to do. It was Becky's suggestion, the day before she left this life, that I come here today: to show support, to stand with Jane, on the right side of justice, a part of this.

We've decided to join the St Oliver's CE Primary School families, the ones who stop your heart with their placards showing the individuals Jane saved. It was Scott who noticed it, when I showed the boys the videos of the protests from the first part of the trial, to prepare them for what to expect:

'Which one's Jane?' It's funny what hits you, tearing into your flesh like a bullet.

Sean added to the impact. 'Yeah, she should be represented. Jane's the only one whose life is *still* on the line.'

I look over at the placard held proudly by Scott. I see Jane. Molly under one of her arms, Joe under the other, all three faces laughing into the camera. I step into position behind my sons, a hand on each of their shoulders. I check Scott seems confident with me here rather than outside him. He twists round to smile up at me and I know we're ready.

'I love you guys. I can't put into words how proud I am of you.'

'You too, Dad.'

We step forward, onto the square, marching strong towards the line we're destined to join. A wave rolls in, flashes blinding us. I didn't expect this, but I suppose I should have – the press conferences and my testimony made me familiar to the press covering Jane's case, and seeing the Detective Inspector who led it joining the protest supporting Jane's release is... significant. I squeeze the boys' shoulders tighter, clinging onto them, propelling us forward. *Propelling us forward.*

SEVENTY-THREE

SIMON

It has all happened rather rapidly this morning – the judge has wasted no time with excessive formalities. I think everyone who knows court was impressed with how settled and competently the jury appeared to come back, so I can only presume the judge followed her instincts in not labouring the reinitiation and instead got us straight back into the thick of things. I outlined to the jury what I would be bringing to them in the defence, clearly staking out the defence of others parameters. Fortunately, I'd asked my first witness, my expert, Dr Melanie McCulloch, to be present in the vicinity all day so that she was ready anytime. I knew she was looking forward to her very delayed chance to testify for Jane.

Mel walks to the witness stand with proficiency – back straight, chin level, eyes soft. She looks muted (for her), in a sky-blue skirt suit with a sunflower yellow silk blouse glowing out from beneath it. She looks over to the jurors and smiles. She nods her thanks to the court usher who led her to the stand. She is grace personified. She is sworn in.

'Dr McCulloch, could you please state your qualifications and credentials for the judge and jury?' the court clerk asks.

'I am Dr Melanie McCulloch, Professor of Psychiatry at Cambridge Medical School. I have worked in academic and patient-based psychiatry for thirty years, specialising in the importance and scope of human identity. During my career, I have led many research trials and studies into ordered and disordered senses of self, as well as writing the main text on the subject used in post-graduate psychiatric programmes across the world.'

'Thank you. Mr Rafferty, please begin,' the judge instructs. I move half the distance between my table and the stand, just as much as I can get away with, wanting to create a bridge between the defence's home and the witness.

'From a psychiatric perspective how is the threshold for what constitutes reasonable force determined?' I begin, keeping my voice smooth and steady, despite the shiver I feel in my chest at the enormity of the next few minutes. I look cool – I hope – but feel clammy.

'It is very similar to the legal stance – if an individual genuinely perceives a threat or attack to themselves or others, and they react with a force that is effective but not excessive for the risk posed by the attack, then we would deem that they have reacted with a reasonable force, regardless of whether the oncoming attack is factually true or not.'

'So, it seems that a crucial element in determining whether the force used is reasonable is the severity of the threat or attack?'

'Generally, yes. It would be my opinion that the greater the harm posed by the threat or attack, the stronger the force that would be classed as reasonable to use to neutralise it.'

'How does Jane Bell's case fit into that spectrum?'

'Ah, that brings a more complicated answer. There are different types of threat an individual can perceive: physical threat, emotional threat, and threat to identity. It is usually the case that if a threat or attack poses a risk to more than one of those areas, there is a cumulative effect that heightens the intensity of the risk perceived. It would psychiatrically be expected that a person in Jane's circumstances would experience all three of those threat types at once, and given her children were under threat of death, I would deem the extent of harm posed by the attack to be perceived by Jane to be the highest possible. Therefore, the level of force that could be used in defence and be deemed reasonable would be extremely high.'

Two of the jurors are a flurry of pens scratching on notepads, I can only hope detailing this list of criteria. The others all look fully engaged and attentive – a great start. I snap back into focussing on Mel, who has twisted slightly in her seat to face the jury more directly. She's good.

Mel has so far done exactly what I knew she would – she's made sure she communicates on a balanced level – so that she can be understood by a rocket scientist or an illiterate person. I suppose a psychiatrist is the most helpful expert witness a lawyer can have, since they understand this need.

'You mentioned that you think Mrs Bell experienced all three threat types, including threat to identity. Could you explain how her identity was at risk with this attack?'

'Of course, I'll outline the general principle first – how a mother's sense of identity can grow to extend to her children, as I believe is the case for Jane. For the first nine months of a child's existence, while it's a foetus, a mother's life is synonymous with her child's life – she is responsible for that life entirely. Physically, her child is a literal part of her body. For the first seven months, if her life ends so does her child's – she feels her life *is* their life. Additionally, as her pregnancy progresses, her most standout and obvious physical characteristic will be that foetus – she'll even be treated differently because of it by nearly everyone she encounters – strangers giving up seats so she can take priority, family possibly being more actively caring or attuned. At this point, her physical identity is significantly taken over by her unborn child. It is also likely that were any physical threat to befall her, she would instinctively act to protect her foetus as her highest priority, even at the expense of herself.' Mel pauses here, to give the chance for absorption. 'Then, once her child is born, her life changes beyond recognition.

'Every waking, and sleeping, minute of the day that baby's welfare is her responsibility and priority. She perceives her body is still attached to her child too – producing the milk it needs to thrive. After that, when her child is young, it cannot protect itself, it cannot make good decisions, it cannot meet any of its own basic human needs, it's nowhere near a fully formed adult. Most importantly, in this case, it cannot *defend* itself against any attack.' There is another, longer pause.

'Some mothers' maternal instincts are stronger than others – these innate maternal drives, which are as much a part of a woman as her drive to eat or her drive to sleep, mean she is fiercely driven to protect her children. In fact, for many women, her instinct to protect her children will override her own necessities – the sound of her child's cry in the night will wake her from sleep, she'll ensure her child eats even if there is no food left for her. The single biggest driving force in her life is the protection and defence of her child.

'Another crucial element is that while her children are young, the woman whose identity extends to include her children will feel that her most significant social role is that of their mother. She may spend nearly all her waking hours with them, even leaving the door open when she uses the bathroom and using a monitor to connect herself audibly while her child sleeps. Her life and their lives are the *same thing* to her. These factors all tend to reduce as a child grows older and reaches a stage of development where it can begin to defend itself physically, make independent decisions, emotionally cope without its mother's presence for a whole day, as a child becomes distinctly its "own" person.'

'Could you explain why you believe those circumstantial factors apply to Mrs Bell please?'

'I've spent some time with Mrs Bell while she's been in custody and have gathered a full clinical history on her, as well as evaluating her thoroughly psychiatrically. I can confirm that the profile I have outlined above – those things I stated could cause a mother's sense of self and identity to include her children – does indeed apply to Mrs Bell. She carried both of her babies very large – there was no hiding either pregnancy from the world. I've seen photos that confirm this. Her pregnancies were both accompanied by significant physical side-effects – acne and severe morning sickness – which changed both her appearance and her lifestyle. She exclusively breastfed both of her babies until they were fully weaned. She stayed at home full-time with her children until her eldest started school, at which point she began working part-time, putting her youngest child in nursery. This was only ever for a maximum of three hours at a time, as he couldn't cope with a longer separation. Her social circle extends only to other mothers, so that she can remain with her children at all times when she is not working. She engages in no activities or hobbies without them, aside from her part-time job, which she took only as a necessity when Mr and Mrs Bell, then having two children, could no longer afford everything they wanted on Mr Bell's income alone.'

'And Mrs Bell's children – Molly, aged five and Joe, aged three – are within the range that would still fall under the shared sense of identity?'

'Age wise, they would be in the prime range for it, yes.'

'So, in your opinion, it is entirely valid, plausible, and natural that Mrs Bell – a mother of two children under the age of six, who has very strong innate maternal drives, would have a sense of self that extends to include her children?'

'Yes.'

'And as such, she would perceive the action of driving a car into a man she knew was planning to bomb her children and nearly three hundred other children to be one hundred percent honestly and instinctively necessary to remove the threat?'

'Yes – being a fairly small woman, with no access to this man, and no assistance from authorities despite her pleas for it, with the threat level she perceived being so high and the outcome so untenable if she failed to prevent it, I would be inordinately concerned psychiatrically if she hadn't responded in the way she had, or similar.' Mel has reached a crescendo of passion.

'In your professional psychiatric opinion, was the force Jane used legally "reasonable" and as such was Jane acting lawfully in self-defence?'

'Absolutely. There could have been no greater threat perceived by Mrs Bell. She had no less forceful ways of neutralising the attack *actually* available to her. She'd tried to use lesser force by contacting helplines and her local police precinct. She only escalated the force when those acts of reaching out were rebuffed. Therefore, she acted with fully reasonable force in her effort to prevent the attack. Given the terror of the circumstances I can't think of a more reasonable way to have proceeded.'

'Thank you, Dr McCulloch.'

Mrs Rigby rises from her seat behind the prosecution table and marches a few paces closer to the witness stand, before receiving cautioning looks from the clerk and judge. Her shoulders are rigid and closer to her ears than on day one, her lips thinner as she holds her face tight. It is a picture of desperation.

'You cannot be genuinely suggesting that there is no difference or division between three clearly separate people, Dr McCulloch – that a mother and her two children are not three entirely individual human beings, for surely that is implying that children are not human people at all?'

This is not relevant to the prosecution's argument, just an effort to undermine Mel's expertise and so undo any progress she's made for the defence with the jury.

'I'm not suggesting for a moment that they're fused together into one physical unit, no, Mrs Rigby, that would be a medical phenomenon to shake the world. I'm talking about the mind's sense of self, which can at times be very separate from the biological boundaries of a body, as in the case of patients who believe their own arm is a monster and trying to kill them—'

'Thank you, Dr McCulloch, that's all,' Mrs Rigby interrupts.

Mel turns to face the judge straight on.

'Is it not possible for me to finish my answer?' she asks the judge directly. 'My example here could really illustrate to the jury the scope of what Mrs Rigby has asked with regards to the difference between the physical body and the psychological perception of self,' Mel asks the judge.

'It's not relevant, my question was asked and answered,' Mrs Rigby contends in response.

The judge turns to address Mrs Rigby head on. 'I think it entirely relevant that the jury hears the full extent of Dr McCulloch's explanation of what the sense of self can extend to, or not, especially since *you* have questioned it, Mrs Rigby.' The judge turns back to Melanie. 'Please carry on, Dr McCulloch,' the judge continues. Bethany doesn't *quite* turn scarlet.

'Thank you, My Lady. There have been cases where such patients have had to be restrained to stop them from attempting to hack off their own limb with any remotely sharp implement they can lay their hands on, because they've been certain that the limb is not a part of themselves. There are other amputee patients I've had who, despite the most obvious visual absence of their limb, truly believe it's still there – still a part of them. It is abundantly clear within my field that the sense of self is in no way limited by the physical body.'

'But those are cases of mental instability, insanity, or malfunctioning, where the individual can't distinguish fantasy from reality, and as such are irrelevant to this case – no such claim is being about the defendant. That will be all, thank you.'

'I disagree, Mrs Rigby, I feel it is entirely relevant, for while those cases may be instances of mental illness and Jane Bell's case isn't, they all show how the biological boundary of self – the physical body – and the psychological boundary of self – the perceived identity – can be entirely separate, which was the exact question you raised earlier. Your point about the mental illness those patients suffer from only serves to strengthen Jane's position, given that her extending her sense of self to her children is entirely sane, valid, and understandable. It is an anthropologically necessary development of the human brain – her children being an integral part of her identity, despite being separate from her physical body – well that's nature at it's very finest, doing what it was always meant to do, what it has spent centuries evolving and perfecting.'

Melanie reached a crescendo with her closing comment: 'Jane Bell's defence of her children and herself as their only protector is the entire history of the maternal human condition crystallised into one act.'

SEVENTY-FOUR

ANEESA

5TH NOVEMBER 2019, *Birmingham Gazette*, Aneesa Khan (posthumously)

JAMES FOSTER, PRIMARY SCHOOL BOMBER PROMISES HE WAS DOING IT "FOR LOVE"

James Foster is the man now infamous for his plans for a murder-suicide bombing of St Oliver's CE Primary School this January; foiled in the eleventh hour by Birmingham mum Jane Bell. On the day of his death, which was the eve of his planned attack, he posted a letter of explanation to me at the Gazette offices.

In the interests of the twins he has left behind, who were the primary targets of his bomb attack, we will not publish his letter in full. However, we will honour his wishes, as laid out in the letter, to communicate his reasons to the public.

Foster's letter opens with an apology. An urging for "everyone to know how deeply sorry I am". Foster describes his plan as "a hopeless man's last resort".

He goes on to explain the history of his twin "miracles" and the circumstances of the five years of their lives. It is a story of challenges – that were risen to; fatherhood – that was chosen and embraced; and loss – that was suffered when his children were taken away; and of the moving of goalposts by Children's Services, making it impossible to get them back.

James Foster presented a history of work as a labourer to earn the living needed to put a roof over the heads of his children. He states he got clean from an addiction in order to be a good father to his children and that he repeatedly asked for mental health support to reach the stability he needed to gain back custody of his twins. He says he filled his son's room with lava lamps because they calmed him; he covered his daughter's room in unicorns and fairies because she talked about them twelve times during one of his visits. He was a man prepared to do "anything" for them.

Who could have known that "anything" extended all the way to a murder-suicide in order for James to be "together now" with them, to be together "for eternity"?

Well, Jane Bell knew of course. Which is why she struck him down with her car to stop him. The police could have known too, if only they had listened to Jane when she told them.

There is no mistaking Foster's intent from the letter. He expressed that he was "truly sorry for all those who have been lost alongside". He explained his reason for the scale of the attack as "I don't know which classrooms my kids will be in and I can't risk my son or daughter being left behind"; but with the preface that "I wish there had been another way". With the intelligence the police have now found regarding the online manipulation Foster experienced by the individual who was behind the attack, perhaps this explanation demonstrates the ways Foster was groomed for the bombing plan.

James Foster "couldn't live without" his children, who were his "reasons for living". He writes of how he couldn't exist without teaching them to ride bikes and knowing their favourite chocolate bars. The news they had been matched with adoptive parents was the catalyst for his plans.

I can make the assurance, being witness to the words he wrote as his explanation to the world, of two things.

First: that Jane Bell saved three hundred children's lives from being taken by James Foster's bombs.

Second: that Foster loved his twins, that his sign off was true to his heart: "I did it for love, I promise."

Editor's note: As many of the Gazette's readers will be aware, the writer of this piece, Aneesa Khan, was killed while covering Jane Bell's murder trial. She wrote this piece before her death. The decision has been taken to publish this in order to honour Aneesa's intended coverage of Jane Bell's story.

SEVENTY-FIVE

JANE

Today it's my turn to speak. Finally, I will get to tell my side of the story. I'll get the chance to dirty my hands in the fight for my freedom. It's very surreal that for so long I've been the only one in this room not actually doing that.

I feel hands tighten around my elbows as I stand up. Flanking me are two uniformed officials who resolutely avoid eye contact. They could be robots, if one didn't smell of Chanel No.5 and the other of summer heat in clothes that don't breathe.

I make sure my strides are a few inches shorter than usual, as if I'm wearing high heels, to give me an extra moment before I stand up there.

It appears to me as a stage of sorts, and I've always suffered with stage fright.

I imagine the smell of my sweet orange and bergamot hand cream just like Simon has coached me, and I feel a sense of peace envelope me. I turn the corner and walk up the steps. As soon as I look up from the ground, I see so many eyes.

There are eyes showing nearly every emotion I can imagine – from admiration to pity; fear to pride; hostility to jealousy.

I feel a gnawing in the pit of my stomach and my breathing shallows and quickens. I make myself find Simon's eyes and I see strength and fire. I seek Neil's and find love. I glimpse Detective Inspector Simmons' and unexpectedly see allegiance. I scan to Rachel's and see hope. It is enough. I take a breath that fills my abdomen, I roll my shoulders back, I blink, and it begins.

'Please state your name for the records.'

'Jane Marie Bell.'

I'm sworn in, hand on the Bible, truth now coursing through my veins via moral compulsion injection.

Simon finds my eyes with his as he stands. I connect with them and feel complete trust.

'Can you tell us the level of fear you felt about Mr Foster in the days before 16th January?' He eases me in.

'I felt fear, more than I had ever imagined it was possible to feel.'

'The court has already heard that you took several actions to minimise or remove the threat from Mr Foster before 16th January – namely, a phone call to a specialist helpline and a visit to your local police station in an attempt to get the police's help in dealing with him, and finally removing your family from your home for a short while. Can you explain now why those were the actions you took?'

'I felt those were the only things I *could* do. I asked for help, sought guidance, and none came. I knew that I was too small and weak to overpower a strong and healthy adult man, and even if I did, I knew that it would only be temporary – that it wouldn't do much to stop him in the long run. I also knew that if I watched him, followed him, and waited until he had the bombs at the school, the risk of the police not making it in time was too great – the bombs would be live, ready to detonate, and in place. The children would almost certainly have died. I felt there really was nothing else I could do.'

Simon asked no more questions. He'd explained to me the plan was to get the prosecutor to ask the important ones – he said it would come across much better than him posing negatives for me to refute, given that our strategy is to positively prove defence of others rather than a traditional defence of poking holes in a murder case's evidence.

The prosecutor rises from her seat, steely and shrewd, with an air about her of a matador pulling out their red cape.

'Mrs Bell, can you confirm for the jury what your feelings were towards Mr Foster on the morning he died?'

I see Simon bristle, and the judge calmly intervenes.

'Mrs Rigby, please avoid repetition – that has already been established. Shall we move to the point?'

'Very well, My Lady, my apologies. Mrs Bell, crystal clear now please, did you want Mr Foster to die?'

'There is no one that I "want to die", Mrs Rigby; I just wanted my children to be safe, all the children at the school to be safe. I just wanted to stop him.'

'The forensic evidence proves that you accelerated into Mr Foster at a rate at which the only possible outcome was instant death. Surely that means you were trying to kill him?'

I've just about gotten used to the energy and speed with which such transactions take place, and how quickly each witness is thrust into extreme intensity but, even so, everything feels thicker and heavier up here.

I take a deep breath. This is where every word counts and will for ever be held in black and white for the world to know.

'The thought of wanting to kill Mr Foster never entered

my head. What was in my mind at every waking moment from learning of his plan to...'

'Excuse me, My Lady,' Mrs Rigby interrupts loudly, which is met with arched eyebrows from the judge. 'May I request that the jury disregard the impact of the victim's alleged plans, given that they were not enacted?'

'I'm afraid not – as we discussed in chambers, Mrs Rigby, the plans of Mr Foster have been confirmed by the police as factual, and said plans formed the motive for his death, so we obviously need to allow them. That being said, as I stated for the jury's benefit earlier, it needs to be remembered that this is not a trial of Mr Foster and that the act of terror itself had not been carried out.' The judge has a definite air of frustration about her. 'Please proceed, Mrs Bell.'

'...From learning of his plan to bomb the children all the way to getting out of my car after I'd hit him, all that was in my mind was the thought that I must remove the threat to my children, that I wouldn't survive anything happening to them.'

'So, did you realise when you pressed down on the accelerator that Mr Foster would be seriously injured, perhaps killed? Then proceed anyway?'

'I never had specific thoughts of what might happen to him, since I never planned to kill him; or hurt him; and I never planned the car hit.' I take a big gulp – the saliva in my mouth has all got stuck in a ball at the back of my throat – I feel like it's choking me. Despite imagining this moment for months on end, now it's here it's like a nightmare I could never have dreamed up. 'The moment before it happened, I realised that *only I* had the chance to stop him, and I knew I had to take that chance, my thoughts did not extend beyond that choice.'

'Did it matter to you what might happen to him?'

'I didn't have time to think like that. However, if I had, I would have cared. I would have tried to strike the perfect balance of scaring him and incapacitating him enough that he couldn't have ever done something as evil as he was planning, and yet not ended up with him losing his life, of course I would.'

'Would you do it again, Mrs Bell, knowing how it did end.'

'Yes, I—'

'Thank you, that is all, Mrs Bell. The prosecution rests.' Mrs Rigby nearly shouts, with a flourish.

'Please, may I finish my sentence?' I know I have to be given the chance to explain, let the jury know what I mean.'

The prosecutor looks at the judge who takes a few moments to answer.

'Since you were mid-sentence, I'll allow it, Mrs Bell, but no more.'

Her eyes connect with mine for the first time since I took the stand and she gives a single nod.

'Thank you, My Lady' I let a pause hang for a brief moment in the room. 'I would do it again, because while I regret that Mr Foster died, I don't regret that the children lived; I would do the same for all of you now, if I saw a gunman burst through the door, bullets flying, people falling, even if I knew the shooter would die by me taking them down, I would try to do that...' I see the prosecuting barrister rise to object and the judge silence her with a raised hand. '...because when someone believes it's their right to take innocent lives, I believe they put their life up for stake too – how could it be any other way? I truly, honestly, and deeply believe in the sanctity of life, but I believe more strongly and fervently that the moment we stand by and let innocent people die at the hands of another we too become monsters, we become complicit in the administration of evil, and everything we have built our society on becomes meaningless, worthless, and ruined. Hope dies with the innocent.'

SEVENTY-SIX

SIMON

Jane did well on the stand. She was passionate, she was vulnerable, she was relatable. Add in the consistency and plausibility and it was an ideal performance.

The prosecution is giving its closing arguments now. It is exactly what I expected – repetitions concerning the 'viciousness' and 'violence' of the 'attack', the claim that there were many other options available to Jane that would have resulted in less harm to Mr Foster. In any other case it might be convincing, but to me it sounds flat and not on the level of feeling needed for this behemoth of a trial that the whole world is following.

It's my turn. I'm ready to rise to the level Jane deserves.

'The world is a complicated and unfair place. In any hospital, on any day, women are aborting their babies, while other women are undergoing IVF treatment. In any hospital, on any day, there are people experiencing torturous chemotherapy treatments to try to get a few more months of life, and others are recovering having just attempted suicide, desperate to be gone from their life this instant.

'Amongst all of that, most every single day of our lives, we have little opportunity to make any tangible difference. However, members of the jury, today you have not just a chance to make a difference, but more than that you have the chance to do what is right; a compulsion to bring some right into all this wrong, to light a candle in the darkness, to resurrect for Jane Bell her life, to make sure that true justice is done.

'The law has become a twisted thing. It is always trying to catch-up. It's always experiencing challenges which urge it to grow to be truly just. It's the bus that's always a minute behind schedule or the coin that always lands heads up. I can almost hear your confusion given that I've dedicated my life to it, but I assure you that's precisely why I know this to be true – I know because I've studied it for decades. I know the endless times it has let people down, stood on the wrong side of the line, said yes to terror and genocide and atrocity. The law allowed men to own other men, to torture them and control their lives, to brand them and trade them like animals under the name of slavery. It was a *crime* to run, a *crime* to be *free*. The law said to all those men, women, and children who were suffering, dying: *no*.' I pause, wanting every shred of impact to hit.

I follow the most basic of my training – the foundation on which this cathedral was built. I make every single juror accountable by looking each one of them dead in the eye.

'I'm here today because I *needed* to show you that Jane did *not* in fact break any law. She acted in self-defence and defence of others by protecting her family. So, even if you disregard the morality and stick strictly to the law, then the outcome is crystal-clear. I'm here to simply assist you to see that, even above this, what is right transcends the law, what is just needs no men in white rolled wigs decreeing it; all it needs is your human heart.

'I know that every single one of you knows that the Holocaust was wrong, regardless of what the law said. I know that every single one of you knows that owning and branding other men, women, and children was wrong, no matter what the law said. I know that every single one of you knows that saving your children's lives, saving hundreds of children's lives, stopping them from being blown into pieces and dying in terror, was *right*.

'I'm saying to you, today, right here and now, that we have an amazing, unique opportunity – what's right and what's lawful have come together into this same moment, they've prevailed. They've given you the chance to be on the *right side*. I'm saying to you today, *make right this wrong*.'

SEVENTY-SEVEN

JANE

There's a way out; but no way back. Whichever my verdict, I will never be the same again, I will never be treated the same. I never chose for James Foster to move in next door, I didn't ask to be the only one who could, would, stop him.

Did I do enough? Did I do too much? Will those twelve jurors who hold my life in their hands be brave enough to make the choice I had to – to go against the system, to do what's right?

I am the plaything of my senses, wound so tightly I'm a robin's sneeze away from snapping. I must walk back in there to hear how they've judged me. I can't trip or falter, I must lift my chin high to stare unflinchingly down the barrel of the gun aimed at my forehead, keep my spine strong in the game of Russian Roulette that is the verdict.

SEVENTY-EIGHT

MARY

This is the first time since the trial restarted that I'm feeling gnawing apprehension at the unknown. Deliberations mean the structure and rules of the courtroom are revoked – and at the climax of this whole process. We twelve must now decide Jane's future. We must find our way to what is right. We sit down with hot drinks, around a large wooden table in the centre of the room, a couple of people reaching tentatively towards the plate of custard creams in the middle of the table, a few more confidently grabbing. Arnie, whose lips are permanently graced with a laid-back smile, refrains and after a minute or two of contemplation he is the first to find his voice.

'How many of us have driven around the corner after a sip too much alcohol? How many have picked up our phones to glance at a text whilst driving? How many have jay walked... how many?' He pauses just long enough for us all to think, to engage with his point. 'Because those are all crimes – each one of those seemingly tiny actions is against the law. And each one could cost a life, each one of those little choices could lead to someone innocent dying because of what we did. The worst part is every one of those things, that let's face it we've all done, is selfish in origin – we did it because we wanted to indulge and feel merry, or we wanted to save a few minutes of pulling over, or we just couldn't be bothered to walk to a crossing. But what Jane did was the exact opposite.'

I feel my pulse quickening with the realisation that I'm not alone in my thoughts. 'It was *selfless*, and it was to *save lives*, and that doesn't factor, nearly enough, in law. What's *right* is selflessness and protection of innocents, what's *wrong* is selfishness and recklessness. We need to find Jane innocent according to defence of others, which is exactly what she did – defended the innocent. Doing that is exactly what's right.'

There is a weighted pause, one in which throats are cleared and eyes are cast downward. The most forthcoming of us – Piet, a construction electrician – is the first responder.

'I get your point, Arnie, I really do, and I hold my hands up and admit I'm guilty of one of those – I've read texts while driving – but I assessed the situation and I knew it was safe. If it hadn't been, and I'd got caught, I would have expected to pay the price of that, to serve my punishment. That's all that's happening here – Jane got caught, and our job is to decide the law, not morals.'

'You could have been wrong about it being safe, Piet,' Arnie replies. 'In a split-second circumstances change, and it could have become unsafe. All that stopped you from being a killer is fate, or God, or chance, whatever you believe. Intention should count for something. What's stopping you from believing in Jane's defence of others innocence?' he beseeches.

'Like I keep saying, I know that she was acting to defend others, I'm just not sure that her level of force was reasonable – you've seen the photos of the victim, you've heard how hard she hit him. I don't see how that could be anything other than a full-blown attack to kill – and I think she needs to be held responsible for taking another life. Otherwise, where will it end? People will be killing each other all over the place based on fabricated suspicions. We can't know for sure that James Foster would have gone through with it. Whatever we think about what's right and wrong, we have to keep basic order in society over the big stuff – like killing – or else I really believe we won't have a society left at all,' Piet finishes.

There is another silence, this time less reserved – looks are exchanged between allies across the table. More custard creams are consumed. I find my voice. This is my time.

'I actually agree with you both to some extent. Arnie, I think you're completely right that we all need to live more according to what is truly right, but I also hear you, Piet, that a life ending is a hugely important thing and it's a heavy burden that we are responsible for determining the lawfulness or not of it. My understanding of it, based on what the judge just told us, is that all we have to work out is whether the action Jane took was "reasonable" defensive action in the circum-stances. I think that the best starting point is to determine how many of us currently feel certain of the verdict we would submit. Is anyone uncomfortable with a show of hands?'

There are no heads nodding around the table, so I continue, 'Those who would be confident in finding Jane Not Guilty?' I scan slowly around the table. There are ten hands raised. Mine would be too, making eleven. It's Piet whose hands are tucked under the table. Based on my research I know this will be enough to return a verdict if it comes to it. My heart soars.

Piet looks aghast. 'No way,' he comments. 'You're all sure?' Ten heads nod. It's the shyest juror who speaks next, our youngest member – a nineteen-year-old who dresses only in black every day.

'I don't see how she could have done anything else. Yes, it was brutal what she did to him, it was major and gory and grim. But that's nothing compared to how dark and twisted and evil what he was planning was. The threat was so severe that I can't and won't believe that what she did was unreasonable. The defence guy made it very clear that she really had no other options. She tried to get the cops to deal with him. She had no other way to stop him. It's like Arnie said, she did what was *right*, and it stands up in the law too.'

As I look around and for a moment reflect on life, on what's happened in mine because of that envelope landing on my mat one ordinary day, I think: we can all grow more beautiful, stronger, and more magnificent than we can ever imagine.

SEVENTY-NINE

NEIL

The jury is deliberating. They've been in there for five hours now. I'm petrified. I'm also angry. There are people in that room who have control over our family, who might not be able to see the goodness in Jane, the innocence; even after she bared her soul to them on the witness stand. My body hums with the tension but I am frozen. All these feelings consume me; there's nothing I wouldn't do to get the outcome for Jane; for Molly; for Joe; for *me*, that we need. Yet it doesn't matter. I can't change anything. I'm more helpless, and more powerless, than I've ever been before, and *this* is the moment I most need to be the opposite.

I used to be a gentle, sweet, maybe slightly rudderless man. I've mentioned the life sentence before; but in these minutes, as I wait for Jane's verdict, I realise my sentence has already settled within me. I'm forever changed. My gentleness has been replaced with bitterness. My sweetness with unrest. My rudderless-ness with a biting fury. I don't know what to do; how to find my way back to the man I liked – the man Jane loved; the man who made Molly and Joe.

Then, out of the blue, I find a speck of a long-buried memory. Hope. Like a sailor being sucked under time and again beside the shipwreck of his life, to see the lights of a lifeboat draw up beside him, I reach out. Comfort. I feel a seed take root inside me and grow through my chest, buoying my heart. Peace. I pray.

Simon's stayed with me, and he gives me odd looks at first, then he asks questions.

'Does it work?'

'I believe it does, or else I wouldn't be doing it.' I manage a wry grin.

'Have you ever known for sure?'

'That's not really the spirit of it... But what harm can it do?'

'I suppose it's a form of positive affirmation, right, and that's scientifically proven?'

'If it helps to look at it that way, then yes.'

'You're not kneeling with your hands together, though.'

'No need to. He can hear what you're saying to Him, however you do it.'

'Right.' Simon gives a single nod. Then he's silent for a while. His eyes close. It all helps Jane.

Rachel calls. She left when the jury went into deliberation, so now it's been half a day with no news. She sounds like she's about to combust or break down. She says Molly and Joe are clueless, enjoying playdough with her boys and my mum. I'm pleasantly surprised. It's strange how sometimes it takes losing a family member to gain one.

'How long do you do it for?' Simon interrupts my thoughts.

'As long as you feel is right.' I smile at him encouragingly.

'Okay. Fancy a coffee?' I nod, and after he's left to get

them, I enjoy a moment of stillness and space to let some tears leak. I don't know how I'll survive if Jane doesn't come home. I need her. I can't exist as a half anymore.

Simon bursts back in, quicker than I was expecting. His eyes are wide, and his hands are not bearing coffees.

'It's time.' He spins around, throwing a handkerchief at me as he does so. It's burgundy... and silk. We might be worlds apart, but I deeply hope we've forged a friendship that will last.

I stand up, wipe my face, and step back into the theatre for the final curtain call.

EPILOGUE
JANE

There is one piece of the story that I haven't told anybody. But someone should know, and that person will be you.

James will for ever be remembered as a monster, dark, deadly. He may be all of those things, he may not – it's not for me to decide. He did have a thread though, a nearly invisible yet definitely present shred, of mercy.

That day, while I did save the children, he saved mine.

Molly was running ahead of me to leave for school. We rarely saw James outside, as you know, but that day he was walking past our driveway, scurrying along. My heart dropped when I realised that Molly had seen him and was skipping over.

'Hello!' she called out to him.

His stride faltered.

'Yes, you!' Molly shouted. She'd reached him by now, and he'd stopped.

Molly gave him a huge grin. I was rushing to them as quickly as I could. Molly was bent over her Dora the Explorer lunch bag and pulling out a cling film wrapped offering.

'My mummy makes the best lemon cake. You just have to taste it!' she implored, holding it out to him. He was immobile for a few moments, so Molly grabbed his hand, uncurled his fingers from their fist, and closed his fingers around the slice of cake. He looked deeply into her shining eyes for a long minute.

'You will love it, I promise,' she sang out.

James looked pained, but he let the corners of his mouth tug up for a fraction of a second and he bowed his head almost imperceptibly.

'They're sick tomorrow,' he said, quietly, looking me dead in the eye for the very first time.

'No, they're very well,' I replied, curtly.

'I mean, they *are* sick. No school,' James ground out slowly. I stood still for a moment, my hands tightening around their smaller ones. That's the moment I knew... that my last shred of doubt about what to do vanished. It may have been his mercy, but it was my evidence. I decided.

End justifies means.

ACKNOWLEDGMENTS

There are several people without whom this story would never have reached you:

My mum – the moon who moved the oceans.

My agent – Jo Bell – who believed in me and the manuscript so deeply, who has guided me, bolstered me, advocated for me, delighted with me, always been 'for' me and who has worked so hard for me and this book. Jo, you have been truly exceptional. I couldn't have done this without you. No thanks could ever suffice. A special mention for Reggie, stories of whom brought much laughter to our calls.

Within my publishers, Aries editors Hannah Smith who commissioned the book and Martina Arzu who carried *The Choice* through final structural edits, into copy edits, proofread, publication, and beyond.

There are many more individuals who contributed to *The Choice*, including:

My dad, who has supported me in so many ways, unwaveringly, and across all the varied chapters of my life thus far.

My brother, whose brainstorms and ideas have been of great value and who has always carried forth steadfast faith in my writing.

My Nan, Valerie, who diligently and with the keenest eye imaginable proofread *The Choice* and who researched and advised on the situation regarding James Fosters and his twins with knowledge and expertise from her career as a social worker.

The professionals of Chester and Birmingham Crown Courts who gave information and advice so generously when I attended for research.

The covers of *The Choice* (both e-book and paperback) were designed by Emma Rogers.

The Choice was copy-edited by Elspeth Sinclair and proofread by Amber Daalhuizen.

Freelance editor Emma Mitchell edited the original manuscript prior to Aries commissioning it, which involved much fact-checking and research as well as the edits themselves. Emma was also instrumental in encouraging me early on in my writing journey, as well as bringing me into the wonderful online book community.

One round of structural edits within Aries was done by Hannah Todd.

The sales and marketing team at Aries who helped *The Choice* reach readers consists of Jessie Sullivan, Amy Watson, Lottie Chase.

ABOUT THE AUTHOR

S.J.Ford has loved words since she can remember, from covering her bedroom in book quotes as a child, to now writing her own. She has been inspired by the simple beauty of the poetry of Beau Taplin, as well as authors who write profoundly, such as Mitch Albom, or who tackle issues, such as Jodi Picoult. In her own writing she focuses on ethical questions and challenging topics which provoke reflection and thought in readers.

In her life up to now she has worked in marketing and copywriting and is now also studying for a degree in Psychology. In her spare time she loves getting into the forest or to the beach as often as possible with her golden retriever.